was born in Bournemouth, Hampshire in 188?. She was christened Marguerite Radclyffe Hall but in adult life called herself John. Radclyffe Hall was educated at King's College, London, and in Germany. She began her literary career by writing verses, collected into five volumes of poetry. Many of these, notably 'The Blind Ploughman', were set to music by popular composers of the day and sung in drawing rooms and on concert platforms all over Britain up to and during the First World War.

In 1907 Radclyffe Hall met Mrs Mabel Batten, the society hostess, under whose influence she became a devout Catholic. She lived with her until 'Ladye' Batten's death in 1916 and through her met Una, Lady Troubridge who was to become her lifelong companion. Radclyffe Hall published seven novels. The first two, *The Forge* and *The Unlit Lamp* were published in 1924. They were followed by *A Saturday Life* (1925), *Adam's Breed* (1926) which was awarded the Prix Femina Vie Heureuse and the James Tait Black Memorial Prize, *The Well of Loneliness* (1928), *The Master of the House* (1932) and *The Sixth Beatitude* (1936). She also published a volume of stories, *Miss Ogilvy Finds Herself* (1934).

In 1930 Radclyffe Hall received the Gold Medal of the Eichelbergher Humane Award. She was a member of the PEN Club, the Council of the Society for Psychical Research and a fellow of the Zoological Society. Her friends included Elinor Wylie, May Sinclair and Rebecca West in England, and Colette, Romaine Brooks and Natalie Barney in Paris. Between 1930 and 1939 Radclyffe Hall lived in Rye, Sussex but she spent much of her time in Italy and France in pursuit of a lover, Evguenia Souline. Radclyffe Hall died in Dolphin Square, London, on 7th

ADAM'S BREED

Radclyffe Hall

With a New Introduction by
Alison Hennegan

PENGUIN BOOKS – VIRAGO PRESS

PENGUIN BOOKS
Viking Penguin Inc., 40 West 23rd Street,
New York, New York 10010, U.S.A.
Penguin Books Ltd, Harmondsworth,
Middlesex, England
Penguin Books Australia Ltd, Ringwood,
Victoria, Australia
Penguin Books Canada Limited, 2801 John Street,
Markham, Ontario, Canada L3R 1B4
Penguin Books (N.Z.) Ltd, 182–190 Wairau Road,
Auckland 10, New Zealand

First published in Great Britain by Cassell & Co. 1926
First published in the United States of America by
Doubleday Page & Co. 1927
This edition first published in Great Britain by
Virago Press Limited 1985
Published in Penguin Books 1986

Printed in Finland by
Werner Söderstrom Oy, a member of Finnprint
Set in Imprint

INTRODUCTION

Food was Radclyffe Hall's working title for the novel which eventually became *Adam's Breed* and *Food* it would have remained had not her publisher, uncomfortably close to publication day, panicked himself into believing that deluded literary editors, libraries and booksellers would either overlook or misjudge Miss Hall's new cookery book.

It was Una Troubridge, Hall's friend and lover for almost thirty years, who gave the book its final name just as she would do for the three later novels, *The Well of Loneliness*, *The Master of the House* and *The Sixth Beatitude*. Quarrying frenziedly in the local W.H. Smith's, she came upon Kipling's poem, 'Tomlinson', a fast moving ballad whose rollicking pace belies its grim subject of a dead man's soul denied entrance first at the gates of Heaven and then at the mouth of Hell. Both St Peter and the Devil reject Tomlinson for he can lay claim to no virtue or sin which is truly his: all his living has been at second hand, guided by others' precepts and example. Truly, he cannot call his soul his own: there is nothing for St Peter to welcome in, nothing for the Devil to burn. Yet the Devil, who in company with everyone else in this mock-Border Ballad speaks Scots, shows more pity to Tomlinson than does St Peter. For the Devil, after all, as he says in a phrase whose repetitions echo through the poem, is 'all o'er-sib [i.e. intimately related] to Adam's Breed'. Through disobedience to God he lost Heaven as Adam and Eve lost Eden. Thereafter, till the end of time, he works—by temptation, trickery, flattery—to keep the offspring they bred from the bliss he forfeited. He is both at odds with humanity and despairingly bound to it: each shares an aching need for reunion with the God so nearly lost.

v

All of which may seem a bewilderingly far cry from a novel originally entitled *Food* and evoking Soho's tightly knit expatriate Italian community of shopkeepers, restaurateurs, cooks and waiters as it goes about its business of 'supplying other people's daily needs' in the last decade of the nineteenth century and first two decades of the twentieth. No room for metaphysics here, it seems, in a world obsessively concerned with the material. The pages of *Adam's Breed* are crammed as full as a Strasbourg goose with food selected, sold and served, meals prepared and eaten, vines tended, grapes harvested and wine drunk, flour milled, pasta made, coffee ground and bread baked. Its characters' lives are punctuated by ceremonious meals eaten at crucial moments—of celebration and consolation, matrimony and mourning—and humbler ones exchanged in simple friendship.

So much food, so much chewing: even the greediest reader may come to feel a trifle oppressed by a world reduced, it sometimes seems, to a 'long vista of jaws', champing their way to eternity. How much more oppressive, then, for those who serve them, doomed to wait upon those never sated mouths. Indeed, that thought was, so Una Troubridge tells us, the genesis of *Adam's Breed*:

> In the middle of a pleasant *tête-à-tête* luncheon John
> [Radclyffe Hall] became abstracted and inattentive. Her eye
> was following our obsequious waiter and presently she told me
> with quiet decision, 'I am going to write the life of a waiter
> who becomes so utterly sick of handling food that he practically
> lets himself die of starvation.'
> (*The Life and Death of Radclyffe Hall*, London 1961, p. 79)

It proved a deceptively simple summary of what was to be a remarkably complex book. In it the powerful accumulation of the painstaking naturalistic detail and psychological perception characteristic of the traditional mainstream novel fuse with a firmly controlled, densely textured allegory of the soul's quest for God.

Gian-Luca, Hall's central character, is illegitimate and his young mother, Olga Boselli, dies in giving birth to him. To the last she refuses to disclose the identity of her child's father. Gian-Luca's coming deprives Teresa, his grand-mother, of her own child and of her religious faith: the Virgin, so ardently petitioned to save Olga, clearly did not intercede on her behalf. Henceforth a state of war, declared by Teresa, exists between herself and God, the Virgin and the Virgin's son. (Her rage and grief are fuelled by long stifled guilt: as a young unmarried woman she once sinned as Olga did but never paid Olga's price.) The plaster images of the Madonna and the eternally bleeding Sacred Heart are ripped from the wall above the bed where Olga died, leaving five gaping holes where the nails once were. Dutifully, but without love, Teresa accepts responsibility for the baby. Love, and a name, come from Fabio, his grandfather, a gentle but timid man of simple, childlike affection who feels more things than he can ever find words to say. Milk and the means of life come from the breasts of Rosa, a young married woman whose own child has just died of croup. Care, interest and concern are provided by neighbours who loved Olga, who love Fabio. Teresa now neither gives nor seeks human love, no longer believes in God's. Her passions are centred on the Casa Boselli, the shop she shares with her husband. Fabio's lovingly expert knowledge and Teresa's ferociously inspired business sense make the shop the finest of its kind. All over London discerning diners eat the salame, paste, cheeses and *funghi*, drink the Chianti, Orvieto and Barolo provided by the Casa Boselli. Here Gian-Luca begins his long apprenticeship to food.

Technically 'fatherless', technically the English grandson of the naturalized Fabio, the blond-haired, blue-eyed Gian-Luca takes his uncertain place in the predominantly Italian community of Old Compton Street. Teresa, con-tinuing her vendetta against God, incurs and ignores her compatriots' wrath by sending him to the Board School, open to all denominations and none, rather than to the Roman Catholic one.

Puzzled by his father's absence, fantasizing a glorious parentage, loving and hating in equal and confusing measure the English to whom he theoretically belongs but who, in the person of his schoolfellows, mock and reject him, the child is outwardly competent and courteous, inwardly desperately alone. He seeks only one person's love and that he cannot have. Teresa, his 'goddess', remains coldly aloof, by a particularly brutal revelation of his bastardy smashes his dreams of an illustrious, loving father, and offers him instead a bleak commandment: ' "Remember", she said, "that you always have yourself, and that should suffice a man . . . You have yourself," she repeated firmly. "No one can take that from you, Gian-Luca—remember that you always have yourself." '

Impressed by a creed which he cherishes all the more for love of its giver, the young Gian-Luca lives by it. It sustains him as adolescent dogsbody in a fifth-rate trattoria, as trainee waiter and, eventually, as *maître d'hôtel* of London's finest restaurant, the mighty Doric. (He is a quite outstanding waiter: born, it seems, to serve. He possessed 'that rarest of all gifts, the instinct for perfect service'.) Even when he marries the gentle Maddalena, fresh from the Campagna, wretchedly homesick in the Doric's still-room and, like him, orphaned, he remains faithful to Teresa's dictum. As a conscript (why rush to enlist for an England as much hated as adored?) he carries it with him into war, brings it back to a peacetime world filled with survivors desperate to dine and dance in a frenzy of forgetting.

And then it stops working. It had never worked too well: it left too many things unexplained. If it suffices a man to have himself, why was the five-year-old Gian-Luca assailed by such terrible anguish at the sight of the neatly slit and bleeding baby goats hanging outside Rocca's butcher shop? Why should the beauty of bluebells at Kew fill the eight-year-old boy with a sadness that remained even after he'd trampled them in revenge? Why should poetry make him cry? What could prompt the fifteen-year-old Gian-Luca to dare to thrash a waiter twice his age and size because he was tormenting a cat? Where do cruelty and pity, pain and beauty come from? And why? Questions which greatly exercised the young Gian-Luca. Briefly, in early manhood, he'd silenced them. When they return, nothing in Teresa's harsh doctrine of self-sufficiency provides the answers.

Not until his early thirties does Gian-Luca recognize the life-denying poverty of her maxim. Gian-Luca 'has himself' as fully as any man may—and it is not enough. His sense of isolation increases, even and especially within his marriage, where the knowledge that he is loved but does not love agonizingly intensifies his apartness. and yet his wish to love has never been stronger. In the days when he 'had himself', he often judged others harshly, arrogantly, was quick to see, condemn and encourage their weakness. With machine-like efficiency he ministered to his diners even as his mind revolted at a vision of the world as one vast feeding trough in which human pigs wallow and trample each other in their greed. But in the last year of his life the vision changes, he sees with new eyes. Contempt yields to pity and it is intolerable. Unable to believe any longer in Teresa's God of Hate, not quite sure where or how to find the God of Love, he sets off on a pilgrimage which brings him eventually to the New Forest and the knowledge he seeks. He has sought it since childhood, finding only disjointed and fragmented pieces, and always coming closest to discovery when he most doubted Teresa's commandment.

Hers is not, after all, a sustaining philosophy. It does not nourish, does not feed those human needs which remain when physical hunger has been satisfied. Teresa cared punctiliously for her grandson's body, cleansing, clothing, feeding, dosing. His soul and heart she starved. Sustain; nourish; feed; hunger; starvation: how readily words describing the body and its material needs come to mind when we wish to speak of the spirit. They come, in part, because of a millennia-long Jewish and Christian scriptural tradition which constantly uses the language of food, sustenance and harvest to describe the relation between God and God's creation. The language remains familiar, re-sonant, even for those who are not Jewish, not Christian, not believers in any deity: key words and scattered phrases are embedded in proverbial lore orally transmitted; in everyday speech; in the words of countless writers who have absorbed the imagery and diction of the Old and New Testaments.

In this bodily language of the spirit, paradoxes abound.

Hall, a deeply devout convert to Roman Catholicism who was steeped in the Bible, takes those that are central to the Christian mysteries and uses them both literally and symbolically to explore the relation between body and soul, pain and love, God and the world. *Adam's Breed* reverberates with echoes from Genesis, Isaiah, Ecclesiastes, Proverbs, St Matthew and St Luke. Above all, and fittingly, the book is filled with the words and images of 'The Song of Songs', traditionally interpreted as a sacred love song in which the language of human sexual love is used to describe the soul's long desired union with God. Here is the divine love, 'better than wine', which Gian-Luca seeks. Here is the child rejected as Gian-Luca was rejected by his schoolfellows because he did not 'fit': ('Look not upon me, Because I am black . . . My mother's children were angry with me . . .') The lover is 'sick of love', as Gian-Luca sickens under his burden of pity. The anguish of the woman denied entrance to her beloved's house is Maddalena's, denied entrance to Gian-Luca's heart ('By night on my bed I sought him whom my soul loveth; I sought him but I found him not . . .'). Gian-Luca's initially despairing prayers to a God who will not, it seems, hear him are those of the lover whose beloved withholds: 'I opened to my beloved; But my beloved had withdrawn himself, and was gone. My soul failed when he spake: I sought him, but I could not find him; I called him, but he gave me no answer.' And, over and above all, the lovers and their love are described in images heady with the abundance of the physical world—lilies, herbs, spices, fish, fruit and vines. There is here no dualistic enmity between spirit and matter, body and soul: they fuse in perfectly balanced union. It is that union which Gian-Luca first dimly perceives, then denies and later seeks and finds.

Food *is* life since, without it life cannot be sustained. But life, or so some stubborn sense maintains, is more than bodies. If we cannot live without bread, we also cannot live by bread alone. We can hunger and thirst for righteousness as well as for food, and Christianity's mysteries culminate in a meal whose bread and wine are the body and blood of One who redeemed by suffering and died to bring eternal life.

If, at one point, Gian-Luca feels himself to be sinking beneath a nightmare vision of a brutally insatiable, mindlessly devouring world which lives to eat and for which food alone has meaning, that is, in part, because food does indeed hold so many meanings. Hall identifies most of them in *Adam's Breed*, using those countless descriptions of meals and those who prepare and eat them to reveal their often complex significance. Food—wanting it, getting it, evacuating it—shapes every new baby's life. Gian-Luca was no exception and in the pages devoted to his first weeks Hall creates a psychologically convincing (and very humorous) portrait of an eternally hungry young creature.

But she also begins to establish a set of extended symbolic meanings. Gian-Luca is not just himself: he is every baby who ever had to learn the hard way that food doesn't always come when you want it, sometimes disappears or even walks away before you've finished. That there is, in fact, a world of which you and your insatiable stomach are not the centre. That you are part of something larger than yourself and must find your place in it. Through food you learn your relation to that larger world: you are important in it (food comes when you yell) or insignificant (it doesn't). Through food you can change—or try to change—your position in the world, as the toddling Gian-Luca tries, unsuccessfully, to bribe an unyielding Teresa into loving him, in exchange for cherry jam. Food is punishment when you hurt someone who loves you by refusing to eat it. It confers status when you dine only at the Doric. It buys you friends who are happy to share your expensive meals. You can serve it, as a waiter does or as a peasant who tends vines. You can worship it, like the gourmet, and worship with it like the communicant. You can cheat with it, by claiming tinned asparagus is fresh or fight with it, by imposing naval blockades which bring starvation. Food, whose preparation generates so much tension, can mean brutality when healthy and efficient young waiters round viciously on older, tireder ones. And food, which means life for those who eat, always means death for what is eaten.

The price of life is always another's death. Language

reflects that: 'consume' contains a dead metaphor. 'We consume; food is consumed' may be translated as 'We annihilate; food is annihilated'. Once recognized, it becomes an inescapable truth. Gian-Luca recognizes it and can neither escape it nor bear it: (even as he listens to grapes being trodden in the vats, he hears 'the soft, slushing sound made by the grapes in dying'). If a man feels that for grapes, how much more must he feel for animals and humans? And how is such an intolerable vision of pain to be borne?

Radclyffe Hall was much preoccupied with all aspects of pain and suffering: physical pain caused by disease or cruelty; mental pain stemming from fear or loss; spiritual pain arising from guilt or a sense of separation from God; and that particular pain which springs from too keen an awareness of the fact of pain itself in the world. Her conversion to Roman Catholicism in 1912 helped to provide her with a framework within which to make sense of suffering, to redeem it with meaning and, sometimes, to make its meaning Redemption. The charge of masochism is often, and, I think, too glibly levelled against her. For much of her life she was simply unable not to see suffering. Subtly tied in with her deeply felt sense of her own 'maleness' was a passionately chivalric desire to protect the weak or wounded. In daily life she was, like most of us, capable of remarkably callous blindness to the needs of those closest to her and self-interest could make her cruel. Nevertheless pain, anguish, need and fear always called forth her strongest responses: the suffering of animals elicited the strongest of all.

So keen a sense of suffering could make her a taxing companion, as Una Troubridge recalled:

Since childhood I had loved animals, had revelled in the scanty opportunities afforded to a London child of country and farm life and had imposed my love of dogs, especially, upon my rather reluctant family. Since my marriage I had owned a number of dogs and they had always been cherished and well-cared for. Moreover I had inherited or acquired from my father a horror of killing and of all blood sports. But it was John, and John alone, who, without any conscious intention, taught me to appreciate the rights of animals and conferred on me the painful privilege of the 'seeing eye', until in the end I also could not fail to remark the underfed or overloaded horse or ass, the chained or neglected dog, the untamed bird in the dirty, cruelly tiny cage. But before my eyes were cleansed, I remember once to my shame saying angrily: 'You spoil everything! We can never go anywhere that you don't see some animal that makes you unhappy. . .'

(*The Life and Death of Radclyffe Hall*, pp. 50–51)

But the truth, horrifically, is that there is always something for the 'seeing eye' to see. As a child Gian-Luca had the seeing eye: children, so Hall believed and frequently said in her fiction, especially *The Sixth Beatitude*, often do. In adolescence and early manhood he lost it or, perhaps, preferred not to use it. He became 'sharp-eyed' instead, banishing pity as a luxury fit only for women and infants: and, anyway, it frightened him. . .

The relation between sight, in its physical sense, and vision, in its spiritual one, was something to which Hall returned again and again in her work: we see it in her earliest and her last. Her poem, 'The Blind Ploughman', was first published in 1913. Later, set to music, it became one of the most popular songs of a war in which so many men had lost their sight. Its sixteen short lines hold references to Ecclesiastes, The Song of Solomon, St Matthew and St Luke: its last verse runs

> God has made his sun to shine
> On both you and me;
> God, who took away my eyes,
> That my *soul* might see.

Her last completed novel, *The Sixth Beatitude*, published in 1936 seven years before her death, again fuses naturalism and symbolism in a remarkably vivid and loving portrait of a Romney Marsh community. The sixth beatitude says 'Blessed are the pure in heart for they shall see God'. Croft Lane's most 'disreputable' and 'immoral' inhabitant, Hannah Bullen, has conceived three illegitimate children by three different fathers. At the book's end she earns something very like sainthood and, indubitably, sees God.

xiii

It was not sentimentality that made animal suffering so terrible to Hall. Animals' greater vulnerability to human abuse, their subjection to human power, enjoins greater responsibility to them. They may not have souls ('It doesn't matter: they're not Christians!', yells Leone, Maddalena's disgusting teenage cousin, as he tortures yet another animal) but they are unquestionably part of God's creation and as such demand gentleness and respect. (Plants do, too: '. . . the sound made by the grapes in dying'.) For Hall, beasts and humans are linked in what the mediaeval philosophers called The Great Chain of Being: that intricately balanced network of mutuality and interdependencies which constitutes the physical world and both manifests and mirrors the God-head's love for its creation. To ignore that chain, despise it or seek to destroy it insults and wounds God.

Humans are indisputably the most destructive creatures in creation and animals their frequent victims. Yet sometimes more unites animals and humans than divides them. An elderly, lame and harassed waiter, in pain and overworked in a job he dare not lose, publicly humiliated by a padrone who calls him 'a lame old mule' in front of a crowded restaurant of diners, has much in common with the little Sardinian donkey whom Leone torments. A herd of cattle goaded uphill to the shambles, and already fear-crazed by the smell of blood heavy on the air, are close enough to men in battle (Rosa's son among them), driven over the top to the death they know waits for them. And both men and beasts are close to the Christ whose wooden roadside image the cattle-driver pauses to reverence before he turns to whip the beasts once more.

Animals become human, humans animal in the vision *Adam's Breed* unfolds. Maddalena is described as 'a trapped rabbit' when Gian-Luca rounds on her, as 'a mothering doe' whose sad eyes register the knowledge she has always known, that he does not love her as she loves him. Roberto, the little wine-waiter, has the eyes of a skylark. Gian-Luca's own heart, overtaxed in a weakened body, beats like the wings of the caged birds he freed because he could not bear to witness their captivity. The Doric's three fine rooms become 'the three verdant pastures for browsing'. Human cattle devour animals, often torturing them first, then themselves become beasts to be devoured: by Moloch, the greedy monster of War who sucks them into his cannon-mouth; by a second monster, an increasingly mechanized world, dangerously alienated from the earth and wrongly called Civilization, which devours the workers who made it:

What did it matter if the things that he saw were the work and the will of these people; all the hideous folly the work of their hands, all the hideous injustice the will of their brains; it was there, they had done it, they had built up the monster, and had called him Civilization. And now they were sweating great gouts of blood, or so it seemed to Gian-Luca—rich and poor, idlers and workers, they were all sweating blood. Ay, and the patient beasts that must serve them, all sweating great gouts of blood.

It is a bleak vision, but not Gian-Luca's final one. It brings him a despair close to madness but in it lies the beginning of his redemption: 'He could not find God in this anguish of pity, he could not find himself, he was utterly lost.' How can a man 'have himself' when he has lost himself? Not until Gian-Luca acknowledges that he is lost can he begin to free himself from Teresa's deluding belief in a spurious autonomy. Only then can he dare to acknowledge his own need to love, only then can he admit his own vulnerability, as love demands.

Deeply affected by suffering though she was, Radclyffe Hall was not, ultimately, despairing about it, because she believed she knew the solution and the solution was love. In the end it will be Gian-Luca's solution, too. 'God is Love', said Hall's unfailingly loving maternal grandmother who helped to bring her up and whom she adored. And God remained Love, despite the death of a lover, the hatreds and obloquy released by *The Well of Loneliness*'s trial for obscenity, a long and destructive triangular love relationship which saddened the last decade of her life, and an agonizing and protracted death from cancer of the bowel. 'I offer it to God', she said of the pain that could no longer be controlled by drugs. And, with a grin and a flash of that humour which so many people assume she never had, said of her imminent and excruciating death, 'What a life!' Momentarily her life mirrors her fiction as we remember Gian-Luca's question to the old Romany woman who befriends him in the New Forest. What, he asks her, is the Romany word for death? ' "Merripen", she said gravely. "And for life?" he inquired. "What is life in your language?" And she answered him: "Merripen".'

Life, it seems, is death and death is life. 'He that findeth his life shall lose it: and he that loseth his life for my sake shall find it', says Christ in St Matthew's gospel and that paradox, one of Christianity's most demanding, weaves its way through *Adam's Breed* and goes to the heart of Gian-Luca's agony. No longer able to bear the spectacle of a suffering world, he had turned his back upon it and gone in search of God. For many months God remained elusive, even though Gian-Luca had sensed that he was drawing nearer. When Maddalena writes, begging him to return to her, everything in him revolts against re-entering a world of pain. And yet he knows he must return—and in that knowledge at last finds God. For what impels him to go back is a courage and endurance greater than himself, based on a love which knows it must respond to Maddalena's human needs yet comes from and is offered to the divine. With the revelation of God's love comes a second revelation. The world's sorrow cannot be escaped: it must be joined and embraced. Gian-Luca's 'pity' was not love: rather, it came perilously close to fear and contempt for it kept a safe distance between him and the world. Now, in truth, he can begin to love:

There were spent, hunted stags; there were blind pit-ponies; there were children without eyes; and to such things he belonged by reason of his infinite pity. He was theirs, the servant of all that was helpless, even as God was their servant and their master. But one helpless thing needed him above all others, the sad, patient woman who waited—it was better to make one poor creature happy, than to mourn for the ninety and nine . . . he had grown frightened because he was lost, because he could not find God. And all the time God was here in himself, that was where he was, in Gian-Luca and in every poor struggling human heart that was capable of one kind impulse. . . The path of the world was the path of His sorrow, and the sorrow of God was the hope of the world, for to suffer with God was to share in the joy of His ultimate triumph over sorrow.

Reconciled at last to the world Gian-Luca, weakened by months of privation, has left it too late to return. As a boy he had lamented the lack of his own country: he was English to the Italians, Italian to the English. His long delayed visit to Italy, invested with so much hope and love, had revealed to him a nightmare of hitherto unimagined cruelty. His final revelation coincides with the beginning of his journey to another country, one that will be thoroughly familiar to him though he has been exiled from it all his life. It is a triumphant departure: even those who miss him most deeply—Maddalena, Rosa and her husband, Mario, the 'lame old mule',—recognize that.

Only Teresa does not. Teresa, who has never wept, only railed. Teresa, who has found no way to bear and thus transform her grief for Olga, found no way to love Gian-Luca. Teresa, who tore the plaster images from the wall and thought that concealing the holes left by the five nails—one for each wound of Christ—could obliterate the meaning of His passion. *Adam's Breed* ends as it began, with Teresa berating the Virgin, demanding the answer she refuses to hear.

Alison Hennegan, Cambridge, Easter 1985

BOOK ONE

CHAPTER ONE

I

TERESA BOSELLI stood at the window staring down at Old Compton Street; at the greasy pavements, the greasy roadway, the carts, the intolerable slow-moving vans, those vans, that to Teresa's agonized ears, seemed to rumble more loudly because of that window. There were men in the street, and women too, mothers—yet they let those vans go on rumbling; they did not know, and even if they knew they would probably continue on their way uncaring.

Teresa's whole being, soul, heart and brain, seemed to fuse itself together into something hard, resisting—a shield, a wall, a barricade of steel wherewith to shut away those sounds. In the street below the traffic blocked itself; protesting horses shuffled and stamped, their drivers shouted to each other, laughing; a boy went by whistling a music-hall song; a dog, perched jauntily on a grocer's cart, sprang up to bark at nothing in particular; and Teresa shook her clenched fists in the air, then let them drop stiffly to her sides. Her eyes, small, black and aggressively defiant, burnt with a kind of fury.

Turning from the window, she looked about the room with its horsehair arm-chair and couch. She herself had crocheted the antimacassars that, slightly out of shape and no longer very white, adorned the slippery horsehair. She herself had chosen the red serge curtains and the bottle-green window blind, the brown linoleum so very unlike parquet and the rug so alien to Persia. She herself had made the spotted muslin hangings over pink sateen that clothed the dressing-table, and she herself had pinned on the large pink bow wherewith they were looped together. She herself had fixed the little wooden bracket that held the patient plaster Virgin, and hers were the hands that had nailed the Sacred

9

Heart directly over the bedstead. A battered wooden bedstead, a battered Sacred Heart; the one from long enduring the travail of men's bodies, the other from long enduring the travail of their souls. In the oleograph the Heart was always bleeding—no one ever staunched it, no one ever worried. To Teresa it had stood for a symbol of salvation; she had sometimes condoned with its sufferings in her prayers, but never—no, not once—in her *life*. She had seen this particular picture of the Heart in a window near the church in Hatton Garden. She had gone in and bought it, three and sixpence it had cost. That had been six months ago this November, while Olga, the belovèd, the only child, the beautiful, had been away in Florence serving as maid to the children of rich Americans, teaching them Italian—*Maledetti!*

On the wooden bedstead lay an old patchwork quilt, the labour of Teresa's fingers, and under the quilt lay Olga, the belovèd, the labour of Teresa's body, and of Fabio, downstairs in the shop below cutting up mottled salame. But when Teresa thought of Olga, the belovèd, she tried not to think of Fabio.

Teresa was forty. For forty years she had stared at life out of fierce, black eyes that had only once softened to human passion, for the rest they had softened when she looked at Olga; but when she had prayed to the Blessed Virgin, to whose gentle service she had once been dedicated, her eyes had been frightened and sometimes defiant, but not soft as when she looked at Olga. 'Mea culpa, Mea culpa!' she had told the Blessed Virgin—remembering the one hot sin of her youth—'Ora pro nobis, Sancta Maria Virgio Mater Dei, Ora pro nobis.' And then: 'Take care of Olga, dear Mother of Jesus, preserve her from temptation and the lusts of men——'

Tall and spare as a birch tree was Teresa, as a birch tree that has waited in vain for the spring. Her wavy black hair was defying time; it shone, and where the light touched it, it bloomed, faintly blue in the light. Her forehead had much that was noble about it, but the brows—thick and coarse as those of a man—all but met above the arch of her nose, a few isolated hairs alone dividing them. A slight shade, more marked towards the corners of her mouth, added to the strong virile look of her. Her dress was sombre and rather austere, it was fastened at the throat by a large mosaic brooch, and in her ears she wore filigree gold ear-rings. A purposeful woman, an efficient woman, a woman who knew well that four farthings make a penny; a woman who liked the feel of those four farthings, who invested them with romance. Farthings, pennies, shillings, sovereigns—always the ultimate sovereigns. Golden things! Some people might like buttercups; Fabio did, for Fabio was simple, but Teresa preferred the cold beauty of sovereigns; sovereigns could buy flowers, but flowers could not buy sovereigns, her practical Tuscan mind told her that. And yet she was no miser, there was method in her saving, she saved for a definite reason, for Olga. Perhaps, too, she saved a little for Fabio, Fabio who was stupid where money was concerned. He could cut up salame into fine transparent slices, but only after Teresa had taught him how to do it; scolding, ridiculing, making him feel humble—Fabio who always replied: 'Sí, sí, cara.'

Long ago now, more than twenty years ago, she had said: 'If you love me, you'll marry me, Fabio, in spite of what you know has happened.'

And Fabio had said: 'I will kill him first, *Cane!*'

But Teresa had said: 'No, marry me first.'

And Fabio had replied: 'Allora——'

After that he had brought her back with him to England. Fabio had already been a naturalized Englishman at the time of his meeting with Teresa in Florence—he had found it convenient in his business—yet never was man more Latin in spirit. Short flares of temper and infinite patience; the patience that sat for hours waiting for trains in the heat of a Tuscan summer; the patience that suffered the hardships of conscription, and later the heart-breaking sunlessness of England, and later still, Teresa's cold marital endurance—Teresa who was always repenting the sin that Fabio had helped her to efface. Once back again in London among his salami, his spaghetti and his Parmesan cheeses, damped down by rain and fog and mud, and a little, perhaps, by Teresa's endurance, Fabio had forgotten to kill his 'Cane,' which doubtless was just as well. Only when Olga was born two years later did he remember how often he had prayed to Saint Joseph, the wise old patron of wedlock, that she might not be born too soon.

Sounds! The room was full of them, the house was full of them! The whole world was full of them—a hell composed of sounds! Footsteps in the shop below, the clanging of the shop bell—voices—Fabio's voice, then others, unknown voices. A door banging, the shop door, people going in and out. And always that ceaseless din of traffic in the street, now fainter, and now louder, more vindictive. Teresa's body tightened to do battle once again, as though by standing rigid and scarcely drawing breath she might hope to subdue the universe.

The figure on the bed moved a little and then sighed, and together with that sigh came a more imperious summons, the sharp, protesting, angry wailing of an infant not yet fully reconciled to life.

Teresa hurried to the bed. 'Olga!' she whispered, 'Olga!'

The girl's eyes opened and closed, then they opened again and remained fixed on Teresa; there was recognition in their gaze.

Teresa bent lower; the nurse had gone out, she would not be back for an hour. 'Who was he?'—the same monotonous question. 'Tell me, my darling—tell Mamma that loves you. Who was it hurt my little lamb?'

Olga's head moved from side to side; feebly, like some sore stricken creature, she beat with her hands on the patch-work quilt.

Teresa's strong arm slid under her shoulders. ' Tell Mamma,' she whispered close to her ear, 'tell Mamma, like a good child, Olga, my darling, and then the Blessed Virgin will make you well again.'

She spoke as she might have done fourteen years ago, when the five-year-old Olga had been coaxed and coerced into making some childish confession.

'Tell Mamma, Olga—tell Mamma.'

But the pale lips remained very gently closed. Olga, slipping back again into oblivion, kept her secret safe in her heart. Then Teresa's will to know rose up stern and terrible, the will of those countless peasant forbears, creatures of hot suns and icy winds, of mountains and valleys and strong, brown soil; creatures who, finding no man to respect them, had made a god of their self-respect, offering the virtue of their women on his shrine, not for that virtue's sake but for their own. And against this god in the days of her youth, at the time of the gathering in of the grapes, Teresa Boselli had passionately sinned, and had for ever after hated her sin; but never more hotly than at this moment when she saw it lifting its head in her child, in Olga, who, having betrayed her mother would not betray her lover. Teresa's thin form towered gaunt above the bed.

'Tell me!' she commanded. 'Tell me!'

The girl's lids had fallen, she was very far away; no sounds from the external world could reach her. Teresa stared down at the drawn young face, and her breast ached as though it would kill her with its pain. Groping for her rosary she tried to tell her beads, the Dolorous Mysteries, beginning in Gethsemane, and as each tragic decade came to a close she demanded the life of her child.

'Give me the fruit of my womb, Blessed Mary.'

Her prayers gathered force as her terror increased; the face on the pillow was changing, changing—it was growing very solemn, very aloof. In a passion of entreaty she dropped to her knees, pressing the rosary against her forehead until the beads scarred her flesh. In her anguish she struck at the gates of heaven, she tore at the garments of the Mother of God.

'Not like this—not like this—you spared me, spare her. I demand it of you—I demand Olga's life! Why should her sin be greater than mine? You who were a Mother, you who knew grief—you who saw death at the foot of the Cross—you whom I have served in penitence and love—I demand it of you—give me Olga's life!'

And Olga, drifting always farther away, lay with quiet, closed eyelids and motionless lips, giving her life's blood, but not the secret of her loyal and impenitent heart.

Then Teresa fell to weeping; she wept without restraint, noisily, heavily—her sobs shook the bed. From time to time she drank in her own tears.

The nurse came back. 'What's the matter, what's happened?' She laid her fingers on the girl's thin wrist. 'I must send your husband for the doctor,' she said, and she hurried downstairs to the shop.

Fabio lifted his head from his hands; he was sitting on a

narrow, high-legged stool behind his sausages and cheeses. A small man, himself as rotund as a cheese, with a mild, pale face, and a ring of grey hair that gave him a somewhat monkish appearance, in spite of his white coat and apron.

'Well?' he said, blinking at her a little.

The nurse shook her head: 'You must go for the doctor—any doctor if he's out.'

Fabio got heavily off his stool, his lips were trembling: 'You go,' he suggested. 'I would wish to be with our Olga.'

'No, I must go back—I'm needed upstairs—but be as quick as you can.'

3

Olga was dying—the doctor came and went; he would call again later, he told them.

'Fetch me a priest!' demanded Teresa, calm as a general now before battle. 'There is yet time enough for a miracle to happen, the Holy Oil has been known to save life.'

She stared across the bed at the kneeling Fabio.

'Don't drive me from Olga——' he pleaded pitifully.

Teresa was relentless: 'Do as I tell you!'

And getting to his feet he obeyed her.

4

That night, in spite of the Holy Oil, Olga went on her journey. After the great love that lay hidden in her heart, after the great anguish that lay whimpering in the basket, the spirit that was Olga slipped silently away to the Maker who would have no need to question, knowing all things and the reason thereof.

5

Teresa demanded to be left alone with her child and the child of her child, and because of her voice and the look in her eyes, Fabio left them alone. The room was shrouded in comparative darkness. Four thin, brown candles guarded the bed. From the little red lamp in front of the Virgin came a fitful, flickering glimmer. Teresa stood over the slender body, gazing down with her hard, black eyes; then she turned and lifted the baby from his basket, a tiny lump of protesting flesh muffled in folds of flannel. From her fumed-oak bracket the Virgin watched with a gentle, deprecating smile. She could not help that deprecating smile—it was moulded into plaster. Majestically, Teresa turned and faced her, and they looked at each other eye to eye. Then Teresa thrust the baby towards her, and the gesture was one of repudiation.

'Take him!' said Teresa. 'I give him to you, I have no use for him. He has stolen my joy, he has killed my child, and *you*, you have let him do it—therefore, you can have him, body and soul, but you cannot any longer have Teresa Boselli. Teresa Boselli has done with prayer, for you cannot answer and God cannot answer—possibly neither of you exists—but if you do exist, then I give this thing to you— do as you like with it, play with it, crush it, as you crushed its mother over there!'

Fabio came up quietly behind her; he had stolen back to her unperceived. He took the baby from her very gently.

'Little Gian-Luca come to Nonno,' he murmured, pressing his cheek against the child.

CHAPTER TWO

I

FABIO REARED himself up in bed. It was past midnight, and the candle was guttering prior to its final extinction. Fabio's hair, a dishevelled halo, stuck out grotesquely above his ears, his nightshirt, unbuttoned, showed the thick, black hairs that gave to his chest a fictitious look of strength, and his eyes so mild and placid by nature, harboured something very like anger.

'I *will* have him baptized!' he shouted suddenly. 'And I will have him called Gian-Luca!'

Teresa, her throat modestly concealed by the collar of her cotton night-gown, her hair brushed severely from her brow and plaited, her hands clasped before her on the red coverlet, looked at her husband coldly.

'Why baptized?' she inquired as though surprised. 'And if baptized, why Gian-Luca?'

Fabio turned to her: 'Is it you who speak so—you who have always been so pious?'

'I have done with piety,' said Teresa quietly, flicking some dust from the bedspread.

'And you would deny him the rites of the Church?'

'I have done with the Church,' said Teresa.

'Ah! Then perhaps you have done with God, too?'

'Yes, I have done with God, too.'

Fabio stared at his wife aghast. He had not been a practising Catholic for years; still, he had had his ideas about things, and God had been one of his ideas. Something angry and pitiful was stirring in his heart on behalf of the small Gian-Luca; a feeling that he was not receiving fair play, that for all he, Fabio, knew he was being deprived of some mystical, incomprehensible advantage, of something that he had a right to, and the more his heart smote him the angrier he grew.

'He *shall* be baptized!' he repeated furiously.

'Forms——' murmured Teresa, 'just meaningless forms——' and she shrugged her angular shoulders. The child began to cry, and stooping down she rocked the wicker bassinette. 'Just meaningless forms,' she murmured again, and then: 'Why Gian-Luca, Fabio?'

'It came to me so—it came to me, "Gian-Luca," I cannot say more than that.'

'It came to you so?'

'Yes, I thought "Gian-Luca," as I took him from you that night.'

'I see—a sign from heaven, I suppose?'

'Corpo di Bacco!' bellowed Fabio. 'Corpo di Bacco! I will baptize him now, I myself will baptize him!'

He lunged out of bed and over to the wash-stand, dipping his fingers in the jug. Bending down to the now quiet infant, he made the sign of the cross on its forehead. 'Gian-Luca, I baptize thee,' he muttered fiercely, 'in the Name of the Father, and of the Son, and of the Holy Ghost.' Then his anger suddenly deserted him. He looked up at Teresa; she was watching the proceedings with a little smile on her lips.

Feeling cold and rather frightened, he crawled back to bed and tried to take her in his arms. 'My Teresa,' he whispered, 'be gentle, my Teresa, don't hate our little grandson so much—be gentle to him for Olga's sake— perhaps, she can see us, who knows?'

'Fool!' said Teresa. 'Olga is dead; it would have been better if the child had died too. I feel nothing any more, neither love nor hate, my heart is broken. Can a broken heart feel?'

'I will try to mend it for you,' he pleaded.

'You!' she said, turning her face away.

The candle guttered and went out. Fabio stared miserably into the darkness; he prayed a little but without much hope, he had always been rather hopeless in his prayers, always a little too fearful of God. And meanwhile the newly baptized Gian-Luca had mercifully gone off to sleep, his crumpled face was pressed into the pillow, his round, shiny head, ridiculously bald, was slightly bedewed with sweat. From time to time Teresa's hand dropped softly and set the cradle in motion; this she did automatically, from a sense of duty and custom. The rocking of the cradle fell into line with a hundred other everyday duties that must and would be accomplished, and presently Gian-Luca would fall into line too. He would never be neglected; like the shop and the house he would always be kept clean and sweet, and like the shop and the house he would come to long at times for the hand that dishevelled, that rendered untidy, in a foolish access of affection.

2

Gian-Luca having no one to talk to, and having no language wherewith to talk in any case, found himself, as all infants must be, at a great disadvantage in relation to life. Had his mind been a blank, as people seemed to think, it would have been easier not to howl; but his mind was a turbulent seething muddle, in which colic and darkness and the sudden flare of gas-jets and ticklings and prickings and stupid grasping hands and uncomfortable confinement in preposterous positions, were all jumbled together in nebulous chaos, impossible at first to disentangle. From this chaos one day there suddenly emerged a creature who was beautifully concrete, a kindly young woman who had always been there and had always borne a relation to hunger and to hunger's ultimate appeasement. But whereas before she, like everything else, had been part of the haze called life, she now emerged a well-defined being that was capable of arousing anger or approval, capable of being smiled at or howled at, capable even, of being thumped. She could open her bodice and give you what you wanted, or she could refuse to do so. In the latter contingency you felt blind with rage, in the former you felt much less than was supposed, much less indeed than you appeared to be feeling; in the former you quickly became atavistic, doing what you must, automatically, because something, somewhere, ordered you to live.

The concrete creature was Rosa Varese, the daughter of Nerone who sold tobacco a little way down the street; she was married and had lost her own baby of croup in the very nick of time to provide you with dinners, but all this of course you did not know, nor would you have cared if you had. Your emotions were entirely concerned with yourself, not through any wish of yours, but by order of that something that commanded you, Gian-Luca, to live.

Side by side with the curious mystery of food was the mystery of safety-pins; the first inanimate objects these to emerge from the nebulous chaos. They could press, they could prick, they could feel hard and cold, in fact they could fill you with fury; but—and this was what was so strange about them—they could fall into your lap and look very alluring—beautiful even when they lay in your lap, so beautiful that you wished to pay homage and in consequence put them in your mouth. Safety-pins, no doubt rather humble in themselves, were nevertheless important; through discovering them you discovered other things such as coal and soap and thimbles; in a word you developed your sense of beauty, and your instinct told you to worship beauty by trying to swallow it.

But although you were fast becoming familiar with the joys and sorrows of life, there were still big gaps in your comprehension; for instance, the things that they put on your feet—they caused you a most peculiar sensation, you wanted to cry, you wanted to laugh, you wanted above all to pull them off. But whenever you succeeded in pulling them off, someone was always there to slap your hands, and this, in view of your awakening perceptions, struck you as outrageously unjust. And then there was that thing they put on your head, it tormented you and tickled your ears; you were fastened to it by something soft, something that went under your chin. One day you discovered that the something soft could be chewed, and in consequence you chewed it—you did not try to swallow it like beauty—and since you could make but small impression with your gums, why did they always pull it away, making sounds meanwhile that you disapproved of?

Sounds! You began to listen for sounds, you tried to make them yourself, you began to feel that it was not enough to crow or to howl or to gurgle. You began to feel that given time, you yourself would make sounds that counted; you were still rather vague as to what they would be, but you knew that somewhere out of the void would come sounds that belonged exclusively to you; others might make them but that would not matter, for with some sort of magic that you did not understand, the fact that you made them would mean that they were yours, as surely as your mouth was yours. One way and another you were full of curiosity, full of a desire to do things. When you had done them they occasionally hurt you, as when you bit the buckle of your pram-strap and made your gum bleed, but taken on the whole you considered it worth while, and the next day you ducked your head and bit the thing again—that was the way to face life, you felt.

3

Rosa spoke seldom but cried very often, so that poor Gian-Luca had not the advantage of hearing those consoling expressions of endearment that presumably help the infant sub-conscious to resign itself to life. Had he not possessed a great joy of living, in spite of colic and other tiresome things, Rosa's tears might very well have damped him; as it was they only irritated. Her tears had a way of dripping on to his head in the very middle of dinner, and he vaguely divined, as it were by instinct, that they spoilt the quality of the dinner itself, which was of course quite inexcusable.

He could not understand the element of tears, they were wet like his bath but they tasted different, and they came for all sorts of unexpected reasons, for instance when you bumped your head. Rosa would stare at Gian-Luca in silence, and then there would come a noise in her throat, sometimes a series of noises even; 'Mio bambino——' and then more noises and something splashing off her on to him. They usually spent the day at the Bosellis', but every night she returned with Gian-Luca to her father's tobacco shop down the street where she and her husband lived. She was young and bereaved; she gave of her milk but not yet of her heart, that was not to be expected; her heart was far away with quite another baby, whose food Gian-Luca was consuming.

Gian-Luca had a queer, old wooden cradle beside the bed shared by Rosa and her husband. He liked Rosa's husband, a handsome young man who roared and slapped his thighs; not so much to please Gian-Luca as to please himself—he had never quite grown up. He did a delightful thing too, every morning, he smeared a species of foam on to his chin; he smeared some on to Gian-Luca's one day, and Gian-Luca licked it off. The tobacconist was not quite so amusing, still, it must be admitted that he had a wooden leg. . . . The leg made a most arresting noise when he walked —thump, thump, thump, thump—Gian-Luca would listen, and rock with excitement when he heard it. If it had not been for a tendency to colic, every minute of the day would have seemed worth while, but of course one's stomach being nearly the whole of one, it is apt to have very large pains.

Rosa's husband was a waiter at the Capo di Monte and when he came home, which he did very late, he naturally wanted his sleep. He suffered from a swollen joint on one foot, and this made him angry at times. Between Gian-Luca's colic and Rosa's tears and the pain in that joint when he took off his shoe, his nights were becoming decidedly unpleasant, which reacted on them all in the mornings. There were mornings now, growing more frequent of late, when his roaring, even to Gian-Luca's ears, did not suggest a game; when he and Rosa would settle down to quarrel, which they always did in English because they both disliked it, and because each knew that the other disliked it. Their quarrel-English was particularly florid and beautifully free from restraint; it largely partook of Saturday nights outside the 'George and Dragon.'

Gian-Luca learnt that certain sounds were ugly, that they made you feel strangely disturbed and unsafe. He also learnt that some sounds might be soothing, as for instance when Mario and Rosa made it up with many soft murmurings and kissings. As the weeks turned into months he became all ears, he became a kind of reservoir for words. The words went filtering into him through his very skin, and finally emerged in one loud, triumphant vocable: 'Gug!' said Gian-Luca, and then—'Gug!'

But 'Gug' was not enough, gratifying though it was, it could only express Gian-Luca, and by the time Gian-Luca had known the world a year, he had come to realize that to make one's presence felt one might have to express a few other things as well—a bore perhaps, but there it was. Gian-Luca looked about him for the next most worthy object, and wisely decided that four legs and a tail, to say nothing of a thoroughly soul-satisfying bark, had every right to his attention. 'Dog!' said Gian-Luca, staring at the mongrel that wandered in and out of Nerone's little shop.

'Doggie!' said Rosa, as one talking to an infant.

'Dog,' repeated Gian-Luca firmly.

'Poveretto!' wept Rosa to Mario that evening. 'That his first word should be "doggie" instead of "mamma," poveretto—what a world of misery we live in!'

'You would think so if you had my bunion,' grumbled Mario; then he kissed her, for of course a dead baby hurt far more than even the most virile bunion.

But though Rosa wept with pity, Gian-Luca did not weep; what the ear has never heard and the eye has never seen, the heart of one year's beating cannot mourn for. In his vast self-satisfaction he walked towards the coal box, fell down, got up, fell down, and finally decided that Nature was not mocked, and that progress on all fours was the only mode of locomotion.

4

Fabio was told the marvel, Gian-Luca had said 'Dog', and Fabio was thoroughly offended.

'Nonno, Nonno, Nonno!' he cried, pointing to himself. 'Little Gian-Luca must say, Nonno!'

Gian-Luca eyed him kindly, he liked his funny hair, and reaching up he pulled it politely.

'Ecco!' exclaimed Fabio. 'He is as strong as any giant, but all giants call their grandfathers "Nonno," don't they Teresa? They say: "Nonno, Nonno!"'

Teresa looked up from a mound of pale grey knitting, then she dropped her eyes again without speaking. She was always knitting something in her spare time these days, knitting had become her obsession. She knitted in the shop, in her cash-desk, during meals, and at night she would knit herself to sleep. She knitted very fast, with a harshly stabbing needle, occasionally raising the needle to her head for a swift, proficient scratch between the stitches.

'Pearl one, knit two, pearl one,' murmured Teresa glancing at a book that lay beside her.

'Nonno! Nonno! Nonno! Say Nonno!' shouted Fabio, shaking a finger at Gian-Luca.

'Poveretto!' began Rosa, with her apron to her eyes, preparing to burst into tears.

But at that Teresa suddenly looked up from her knitting. 'Basta e supera, you hear?' she said sharply; then, as though she had forgotten Rosa, 'Knit one, pearl one, slip one.'

Gian-Luca considered 'Nonno' for some weeks before he finally said it, and when he did so he made a grave mistake; he applied it, not to Fabio, but to the wooden leg of Fabio's friend and rival down the street. The leg had been particularly active for some time, Gian-Luca had heard it for an hour, and when its owner, balancing himself against the counter, had actually lifted it and waved it in the air— 'Nonno!' screamed Gian-Luca, beside himself with pleasure.

It was very unfortunate that Fabio should have entered to buy some 'Macedonia' at that moment. It was even more unfortunate that Nerone should have laughed, with something like triumph in his eyes. Fabio surveyed the group, thrust his hands into his pockets, and left the shop without a word.

'Ma che!' exclaimed Nerone, in an access of delight, 'Ma che! I think him jealous of my stump!'

For fifteen years these two had behaved like ageing children; quarrelling, boasting, teasing, and loving—always loving—but quick to take advantage of each other whenever it offered.

'That salame—very bad, your place is going to pieces, Fabio. You naturalize yourself and then you sell us bad salame, the salame looks at you and then goes bad.'

'I do *not* sell bad salame—mine is the best in England. As for you, you talk and talk, then sell rotten cigarettes, all powder, one might as well smoke snuff.'

'You accuse my cigarettes, straight from Italy they come.'

'Teresa says they come more likely from the Ark. Teresa says I cough—"That is Nerone," she says, "with his rotten Macedonia all dropping out one end." She says: "That is that old fox Nerone."'

'Ah! So that is what Teresa says. Well now, tell me this

my Fabio, you find tobacco in my smokes, is it not? What else do you find, beside tobacco?'

'The dust from the shop.'

'Oh, I find much more than that—oh, much more, in your salame.'

'And please, what do you find?'

'If I tell you you will get angry.'

'Not at all, I know my salame, he is prime.'

'Prime you say? Santa Madonna! Listen to him, prime he says! Very well, then, it is prime, but—I find a little worm. He looks at me, I look at him, he bows, I lift my hat. I have him in a tumbler, come and see!'

For fifteen years these two had played dominoes together, drinking Amarena in the evenings. When Fabio lost the game—as he nearly always did—Nerone would openly rejoice; if, however, Fabio won it, Nerone lost his temper, and that made Fabio happy for a week. When both their wives had been alive, before Nerone became a widower, they had managed to quarrel over them:

'My Lucrezia, what a cook! What a marvellous risotto! Why do you let your Teresa boil her rice into a pulp? You should send her here, Lucrezia will teach her how to boil it.'

'Then you send us your Lucrezia, and we will show her zabaione, we will teach her not to turn it into lumps like scrambled eggs!'

But when sorrow had come upon them—and to Fabio shame as well—they had ceased to nag each other for the moment. They had turned away their eyes, while their hearts grew kind and shy, neither had wished to see the sorrow of the other. They had found no words, or if they spoke they did so fearfully, timid of saying the wrong thing. And when Lucrezia died, Fabio sent a wreath of iris, so large that it ousted all the other floral tributes. And when Olga died, Nerone sent a splendid cross of roses, and: 'I will have them white, all white,' he told the florist.

5

No sooner had Gian-Luca found his tongue, than he found his feet with a vengeance; there were set-backs, of course, but to all intents and purposes he quickly became a biped. His adventures increased and multiplied, leading him now into strange, alluring places: the backyard, for instance, where the empty cases stood, festooned with flue and smuts. These empty packing-cases attracted him greatly; they were dirty, they were hollow, and queer, fantastic labels, together with all sorts of scrawls and lines and crosses appeared on their battered sides. To do them justice, they were very wise old cases, having travelled with aplomb all the way from Italy. Gian-Luca, of course, was not aware of this, still he felt that there was something about them. . . . This conviction of his grew and grew, until he longed for a fuller communion, a communion only to be properly attained by filling the void with himself. Into the lowest and kindest of the cases Gian-Luca heaved his minute proportions, to discover—as occasionally happens—that in life it is simpler to get in than to get out, and this revelation when it came was terrific; he was rescued half an hour later by Teresa; still, there had been that half-hour——

At about this time they weaned him from Rosa, and Gian-Luca made his first acquaintance with sorrow. Rosa came daily to push his perambulator, but Rosa, without the comfort of her breasts, was not Rosa to him any more. She seemed cold and aloof; 'tout passe, tout lasse . . .' but naturally Gian-Luca did not know this fact as yet. Though Gian-Luca sorrowed, yet his Rosa rejoiced, she no longer splashed him with tears; if her lips trembled now they did so with smiles, nay more, she was constantly laughing. 'I will bring you a little new friend, one day soon!' she had taken to whispering in his ear; and sometimes she led him into a church, and sat clicking her rosary just above his nose, while he kicked and protested on her lap. 'You must not tell Nonna where we have been,' Rosa would caution, holding up her finger; just as though Gian-Luca knew where they had been, or could have told Nonna if he had!

Sometimes Rosa would stay on and play with him a little in the room that had once been Olga's, but more often he would be shut up there alone, and this, for some reason, he did not object to—he liked the room that had been Olga's. There were bars in front of the window now, and a high nursery guard for the occasional fire, but beyond these two drawbacks the room was all his, his to do with as he listed. He could twist the large knobs on the wash-stand by the window, he could crawl away under the bed, he could climb along the charming slippery horsehair sofa or toboggan down the seat of the chair. He could stare in fascination at the deep wounds in the wall; one just above the bed and four just opposite. He longed to put his finger into these deep wounds, but found that they were too high up. In the region of the wounds the paper hung torn and jagged— it looked like mutilated skin; and Gian-Luca, all agog with primitive instinct, would ache and ache to tear it away.

'Gug!' said Gian-Luca, returning fiercely to his first form of self-expression, 'Gug! Gug!' And his small hand would grasp the empty air in its eager will towards destruction. Except for those five wounds the walls were quite bare; Teresa had left them just as they had been on the night when Olga died. Only the Virgin, together with her bracket, and the Heart—whose bleeding no hand ever staunched— had gone, and in their place were the wounds that Gian-Luca longed to prod.

CHAPTER THREE

I

WHEN HE was four a splendid thing happened; Gian-Luca was given the freedom of the shop. It had been impossible to do other than accord it, short of tying up Gian-Luca's legs, so Teresa threw open the door from the parlour and said: 'Go—but do not steal the pickles.'

This occurred one morning in July, when the warmth of the sun was busily engaged in coaxing out endless smells. The street door was also standing wide open, and through it came a series of rumblings and shoutings that expressed the spirit of Old Compton Street.

The shop! All his life Gian-Luca remembered those first impressions of the shop; the size of it, the smell of it, the dim, mysterious gloom of it—a gloom from which strange objects would continually jump out and try to hit you in the face—but above all the smell, that wonderful smell that belongs to the Salumeria. The shop smelt of sawdust and cheeses and pickles and olives and sausages and garlic; the shop smelt of oil and cans and Chianti and a little of split peas and lentils; the shop smelt of coffee and sour brown bread and very faintly of vanilla; the shop smelt of people, of Fabio's boot blacking, and of all the boots that went in and out unblacked; it also smelt of Old Compton Street, a dusty, adventurous smell.

Gian-Luca stared about him in amazement and awe, he had never known before this moment how truly great Nonno was, but he saw now that Nonno distributed like God, and that what he distributed was good. From the ceiling were suspended innumerable coils of what looked like preserved intestines. They may possibly have been intestines at one time, but when Fabio sold them they had beautiful names: 'Bondiola,' 'Salsiccie,' 'Salami di Milano,' in other words they were sausages. The sausages varied as much in figure as they did, presumably, in taste; there were short stumpy sausages; fat, bulging sausages; sly, thin sausages; anatomical sausages. There were regal sausages attired in silver paper, there were patriotic sausages in red, white and green, and endless little humble fellows hanging on a string, who looked rather self-conscious and shy.

And the pasta! There were plates of it, cases of it, drawers of it, and all the drawers had neat glass fronts. The glass-fronted drawers were entirely set apart for the aristocracy of pasta. One saw at a glance that social etiquette was very rigidly observed, each family of pasta kept strictly to itself, there were no new-fangled ideas.

There were paste from Naples, marked: 'Super Fine.' —Tagliatelle, Gnocchi, Zita, Mezzani, Bavettine, and the learned Alfabeto. There were paste from Bologna— Cestini, Farfalle Tonde; and from Genoa, the conch-like decorative Bicorni and the pious Capelli di Angelo. There were paste shaped like thimbles and others shaped like cushions and yet others like celestial bodies; there were rings and tubes and skeins and ribbons, all made of pasta; there were leaves and flowers and frills and ruchings, all made of pasta; there were yards of slim white paste that suggested vermifuge, and many leagues of common macaroni. The common macaroni had to fend as best it could—it lay about in heaps on the floor.

But not alone did Fabio deal in sausages and pasta, he dealt in many other things. Providing as he did a smell for every nose, he also provided a taste for every palate. Huge jars of plump, green olives, floating in turgid juices, stood ready to be fished for with the squat, round wooden spoons; a galaxy of cheeses, all approaching adolescence, rolled or sprawled or oozed about the counter. Tomatoes, in every form most alien to their nature, huddled in cans along a shelf; there were endless sauces, endless pickles, endless pots of mustard, endless bins of split and dried and powdered peas. There were also endless bottles containing ornate liquids—Menta, Arancio, Framboise, Grenadine, Limone—beautiful, gem-like liquids, that when a sunbeam touched them glowed with a kind of rapture—came alive. Chianti in straw petticoats, blinked through its thin-necked bottles, suspended from large hooks along the walls, while beneath it, in the shadowy bins, lurked yellow Orvieto, full-blooded, hot Barolo and the golden Tears of Christ. Apples, nutmegs, soups and jellies, herring-roes and tinned crustacea, rubbed shoulders with the honey of Bormio. A kind of garden this, a Garden of Eden, with a tree of life on whose long-suffering sides had been grafted all the strange stomachic lusts of modern Adam. And as God once walked conversing with His offspring in the garden, so now, the worthy Fabio moved among his customers; a mild-faced, placid Deity, himself grown plump with feeding—smelling of food and wine and perspiration.

In the little wooden cash-desk sat Teresa at her knitting, with a pen-holder stuck behind her ear. A black-browed, imperturbably austere, regenerate Eve, completely indifferent to apples. From time to time she laid aside her knitting, found her pen, and proceeded to make entries in the ledger. Gian-Luca, looking at her, felt that Nonno might be God, but that Nonna was the source from which he sprang. Nonna controlled a drawer from which flowed gold and silver; enormous wealth, the kind of wealth that no amount of saving could ever hope to find in money-boxes.

Gian-Luca had suspected the omnipotence of Nonna, and now his suspicions were confirmed. He knew, had always known, that Nonna must be worshipped, that moreover, she was worthy of his worship. For one thing she was beautiful, she had small, black, shining eyes, and hair that reminded him of coal. He often longed to rub his cheek against her glossy hair, only somehow that would not go with worship. He adored her bushy eyebrows—one eyebrow when she frowned—not unlike Nerone's moustache—and the downy, dusky look just above her upper lip, and the tallness and the gauntness of her. He admired her long, brown fingers with their close-pared, oval nails, and her heavy ears that held the filigree gold ear-rings. He admired her blue felt slippers and her flannel dressing-gown, and most of all the queerness and the coldness that was Nonna in relation to Gian-Luca himself. It would be:

'Nonna, Nonna!'

'Yes, Gian-Luca, what is it?'

'See my horse! Look, I will make him run!'

And the horse would run, would gallop, on his little wooden wheels, but Nonna would go on with her knitting.

Or:

'Nonna!'

'Yes, Gian-Luca?'

'I want to kiss your finger.'

'Do not be foolish, fingers are for work.'

'Then may I touch your ear-rings?'

'No.'

'Then may I see your knitting?'

'Gian-Luca—run upstairs and play with Rosa.'

She was conscientious, quiet and she never lost her temper; Nerone had large rages, even Fabio had small rages, but Nonna very seldom raised her voice. And he loved her. With the strange perversity of childhood, he found her a creature meet for love. Her aloofness did but add to the ardour of his loving, to the wonder and fascination of her. From the room that had been Olga's, he would often hear her footsteps passing and repassing on the landing; now surely she was coming—she was coming in at last; but she never came—Gian-Luca wondered why. It was Rosa who swept that room and tidied up his toys; it was Rosa who washed his hands and slapped him and caressed him. Rosa would call him: 'piccolo,' 'amore,' 'cuore mio,' but Teresa called him Gian-Luca. Fabio would call him 'angiolo,' 'tesoro,' 'briccone,' but Teresa called him Gian-Luca; and in this there lay great loneliness, great cause for speculation, and yet greater cause for further loving.

2

Teresa looked up from her knitting one evening, and her eyes rested long on her grandson.

'Gian-Luca, come here.'

He slid off his chair and went to her, shy but adoring. The light from the lamp lay across her long hands and fell on one side of her hair. It fell on Gian-Luca and illumined him also—a thin little boy in a black overall with a large smear of jam down the front.

'You have spilt your jam, Gian-Luca,' said Teresa promptly, but her eyes were not on the stain; then she did a very unexpected thing, she suddenly touched his hair. For a moment her hand lingered on his head, feeling the ashen-fair mop, feeling as one who is blind might feel, seeking for sight through the fingers. 'This has nothing to do with us,' she said slowly.

Fabio put down his paper and frowned: 'You mean?'

She was silent for a moment, pointing. Then: 'This hair has nothing to do with us,' she repeated in her flat, even voice.

Fabio's frown deepened. 'What of it?' he muttered. 'What can it matter, the colour of his hair?'

But Teresa had turned the child's face to the light and was staring down into his eyes.

Gian-Luca's eyes, neither grey, blue nor hazel, were a curious compound of all three. They were limpid, too, like the cool, little lakes that are found high up in mountains. His were the eyes of Northern Italy—the eyes that the vast barbarian hordes, sweeping over the vineclad fruitful valleys, had bequeathed to the full-breasted, fruitful women —the eyes that they would see in their sons.

'Nor have we such eyes in our stock,' said Teresa, and she pushed Gian-Luca away.

He stood and surveyed her gravely, reproachfully, out of those alien eyes.

'It is bed-time,' she told him. 'Little boys must go to bed.'

'Sí, sí', agreed Fabio anxiously. 'They must.'

Gian-Luca went up and kissed Teresa on both cheeks; every evening he kissed her like this, on both cheeks, as family custom demanded. Then he turned and kissed Fabio also on both cheeks; Fabio was very prickly to kiss, for he shaved only twice a week.

'I will come and turn out the gas,' Teresa told him, 'and do not take too long undressing yourself, and do not eat the orange Nonno gave you until to-morrow, it would make your stomach ache.'

Gian-Luca nodded and went towards the door, but in looking back he felt anxious and perturbed to see that Nonna had dropped her knitting and was staring blankly at the wall.

Gian-Luca was usually quite happy in the darkness, after Teresa had put out the light. The darkness had never held terrors for him; he liked it, he found it friendly. Moreover, when he closed his eyes and lay half dozing, he would sometimes see pictures inside his head; vivid and clear and beautiful they were, like a landscape after spring rain. Gian-Luca knew something of trees and grass—once or twice he had been on excursions out of London with Rosa and her husband—but nothing he had seen then came up to his pictures; the only trouble was that they faded away if he so much as drew breath. In Gian-Luca's pictures there were wide green spaces, and once there had been running water; sometimes there were low-lying, far-away hills, and sometimes a kind of beautiful gloom—green, from the leaves that made it. The pictures were happy, intensely happy, and Gian-Luca grew happy as he saw them. By the next day, however, he had always forgotten their most alluring details; he would have to wait until he went to bed again, and then the darkness would remind him; back would come memory and sometimes new pictures, and that was why he liked the darkness.

To-night, however, the pictures would not come, though he shut his eyes and waited. The act of shutting his eyes disturbed him, it reminded him suddenly of Nonna. Nonna had stared down into his eyes; she had felt his hair too, and had said things about it—she had said things about his hair and his eyes, things that he had not understood. For a moment, when her hand had rested on his head, he had thought that she meant to caress him; Nonna was not at all given to caresses, still, for one moment he had thought . . . Well, then he had realized, without knowing how, that Nonna was not being kind—she was not being actually unkind either, only—she hated his hair. He lay and pondered these things, bewildered, and his heart felt afraid because of its love. It was dreadful to love a goddess like Nonna—a goddess who hated your hair——

He began crying softly to himself in the darkness, a sniffling, lonely kind of crying. The pictures would not come and Nonna would not come; why should she come when she hated his hair? Still crying, he drifted away into sleep and dreamt of hair and eyes; quantities of fair hair that blew about him, strangling; two strange, pale eyes, that snapped themselves together and became one enormous, threatening orb, watchful, coldly vindictive.

He woke because there were voices in the room; Fabio and Teresa were undressing. From his cot that stood beside their double bed, he could see them moving about. They spoke in hissing, insistent whispers, doubtless lest they should disturb him. He closed his eyes again, pretending to sleep, he did not want Nonna to look at him just then. Her voice sounded different, perhaps, because she whispered, perhaps because she hated his hair. The same words recurring over and over—'Olga,' and then: 'But his hair—his eyes——' over and over again. Long after both of them had climbed into bed they continued whispering together; they always seemed to be whispering about Olga, and once Nonno said, 'How lovely she was!' And Gian-Luca thought that Nonna sighed. No, he *could* not bear it; he put out his hand and tweaked the sleeve of her night-gown. He could hear the swift movement of surprise that followed.

'Go to sleep, Gian-Luca,' she said coldly.

After that they did not whisper any more, and he must have obeyed her and fallen asleep, for the very next moment it was morning.

4

That day he said: 'Rosa, tell me, who is Olga-how-lovely-she-was?'

Rosa went crimson. 'You listen!' she chided, frowning at him darkly.

He ignored this remark and clung to his point: 'Who is Olga?' he persisted. At the back of his mind was a far, faint memory of having heard that name before.

'You come quick, or I go tell Nonna! You come quick out!' scolded Rosa; and then relenting, 'Oh, look, look, caro! See those pretty flowers, Rosa buy you a bunch.'

He was not deceived, though he took the flowers and allowed her to stoop and kiss him. For some reason she did not like Olga, that was plain—perhaps because Olga had his sort of hair.

At dinner he looked up from a plate of macaroni and said suddenly, 'Who is Olga?'

There ensued a long moment of deathly silence while Teresa and Fabio stared at each other; then Teresa said quietly:

'Where have you heard?'

And Gian-Luca answered: 'Last night.'

'Olga,' said Teresa, 'was my little girl. She is not here, she is dead.'

'Olga,' said Fabio, 'was your mother, Gian-Luca.' And getting up slowly he went to a drawer. 'This is her picture when she was small—this is Olga, Gian-Luca.'

Gian-Luca clapped his hands: 'Pretty, pretty!' he babbled, delighted with what he saw.

Teresa and Fabio exchanged a quick glance, then Fabio put away the photograph. Teresa took up her knitting again—she was knitting a waistcoat for Fabio. Gian-Luca watched her efficient brown hands moving in the bright-coloured wools; he was thinking of Nonna's little girl. Nonna's little girl was a matter of importance, was something that he could understand; moreover, it was comforting, it brought Nonna nearer, it made her seem so much more accessible somehow, and more—well, a trifle more like other people. Rosa, for instance, had a little girl now, a plump, fretful creature of two and a half; her name was Berta, and she grabbed Gian-Luca's toys with amazing acquisitiveness for one who was so young. Rosa would dump her down on the floor while she swept and dusted his room in the morning, pausing now and then to exclaim in admiration:

'Bella, la mia Berta!' And then to Gian-Luca: 'Bella, la mia bambina, non è vero?'

Gian-Luca thought that Berta was cross and fat and ugly, and in any case he was rather jealous of her, she took up too much of Rosa's time. But Nonna's little girl looked neither cross nor ugly; on the contrary, she was pretty and had masses of dark hair. He stared across at Nonna; had she ever played? he wondered—with him she was anything but playful!

Nonna must have felt that his eyes were upon her, for she raised her own eyes and said, not unkindly: 'We will not talk of Olga, Gian-Luca.'

34

'Why?' he protested.

'She is dead,' said Nonna: 'one does not talk of the dead.'

And after that nobody talked any more, so the meal was finished in silence.

5

In the afternoon Fabio reached down his hat and went in search of Gian-Luca: 'Come, tesoro, I will take you for a walk, Nonna will guard the shop.' He held out a friendly hand to the child, and together they turned into the street. 'Would you like to go and play with Berta?' inquired Fabio, anxious, as always, to be kind.

Gian-Luca shook his head, but after a moment: 'I would like to play with Olga.'

Fabio said dully: 'Olga is in heaven, she cannot play, piccino.'

'No?' Gian-Luca's voice sounded doubtful. 'Do they not play in heaven, Nonno? Do they not want to play?'

'They are with God,' Fabio told him gently.

'And will not God play with them?'

'God does not play.'

'I do not like God,' said Gian-Luca.

'And yet He is good——' murmured Fabio to himself. 'I am almost certain He is good——'

They walked on in silence for a while after that; it was hot, and Gian-Luca's legs began to flag, Fabio stooped down and took him in his arms.

'Nonno is a horse, you shall ride!' he said gaily, as though to reassure the child.

Fabio ran a little and Gian-Luca laughed, thumping to make him go faster. In this manner they returned to Old Compton Street; the sweat was pouring down Fabio's face. At the door of his shop stood Rocca, the butcher, enjoying the balmy air. Rocca saw Fabio:

'Buon giorno, Capitano!' Rocca had been a good soldier in his day, and now he used military titles for fun. 'Buon giorno, Capitano!' he shouted.

Rocca was much esteemed for his meat, which was usually both cheap and tender. He was also much esteemed for himself—an honest fellow if somewhat lacking in the

35

gift of imagination. As a rule, his display of edible wares was moderately unobtrusive, but to-day he had something arresting to show; Rocca had purchased a couple of kids, which dangled outside his window. The kids were very realistic indeed, they hung there complete, pelts and all. Their little hind legs were bent back over sticks, their noses pointed to the pavement. They looked young but resigned, and their patient mouths had set in a vaguely innocent smile. In their stomachs were long, straight purposeful slits through which their entrails had been drawn. Despite that innocent smile on their mouths, their eyes were terribly dead and regretful, and as they swung there, just over the pavement, they bled a little from their wounds.

'Belli, eh?' demanded Rocca.

'Ma sí!' agreed Fabio, lifting Gian-Luca higher in his arms, whereupon Gian-Luca burst into tears.

'Oh, poor—oh, poor——' he sobbed wildly.

'Ma che!' exclaimed Fabio, genuinely astonished, 'what is the matter, piccinino?'

But Gian-Luca could not tell him, could not explain.

'Can it be the little goats?' inquired Fabio incredulously. 'But do not cry so, my pretty, my lamb, they cannot hurt you, they are dead!'

'Ecco!' roared Rocca in his voice of a corporal, 'Ecco!' And producing some fruit drops from his pocket he offered them to Gian-Luca.

But Gian-Luca turned away. 'Oh, poor—oh, poor——' he wailed, until Fabio, shaking his head, carried him home, still weeping.

'No doubt it was the heat,' he told Teresa afterwards. 'I thought he might be feeling the heat.'

CHAPTER FOUR

I

At about this time Gian-Luca developed his first real signs of temper. This may have been due to heredity, of course, but Teresa certainly contributed. It struck him one day that even a goddess could not be quite indifferent to devotion; the thing to do, therefore, was to worry her with love, and Gian-Luca acted accordingly. He evolved the idea of climbing into her bed, and when ordered to desist, cried loudly. He constantly followed her round the house, never very far from her heels, like a puppy, or running just ahead in the region of her toes until she fell over him. If she went into her cash-desk Gian-Luca would be there, squatting by her stool; if she went into the shop to help Fabio with the serving, out would come Gian-Luca like a Jack-in-the-box, and she would find him clinging to her skirts. But these signs of devotion were only a beginning, there was more, much more to follow, for Gian-Luca decided that he wanted to be petted continually, all the time. Not an evening now but he would sidle up to Teresa and stand there waiting to be petted; sometimes he would reach up and gently stroke her arm; once he got as far as stroking her cheek. When this failed to elicit the proper response, he would hurl himself into her lap. She would say: 'Gian-Luca! What are you doing?'—not crossly, but in a voice of surprise; and then, while he still clung, her thin arms would go round him and her hands would continue their knitting on his back, he would hear the clicking of the needles. Fabio would call him.

'Come here to Nonno, caro.'

But Gian-Luca, would reply: 'I want Nonna!'

And at that, as like as not, Teresa would put him down: 'Run away, Gian-Luca, Nonna wants to go on knitting.'

37

And when he made to clamber on her knee again, she would shake her head and say: 'No, no, Gian-Luca.'

One morning he gallantly offered her his jam on a half-consumed slice of bread and butter.

'Please eat my jam, Nonna.'

'No, thank you, Gian-Luca.'

'*Please*, Nonna.'

'But I do not want your jam, my child. You eat it, it is nice cherry jam.'

Of course he knew that it was nice cherry jam, that was why he wanted her to eat it. She never allowed herself butter and jam, and this pained him as unworthy of a goddess.

When she told him, as she often did, to run away upstairs, he now invited her to follow: '*You* come, Nonna.'

'No, I cannot, Gian-Luca, I must go and help in the shop.'

'Oh, *please*.'

'Do not worry me so, Gian-Luca.'

And then he would begin to cry. His crying would reach Fabio, who would hurry from the shop to see what was happening in the parlour, and he and Teresa would argue in Italian in order that Gian-Luca should not know what they said; but as Rosa had been busily teaching him Italian, their little ruse was often unsuccessful. He understood enough to know that Fabio sympathized and considered that he ought to be petted, and, of course, at this discovery would come yet more tears, the rather pleasant tears of self-pity.

'Dio!' grumbled Rosa. 'You nearly five years old, and yet you cry and cry like a baby; you soon will be all washed away with your tears—Gian-Luca will be melted, like the sugar.'

The thought that he might melt like the sugar was attractive; he now took much more interest in the sugar in his coffee. If he could melt away before Nonna's very eyes! 'Oh! Oh! Oh!' he sobbed in a kind of ecstasy, choking himself with his tears.

'You shut it!' scolded Rosa, who was again nearing her time, and whose Mario was making her jealous with a barmaid. 'You shut it up at once, you make such dreadful noise, I think my poor head split in two!'

But well launched, Gian-Luca found it very hard to 'shut it', for his crying would become automatic; a series of chokings and gulpings and coughings that went on independently of any will of his.

Then one day he made his most stupendous effort; he had sixpence, and with it he bought a bunch of flowers. He carried them with unction, using both hands in the process.

'Why you want?' demanded Rosa, who felt cynical and cross.

But Gian-Luca would not answer that question.

Nonna was not in the shop on his return, she happened to be knitting in the parlour. He approached her very slowly with the offering extended; his face was rather red and his breath came rather fast. Nonna looked up.

'For you!' said Gian-Luca. 'I bought them myself——' And he waited.

'Thank you,' said Nonna. 'What very pretty flowers— it was kind of Gian-Luca to buy them.' But she did not even smell them, she put them on the table and quietly returned to her knitting.

Still he waited. Nothing happened, nothing was going to happen, no rapture, no expressions of delighted gratitude, no clasping, and no kissing of himself. There lay the fading flowers, and there sat Nonna, knitting, and there stood Gian-Luca, always waiting. . . . Then suddenly he broke, something went snap inside him. He looked about him wildly for what he might destroy. His eyes came back to Nonna, to her long brown hands, her knitting, the thing that she preferred before his flowers. His arm shot out, he seized it and tore it from her hands; he hurled it to the floor and stamped upon it: 'Bestia!' he choked, as though the thing had ears. It parted from its needles and unravelled as he stamped; at the sight of this his fury increased beyond control, and hurling himself down he tore and bit the wool, like a small wild beast that worries at a victim.

Teresa sat very still; her empty hands were folded, they did not strike, nor did they rescue. When she spoke she did so gently, and quite without emotion:

'Gian-Luca, you will go at once to bed.'

He looked up at her: 'I hate you! You do not love my flowers—you do not kiss me, not ever——'

39

'You may take away your flowers, I do not want them now,' she told him. 'I find you a very naughty child.'

And that was all—she found him a very naughty child—he was conscious of wanting her to hit him. If Nonna would not kiss him, then he wanted her to hit him; he wanted to try and make her hit him. Words, heard, but half forgotten until that moment leapt from him, he screamed them at her: 'Vipera! vipera! Vecchia strega!' And screaming still, he waited for the blow. But Nonna did not strike, did not raise her eyes or voice—she merely raised her finger and pointed to the door. And Gian-Luca, exhausted now in spirit, mind and body, left her and went stumbling upstairs to put himself to bed.

2

It was just as well, perhaps, that the following winter Gian-Luca had to go to school, for though beaten in his one supreme contest with Teresa, he still clung to the hope of imposing himself upon her, if not by one means then by another. Thus it happened that his active and versatile mind concocted quite a new scheme; the scheme was simple, it consisted in the main of becoming extremely naughty, and in this, it must be said that Gian-Luca succeeded beyond his own expectations. Just as his weeping had become automatic, so now did his naughtiness; once launched he found it difficult to stop, and scrape followed scrape with such startling rapidity that even Teresa had to put down her knitting in order to interfere; and in this lay Gian-Luca's miniature triumph; Nonna no longer ignored him.

The shop was a fruitful source of mischief, there were so many things you could do. For instance, you could dip into the huge jar of pickles and consume large quantities of onions and gherkins, after which—with an effort—you could make yourself sick, an arresting form of disturbance. Then, of course, there were the cheeses; the hard, manly cheeses could be surreptitiously bitten; the more feminine kind that swooned on wooden platters, could be prodded or partly consumed by the tongue. Salame, when eaten in course brown chunks, was an almost infallible cure for digestion, and the essence of peppermint that Nonna administered, when properly sweetened and diluted with hot water, was really rather in the nature of a treat—you sipped it out of a spoon.

And then there was Rosa. Rosa, grown cross, could easily be induced to make scenes. One could always torment Rosa and Rosa's watch, especially the watch, which was very ornate. If, as sometimes happened, she would take it off while she swept and forget to put it on again, it was almost sure to attract your attention, and then—well, you naturally wound it up, whereupon it had a habit of stopping. This suggested that you might not have wound it enough, so you wound it again with more vigour——

Rosa would scream: 'Mascalzone! birbone! I tell Nonna, you see if I not tell Nonna!'

And as this was precisely what you hoped she would do, you laughed, not in malice but in pleasure.

When it rained, as, of course, it did constantly—you could dart away from Rosa and plump into a puddle. There was also Rosa's Berta who grew uglier every day, and whose yells when pinched were most gratifying.

Then would come the longed-for evenings when Nonna would look grave, and when Nonna would say:

'Come here, Gian-Luca.'

You went at once, and standing very still beside her knee, you tingled with excitement and pleasure at the sound of her voice, retailing all your sins. Nonna might remark upon the fact that you were smiling:

'There is nothing whatever to smile about, Gian-Luca.'

Nothing? There was everything! You were smiling because Nonna had at last been brought to recognize your sins. The more you sinned the more you swelled with pride and self-importance, the more you knew that you were brave. With this knowledge of your prowess came a knowledge of yourself, a very soul-satisfying knowledge. In your mind's eye you saw Nonna being rescued from a dragon, and you were her rescuer. Once rescued, how she wept on you for love and gratitude! With what humbleness she kissed you, and with what timidity she asked to be allowed to hold your hand while crossing streets——

There was just one thing, however, that you simply

could not do—you could not pass Rocca's, the butcher's; and this, while it figured in the list of your sins, had nothing at all to do with sin. It bewildered you a little, you yourself were not quite clear as to why you felt so tearful at the thought; you would shut your eyes, because a dragon-slayer never cried, and then up would come the picture of those goats! Rosa would try persuasion, she might even apply force—no good, you simply could not do it. You kicked and screamed and finally lay flat down on the pavement, but—you did not pass Rocca's the butcher's.

'You wicked, you do it all on purpose!' blubbered Rosa, distracted by the scene that you were making.

But you answered: 'No—I hate it! It bleeds—I hate the dead-shop!' That was what you called it: 'The dead-shop.'

3

Strange days; Gian-Luca himself thought them strange, filled as they were with new excitements; indeed, when he finally had to go to school it seemed rather flat by comparison. He was naughty at school, but not really very naughty, there being no Nonna there to see, and on the whole he liked it, there were lots of other children; not small, fat, silly children like Rosa's ugly Berta, but large, thin, clever children like himself.

It had been arranged to send him to the Board School, which was undenominational and took all creeds alike—only Gian-Luca had no creed. Beyond Scripture lessons therefore, which left him rather cold, his mind was quite undisturbed by doctrine. Teresa shrugged her shoulders.

'Can it matter either way?'

'I am not quite sure——' said Fabio doubtfully.

'In that case I will judge, and I say it cannot matter.'

And as usual Teresa decided.

Fabio was rather tired, life was tiring him a little, and the business was growing every day. He had long since ceased to take an active part in his religion, that had been the duty of Teresa in the past; religious forms were made, he felt, for women. Teresa's secession from the Church had grieved and shocked him, he had grown to depend on her prayers. He suspected that Teresa's prayers had been both loud and fierce, the kind that would be heard for the sake of peace alone, if for no other reason. Fabio could not pray like that; perhaps he lacked conviction, he had always been a shy and doubtful man; it had solaced him, however, to know that his Teresa stood up to God and asked for what they wanted. At times, of course, Teresa prayed only for herself, as when she knelt beside the bed demanding God's forgiveness. She had done continual penance, and so, via her, had Fabio; and although this had contributed to wearing down his manhood, at the same time it had brought him more in touch with God, by proxy; that is with Teresa's God. Left to find God for himself, by reason of Teresa's disaffection, he could only grope for something that was kind; something that was softer and more loving than Teresa, something that would understand his needs. Freed from her religious spells he no longer liked her God, though the fact that he disliked Him made him fearful. He felt angry with Teresa, who had thus disturbed his peace, who had suddenly left him in the lurch. So, partly in anger, partly in pity, and a little in superstition, Fabio had baptized Gian-Luca. It had been his final act of defiance against Teresa, there would never be another—not now.

Fabio had grown much older—it was Olga's death that had aged him—this winter he had suffered from pains across his back. The pains had been lumbago, or so the doctor said, and when they caught him, Fabio had some ado to move, had just to stand quite still and call Teresa. For some reason the lumbago would make him think of God. God—lumbago, lumbago—God; that was how it came to Fabio.

'I do believe He is kind——' thought Fabio in self-pity, clinging to the counter in acute distress.

He was frightened when he thought of God, and when he got lumbago he was even more frightened of the pain across his back—that, no doubt, was why he coupled them together.

There had been a final argument about Gian-Luca's school, when Fabio, lying prostrate with red flannel round his middle, had suggested that they might consult a priest.

'That I will not,' said Teresa. 'You may if you wish, my Fabio, but the time is short, the child must go next week.'

'Corpo di Dio!' bellowed Fabio, who had tried to move in bed, and whose face was bedewed with agony. 'I care not what you do—only bring my liniment! I care not where you send him, so you rub me!'

4

Rosa was deeply shocked and so was Nerone, while the Signora Rocca was appalled. She announced her intention of calling on Teresa for the purpose of expressing her disgust.

'Leave them in peace, for God's sake!' advised her husband. 'Have they not already had their troubles?'

'And have I not had mine?' inquired his wife severely, and whenever she said this, Rocca's tardy conscience smote him, and he thought it wiser to be silent.

Rosa spoke to Mario, who, although not very pious, had been known to make Novenas for his bunion. 'Is it not dreadful, Mario, the little Gian-Luca—no father and now no religion, not at all!' And finding her Berta, she began to kiss her warmly, whereupon her Berta yelled.

Rosa gave Gian-Luca a little Rosary and taught him to say his beads; but Gian-Luca sucked and bit the beads until they came apart, and one of them got swallowed by mistake.

Nerone stumped round to Fabio on an angry wooden leg: 'First you naturalize yourself, then you neglect yourself the Church, then you take Gian-Luca away, what next I ask? You become a Protestant perhaps? No wonder you sell us bad salame.'

Except for Signora Rocca, they all attacked poor Fabio; not one of them dared tackle Teresa. The butcher's wife was different, she had money of her own, she went to Mass in purple silk on Sundays. Teresa was busy in the cash-desk when she arrived, but together they went into the parlour.

'A little glass of wine?'

'No, I thank you.'

'What a pity, we have some such excellent Chianti!'

'I have come,' said the signora, taking the easy-chair, 'to discuss the wine of the spirit.'

'Ah!' murmured Teresa. 'Do you think that we should stock it?'

'I have come,' said the signora, 'to speak about Gian-Luca, whose soul is in the greatest peril.'

'How so?' inquired Teresa.

'Can you ask?' Signora Rocca opened her enormous eyes as far as they would go. 'Can you ask, when I hear that you have sent him to the Board School where they teach the worship of the devil?'

'I have not heard that,' said Teresa very mild, 'but no doubt it will come in useful.'

'You appal me, signora!'

'Do not let that be so—I wish only to reassure you.'

'But I beg you to listen—a child born in our midst, and a child already at so grave a disadvantage—through the misfortune of his birth——'

'But should not that recommend him to God—if, as they say, He takes care of the afflicted?'

'God works through His Church alone, signora—would you snatch Gian-Luca from the Church? Consider!'

' "Consideration is a constant source of error," ' murmured Teresa gently.

But Signora Rocca was also versed in proverbs. ' "You give the lettuce into the keeping of the geese!" ' she quoted in her gutteral Genoese.

'I do nothing,' said Teresa, and her tone was quite unruffled. ' "He who does nothing makes no blunders." '

' "He who does evil never lacks for an excuse," ' retorted the signora promptly.

'It is also said,' Teresa reminded her, smiling, 'that: "The elephant cannot feel the biting of the flea." '

5

It was natural enough that the small community gathered together in Old Compton Street should have found a fruitful source of scandal in the open withdrawal of Gian-Luca from the Church. Of late years the Bosellis had kept all tongues wagging; there had been Olga's trip to Italy, her misfortune, her death, and now this almost unheard-of happening—a child that they looked upon as one of themselves, was being sent to a Board School. They were stranger-people, all just a little homesick, all slightly misfits and thus on the defensive; and because of this they belonged to each other, bound firmly together by four most important things, their cooking, their religion, their will to make money; and last but not least by the love of their language—they came together to speak it. No one approved of naturalization, yet in Fabio's case they forgave it; had he not been naturalized to help on his business? And this, though they might not follow his example, they could at least understand. Fabio had long been lax in his religion—this they also understood up to a certain point, and Teresa's disaffection after Olga's death they pitied rather than condemned; but to take Gian-Luca and put him at a Board School, to dump him willy-nilly among purely foreign children, quite apart from the religious aspect of the case—no, this they did not understand.

Rosa, who was pious, had often said to Mario: 'All will be well when Gian-Luca goes to school; the good little Sisters will teach him how to pray, and presently he will make his first Communion, then all will be very well.'

And Mario had nodded: 'That is so, my Rosa.'

For although her Mario was occasionally weak in regard to the sins of the flesh, he was nevertheless a good son of Holy Church, attending Mass with Rosa every Sunday morning; accompanying her to Confession every Easter, when he underwent a kind of spiritual spring-cleaning—after which he would be good for a little.

Nerone's religion, like his love of Italy, was purely an accident of birth. Nerone was a man who clung to early associations as a child may cling to sucking its thumb long after it has left the cradle. Nerone had been poor, disastrously so; as a boy he had often gone hungry. His natal village had consisted of one street whose chief characteristic was a smell. Its church had been tawdry and shamefully neglected, its priest discouraged and untidy, its population hard-bitten to the bone by ceaseless poverty and toil. In the summer Nerone had grilled in his attic and in the winter he had frozen. Italy had given him nothing but hardships, whereas England had provided comparative ease. But Italy had bred him, her soil was the first that his flea-bitten feet had trodden; her religion had grown like him from that soil, and both she and her religion stood for associations that Nerone worshipped in his mind. If he did not always worship them in his business—oh, well, a man had to live!

Nerone loved his country, but he lived in England above his tobacco shop; Nerone loved his Church, but he gave her very little; when approached for subscriptions his attitude was that of a man who was well acquainted with God and was not to be taken in. Nerone loved his people, but refused Italian money, even from new arrivals. To Lucrezia, in her lifetime, he had been wont to say:

'You be careful, Lucrezia, you never take the lira, you always ask for the shilling. We send the shilling home, and behold, he has children! We make him an Italian, and when he is a lira he has little centesimi!'

So the shillings all went home to a bank in Siena, where they promptly bred offspring for Nerone. Some day Nerone would follow the shillings, but not before the uttermost farthing had been squeezed from the place of his temporary exile. And Nerone had his dreams—he was very full of dreams in spite of his astuteness in business. He dreamt of the village with one long, straggling street; he dreamt of the church where he had served his first Mass; of the candles, the Madonna with her faded tinsel flowers, the smell of dust and garlic and stale incense on the air, the kneeling figure of his mother. And because of his dreams which might some day come true, Nerone sold tobacco at a shop in Old Compton Street; and because of his dreams, he refused Italian money and had never been known to lend; and because of his dreams he was bigoted and proud and detested all things English. But, because of his dreams—and this was so strange—he had ordered white roses for Olga's funeral; he had said: 'I will have them all white.'

Nerone loved Fabio and small caged birds and risotto and Amarena. He bullied Fabio and petted his birds; their perches were too narrow and so were their cages, but he fed them with groundsel and lettuce. He also loved children, even little English children who laughed at his wooden leg, and Gian-Luca he very particularly loved; had not Gian-Luca called him 'Nonno'? It was therefore a personal outrage to Nerone that Fabio's weakness had permitted, and for more than a month he never spoke to Fabio without bitter allusions to Gian-Luca's soul, to the fact that Fabio was a traitor to his country and had once sold salame with a worm thrown in. Their evenings together had ceased abruptly, they no longer played dominoes now; but at nine o'clock every night Fabio sighed, and Nerone down the street became terribly restless. Nerone would go to a little cupboard and get out his dominoes; he would throw them on the table and begin to stir them as though he were making zabaione. 'Ma che!' Nerone would pick up his dominoes and put them away in their box; he would try to read the paper, or go for a walk, or find fault with the dutiful Rosa.

In the little back parlour behind his shop Fabio's sighs grew louder; he would presently get up and begin touching things, until even Teresa, so calm since Olga's death, had been known to look up and scold. On the thirty-fifth evening of this mutual torment, came Nerone stumping on his wooden leg.

'Good evening, Fabio!'

'Good evening, Nerone.'

'You come and play a little game of dominoes, Fabio?'

'Ecco! Perhaps I will.'

'Of course I beat you, but that you expect. . . .'

'And perhaps you do not beat me!'

'Very well, then, suppose we go now and see.'

'I am ready—I am not at all afraid!'

It was over; Gian-Luca's soul might be lost, but not Nerone's game. Arm in arm they hurried out into the fog.

'You old fox!' said Fabio, by way of endearment.

'You old brigand!' chuckled Nerone.

Rocca took his Church in a swinging, jaunty stride, and occasionally slapped it on the back. His oaths were lewd and varied and most personal to God; he sharpened his wits on priests and nuns. Rocca had been a soldier and now he was a butcher—he was pleasantly familiar with death; and as the Church, to Rocca, stood more for death than life, he was pleasantly familiar with the Church. He thought it a great pity that Gian-Luca should be sent to a Board School, because he mistrusted new ideas—vegetarianism and the like. Roccas's only comment had been short and to the point:

'Give me the devil I know!' he had remarked. Beyond this he would not discuss the subject except when in a fury with his wife. On such occasions Rocca lifted up his voice:

'Giurabbaccaccio! But leave them in peace; is he your grandson? Alas, no!'

And at this Signora Rocca was forced to be silent; she was childless, a reproach among women.

Rocca jeered at priests, but he continually fed them, and many were the sirloins and legs of English mutton that found their way to the Old Italian Church. Rocca jeered at nuns, but the little 'Flying Angels' had good cause to bless him on more than one occasion, for the wherewithal to brew beef-tea for their poor. Rocca jeered at God, but when one bitter winter, Rocca had managed to get double pneumonia, when he had lain there gasping and despairing —fearful of living because of his anguish, fearful of dying because of his transgressions—Rocca had invited God into his house, and God, being what He is, had not refused to come.

CHAPTER FIVE

I

BY THE time that Gian-Luca was eleven years old, the
resentment felt against the Bosellis for their choice
of a school had all but disappeared. It could not
well be otherwise; people still deplored it, but
Fabio and Teresa were cogs in the machine that
turned out the happenings of everyday life for the little
group of exiles. And then, there was Fabio's salumeria, no
one could get on without his wares—the sausages, the paste,
the rich yellow oil, the straw-covered bottles of Chianti; nor
could they get on without Fabio himself—Fabio always so
mild and friendly, with his halo of rough, grey hair. He had
shown no resentment at their criticism, indeed he had
seemed to feel that it was just; on the other hand, he had
taken no steps to undo his grievous error. Against such
humble but stubborn placidity the storm had raged in
vain; now it had practically beaten itself out, and Fabio,
Teresa, and the young Gian-Luca were once more at peace
with their neighbours.

To this happy and desirable state of affairs Gian-Luca
himself contributed not a little; people liked him, he was
amiable and good on the whole.

'Can it be,' they murmured, 'that the English Board
School is not so infernal after all?'

Certainly Gian-Luca was not at all infernal, his temper
was less violent than it had been. His manners were no
worse than those of other children, indeed, they were
rather better; he shone by comparison with Rosa's son,
Geppe—a turbulent creature of six years old, born just
before Gian-Luca's first term at school. Moreover, Gian-
Luca was a handsome child; he was slim and tall for his age.
His hair had retained its ashen fairness, and grew low on
his forehead from a little cap-like peak—the boys made

fun of this at school. His mouth was well modelled, but the underlip protruded slightly; a wilful mouth, a mouth that might some day harden to endeavour or soften to dissipation. He was pale, with that curious southern pallor that turns to bronze in the sun. His hands were long-fingered and strong, like Teresa's, but more firmly and delicately fashioned.

People whispered together: 'He is beautiful, Gian-Luca, but not with the beauty of Olga Boselli.'

And their pleasure in his beauty was another ground for kindness; did they not spring from the race that had bred Donatello, Verrocchio, and the Della Robbias?

One thing only in Gian-Luca could they find to resent— he seemed to them strangely aloof. They could not be certain of what he was thinking—his eyes gave no clue to his thoughts. Other children looked tearful, or merry, or greedy, or sly, as the case might be; but Gian-Luca's expression was calm and distant—he always seemed to be staring through people at something they had not perceived.

'What are you staring at?' Nerone would grumble. 'Dio! One would think that you knew me by now! Is it that you find me so handsome a fellow? Or is it that you look at something beyond me—and if so what do you look at?'

Gian-Luca would flush with embarrassment; conscious perhaps, that in staring at Nerone his eyes had merely sought an object to rest on while his thoughts were busy elsewhere.

At this time in his life he was very full of thoughts— almost as full as he had been when an infant—only now the thoughts were more definite and hard; they came striking at his brain like so many pebbles; he could almost feel them as they struck. Two thoughts in particular had begun to obsess him; the thought of his father and the thought of his country. No one at home ever mentioned his father, he might never have had a paternal parent—he began to think this was very strange. Certain awkward questions that he could not answer were occasionally asked him at school; the boys wanted to know if his father was dead, and if he had been an Italian.

Gian-Luca knew a little about his mother, but nothing about his father, and since every other child appeared to own a father, he supposed that he must have owned one, too, and further that his father must naturally be dead, otherwise why had he never seen him? Very well then, that was settled; his father must be dead, but he wanted to ask Fabio what to call him; a name was a very great assistance, he felt; it helped you to visualize the person—meanwhile he invented a name for his father, and after a little it became so familiar that it sounded quite true when he spoke it.

'My father was called Leonardo,' said Gian-Luca, in reply to a question at school one day.

'Then you're an I-talian,' was the prompt retort. 'What's the good of pretending you're English!'

And this was another thing that worried Gian-Luca, he *had* pretended to be English—a kind of betrayal of something or someone in order to appear more like his schoolmates. This betrayal of his would haunt him at night when he lay in bed waiting for his pictures; they very seldom came now, which also disturbed him; his nights were just sleep, or those hard little thoughts that struck against his brain like pebbles. He often heard Nerone inveighing against Fabio, for what he called 'the desertion of his country'. But Gian-Luca could never understand what he meant; who could be more Italian than Fabio? Did not Fabio eat pasta and drink good red wine that came in big cases from Italy? As for Gian-Luca, it was only when at school that he ever thought of being English; he was lonely at school, they left him out of things—and moreover they called him 'Macaroni.'

Fabio had taken to remarking lately: 'You grow so very English, Gian-Luca.'

And Teresa would say: 'You speak now as they do, you will soon have a Cockney accent.'

'That is not so,' Gian-Luca would protest. 'I do not like their ugly accent.'

Nerone would pity him: 'Poor Gian-Luca, you have no Church, what a disaster!'

But this fact did not worry Gian-Luca in the least, what he wanted was a country, not a Church.

'If I am English I cannot be Italian,' he argued, bewildered and distressed, 'and yet if I am English I am like the other boys—then why do they leave me out of things?'

He finally decided that he hated the English who always left him out of things. In spite of this, however, he made colossal efforts to model himself on their pattern; he longed with the unfailing instinct of youth to be like his companions at school. He yelled, he shoved, he kicked out his boots; if the other boys swore, Gian-Luca swore too. Whatever they did, he would follow suit, hoping against hope to win their approval. But although they liked him, it was only as a stranger who had suddenly appeared within their gates; his grandfather sold queer, outlandish foodstuffs, while Gian-Luca himself had been heard to speak Italian—enough in all conscience to set him apart as a kind of unnatural freak!

Gian-Luca grew an outward crust of indifference, which however, did not deceive them; they suspected that underneath it he was soft, and they prodded to find the softness. He still disliked passing Rocca's shop, and this they quickly divined. They went out of their way to make him pass it whenever occasion offered. Rocca, these days, had relays of kids all hanging with their heads to the pavement; he was even more prosperous than he had been, a fact that he attributed entirely to the kids—he said that they had brought him luck. The boys made a habit of punching the kids for the pleasure of seeing them swing, for the pleasure also of laughing at Gian-Luca, who invariably turned a little pale. But one day Gian-Luca, in a kind of desperation, doubled up his fist and punched too. He punched until Rocca came out to protest, and even after that he still punched.

'Take that! And that! And that!' he spluttered, panting and white to the lips.

'Look at young Macaroni!' applauded the boys. 'Go it, young Macaroni!'

Then Gian-Luca turned on them like a thing demented:

'Beasts!' he yelled. 'How I hate you—you beasts! Porci! Sporcaccioni!'

And naturally after this incident there was a coldness between Gian-Luca and his schoolmates.

2

That winter Gian-Luca decided to speak to Fabio regarding his two greatest troubles. Fabio could tell him about his father; he could also reassure him about his country; perhaps he might even be able to explain why the boys at school treated Gian-Luca like a stranger—why they so often left him out of things. Fabio would speak in the soft, happy language that always set the heart beating just a little faster; the language of deep-sounding, beautiful words— familiar, reassuring, fulfilling. Gian-Luca rehearsed the scene in his mind.

Fabio would say: 'But you *are* an Italian, what need you care for the foolish English, they have nothing to do with us!'

And he, Gian-Luca would reply: 'That is so. I hate the English as Nerone hates them; they are stupid, they have the brains of pigs, they think only of beer and roast beef!'

Then Fabio would pat him on the back with approval: 'It is good to be Italian, very good,' he would say; 'your father was also an Italian. Your father was a very great man, he was a soldier; he also owned vineyards, enormous vineyards, from which comes the finest Chianti. When he died, he said: 'Take care of my Gian-Luca and tell him how splendid I was!'

Gian-Luca decided to speak on a Sunday, when Fabio would be free to attend. It should be in the morning before Fabio went out. Teresa would be sitting by the fire; Teresa would look up from her knitting for a moment; she might even wish to join in their conversation, adding some reasuring words of her own. . . . In any case Teresa must be there. They would tell him those glorious things about his father that he had imagined for himself: they might even say that his father's name was none other than Leonardo.

But when the momentous occasion arrived, Gian-Luca felt strangely shy; Fabio was reading his paper by the window, Teresa was knitting by the fire as he had pictured; it was all as it should be, it was all quite perfect, yet Gian-Luca felt strangely shy. He began to fidget with this thing and that, moving aimlessly about the room, picking up objects and putting them down—much as Fabio did when mentally distressed—until at last Teresa, who disliked this habit, looked up from her knitting with a frown.

'Can you not find what you want, Gian-Luca? I wish that you would read your book.'

He hesitated with a vase in his hand; it fell and was broken to pieces.

Teresa's frown deepened: 'Dio! Gian-Luca, now see what foolishness you do!'

He caught his breath, staring down at the vase; then suddenly he began to speak wildly. 'I am not happy—I am very unhappy—I want to know about my father!'

In the silence that followed he could hear his own heart beating. Fabio had crushed the newspaper in his hand.

'Your *father?*' Fabio's voice sounded very far-away, and the eyes that he turned on Gian-Luca were frightened.

But now Gian-Luca was feeling less afraid; he was able to go on almost calmly: 'You knew my father, Nonno— I would like to hear about him—I have often thought that his name was Leonardo, I have thought that my father was a soldier.'

Then Fabio told the truth in a moment of panic: 'But I never knew your father, Gian-Luca, I never knew your father's name.'

Gian-Luca stood quite still staring at him: 'You knew my mother——' he began.

'Your mother was my child——' said Fabio unsteadily. 'Your mother was my own poor child!'

Gian-Luca considered for a moment, then he said: 'And she never brought my father to show you? That was strange, for Rosa showed Mario to Nerone—she says so— Rosa showed Mario to Nerone, she says, a long time before they got married.'

'I think he is old enough to know,' said Teresa. 'The children of our country age sooner than the English——' Her voice was quiet; it was almost detached, as though she were speaking of a stranger.

'Not yet,' protested Fabio quickly.

'I would like to know,' said Gian-Luca.

Teresa surveyed him in silence for a moment, then: 'You have a right to know—come here.'

He went and stood patiently beside her, while she picked up a stitch that she had dropped; this accomplished, she looked him full in the eyes:

'It is I who must tell you, it seems, Gian-Luca.'

'Too soon! Too soon!' muttered Fabio from the window.

But Teresa shook her head: 'He has asked—he has been thinking—it is therefore not too soon—it is I who must tell him, it seems——'

Her fingers were moving with incredible swiftness, the sound of her needles was rhythmical, precise—like the tapping of a small machine. The eyes that met Gian-Luca's were defiant, unafraid—but they made Gian-Luca feel afraid.

'Listen,' she said, 'listen carefully, Gian-Luca—we never knew your father—we do not even know whether your father is dead or alive. He did not marry Olga as Mario married Rosa—he did not wish to give you his name. We do not know your father's name, and that is why we call you by ours; that is why when Olga died at your birth you remained here and lived with us. Mario was good, he had love for Rosa, so he gave her his name in marriage. Your father had no love for you nor for your mother—he gave neither marriage nor name.' She paused to allow her words to sink in.

'Then he was not good?' faltered Gian-Luca.

'He was bad,' said Teresa. 'He was cruel and bad; have I not just told you so?'

Gian-Luca stared at her, pale and aghast: 'Then my father was not a great man—not a soldier?'

'Who knows, Gian-Luca; to be great in this world does not mean that a man is good.'

'But——' he said miserably, 'you do not know his name—and I thought that his name was Leonardo——'

'We shall never know your father's name, I am afraid; your mother kept it a secret.'

'Then was she also bad?'

'Your mother was all goodness,' Teresa's sallow cheeks flushed with a painful crimson.

'And yet I have not got a name——' he persisted. 'You say that I have not got a name——' Then a sudden thought struck him and he too flushed crimson: 'Does that make me different from other boys, Nonna? Is that why they leave me outside?'

'I think not, Gian-Luca—they may not know—and yet you are not quite as other children—but if you are honest and good and hard-working that will not harm you, my child.'

'Yes, but how am I different?' he questioned anxiously. 'I cannot myself see any difference.'

'Some day you will understand,' she told him, 'and meanwhile be patient—work hard.'

'Yes, but how am I different? Why am I different?' Gian-Luca suddenly wanted to cry.

'You are all that we wish you to be,' broke in Fabio. 'Is it not so, Teresa?'

'He is all that he can be,' she answered slowly. 'Gian-Luca is all that he can be.'

Gian-Luca forced back his tears with an effort: 'You do not know if my father is alive?'

'No,' said Fabio, 'we do not, piccino—but we sometimes think that he is.'

'And he does not wish to see me, who am his son?'

'It would seem not, my little Gian-Luca.'

'But why?'

'Because,' intervened Teresa, 'he does not love you, Gian-Luca.'

'Dio Santo!' exclaimed Fabio; 'you tell things too soon.'

'I think not,' she answered coldly.

Gian-Luca looked from one to the other; he was trying to understand; he was trying to visualize quite a new world, a world where the most unheard-of things happened—where fathers, for instance, might not love their children. He thought of Nerone's affection for Rosa, of Mario's devotion to Berta and Geppe; of Rocca, who would shake his head and say sadly: 'If only I had a son!' For with all these people among whom he lived, the love of children was a primitive instinct like that of eating and drinking—no higher and no lower—just a primitive instinct. A man loved his body and in consequence he fed it; a man loved the children who sprang from his body, because they were part of himself.

Gian-Luca, aged eleven, could not know all this—nor would he have cared very much if he had. All that concerned him deeply at the moment was the love that he felt himself to be missing. His thoughts turned to Berta and Geppe with their howls, their rages, their insatiable greed; and then to Mario with his tiredness, his bunion, and his infinite, long-suffering patience. He himself had found such patience in Fabio—he remembered this now—he had found it in Fabio. And Teresa? She had been patient with him, too, coldly, enduringly patient. But something had been lacking even in Fabio, and all in a moment he knew what it was; Fabio's patience had lacked a certain quality of joy—the quality of joy that made Mario laugh sometimes at the sins of his small man-child. And as though Teresa had divined Gian-Luca's thoughts, she turned her gaze full on his face.

'Remember,' she said, 'that you always have yourself, and that should suffice a man.'

He nodded. He drew himself up, grateful to her for thinking of him as a man. 'I am Gian-Luca,' he announced quite firmly, 'also, I am an Italian!'

'You are not that,' she told him. 'Nonno is naturalized—your mother became English, so you are English—you are English in the eyes of the law.'

'But I do not feel as they do!' he exclaimed in quick resentment. 'At school they know that I do not feel as they do and they always leave me outside!'

'Nevertheless you are English,' said Teresa, 'and perhaps it is better so.'

Then Gian-Luca forgot that she had called him a man, forgot to be more than eleven years old. 'Non voglio! Non voglio!' he wept in fury. 'I wish to be as Geppe is—Italian. I shall say to them all that I am an Italian—I will not pretend any more.'

'That is foolish,' Fabio told him gently. 'In the eyes of the law you are English.'

'I am *not!* I wish only to be an Italian—I hate the English and Nerone hates them too——'

'And that is also foolish——' said Fabio patiently, 'for the English provide us with money.'

'And some day you will earn their money,' said Teresa, 'and by doing so you will grow rich.'

Gian-Luca stopped crying and eyed her gravely: 'Is it not that I have no real country, Nonna, just as I have no real father?'

There was silence for a moment while she too looked rather grave. 'You have yourself,' she repeated firmly. No one can take that from you, Gian-Luca—remember that you always have yourself.'

That evening Rosa came in to supper, bringing her Berta and Geppe. Berta was now nearly ten years old; her locks as stiff and as black as horsehair—they were tied up with pale pink ribbon. Berta had enormous, flashing brown eyes, and large round calves to her legs. She was wearing a number of silver bangles and a pair of minute coral ear-rings. Berta was already decidedly feminine—she looked at Gian-Luca, who was reading, and she frowned. Presently she went up and snatched at his book, then she darted away as though frightened.

Gian-Luca felt unfriendly. 'Get out!' he muttered. 'Get out and leave me alone!'

At that Berta ran and complained to her mother. 'He has pinched me!' she whined mendaciously.

'What is the matter with Gian-Luca?' inquired Rosa. 'I think he has a devil on his back! Why will he not show his book to Berta? When she asked him so prettily, too!'

Geppe, as always, was busy sucking something, and what he sucked oozed down on to his chin. He looked like his father—very red, very black—and he clung to his mother's hand with the persistence and the vigour of an octopus. Rosa made as though to disengage her hand whereupon Geppe started to howl.

'He is timid,' said Rosa, smiling round the room, 'and moreover he adores his Mammina.' She lifted her son to a chair at the table, then seated herself beside him. Having tied a large napkin under his chin—'You must eat, tesoro!' she commanded.

The supper consisted of a cake of polenta, pastasciutta, a salad, some gruyère cheese, and a stout *fiaschone* of Chianti. Berta was greedy and kept asking for more—Geppe was greedy but he took without asking.

'Com'è carino,' laughed Rosa, beaming at him. 'Com'è carino, il mio maschiotto!'

Geppe choked himself and in consequence was sick, so when Rosa had carefully wiped his chin, she gave him a drink of Chianti and water, by way of settling his stomach. They all went on eating; Fabio chewed his salad with the sound of a mule munching beans. At the head of the table sat Teresa with her knitting; from time to time she would put down her fork in order to knit off a row.

'Mario is suffering from his joint,' announced Rosa. 'It is very swollen and red.'

'He should rub it with soap,' Fabio muttered, with his mouth full. 'They say that soap hardens the skin.'

'The chemist gave us iodine and a plaster, but I think that the plaster draws.'

'Soap!' repeated Fabio. 'I believe in soap! Myself I have got tender feet.'

'No doubt you are right. I will surely tell Mario—poor fellow, his new shoes pinch. It is difficult to find any shoes to fit him, unless we make slits for the swelling.' Rosa sighed, 'He cannot move quickly enough, and that is bad for a waiter; a waiter should always get about quickly, especially when clients are hungry!'

'It is good that they are hungry,' said Teresa, looking up. 'We gain money by way of their stomachs.'

'That is so,' laughed Fabio, cutting himself some cheese. 'That is how we are able to fill our own stomachs.'

'A boy at Geppe's school has got pidocchi in his head,' chirped Berta, licking her fingers. 'I think that Geppe will get them too, and if he gets pidocchi, perhaps I may catch them—I do not wish to catch them, they tickle.'

'Be not so silly, tesoro,' smiled Rosa. 'I am sure that you will not get pidocchi. Mamma will comb your hair every day; that will make it beautifully shiny.'

'Scema!' spluttered Geppe. 'I have not got pidocchi, and if I get them I will give them to you. I will rub my head against yours!'

'Then I will scratch you,' said Berta firmly, and proceeded to put the threat into action.

There ensued a deafening shriek from Geppe, and a mild-voiced protest from Rosa.

'The good Saint Berta will not love you if you scratch,' she reminded her elder offspring.

'Give me some Chianti,' said Berta, quite unmoved. 'I am thirsty; give me some Chianti!'

Fabio filled her glass with red wine and water, which she drank in a series of gulps.

60

'It is excellent Chianti,' murmured Fabio thoughtfully, 'the best I have tasted in years.'

'The price of pasta has gone up,' remarked Teresa; 'I blame the Italian Government for that.'

'If it rises much more we are ruined,' sighed Fabio, who, being replete, could afford to be gloomy.

'Mario's Padrone is buying French pasta, because of the rise,' Rosa told them disapprovingly; 'but I myself do not think that is right. After all, the Padrone is Italian!'

'One must live as one can,' Teresa retorted, 'and the English will eat it just the same.'

'That is so,' agreed Rosa. 'The English are stupid; my father thinks them very stupid.'

The meal finished, they wiped their mouths on their napkins and Fabio fetched a cigar.

'Even tobacco has risen,' he grumbled, burning his fingers with a match.

'Everything is always rising,' frowned Teresa, 'but Fabio and I will rise with it. For those who have got the will to succeed there is nearly always a way. Our business grows, we have not enough room; soon we must hire a new shop.'

'That is your fine business head,' Rosa told her. 'I sometimes think that my Mario's is less fine, but then he is always so patient and kind, and moreover he suffers with his bunion.'

'Nerone should buy him a business of his own,' grunted Fabio. 'I will speak with him about it.'

'That I fear he will never do,' sighed Rosa. 'However, we are very well off as we are—the children have plenty to eat. . . .'

4

Gian-Luca escaped upstairs to his room—Olga's room, in which he now slept. He wondered why Rosa's children always howled; he could never remember them other than howling. He thought Geppe greedy and Berta a bore; he did not like either of them very much, and yet they had Mario for their father, and Mario loved them—that was so strange, for he, Gian-Luca went unloved. There was Fabio, of course, but Fabio did not count, or at least he counted very little. Fabio felt old when you touched his skin, he had pains in his back, he was timid of Teresa—Teresa who might have counted.

Gian-Luca sat down on the well-worn sofa and began to think over Teresa. With a queer, tight feeling round his heart, he realized that he no longer loved her. She allured him still, and that must be why he had that tight feeling round his heart. When she spoke in her quiet, flat voice, he had to listen; when she wished something done, he had perforce to do it, willing and eager to obey; but he no longer loved her or wished for her love—and that made him feel the more lonely.

He tried to picture Teresa as she had been, or rather, as he had once seen her; to recapture some of the sense of beauty that had shrouded her presence like incense. His head fell back and he closed his eyes, the better to conjure up the vision, but all that he saw now was a gaunt, ageing woman with beetling brows and a high, pinched nose; a woman whose hair showed the scalp at the temples, whose lips were too pale, whose chin sagged a little, and whose teeth were no longer very white. And something in all this was intolerable to him, so that unwilling tears trickled under his closed eyelids—tears for himself, but also for Teresa—because he no longer found her fair.

He could hear the sound of laughter coming up from downstairs; then of quarrelling—Berta and Geppe—Fabio's voice, heavy and soft after supper; Rosa's voice, loud, rather shrill; and from time to time Teresa's slow words, spoken in a pause between stitches. A door banged; thump—thump—that would be Nerone, come to fetch Fabio for their game of dominoes—'Buona sera! Buona sera; vanno bene tutti?' Then more talk, more laughter, and Nerone's wooden leg stumping away with Fabio.

Gian-Luca put his head on one side and listened. His people! But were they his people? If he was English then they were not his people; and at this thought his weeping broke out afresh, he buried his face in his arm. All that was nearest and dearest about them came back to him in a flood; he wept for them now as a small child will weep for faces lost in the dark. Even Rocca and his goats seemed less to be condemned; had not Rocca offered him fruit drops?

There was something worth loving then, even in Rocca—something that he wanted to cling to.

He lifted his face and stared round the room, his eyes wandered over to the wound above the bed; it had grown in dimensions, for the thin, dry plaster had crumbled still further with the years. Gian-Luca no longer wished to prod it with his finger; he merely thought it very ugly; it seemed to add to his own desolation, itself so desolate a thing. He rubbed away the tears with the back of his hand—resentful, almost angry—then he suddenly remembered Teresa's words—courageous words, coldly courageous. Going over to the table he found pencil and paper: 'I have got myself,' wrote Gian-Luca. Climbing on to the bed, he pinned up his motto, then he climbed down again the better to see it.

And that was how Gian-Luca tried to cover up the wound in the plaster—and in his own heart.

CHAPTER SIX

I

THERE WAS someone who always wanted Gian-Luca, and that was Mario Varese; he had a good-hearted, pitiful affection for Rosa's foster-child. Mario no longer slapped his thighs, he no longer roared in play; indeed, it might be said that he was now quite grown up—he had broadened out somewhat in the process. Mario was nearly thirty-three, and his hair was receding a little. At one time his dress-suit had hung loosely on him, but now it was rather tight. His cheeks, always red, were redder than ever, and his eyes, that had bulged only slightly in the past, now resembled two brown balls of toffee. But for all this, Mario was still good-looking—and when he could afford it, flashy; on the plump little finger of his large left hand he wore a gold ring with a rhinestone.

Mario was very much the man of affairs when reposing in the bosom of his family; to hear him talk of his prowess as a waiter was to know that the Capo di Monte without Mario would merely have ceased to exist. Mario explained at considerable length the art of dealing with clients, the methods of tempting a poor appetite, or soothing an irritable temper.

'You assert yourself—but with grace,' said Mario. 'You expatiate on the food. You say: "I will *stroke* the lettuce with garlic—no more than that, a caress of garlic—"' Then you say: "I observe that the signore is not hungry, that he feels no great wish to eat—in that case, I suggest Fegato alla Veneziana, fried with onions and plenty of butter—but fried, oh, so very gently!" You watch him, and if he swallows the lot, you step forward and remark with a smile: "Good, very good; is it not so, signore?" If he agrees, then you whip out the menu and tempt with another dish. It is all very easy, and you make them drink too; you observe—as though you were thinking aloud—"The cellar contains some marvellous wine!" then you smile: "But, alas! the Padrone has his whims; it is only the few who are permitted to taste it. He is like a hen with her chicks," you say: "He is like a great artist who will not sell his pictures; he rejoices but to look at the outside of the bottles—the insides he reserves for those who have a palate—however, I will do my best for you, signore; I myself will speak with the Padrone"!'

Mario said that the Padrone was sly, but that Mario Varese was slyer. 'It is wonderful,' laughed Mario, 'how the little round tins contain only that which is fresh! They say: "Listen, Mario! I want something light—what about a plate of that good consommé? I am rather afraid of tomato soup; it usually lives in a tin!" "Signore!" I exclaim, as one who is wounded, "here we make all things fresh!" The chef, he it is who opens the tin in which that excellent consommé lives; they drink it up quickly, perhaps they ask for more— Ma che! They do not know the difference!'

Mario said that the Padrone had sworn to bring all London to the Capo di Monte. 'We have red cotton curtains at the window now, but soon they will be silk!' bragged Mario. The Padrone, he said, was one who would rise; he had a beautiful wife—her hair was golden and she took in the dishes from the little door just behind the bar. She was not quite a barmaid, but she stood among the bottles and bowed to the clients as they passed. Her manner was aloof and she smiled very seldom, therefore when she did smile it made an impression, and those upon whom she smiled were pleased. The Padrone was like that, he also was aloof: he had the bump of selection. 'You'll see! You'll see!' chuckled Mario delightedly. 'One of these days we become the fashion, then we put up our prices, we make them pay high for the fat green snails at the Capo di Monte; and we grow like the snails, fat and rich!'

Rosa never listened, but Gian-Luca did, and he came to the conclusion that all men were foolish, except of course the Padrone and Mario, who must be unusually wise. The matter of the tinned soup troubled him a little, but not, it must be said, for very long. If, as Mario had explained, they did not know the difference, then what difference could it make to them? However, he consulted Fabio about it.

'I myself do not take it, but I sell it,' Fabio told him. And although this left the ethical question rather vague, it appeared to satisfy Fabio.

Mario was so indispensable, it seemed, that holidays were few and far between; when he got one, however, the occasion was momentous—it called for a gathering of the clan. A holiday was not a real holiday to Mario unless it was accompanied by toil; that was the way the good Mario took his pleasures; he planned, he worked, he wore himself out—but after it was over and he lay abed with Rosa, he could count up on his fingers all the things they had done in the course of a brief nine hours.

Mario declared that a little glimpse of green was better than a bottle of Asti; but when he found the green there was never time to see it. He sat under it, he walked on it, he lay on it perhaps, but only until he got his breath. On those very rare occasions when Mario found a meadow he would scamper over to the next. He had the sort of mind that goes with large adventure, preferring always that which lies beyond.

This mind of his, imprisoned for the best part of the year within the narrow confines of his business, broke loose the very moment it could sniff the country air; off it went and Mario with it, always seeking the beyond, always trying to go just a little farther.

Mario was eloquent regarding country air; he said that it took at least ten years off his age. But at times the spirit led him so far afield to find it, that the day would be spent in a third-class railway carriage—then it would be time to go back. He adored his children, so they too must be considered; he was never quite happy without them. He was not quite happy with them, but Mario shrugged his shoulders and supposed that that was often the way in this world.

2

It was spring, and even in Old Compton Street the spring is apt to be exciting. Nerone's new skylark sang and jumped

and sang. Nerone had made a felt top for its cage, the better
to shut out the sky.

'Ma guarda! Is he not joyous?' said Nerone. 'It appears
that he too feels the spring.'

The skylark felt the spring, Gian-Luca felt the spring,
and Mario felt the spring and grew restless. Gian-Luca
looked at his motto every morning: 'I have got myself,'
and the words, lit up by sunshine, seemed to glow with a
new and exciting meaning, until, what with youth and the
spring in his bones, he almost forgot his troubles.

Mario, perspiring at the Capo di Monte, broke a dish,
for which he had to pay. He grew less subtle in dealing with
the clients; when he cleared their tables now he would whisk
with his napkin until the crumbs flew into their laps.

'Sapristi!'—the Padrone was proud of his French—
'Sapristi! You imbecile, what are you doing?'

And Mario would laugh—yes, actually laugh, right in the
teeth of the Padrone!

In the mornings, when he shaved, he did so with vigour,
cutting his chin in the process. The blood might drip on
to the rim of his collar, but Mario did not care; he would
go to the washstand and rub off the stain with an old
flannel wash-rag—after which his collar would look limp.

' I will not have a clean one, it costs so much, the washing,'
he would say. 'We must save, we must put by the pennies
for when we can go into the country.'

Berta got nettle-rash and cried a good deal; she got it
every spring and autumn.

'Geppe has given me pidocchi!' she insisted, whenever
Rosa would listen.

Geppe pretended to grope in his head and to throw the
results at Berta.

'Oh! Oh!' shrieked Berta in a panic of fear. 'Oh! Oh!
He is throwing me pidocchi!'

Rosa scrubbed up the house, and forgetting it was
London, she put the bedding out in the sun. When she
brought it in it was covered with smuts.

'Accursed country!' said Nerone, and he swore: 'We
live in an accursed country!'

Teresa was constantly busy in the cash-desk, the money
went jingling through her fingers. Whenever a sunbeam

67

touched a golden coin she smiled and stroked it gently with her thumb. For the habit of thrift had persisted in Teresa; now she saved for the pleasure of saving. Every Saturday morning she went off to the bank with a little bag hidden in her cloak.

As for Fabio, his halo looked wilder than ever, but the pains in his back had disappeared. He served in the shop without coat, or even waistcoat, his shirt bulging out between his braces.

'God be praised,' smiled Fabio, well content with the gastronomical effects of the fine weather. 'God be praised; we are selling more this spring than we have done for many years past.'

Even Rocca grew poetical, a mood which found expression in his garnishing and laying out of meat. Rocca bought a calf's head to which he pinned rosettes, then he thrust a spring of parsley in its mouth.

The Signora Rocca said very many prayers; it was May, the month of Our Lady.

'Oh loving, oh clement, oh sweet Virgin Mary,' she murmured, and then, bethinking her of Michael the Archangel, and, via him, of Satan: 'May God rebuke him—and do thou, Prince of all the heavenly host, by the power of God, thrust down into hell Satan and all wicked spirits.'

3

Late one afternoon came Mario and Rosa, accompanied by Nerone and the children. They walked solemnly into Teresa's back parlour; their faces were preoccupied and grave.

Mario said: 'Two weeks from to-morrow the Padrone had made me the present of a day. It is very important that we all discuss the matter; the question is, where do we go?'

'Yes, that is the question,' murmured Rosa dutifully; 'as Mario has said, we go, where?'

They sat down, staring at Fabio and Teresa: 'Where do we go?' they demanded.

'There are many nice places,' suggested Fabio.

'It is beautiful weather,' said Teresa.

'Now first,' began Mario, 'we must have the Gian-Luca.

You consent to his coming, I hope, Teresa? The day will of course be a Sunday.'

Teresa nodded and went on with her knitting.

'That is good,' Mario smiled. 'You hear that, Gian-Luca? You accompany us once again.'

Gian-Luca trod slyly on Geppe's toe, and Geppe screamed like a siren. Mario waited for the hubbub to subside, after which he went on speaking slowly:

'I have long wished to visit a certain place which I know is of very great interest; to begin with its name is full of romance—it suggests the sea and the sky.' He paused and made a wide gesture with his arms. 'The sea and the sky——' he repeated.

'And where is this place you speak of?' inquired Rosa.

'It is called Land's End,' said Mario.

No one laughed, no one seemed very much surprised; they had all known quite well what sort of thing was coming, for when Mario thought of a holiday he invariably longed for those far-away places that his mind had yearned over for years. Perhaps he had less imagination than the skylark, for he seemed to enjoy discussing every detail. 'I have heard——' he would say—and then he would be off! As he talked his eyes would grow rounder and rounder, and his face would shine with enthusiastic sweat until even Rosa would hush Geppe into silence the better to fancy herself there. A harmless diversion, a game of make-believe in which Rosa joined to please Mario.

Mario looked from one to the other.

'There are rocks at Land's End!' he announced.

'And the sea!' chimed in Rosa.

'And a beach,' said Gian-Luca.

'I have heard that the beach is stony,' mused Mario; 'however, no doubt there are sea-gulls——'

'Is it not in Cornwall?' Fabio inquired.

'Precisely,' said Mario complacently, 'and Cornwall is a place of historical interest because of that king they call Arthur. Though I do not think Arthur lived at Land's End, but of that I am not quite sure.'

'You shall tell me about him some day,' said Rosa; 'you have always been clever at history. But is it not rather far for the children—have you considered that, Mario?'

Mario frowned. 'Could we not start early. Can it matter *how* early we start?'

'It will cost——' murmured Rosa. 'It will cost a great deal, and we should not have much time there, I am afraid, even if we did start early.'

'That is so,' sighed Mario, suddenly depressed, because Rosa was not quite playing the game. . . . But after a moment he grew more hopeful. 'There are castles,' he told them, 'wonderful castles; I have seen the picture of one they call Corfe. What if we all go and visit the Corfe?'

'There is also Folkestone,' suggested Rosa, tactfully edging a little nearer home. 'At Folkestone one watches the boats coming in—there are sometimes Italians on board!'

'Mi stufano!' Mario burst out rudely. 'Why should I wish to see Italians?'

'It has come to me!' suddenly shouted Nerone, waving a triumphant hand. 'As you cannot go to Land's End, then why not go to Southend? To me it sounds all the same thing.'

But Mario shook his head. 'No, I think not, Babbo; I do not much like the winkles. Moreover, there is mud and many, many, children, and some of them——' He finished the sentence in English, because Berta, who was said to be frightened of illness, might not understand medical terms in that language. 'And some of them cough with the whoop.'

Teresa glanced up at him from her knitting: 'Epping Forest——' she murmured.

'There are too many trees,' said Mario discontentedly; 'it is difficult to get beyond trees; they come in so close; they confine, they molest you—and besides, they shut out the view.' His mouth drooped a little—he was gentler than Geppe, but he looked rather like him at that moment ——'I desire to go somewhere wide,' he muttered, 'somewhere enormously *wide!*'

Then Rosa spoke gently, stroking his hand the better to soften her words: 'Let us go to Kew Gardens and have lunch on the grass; we will take the big hamper with us. In the afternoon we can find the cake shop we went to once before—they had nice little tarts with raspberry jam—I remember because Geppe ate so many. We can travel on top of the omnibus, and you always like that, don't you Mario?'

For a moment Mario's face grew darker, his expression was sombre and resentful. Then all of a sudden he cheered up completely: 'Ecco!' he exclaimed, 'my Rosa has solved the problem! It is not quite Land's End, but there is much to see—we will study the plants and the Chinese Pagoda; after all, there is very much to see. And now we must consider what we take with us to eat—Fabio shall give us a sausage!'

CHAPTER SEVEN

THE MORNING of Mario's holiday ushered in the beginning of a heat wave. Rosa was up by five o'clock preparing the luncheon basket. A large panettone had arrived the previous evening, sent by a friend of Mario's; it had to be cut into four fat quarters before it would fit into the hamper. Fabio had sent round a length of salame and a very ornate pork pie, while Nerone had made no less a contribution than two large bottles of Orvieto in honour of the occasion.

'For,' said Nerone—to console himself at parting with a wine of so excellent a vintage—'it is not very often that a holiday occurs, and when it does one should be generous.'

Rosa, her fringe done up in curl papers, her nose already pink and shiny, rushed hither and thither in a flannel dressing-jacket worn over her petticoat.

'Via! Via!' she was always exclaiming, pushing Berta and Geppe out of her way: 'Via! Via! Who told you to get up? I command you to go back to bed!'

But Berta and Geppe were not thus to be disposed of, nor for that matter was their father. Mario kept wandering in and out of the kitchen—he was bursting with foolish suggestions.

'I would pack the hard-boiled eggs at the *bottom* of the hamper; that way they will not get so cracked; they will be steady.'

'Via! Via, Mario!' cried Rosa, frowning. 'I shall put all the eggs on the top of the hamper; the bottles of wine must go at the bottom, under the panettone.'

'I would like my tobacco put in the hamper, too, so that it will not bulge my pocket. I do not wish to spoil my best suit, and my rubber pouch has just split.'

'We do not wish to eat your tobacco,' Rosa snapped, 'nor do we wish to have it as a flavouring. Can't you go and find something useful to do instead of getting under my feet?'

'I am hungry *now*, very hungry!' teased Mario. 'When will you get us our breakfast?'

'We are hungry! We are hungry!' chanted Berta and Geppe, beginning to jump up and down.

Then Mario laughed and went off to his bedroom; his face was beaming with pleasure. 'What a day!' he exclaimed, throwing open the window. 'Holy Mother of God, what sunshine!'

The hamper packed and their breakfast eaten, Rosa washed both children.

'Ow!' grumbled Geppe as Rosa's large finger entered his ear with the wash-rag.

She shook him slightly and prodded again. Presently she oiled down his hair; when she had finished it looked like black paint, but Rosa was pleased with the effect. She dressed him with care in his best sailor suit, the one that was trimmed with white braid.

'If you dirty yourself I will beat you!' she lied. 'Go and sit over there on that chair.'

Berta's toilet was much more complicated; Berta herself saw to that. 'I wish to wear my white muslin dress, the one that they gave me at the convent,' she stamped.

'That you shall not,' announced Rosa with decision.

'It was given you to honour Our Blessed Lord, when you take part in His procession.'

'Nevertheless, I will wear it,' said Berta, and she promptly sat down on the floor.

'Cattiva! You will wear your pink print.'

'I will wear my white muslin,' said Berta mulishly. 'I will wear nothing else but that.'

'Mario!' called Rosa, 'come and speak to this Berta; she refuses to put on her dress.'

'And what does she wish to wear?' inquired Mario, sauntering in from his bedroom.

'The muslin that the good nuns gave her last year for the Blessed Sacrament procession.'

'And why not?' smiled the father, filling his pipe. 'Why may she not wear the muslin?'

Rosa looked shocked. 'Because,' she said gravely, 'it belongs to Our Blessed Lord.'

'He will not object, I am certain,' said Mario. 'He would wish his little Berta to be happy.'

So Berta got her way and wore the white frock, blue bows, silver medal and all.

'And see that you do not lose the medal or soil the ribbon,' cautioned Rosa.

Mario retired to make his own toilet. He examined his clothes that lay ready on the chair; a dove-grey suit, a pink shirt and collar and a brand-new crimson silk neck-tie.

'Va bene,' said Mario, 'but where are my boots? Where are my new brown boots? Rosa!' he bawled, 'come and find me my boots—I have looked, but they are not here!'

Rosa came in with her mouth full of pins; she too had been dressing at that moment. 'Here are your boots, cretino,' she said crossly, producing them from the wardrobe, 'but I would not advise you to wear them; it is hot, they are certain to draw your feet.'

'That is nonsense!' he told her, 'I *wish* to wear them; what one wishes to do never hurts.'

He fondled the yellowish leather with his hand, then he rubbed it on the bedspread.

'Magari!' sighed Rosa, 'between you and the children, I think we shall never get off. I so carefully warned Geppe to keep himself clean, and now he has spilt coffee all down his blouse.'

At that moment Gian-Luca arrived, looking hot in a knickerbocker suit of brown tweed. He was wearing a spotlessly clean Eton collar and a ready-made blue satin bow.

'Ah! Gian-Luca!' exclaimed Mario, 'you are fine this morning, almost as fine as I am!' and Mario surveyed himself in the glass, turning first this way, then that. 'Now you have come, it is time we start,' he continued, straightening his neck-tie. 'Let us go and collect the luncheon-basket, also Rosa and the children.'

2

They walked as far as Piccadilly Circus, Mario carrying the hamper. At the Circus they climbed to the top of a bus bound for Hammersmith Broadway.

'Be careful! Be careful!' shrieked Rosa to Geppe, who was trying to swing himself up by the hand-rail.

'He will hit me in the face with his heels,' fussed Berta; 'I wish you would make him behave!'

Mario was stopped at the bottom of the steps by a kindly but firm conductor. 'You must leave that 'amper with me,' said the conductor; 'no 'ampers allowed on top.'

'Not so,' retorted Mario; 'I will take him on my lap— I will nurse him—he cannot be left!'

The conductor pulled the cord and the bus moved off slowly behind the stout, sweating horses.

'I will not leave him!' cried Mario, still clutching his hamper; 'you see, I take him on my lap.'

'Oh, all right.' The conductor stood aside for him to pass, and Mario struggled up the steps.

The bus was very full—Geppe sat on top of Rosa. 'Here we are!' shrilled Berta from her seat beside Gian-Luca. 'You will have to go over there and sit beside Mamma.'

Mario squeezed in with the hamper on his knees; it grew heavier every moment. 'Dio!' he groaned, 'what is living in this hamper? Is it perchance a giant?'

'You take Geppe and give it to me,' suggested Rosa; 'I will now hold it for a little.'

Their burdens exchanged, they began to mop their faces —it was growing exceedingly hot.

At Hammersmith Broadway the crowd was enormous, and most of it was waiting for the bus to Kew Gardens.

'You had better carry Geppe,' said Rosa to Mario; 'I fear that he may get lost.'

Geppe objected, beginning to cry: 'I want to walk with Gian-Luca!'

As his father picked him up, he beat with his heels: 'Put me down, put me down, I tell you!'

Rosa dragged Berta along by the hand, while Gian-Luca struggled with the hamper.

'No more room on top!' yelled the harassed conductor. 'Inside only, please.'

By dint of superhuman exertion, they managed at last to get in.

'Now then, young 'un, don't gouge out my eyes with that basket!' protested a voice to Gian-Luca.

There were several other children on the knees of their parents, all fretful and on the verge of tears.

'It's this terrible 'eat,' said a mother to Rosa; 'it do try 'em, don't it, the 'eat?'

The smell in the bus suggested that it did—the sun was blazing through the windows.

'Phew! Ain't it awful!' a lady complained, clinking her black jet bugles.

Berta sat scratching her nettle-rash, and Geppe's nose required attention. Gian-Luca peered over the top of the hamper, his collar was feeling rather tight.

'May I undo my collar?' he whispered to Rosa.

But Rosa shook her head: 'No, no, caro, you look so nice as you are; you cannot undo your collar.'

He subsided behind the hamper again, so as not to see Berta who was making him itch. He wished that Mario would observe Geppe's nose—it really did require blowing. Rosa's fringe had begun to come out of curl—Gian-Luca noticed that too—one long, black strand was gradually uncoiling; very soon it would be in her eye. Her hat—last summer's—looked rather jaded, the roses no longer very red; however, by contrast, Berta's headgear was a triumph; a yellow poke bonnet trimmed with cornflowers and daisies and tied under the chin with white ribbon. Berta's hair stuck out in a bush behind; her eyes stared, inquisitive and greedy.

'I am hungry,' she was saying; 'how long does it take?'

'We are nearly there,' consoled Rosa.

3

Kew Gardens lay like a jewel in the sun, the grass green and gleaming as an emerald.

'Ma guarda, guarda!' cried Mario in delight; 'have we walked into Paradise?'

Gian-Luca paused to examine a magnolia that grew just inside the gate.

'Come on!' ordered Mario; 'we have very much to see; we cannot waste time, we must hurry!' He was walking a little lopsidedly now, by reason of the hamper that he had taken from Gian-Luca. His boater straw hat had slipped back on his head, his shoulders were hunched with effort.

They passed a hothouse and a small museum. 'Those are for later,' said Mario; 'I think now we will make for the large museum; that is of interest, I remember.'

On the way Geppe spied some enticing-looking ducks, swimming on an artificial lake.

'Come on! Come on!' called Mario, sharply; 'we have no time to play with ducks.'

The museum was stuffy and very dull, two cases only were amusing. These stood by the door; they contained little people—natives with carts and oxen. The children stopped in delight before them.

'What funny clothes!' remarked Berta.

Gian-Luca agreed.

'Oh, look, oxen!' piped Geppe, blurring the glass with his breath.

'Come, piccini!' came Mario's voice in the distance.

'Come, Rosa, there are two more floors.'

They turned reluctantly to follow the voice, which seemed always to soar on just ahead. At the foot of the stairs they caught it up.

'I think I will stay here,' said Rosa.

'As you please,' Mario smiled; 'but *we* will see all. Come, children, come on, Gian-Luca!' And he and the children disappeared up the stairs, leaving Rosa to wait at the bottom.

The tour of the museum completed at last, Mario bethought him of luncheon. 'I think we might go to the Pagoda,' he suggested; 'do I not see its top across there?'

'It is such a long way off, and already it is late,' complained Rosa; 'let us find a place nearer.'

In the end they sat down in the shade of a wood. It was only a small imitation wood, an incongruous and rather pathetic thing, trying to look wild and romantic and careless, a few hundred yards from a hothouse. However, there were beech trees and many sanguine birds—there were also bluebells in the grass.

'Look, Mario, are they not lovely?' exclaimed Rosa.

But Mario's gaze was very far away. 'We ought to have gone to that Pagoda——' he said slowly, 'I can see it over there against the sky.'

Gian-Luca was staring intently at the bluebells; he

77

stooped and touched them with his finger. They were cool and fine as though wrought in wax, their heads bent sideways a little. Something in the blueness and coolness of them reminded him of his pictures—the pictures that never came to him now when he lay between sleeping and waking—but something in this blueness and coolness made him sad, not happy like things seen in his pictures. He resented this sadness; he frowned at the bluebells and suddenly pushed them with his foot.

'Have I not got myself?' thought Gian-Luca; then wondered what that could have to do with bluebells.

Rosa was unpacking the luncheon-basket and Mario was opening a bottle of wine. Berta and Geppe were trying to quarrel, but they could not settle down to it, their attention kept on wandering in the direction of the food.

Gian-Luca accepted a large hunk of pie, and began to forget his depression; for after all, at eleven years old, many mysteries—like bluebells and sudden sadness and belonging to one's self—seem much less disturbing once the cry of the stomach is appeased.

'Madonna! What excellent wine!' gurgled Mario, drinking his second glass. 'Your father is as mean as a Genovese, Rosa, but to-day he has been generous like an emperor.'

They gorged until Berta and Geppe grew sleepy, and Rosa's head nodded on her bosom. But Mario was not sleepy; like a lion refreshed, he began to pace up and down.

'Come on! We must go to the Pagoda,' he urged. 'Avanti! There is not much time.'

They struggled to their feet. Rosa repacked the hamper, then she wiped Geppe's mouth and tied on Berta's bonnet, after which they had to hurry to catch up with Mario, who was out of the wood already. On the way to the Pagoda there were prunias in blossom, a sight to rejoice sore eyes, but Mario stumped forward with never a glance.

'Come on, avanti!' he kept on saying.

However, when at last they reached the Pagoda, Mario's thoughts appeared to stray. 'We have not seen the hot-houses yet,' he told them; 'and they are not to be missed.'

The first houses that he chose stood all in a row; five broiling, progressive hells. No need to go out into the air for a moment; you could pass from one to the other. At the fourth degree of torment, Rosa protested:

'I cannot support it,' she gasped.

'I feel sick,' put in Berta, hoping for attention.

'As for me, I like it!' bragged Geppe.

Gian-Luca was not sure that he himself did like it; he felt rather sorry for the trees. They were tall, anxious trees, always doomed to look through windows; and, moreover, they had grown and grown, until their heads were pressing against the glass roof. But Mario, once started on a quest for knowledge, was not at all easy to coerce; he might pause for a moment to read out a label, to elicit some scrap of information from a keeper; but before there was even time to draw breath, he would be off again, faster than ever.

There were many other houses, some cooler, some hotter, but all of great interest to Mario, it seemed.

'I know I am going to be sick!' announced Berta, punctually every five minutes.

At last Rosa struck; they had now reached a house that was tactlessly known as: 'The Stove.'

'Into this, my friend, you shall penetrate alone; we will wait outside,' she said firmly.

Even Mario showed signs of wilting a little when he finally emerged from 'The Stove,' but not for very long; having dried his drenched forehead, he suggested a tour of the gardens.

'I am told,' he remarked, in the pompous voice of one who imparts information, 'that these wonderful gardens extend for many acres—two hundred and eighty-eight, I believe—and at every few yards there is something of interest; we missed a great deal when we came here last time.'

His eyes were so round and his face was so eager that Rosa forbore to protest; so once more he started his caravan in motion, and they went for a tour of the gardens. It would not have been so tiring had he been content to investigate objects of interest as they came, but his mind worked faster even than his legs; he was always breaking off in the middle of one thing in order to push on to the next. Then his conscience would smite him:

'Let us go back a minute to King William's Temple,

it is not very far.' Or: 'Perhaps we should have gone to the other museums; up to now, we have seen only one.'

In the very middle of the Rhododendron Dell, he stood still abruptly and groaned.

'What is the matter?' inquired Rosa in alarm.

Mario did not answer, but when he walked on he was limping like a horse with a splint.

'Did I not tell you that those new boots would draw?' inquired his wife, almost crossly.

'You did,' he admittted, 'and, as usual, you were right; they draw with the strength of the devil!'

Berta and Geppe began to hang back.

'I am tired and my head aches,' whined Berta.

'I have got a stone in my shoe,' whimpered Geppe, 'and that hurts much more than a bunion!'

Gian-Luca's collar got tighter and tighter; he felt as though he must burst. It was his turn to carry the hamper again, and his arm was beginning to grow stiff. Rosa's hat had slipped to one side of her head, her fringe was completely out of curl; her kind, plump face looked dusty and sallow, there were rings of fatigue round her eyes. Berta's white frock had a rent in the side—caught on a branch in passing. Geppe limped along in imitation of his father, and as he limped, he complained. But Mario, still happy in spite of his anguish, pushed on with the courage of an explorer.

'There are still some museums, and then the Kew Palace,' he smiled, taking Rosa's arm.

'My dear,' she murmured; 'my very dear Mario— are you not worn out, amore?'

'I am splendid,' he told her. 'Just a little bit lame, but otherwise I am splendid.'

They were gentle with each other, the two of them, these days—now they seldom, if ever, quarrelled. The passions of their youth were cooling a little, and with their passions, their tempers. Then the frequent quarrels between their offspring left little time for their own; they were too busy coping with Berta and Geppe to devote much thought to themselves.

Mario said: 'It is very pleasant to get out of London for

a little—even if one only comes to Kew Gardens; still, it is very pleasant.'

She nodded: 'But I wish you had let me slit that boot, I cannot endure to see you hurt——'

He patted her hand: 'Do not worry, donna mia; it would spoil the new boot to split it.'

They dragged themselves on through the last museums, and, finally, over the Palace; after which they found Rosa's cheap little cake-shop, where Geppe once more ate jam tartlets.

4

On the way home that evening Geppe fell asleep, leaning against his mother. His small hand was quite incredibly sticky, but Rosa held it in hers. Berta, very upright in the corner of the bus, blinked hard to keep herself awake.

'Look at that Geppe,' she whispered to Gian-Luca; 'he sleeps—but then, he is so young!'

Having left Gian-Luca at Fabio's side-door, they betook themselves slowly homeward. Rosa was carrying Geppe, still asleep, Mario was leading Berta; with his other hand he clung to the hamper, which bumped against his leg as he hobbled. A quiet May dusk, the friend of tired faces, went with them down the street.

5

'And have you enjoyed yourself?' inquired Rosa, when at last she and Mario lay side by side in bed.

'Ma sicuro,' he assured her; 'oh, very much, my Rosa—only think of all that we have seen!'

Turning over he checked off the items on his fingers, calling them out one by one. There were not enough fingers, so he tapped on the bedspread, while she lay and watched him—smiling.

CHAPTER EIGHT

I

GIAN-LUCA left school the following Christmas, having made neither enemies nor friends. He was missed a little by both teachers and students; by the former because of a quick intelligence that had made him an interesting pupil, by the latter because there was now no 'Macaroni' to be teased and left out of things.

For a few weeks he experienced the novel sensation of having nothing to do. Just at first this was rather a pleasant sensation; he could lounge in and out of the shop as he pleased, or better still, stroll down the street to Nerone's and hang about bothering Rosa in her kitchen until she drove him away. But after a time this enforced idleness began to pall on Gian-Luca, and then it was that he formed a new habit—he formed the habit of books. Hitherto all books had meant lesson-books, he had read scarcely anything else, and lesson-books had been part of a rule imposed not by himself but by others. Now, however, it was different, he himself was the rule, he could read or not read what he chose; and this fact gave Gian-Luca a pleasant sense of power, so that even the volumes which he had brought from school became suddenly much more interesting.

From his early childhood he had loved the sound of words, and now he began to discover things about them; their length, their shape, their colour, their balance, their relation one to the other. He discovered the felicity of certain groupings, the strength and virility of others; the power of a name, the clamour of a line, the solemnity and vastness of a stanza. For the magic that unsealed his ears and his eyes, lay for him in a volume of verses; the verses were Italian; he had found the book one day, quite by chance, in Mario's bedroom. No one had ever heard of the author, or at least, so Mario said:

'Non lo conosco,' said Mario with a shrug. 'He is doubtless somebody new.'

When Teresa and Fabio had retired for the night Gian-Luca had relighted his gas, which was forbidden, and then he had crept back to bed with his book. As he read he began to see pictures again—yet now he was very wide awake—these were pictures that someone unknown had seen first, and left for Gian-Luca on the pages. The next morning he was knocking at Mario's door before that good fellow was up.

'It is I, Gian-Luca.'

Mario's voice came, rather husky: 'Per carità! What do you want?'

Gian-Luca put his head into the room, then his hand which was clutching the book. Mario reared up in bed like an angry retriever, his curly hair standing on end.

'Is it not enough that I work half the night because the Padrone has decided to serve suppers? Is it not enough that Rosa must wake me at six to do her infernal washing? Is it not enough that Geppe has a cold and coughs and weeps without ceasing? And now you! Come in, there's a draught in my ear; I shall have the earache in a minute!'

Gian-Luca obeyed him; closing the door, he went over and stood at the foot of the bed. His face was so solemn that in spite of his temper Mario began to smile:

'Have you decided to visit the North Pole or has Fabio swallowed a yard of salame? I am wide awake now—what has brought you so early, and why do you look so grave?'

'I came,' said Gian-Luca, 'to ask you for this book—I find it has beautiful verses.'

'What book? Oh, that thing! Ma sí, you can keep it. I cannot recall at the moment who gave it—a friend of Rosa's, I think; but put it in your pocket, Rosa disapproves of verses, and I hear her coming upstairs.'

As a matter of fact the book had been a present to Mario from his barmaid, given in the days when sentimental tokens had passed very freely between them. But Mario had never read one of the poems, and moreover, he now wished to deny the barmaid who, being a Latin, was causing him trouble by refusing to be denied.

Rosa came in: 'What has happened?' she demanded. 'I hope that no one is ill.'

'Not at all,' said Mario, winking anxiously at Gian-Luca, 'it is only that this imp here has come to torment us, having nothing better to do——'

'Oh, well,' sighed Rosa. 'I must not be idle, *I* have very much to do.' And she left them.

'Now go!' commanded Mario, glaring at Gian Luca, 'but first, have you hidden that book as I told you? You have? That is well; I am glad that you take it; I wonder that Rosa has not found it already—I thought I had burnt it up.'

2

Gian-Luca's unknown Italian poet was a wonder-worker, it seemed, for he wove a spell not only for himself, but for all his fellow craftsmen. Having read and re-read what he had to say, Gian-Luca bethought him of Browning, and found to his delight that though Browning was English— a very great drawback he felt to any poet—yet, nevertheless, he could make the heart beat and the eyes fill with sudden tears. From Browning he turned to Tennyson and Words- worth, and finally rediscovered Kipling. He had studied them all while he was at school, but now when he read them they seemed different.

Alone in the room that had once been Olga's, Gian-Luca made friends of his books. He would talk to them, pet them: 'Oh, bello!' he would say, stroking a page with his hand. Or he might feel disapproval, in which case he would scold: 'That is ugly, I do not like that line; if you were in Italian it would fit much better, it would not have so many small words.'

He made a shelf from an old packing-case, so that his friends might be well lodged, and when it was finished he nailed it to the wall directly opposite his bed. The shelf was just long enough to cover the wounds that had gaped in the plaster for years.

'Bene!' smiled Gian-Luca, 'I have hidden them all now; they were ugly, I am glad that they are hidden!'

One morning he sought out Fabio in the shop, asking him gravely for books.

'Ma che! I have none, but here are macaroons!' laughed Fabio, giving him a handful.

Gian-Luca ate the macaroons with much gusto, but the next day he sought out Mario.

'Can you lend me some books?' inquired Gian-Luca.

'Ma che! I have none,' said Mario.

Then, seeing Gian-Luca's look of disappointment, Mario scratched his chin, thinking hard: 'I have it, Gian-Luca! I know where you must go, you must go to the Free Lending people; there they have hundreds and thousands of books; you can bring away with you a sackful.'

Gian-Luca discovered the Free Library, but he asked for books in Italian.

The Librarian smiled. 'We have nothing in Italian—plain English, my child, that's what we keep here—try Shakespeare, he's not bad you know!'

As the days went on the Librarian grew more friendly. 'Do you write yourself?' he inquired without a tremor. Gian-Luca shook his head. 'You should try,' said the Librarian, 'it's never too young to begin.'

'So far I am reading,' Gian-Luca told him.

'So I have observed,' said the Librarian.

'Some day I shall make money, and then I will write,' Gian-Luca remarked confidentially. 'It is better to grow rich before writing lovely things, otherwise one might starve.'

'Out of the mouths of babes and sucklings——' began the Librarian, and he laughed. 'I see that you appreciate England, my child; however, I believe that some writers make money——'

'It is dangerous, my grandmother says that it is dangerous, and she is very clever,' said Gian-Luca. 'You see, I have only got myself, so I cannot write until I am rich.'

'I wish *I'd* only got myself,' sighed the Librarian; 'there are quite a number of me.'

'How many?' asked Gian-Luca, rather surprised.

'Five girls and two boys,' said the Librarian.

It was true that Teresa had mocked at poets when Gian-Luca had mentioned quite vaguely one evening that it must be rather fine to write verses.

'That is not for you,' she had told him firmly. 'For you is a business life—some day you may inherit this shop of ours, when Nonno and I are dead. Although,' she had added, 'we see no reason why you should not read if you find it amusing, but never read so much that you neglect other matters. Poets are very foolish people as a rule—they must also be very conceited. Nonno and I are not young any more, so you must be self-reliant, a worker—you cannot afford to start scribbling nonsense, for you stand very much alone.'

This had neither surprised nor shocked Gian-Luca, indeed he agreed with Teresa. A person who was minus even a name would have to fight hard for a place in the world, and something in this thought made him stubborn and defiant—his arrogant underlip shot out a little whenever he remembered himself.

He was old for his age, every day he felt older; perhaps it was because he now knew life so well, knew all sorts of queer things about fathers and children—children who had no real names. Every morning on waking he looked at his motto, kneeling up in bed the better to see it; and every night he would examine it afresh—he found it so reassuring.

'I have got myself,' he would mutter softly, and his muttering was not unlike a little prayer, and then: 'I am neither Italian nor English—not anything at all—I am just Gian-Luca.'

At times this made him feel very lonely, but at others it struck him as being rather splendid; and when this happened his mouth would grow wilful, with its arrogant underlip.

However, Gian-Luca did try to write verses, though shy and shamefaced about it. He felt quite sure that it was a waste of time, but as he had nothing very useful to do and something inside him kept asking and urging, he decided to give it its own way. Of the poems by that unknown Italian poet, there was one that Gian-Luca particularly adored: 'Gioia della Luce' the poem was called, 'The Joy of

Light,' and the more he read it the less he understood its meaning, and yet somehow he felt that he did understand it—but not exactly with his brain. The poem was long, it went on and on in a turbulent torrent of words. The great, ringing words stumbled over each other, shouting, proclaiming, lifting up their arms—at least that was the idea that came to Gian-Luca—the words were lifting up their arms! It made him want to laugh, it made him want to cry, it made him want to run for miles and miles. It reminded him of bluebells and blossoms at Kew Gardens, of the longings that Mario had sometimes for the sea, of things that he himself had only half imagined, of things so vast and splendid that imagination failed. Yes, that was what he knew to be so queer about the poem, it was full of little happenings like the bluebells and the blossoms, it was also full of bigness like most of Mario's longings—and of something that Gian-Luca knew to be within himself.

With the blessed self-assurance and temerity of youth, he selected this poem as his model. 'I will write about myself,' he thought complacently; 'I will write in big and lovely-sounding words.'

' "Sono Gian-Luca—Gian-Luca—" ' he began, and he suddenly added, ' "poverino." ' Then he tore up the paper; no, it was not quite right, the words sounded neither big nor lovely. He re-read his model and started again, this time he composed four verses.

'Dio!' said Gian-Luca, 'they are very bad indeed.' And once more he tore up the paper.

By the end of a week he had written an epic with which he was not at first ill pleased; but the more he admired it, the more he became certain that the epic ought not to be admired.

'Che, che!' he grumbled; 'how is this, I wonder? I feel but I cannot express; perhaps I had better try something little—I will write about the bluebells at Kew.'

The bluebells at Kew proved still harder to express, for he felt that they required so few words. He knew just what they looked like and just what they meant, but when he had finished his lyric about bluebells, it might have been written about onions. He consulted the 'Gioia della Luce' once more, and this time while he read it he scowled; he was growing very angry, and he swore a fat oath that Rocca occasionally used. He wanted to punish the 'Gioia della Luce,' and proceeded to slam to the book.

'Now you cannot get out to annoy me,' he said fiercely; 'I will keep all your beautiful words in prison, I will keep them shut up for a month.' After which he hurled the book under the bed, where it lay amid old dust and boxes.

'It is no good,' sighed Gian-Luca, feeling calmer now, but sad; 'I can read but I cannot write.'

And some instinct told him that he would never write, however hard he might try. He might live to grow rich, to grow very, very old—older than Fabio and Teresa; he might do many splendid and wonderful things, but one thing he would not do, he would never write a poem that in any way equalled 'Gioia della Luce.'

CHAPTER NINE

I

'FABIO,' said Teresa, 'come here, my Fabio, there is something I want to show you.'

She was sitting at the table which was strewn with papers; a ledger and two pass-books lay open before her, and her voice when she spoke was unusually gentle, there was something caressing about it. Fabio drew up a chair to her side and adjusted his steel-rimmed glasses.

'So many papers!' he exclaimed with a smile.

'So much good money,' she answered.

Her hand began straying among invoices and bills, letters and order-sheets: 'Today I have heard from yet one more restaurant; they send a large order for immediate delivery— I am thinking we had better get another cart and horse, and another young man to drive it.'

Fabio scratched his head and looked rather frightened: 'It seems that we grow,' he murmured.

'We grow,' agreed Teresa; 'we are getting quite well known; the Casa Boselli prospers.' She let her eyes dwell on one of the pass-books, then she pushed it over to Fabio. 'The total will show you that we grow,' she said, pointing; 'that sum represents our deposit alone, and here is the drawing account.'

He stared incredulously, frowning a little. 'I had not realized——' he stammered.

'We have not gone over the accounts together for more than a year,' she remarked, smiling quietly. 'Will you now check these figures, Fabio?'

He fished a stump of pencil from his waistcoat pocket and wetted the lead with his tongue.

'First the ledger,' said Teresa, 'and then the two pass-books, after which you might total up the orders.'

Fabio ran his pencil down the long columns: 'Trenta, trentotto, cinquanta——' he muttered, then: 'Cento, cento dieci, duecento, trecento——' From time to time he sucked at his pencil or licked the end of his thumb. Presently he raised his eyes to Teresa. 'Our Lady is good,' he said softly.

Teresa shrugged her shoulders: 'Our wares are good, you mean; I am very well pleased with our business.'

'It would seem,' said Fabio, 'that you and I grow rich.' But his voice lacked enthusiasm. He was thinking: 'We grow rich—yes—but Olga is dead—the dead have no use for money.'

Perhaps Teresa divined his thoughts, for her face closed up like a secret door that, in closing, is one with the surrounding structure; when she spoke her voice was no longer caressing. 'I have not let life crush either of us, Fabio.'

'That is true,' he said humbly; 'you speak the truth, Teresa—but somehow——' He paused and began to rub his eyes. 'But somehow, those pains in my back, when they come, make me timid—they make me feel old. I am old to to be useful in so large a business, it begins to frighten me a little. I am stupid about money, and the pains in my back——'

'They are only lumbago; you drink too much red wine,' she told him, closing the ledger.

He nodded: 'I know—but I love my Chianti, it takes my hand like a friend—when I feel it in my gullet I am more of a man—however, those pains in my back——'

Teresa, strong as a tall steel girder, surveyed him a moment in silence. 'I will rub you to-night. Does it pain now?' she inquired.

He shook his head.

'Very well, then, that is good, for I want to talk about Gian-Luca.'

He had known that this was coming, that it had to come—the boy had been idle for weeks. But Fabio, these days, shrank from all mental effort as a sea-anemone will shrink from a touch—he had lived too long with Teresa. Something told him that he would be left to decide upon a career for the child; that now that Gian-Luca was no longer a baby,

Teresa would feel even less obligation towards him than she had done in the past; and his fears were confirmed, for Teresa was saying:

'He is not a baby any more; it is now your turn, Fabio— I have done what I had to—it is time that you took a hand.'

'You mean——?' he faltered.

'That Gian-Luca must work; we are not like the English —idle.'

He nodded; she was right, Gian-Luca must work— Fabio had no doubt at all about this, for Fabio came of a thrifty peasant stock. They might spoil their children while they were little, but once they left school they no longer spoilt them; their children then, as a matter of course, became part of the earning machine. Nor did it occur to Fabio to consider those sums lying at the bank; that had not been the way with his peasant forbears, it was not the way now with Fabio. He loved Gian-Luca, patiently, tenderly, bearing him no resentment; but the idea of giving him a better education than that provided by the local Board School never crossed his horizon. When he himself had been Gian-Luca's age he had worked at any employment that offered; that had been and still was the way of his people, they were not afraid of small beginnings. Adaptable and infinitely painstaking in business, with an eye always on the future, they respected hard work, sagacity and money, but completely lacked imagination.

Fabio laid his hand on Teresa's arm: 'Will you not advise——?' he began.

Teresa shook her head: 'I have no advice to give; now it is you who must decide. The boy is twelve years old, he will soon be a man, he will not be backward, I think. While he was little I did my duty, I saw that he was clothed and fed and kept clean—he is no longer little, he needs me no more, therefore I may rest from Gian-Luca.'

'How you hate him!' exclaimed Fabio in spite of himself.

Teresa looked surprised: 'You are wrong, I do not hate him, but to me he is alien—from the moment of his birth he has always been alien flesh.'

Fabio stared at her dumbly, then he cleared his throat and turning, spat into the fire. He was thinking: 'I must go and consult with Nerone, perhaps he will tell me what to do.'

On the following day he sought out Nerone at an hour when he hoped to find Mario at home. Mario, he knew, was fond of Gian-Luca, and no doubt he also would be willing to advise. The three of them retired to a room behind the shop, in which Nerone kept his birds; the skylark, brought in because of the weather; a bullfinch that suffered much from its feet, two Norwich canaries that would very shortly breed, and a box cage of avadavats. The avadavats were huddled together in a long, ruffled melancholy row. Mario began to tease the bullfinch with his finger, but kindly, because of its feet.

'I wish that I too could stand on one leg!' he said, almost enviously.

'I have come to talk about Gian-Luca,' began Fabio; 'he must work, the moment has arrived.'

'You are right,' agreed Nerone, 'we spoke of it last night; it is most unnatural how he reads.'

Mario stopped teasing the bullfinch for a moment: 'What does Teresa say?' he inquired.

'She will not say anything at all,' sighed Fabio. 'I have come to you two for advice.'

'Advice? Can you yourself not decide?' demanded Nerone sternly.

'There is so little choice,' Fabio temporized; 'for Italians of our class there is very little choice, when we want to find work in England.'

'Oh, oh, but I thought you were English!' gibed Nerone.

'There is very little choice——' repeated Fabio.

'There is of course tobacco,' Nerone smiled complacently; 'but tobacco I am keeping for Geppe. When Geppe leaves school he will come into the shop, which is lucky for his father, eh, Mario?'

'After meals one smokes——' mused Fabio, gently. 'It is always much the same thing——'

'So it is!' laughed Mario. 'They may say what they please, but when a man is starving will he think of his soul? I say no, he will think of his stomach; therefore, empty or full it is all the same thing—stomachs and nothing but stomachs.'

'Some people will even chew tobacco,' remarked Nerone; 'everybody does in America, I am told.'

'There you are!' broke in Fabio; 'what did I say? For us it is always the same.'

'You prosper, I believe,' Nerone said jealously; 'I hear that you will soon be very rich. Why not let Gian-Luca work in your shop for a little? After that he could go as a waiter if you do not require him at home.'

'He may wish to be a cook,' suggested Fabio, 'or perhaps a hall porter at a restaurant.'

'If he wants to be a waiter, I can help him,' put in Mario; 'there is no doubt at all about that!'

'*You!*' sneered Nerone; 'are you not well over thirty, and still at your Capo di Monte? Per Bacco! I think Gian-Luca could help you; I think it is the other way round!'

Mario flushed darkly. 'You go too far, Babbo; insult me if you must, but not my restaurant. How often have I told you that the Capo will be famous, very famous, one of these days?'

'Many times you have lied thus,' Nerone said rudely; 'many times have I spat out your lies!'

'Basta! Basta!' cried Fabio, dreading a quarrel; 'I implore you not to get angry.'

'Who would not get angry?' grumbled Nerone. 'Am I not a long-suffering man?' Presently he said: 'Have you thought of our Rocca? I hear that he is wanting a boy.'

'I had thought of that, of course,' replied Fabio, 'but I do not think it would quite suit Gian-Luca; he is still rather funny about those small goats.'

'Let me ask the Padrone to take him at the Capo,' Mario insisted eagerly.

'Sacramento!' yelled Nerone. 'You and your Capo! And nothing you are, no, less than nothing! It is I who provide for Rosa and the children, it is I who scrape and save. As for you, you have nothing so far as I can see but a bunion on your left foot. I would not exchange my good wooden leg for your bunion—no, that I would not!'

'I am thinking, Mario,' said Fabio slowly; 'I am thinking of what you have said. If I kept Gian-Luca for two years in the shop, he might go to you afterwards. Already I can see him in a neat white waistcoat and a little black satin tie; I can see him in a fashionable restaurant after he has learnt at the Capo. He is one of those boys who is bound to rise;

he will have such a fine appearance, I cannot promise that you will keep him long; still, no doubt it would be good training——'

'As for that, no better exists,' bragged Mario. 'Will he not be under me?'

'Ah!' exclaimed Fabio in enormous relief; 'then I think we can take it as settled. I have always intended to make him a waiter; I have my ideas for Gian-Luca!'

'Then why did you come to consult us, Dio Santo!' bawled Nerone, now thoroughly roused.

'I wished to hear what you would say,' Fabio told him. 'We are such old friends that I thought it only courteous to tell you of my plans for the boy.'

3

Everyone thought Fabio's decision a wise one, including Gian-Luca himself. Gian-Luca, aged twelve, had no exalted ideas, and very few illusions about life. It seemed to him perfectly natural and right that he should help Fabio in the shop, and that afterwards he should work under Mario at the celebrated Capo di Monte. Most people that he knew did just that sort of thing, or at all events, something very like it. 'And,' argued Gian-Luca, 'if I cannot write well, perhaps I can serve well—even better than Mario.' For at twelve years old he already had great confidence in his own ability to serve.

'What fun you will have!' said Berta enviously, with her eye on a jar of fruit toffee from Turin. 'There are so many things one can eat in this shop, it is ever so much nicer than ours.' She and her brother had wandered in one Saturday afternoon, to find Gian-Luca in a little white jacket, importantly installed behind the counter. He looked at her disdainfully.

'We do not eat, Berta, that is not the way to grow rich; we offer our sweets to our customers, they eat and we keep the money.'

'Oh, but think——' persisted Berta. 'Just one little bit! That cannot be worth a farthing.'

'You are not to!' cried Gian-Luca, catching at her hand. 'You are not to go stealing our toffee!'

'Dirty pig!' retorted Berta; 'I do not want your toffee, we have much nicer toffee at home.'

'Then leave it alone, and do not touch those raisins, you are squashing them soft with your fingers!'

Geppe strolled round with his hands in his pockets: 'Good day,' he said, nodding in the manner of Nerone; 'it appears that we shall have some fine weather.'

'Good day,' said Gian-Luca, bowing a little; 'it appears that we undoubtedly shall.' Geppe's game was certainly very appealing, Gian-Luca's eyes began to sparkle. 'And now,' he said pompously, 'I will show you how I serve; you go out and come in again.'

At that moment, however, Teresa appeared: 'Be off, you two children!' she commanded. 'Have you sorted that wrapping-paper, Gian-Luca? You have not? Then do so at once.'

'Ha, ha!' mocked Berta. 'He is so very grand and he does not know how to sort paper!'

'I do!' said Gian-Luca.

'You do not!' sneered Berta. 'It is obvious that you do not.'

Gian-Luca's arm shot out across the counter and he tugged at a lock of black hair.

'Take that!' yelled Berta, slapping his face.

'And that!' he retorted, with a truly frightful pinch.

'And that!' spluttered Berta, beginning to scratch, whilst Geppe ate olives in a corner.

'And this!' remarked Teresa, as she seized Rosa's off-spring and thrust them forth into the street. 'And now,' she said, turning again to Gian-Luca, 'if you think you have finished behaving like a baby, I will show you how to sort paper.' She proceeded to explain the art of saving, as applied to paper and string. 'One does not always give a new piece,' she told him. 'One uses one's discretion according to the order; small orders may be done up in old bits of paper— say anything under two shillings.'

Gian-Luca nodded, rather red in the face and considerably humbled in spirit. 'And what must one do, Nonna, if they ask for something that does not exist in the shop?'

'In that case one persuades them to take something else; they should never go away empty-handed.'

'But if they do not want it?'

'You must make them think they want it; that is the art of good selling.'

'I will try——' he murmured doubtfully, forgetting for the moment how proficient in all things he was.

4

There was much to learn about the art of selling, as Gian-Luca was soon to discover. There was also much to learn about the ways of people who came for the purpose of buying. There were people who spoke with habitual rudeness, who ordered you about your own shop. When you handed them the parcel they never said 'Thank you,' they just turned and went out of the door. You longed to make faces at these sort of people or to pinch them like you pinched Berta; however, you remembered that at least they had to pay, and that consoled you a little. There were people who never knew quite what they wanted, who could never make up their minds. They asked you for tomatoes, but their eyes strayed to funghi; when you showed them the funghi they inquired about biscuits: 'I wish to take home a small present,' they told you. In the end, as like as not, they bought cheese. There were people who never fancied anything handy, anything that lived low down: 'Let me see that honey up there,' they would say, pointing; 'no, not this— that honey up *there*, if you please, I think it looks fresher than this.' There were people who believed in always being friendly, no matter how busy you were. They usually arrived when the shop was quite full, and engaged you in long conversations about nothing—but they always counted their change. There were people who seemed unable to see you, who looked over your head at Fabio or Teresa. You leant across the counter in your most approved manner: 'Are you being served?' you inquired politely, but they answered: 'I think I'll wait, thank you.' But the worst kind of people were those who did see you, and appeared to be amused at what they saw. These people made you nervous as you struggled with their parcels or tried to make out their bills. They would thank you profusely with mock gravity, they might even tweak your ear, and they frequently called you objectionable names like 'Kiddie,' 'My lad,' or 'Infant.' After such people left you began to grow downwards, you began to get smaller and smaller. In the end your head barely reached above the counter—at least, that was the way you felt.

On the whole, however, you enjoyed serving people; you could study them while you served. You realized quite soon that you never knew people until you began to serve them.

5

During Gian-Luca's two years at the shop, he learnt about all sorts of things. England was busily fighting the Boers, so Gian-Luca learnt a little about war, and a little about Death, from hearsay. The Boer War in no way affected his people, it scarcely even touched their trade; but into Old Compton Street there crept a sense of sadness —Rosa was constantly wiping her eyes for the mothers she did not know. He learnt about Teresa, and in place of his love there grew up an aloof respect. He saw her as she was when she stood at the helm, hard-headed, close-fisted, fearless in business, with a kind of genius for affairs. He learnt about Fabio; about his little fears, his weariness, his sense of growing old, the pains in his back that made him think of God, that God Who was part of the pains in his back, but never quite a part of Fabio. And Gian-Luca, very young, very strong, and very gallant as he seized the long knife and sliced the salame, began to pity Fabio and, in pitying, despised him—as is sometimes the way of youth.

All his life he had seen packing-cases arrive, and had often watched Fabio unpack them. But never before had he quite understood the full significance of all those large cases, that now arrived in their hundreds. There were certainly more than there used to be, and this fact was rather exciting; for in each was a smell or a series of smells, a taste or a series of tastes. Every case contained something that someone would eat, an astonishing quantity when seen all together, and this meant that the whole world was always hungry— incredibly hungry, preposterously hungry, ready and eager to consume every morsel that Teresa and her kind could

97

produce. He found this thought amusing; he would look at a cheese and begin to speculate about it: 'I wonder who you will go to,' he would think; 'I wonder whose palate you will tickle.' He visualized millions of red, gaping caverns, into which must be poured something pleasing to the taste. 'We are right who take up this business,' he would think; 'they could never get on without us!' And then there would come a sense of secureness, he would feel less alone in the world.

6

Gian-Luca still went to the Free Library, and this surprised the Librarian. 'I should think you'd have no time for reading,' he remarked, 'now that you're such a man of business. I should think that you must feel rather bored with books, considering there's no money in them——'

'What has that got to do with it?' inquired Gian-Luca, staring at him in surprise; for at this time he was very much a Latin; he kept two distinct Gian-Lucas, one for beauty, one for business, and so far they had never collided.

'I can't make you out,' said the puzzled Librarian; 'it's so queer that you like books at all.'

'Rocca likes music,' Gian-Luca told him, 'he goes to the gallery at Covent Garden; Rocca is mad about Opera!'

'And who is Rocca?' inquired the Librarian. 'He sounds very hard, somehow.'

'Rocca's our butcher, he used to be a soldier. When he was a little boy he knew Garibaldi,' said Gian-Luca, defending Rocca.

'Ah, well,' smiled the Librarian, 'it's a very large world, there must surely be room for us all—Come and see me some day, I live in Putney; perhaps you could come to tea?'

'It would have to be a Sunday,' Gian-Luca told him gravely. 'I am very busy all the week——'

'That will do; you can come next Sunday at four—I will show you my own special books. What would you like for tea—Chelsea buns? Or do you prefer Swiss roll?'

'I prefer Swiss roll, apricot,' said Gian-Luca.

'I will tell my wife,' promised the Librarian.

Gian-Luca arrived at the Librarian's house punctually at four the next Sunday. Fabio had laughed when bidding him good-bye:

'It seems you make new English friends, piccino. Now I have never been the friend of a Librarian, though perhaps I may have fed one—it may be so—unless they eat only books!'

The Librarian lived in one of a row of neat little red-brick villas; its name was 'Balmoral', and each side of the gate stood a foolish-looking acacia. The Librarian opened the door himself, his feet were in carpet slippers; an old briar pipe was gripped between his teeth, and he wore neither collar nor tie.

'Come in, come in! I am so pleased to see you,' he exclaimed, holding out his hand.

A small, rosy lady of uncertain age, was awaiting them in the drawing-room. The walls of the room were lined with books, as had also been those of the passage. She shook hands with Gian-Luca and smiled at him kindly with her head a little on one side. Her eyes were the eyes of a tame city bird—she reminded Gian-Luca of a sparrow.

'My husband has talked so much about you that I feel as though I knew you quite well,' she said.

At which Gian-Luca made a stiff little bow and brushed her hand with his lips. Teresa believed in punctilious good manners, and considered the English very boorish.

'You have very many books!' remarked Gian-Luca, quite unable to hide his curiosity.

'We have,' she agreed, 'very, very many books.' And unlike a sparrow, she sighed.

The books had a somewhat rakish appearance, caused by the sagging of the shelves; in one corner of the room a shelf had collapsed, and its contents were stacked on the floor.

'A slight accident, you see,' observed the Librarian, 'it happens occasionally here; I made all the shelves in this room myself, and they're really not so bad considering——'
Tea not being ready, he took the boy's arm, and proceeded to conduct him over the house. 'If you want to see *all* my books,' he said happily, 'I shall have to take you even

into the bathroom. We have to be careful not to have our baths too hot, otherwise the steam might spoil the bindings.'

Gian-Luca was astonished; every room they went into was packed and bulging with books; they elbowed the wardrobes, edged up close to the beds, or lay in untidy heaps on the chairs. The queer, bookish smell of them filled the air—it was pleasant to Gian-Luca's nostrils. Presently they went downstairs to the study, an absurdly small apartment overlooking the yard. Its sole furniture consisted of a roll-top desk, an arm-chair and a reading-lamp.

'Here,' said the Librarian in a very solemn voice, 'are all my old first editions. They deserve a veritable palace to themselves, yet I find them wonderfully uncomplaining——' He looked round at his treasures with the eyes of a parent who marvels at the sweetness of his offspring. 'They are so full of wisdom, it must be that,' he murmured, 'the wise are seldom self-assertive.'

'Are they not worth much money?' said Gian-Luca.

'Hundreds!' the Librarian told him; 'but no money could buy them,' he hastened to add, in the tone of one on the defensive. He placed a slim volume in Gian-Luca's hands. 'Take this, for instance, it is almost unique; they haven't got this one at the British Museum, and they won't have it until I am dead! I should like to take it with me for my library in Heaven, but that I fear wouldn't be allowed.' His quizzical eyes were watching Gian-Luca, who by now was staring round him in open amazement.

'So many, so valuable, so expensive!' said Gian-Luca; 'I have never seen so many owned books before—at home they have none at all.' He went over to a shelf and took out a volume which he opened, beginning to read. The Librarian noticed his gentle hands, and forbore to protest at his action. In a minute or two Gian-Luca looked up:

'I very much love their smell. It is such an old smell and yet it seems alive—do you think that perhaps they may breathe?'

'Who knows?' said the Librarian, smiling at the thought. 'They feel very much alive to me.'

Then Gian-Luca's mind became practical again. 'Did you buy them all yourself?' he demanded.

The Librarian laughed: 'Do I look as though I had? Do I look as though I could afford them?'

Gian-Luca examined his friend more closely, and observed that his clean-shaven face was much wrinkled, as though from continual smiling. Two funny, deep lines ran down into his chin, and his hair had a tuft like a schoolboy's. But although he appeared to have amused himself vastly—over what Gian-Luca could not conceive—his clothes would have thoroughly shocked Teresa, so frayed and untidy were they.

'No,' said Gian-Luca, who felt bound to tell the truth, 'you look terribly poor to me.'

The Librarian nodded: 'You're right, I am poor—we're all as poor as rats. But when I was younger a dreadful thing happened—I had a most wicked old uncle. He left me no money but all his books, I'm afraid he must have done it out of spite! It was rather like leaving a cellar to a drunkard, he probably knew that I'd read myself to death, as I have done financially.'

Gian-Luca was silent for a moment, then he said: 'Could you not sell your fine books? After all, one must live and one cannot eat books, and at times one feels very hungry.'

'Good Lord!' sighed the Librarian; 'now I'm disappointed in you. Do you always think only of your stomach?'

'We think of other people's at the Casa Boselli—that is what really pays. My grandmother says that your money is your best friend, and as she has much she must know.' Then Gian-Luca's heart softened quite suddenly, and he smiled at the shabby Librarian. 'All the same,' said Gian-Luca, 'I would like you for a father—I think you would make a nice father.' And he meant it.

The Librarian surveyed him very kindly. 'You're wrong there,' he said, shaking his head. 'I'm a rotten bad father, and in any case, I've got far too many children as it is!'

'Which do you like best, books or children?' Gian-Luca inquired, a little puzzled.

'That,' said the Librarian, 'is a difficult question—I've never been able to decide.' As he spoke, something bumped against the door, which opened rather abruptly. A very fat child lurched into the room, and seeing Gian-Luca, began to suck its thumb. 'My latest folly!' said its father, pointing.

'It's three, the others are all grown-up. Go away at once, folly!' he commanded sternly; 'you're much too corpulent to fit into my study, in another minute you'll get stuck.' But the infant continued to stare at Gian-Luca, and its father apparently forgot it. 'You were saying,' he went on, 'that you think of people's stomachs—a revolting portion of the body.'

'Why?' said Gian-Luca, a little offended. 'I cannot buy books and I cannot write them; so I am going to be a waiter.'

The Librarian seemed to be thinking aloud: 'Dull, very dull, very ugly——' he murmured.

'It will interest me,' said Gian-Luca, with dignity, 'to see where all the food goes to. We have hundreds of pounds of food at our shop, it arrives in enormous cases!'

'I know where it ultimately goes,' said the Librarian; 'but come on, I expect tea's ready.' And seizing his latest folly by the hand, he led the way to the dining-room.

'You observe,' he smiled, motioning Gian-Luca to a chair, 'that we have not forgotten the Swiss roll!'

The plump little lady who looked like a sparrow, beamed across the table at Gian-Luca. She seemed to feel that he must need comforting, and put four lumps of sugar in his tea. Gian-Luca preferred two, but he drank his tea politely, he was obviously growing very thoughtful.

'If you had fewer children, could you then not buy more books?' he suddenly inquired of the Librarian.

'Dear me!' said the hostess, looking rather startled. But Gian-Luca continued to be thoughtful.

'Or suppose,' he went on dreamily, 'that you read fewer books, could you not afford to have more children?'

'I'm greedy!' smiled his host; 'I'm greedy, I want both; that's why I wear carpet slippers on a Sunday—it's not to ease my feet, but to save my boots—and that is what comes of being greedy!'

'I do not understand you,' said Gian-Luca, frowning.

'I don't understand myself,' said the Librarian. Then he looked at Gian-Luca: 'Now, you're what the world calls wise, you don't neglect the substance for the shadow; that's what we all do here, we all neglect the substance, in spite of this disgracefully stout offspring whom you see. However,

if at moments you should come to long for the shadow—
well, Gian-Luca, we'll be very glad to see you.'

'Yes, indeed, always glad,' said the hostess gently; 'you
must come very often, Gian-Luca.'

She was looking at her guest with pity in her eyes, a
pity that she could not have explained. 'Undoubtedly, a
very prosperous child,' she was thinking, 'he's well dressed
—I suppose his grandparents must be rich, these Italians
only come here to make money!' Yet the mother that was
in her was not quite satisfied, it was thinking too, but not
about prosperity—it was thinking that never in its life had
it seen such a queer, unresponsive and lonely little boy—
so self-sufficient and so lonely.

8

That evening Gian-Luca went up to his room and found
his pencil and paper. A vague spirit of discontent was upon
him, a vague longing to find self-expression.

'The Librarian lives in the shadows,' he wrote,

'But Gian-Luca must live in the daylight.'

Only rhymes could appease the ache that was in him,
he disdained the idea of prose. But the rhymes would not
come; there was no rhyme for shadows and nothing that
seemed to go very well with daylight. So Gian-Luca lost
his temper and tore up his paper, and hurled his pencil to
the floor. He sat glaring into space:

'It is all wrong!' he muttered. 'Something is all wrong
with me. I wish to write poems, I wish to be a waiter; yet
a waiter cannot write, and a poet cannot wait—I am greedy
like the Librarian. Also, I am sometimes greedy over food,
I should very much dislike to go hungry.'

'Piccino!' came Fabio's voice up the stairs; 'come quick!
We have minestrone for supper!'

The would-be poet got up with some haste, he was feeling
very hungry at that moment. A most enticing odour was
pervading the whole house.

'I come now at once!' replied Gian-Luca.

CHAPTER TEN

I

THE CAPO DI MONTE was in Dean Street, Soho. It occupied the whole of a tall, blistered house that had once been painted brown, and on either side of its swing glass doors sat two white Capo di Monte cherubs, perched on pedestals of carved Italian walnut. Judging from their smiles and the contours of their figures, the food at the Capo was good, a fact which they proclaimed to the hungry of Dean Street—or at least had been put there to proclaim. The Padrone was intensely proud of his cherubs, he dusted them himself every morning; they had come with him all the way from Italy, and had given their name to the restaurant.

The Padrone was still quite young in years, but old in the ways of business. He had soft brown eyes and a devilish temper. His skin was sallow and luminously greasy; his nose was aggressive, his mouth over-ripe, and his teeth were magnificently healthy. He was tall, but already his soiled white waistcoat showed signs of a little paunch. For the rest he was obviously born to succeed, being quite untroubled by scruples.

Fabio had felt a little doubtful about him when it actually came to the point, but Gian-Luca had preferred the life of the restaurant to the more monotonous career of the shop.

'I would like to see things outside,' he had said, 'a waiter sees all sorts of people, Nonno; I think I would rather go to the Capo, Mario likes it so much.'

So Fabio had nodded and murmured: 'Sí, sí——' as he usually did when afraid of an argument, and one morning Gian-Luca started off with Mario *en route* for the Capo di Monte.

Gian-Luca was carrying a brown paper parcel which contained his exciting new clothes; a black suit with a species of Eton jacket, some stiff shirts and collars, and four white cotton bows which fastened with a clip at the back. In addition to all this he had six enormous aprons that would cover him down to his feet; in fact he had been very generously equipped for his duties as 'piccolo'. The March wind blew clouds of dust in their eyes as they turned the corner of Dean Street.

'Now listen,' said Mario, halting on the pavement; 'I would say a few final words.'

Gian-Luca stood still obediently, though he secretly wondered what there could be left to say, so much had been said already. It was ten o'clock, and since seven that morning Mario had never stopped talking. However, he was evidently still full of words which were no doubt better out than in.

'Now first,' said Mario, removing some dust from the corner of an eye with his thumb; 'now first, you observe me in all that I do, and whenever you can, you do likewise. Now second, you are always smiling to the clients, even if they spit in your face—they do not quite spit, I speak figuratively, but one feels sometimes that they would like to. Now third, you move quickly; whatever you do, do it quickly and do not make a noise; a plate should be given or removed with a flourish, and yet it should seem to be arriving out of space—do not fumble with the hand, the hand should appear superfluous, but be careful not to spill the gravy. Now fourth, keep a quarter of an eye on the clients, but an eye and three-quarters on the Padrone; he has many little ways that are purely his own, for instance, a language of gestures. You must learn all his gestures and exactly what they mean, otherwise he may lift his voice—I have found it better to understand his gestures, it often saves trouble later on. The Padrone is a genius, and as such he has his moods, that is only to be expected; he appears to be impatient, that, however, is not so, he is probably thinking about a new dish that will some day make him famous. Now fifth, you must always wait on the Padrona and do whatever she asks you; she is beautiful, so the Padrone loves her—I do not think she on her part loves him, but that is none of our business. If you win the Padrona, you win the Padrone, and that makes an easier life; I myself am always most careful to win her, I have found that it more than pays. The Padrona controls all the dishes from the lift, you will have many dealings with her; she also controls all the wines and the spirits, but that need not concern you just yet. And sixth, never give away any secrets regarding the business of the house; every house, you will find, has a few little secrets; they are not for the public, they are not for the clients——' Mario glanced at his watch. 'Come on, come on! Already it is late,' he said, pushing Gian-Luca; 'we have no time to stand here talking in the street!'

They began to hurry against the wind, Gian-Luca clutching his parcel. 'This way!' cried Mario, as, arrived at the Capo, he led Gian-Luca through a grimy side-door, and down some steep stairs to the basement.

Gian-Luca had often been past the restaurant, but had never until now been inside its portals—the Padrone did not encourage visits from the friends and relations of his staff. Gian-Luca found himself standing by Mario in a narrow passage lit by one electric globe; the uneven stone floor was very far from clean, the walls were discoloured with damp and mildew, and from somewhere out of sight came a furious voice, swearing loudly in Italian.

'The Padrone,' whispered Mario, in the awed tone of one who hears God speaking in His thunder.

They stood very still while the storm subsided, or rather until it betook itself upstairs, then Mario smiled nervously: 'Come along to the kitchen, I will show you our chef, Moscatone.'

The kitchen was a vault quite devoid of daylight; like the passage it had one electric globe; in this case, however, the globe was more powerful, so that every defect jumped at once to the eye, and Gian-Luca decided that there were many. The cooking appeared to be all done by gas, judging from the huge gas stove and the smell; the smell of the kitchen was far from appetizing, consisting, as it did of greasy gas ovens, a stopped sink, and last night's black beetles. Moscatone, a gigantic Neapolitan, was standing in the middle of the floor; his huge face was shining and splotched with temper:

'I will slay him! Corpo di Dio, I will slay him!' he rumbled, like a bursting volcano.

A scullion, busily peeling potatoes from a pan gripped between his knees, looked up with a smile.

'He is offal,' he murmured; 'he is even less than offal——' And he mentioned with some detail exactly and precisely what he was.

'Here is my friend Gian-Luca,' said Mario; 'Gian-Luca, this is Moscatone; the very best chef in England we have here, that is why some day we will be famous.'

Moscatone's anger blew away like a cloud, dispelled by his enormous guffaw. 'Famous, the Capo! I think not, however—how do you do, Gian-Luca?'

Gian-Luca took the extended hand, which felt soft and unpleasantly greasy.

'He is going to learn to be a waiter under me,' put in Mario, with pride in his voice.

'Is that so?' said Moscatone, as though surprised. 'He will learn under you, you say?' Then he changed the subject, for in spite of his temper he was really a kind-hearted giant.

'Come along, you must change your clothes,' ordered Mario; 'I will show you the way to the dressing-room, Gian-Luca.' And he led the way to a green baize door at the end of a long dark passage.

What Mario had called the 'dressing-room' was a small composite apartment; part wardrobe, part storeroom for boxes and rubbish, part dustbin, and part lavatory. A fair young man with a round, foolish face, was already very much in possession. He was standing in front of a bit of cracked mirror, in his shirt sleeves, adjusting his tie.

'Here we are!' announced Mario, as though they were expected; 'Gian-Luca, this is yet another waiter. His name is Schmidt, and moreover he is Swiss, a very excellent fellow.'

'Good Morgen,' said Schmidt, who spoke no Italian, but who prided himself on his English; 'I vill not be a tick, not ein half a tick—it is nearly completed already.'

'Do not hurry,' said Gian-Luca, surveying him gravely; 'we can wait while you finish your tie.'

Schmidt grinned. 'Do not hurry? Vell, my friend, I must hurry; if I do not I get in the soup.' He turned from the glass to put on his coat, and pushing past Mario was gone.

'He is always like that,' said Mario disapprovingly. 'He

is always in too great a hurry; a waiter must be quick, but never in a hurry. They are foolish people, these Swiss.'

He began to unearth some old dress clothes from the crowded peg on the door. Gian-Luca undid his brown paper parcel, and together they struggled to dress. There was so little room that whenever they moved they promptly collided with each other.

'Pazienza!' sighed Mario in a vague, patient protest, as Gian-Luca bumped him with his elbow.

'I do not understand my apron,' said Gian-Luca. 'It seems to me very wide.'

'I will show you,' Mario told him kindly. 'The wider it is the better.' He folded Gian-Luca into the apron which swathed his legs like a shroud. 'Ecco!' exclaimed Mario. 'And now you are ready, and very fine indeed you look, piccino,' and he smiled with affection and approval.

2

Upstairs it was certainly more cheerful than the basement, it also smelt less of stopped sink. The restaurant was a long, low, well-lighted room, with a stand of aspidistras in the centre. Here and there, in a pot tied up in pink paper, a fern was trying not to die; there were many little tables, and the one good-sized window was embellished with red cotton curtains.

'Some day they will be silk,' thought Gian-Luca when he saw them, remembering Mario's words.

'Ah!' exclaimed the Padrone, jumping up from a table at which he had been drinking vermouth. 'You are late as usual, accursedly late. I am sick of you and your lateness!'

Mario's eyes goggled: 'I am sorry——' he faltered.

'My apron delayed us,' piped Gian-Luca.

The Padrone stared. 'And who may you be? Ah, yes, I remember, the new piccolo.'

'At what time would you wish me to arrive?' inquired Gian-Luca, assuming the air of a man.

'Half-past nine and not a minute later,' he was told.

'I will come,' said Gian-Luca calmly.

'That is well,' growled the Padrone, rather taken aback, 'that is well. Time is money at the Capo. And now go and

wash the glass in those doors; after that you must sweep out
the restaurant. Come here you, Schmidt, and give him a
baize apron and show him the buckets and brooms!' he
bellowed. 'Corpo di Bacco! Where is the fool? Santa Madonna! where is he?'

3

Gian-Luca washed the glass, and then, just for fun, he
polished all the brass as well. He brushed down the steps
and finally retired to sweep up the restaurant floor. From the
corner of his eye he watched Mario and Schmidt scuttling
in and out of the pantry; they were very busy laying the
tables for luncheon, and Mario puffed a good deal. Schmidt,
who was rather a painstaking fellow, had a habit of breathing
on things, especially the glasses, which he always suspected,
and once, when he thought he detected a smudge, he spat
on his finger and removed it. Gian-Luca, thumping about
on his knees, watched the proceedings with interest.

'Nun was! You not got those clean serviettes yet? Mein
Gott! You take long, venever you be ready?' he heard
Schmidt grumbling at Mario.

'Mind you your business!' shouted Mario hotly. 'I know
how I set the table!' Schmidt laughed. 'You not spit on the
glasses,' went on Mario, who had looked up and caught
him in the act.

'Then why you bring them in dirty from the pantry?'

'You not make them any cleaner with spit!'

'Was? Do you say then that my mouth is dirty?' Schmidt's
face was now red with temper, 'Ich ask; you perhaps would
accuse my mouth?'

'Dio!' groaned Mario, who was limping a little. 'What
do I care about your mouth!'

Schmidt went back to the pantry, muttering in German,
and Mario stood still for a moment; very gently he began
to rub his sore joint against the calf of his leg, then he sighed,
and mopping his brow with his napkin he too hobbled off
to the pantry.

Gian-Luca, left alone, settled into his stride—the proverbial new broom sweeps clean. The dust rose in clouds, in
less than five minutes he produced a miniature dust-storm.

Through the haze he could see a woman approaching:

'Santa Madonna!' she was saying. 'Santa Madonna! Do not use so much force. Have we imported a Samson?'

He paused with the brush firmly gripped in his hand and, still kneeling, stared up into her face. Then he sneezed and she sneezed; after that he stood up.

'The floor is very dirty,' he told her.

The Padrona laughed softly. 'Do I not know as much? Naturally the floor is very dirty.' And then, speaking in Italian: 'But you must brush gently. One flicks with the brush to make the top clean; one does not disinter all the filth of a year—see, like this, I will show you, like this——' And together they both went down on their knees.

The Padrona smelt nice when she came close to you. Gian-Luca could smell her through the dust. She had very small hands with pink-tinted nails; her feet were small, too—she wore little bronze slippers and thin silk stockings to match. She laid her hand gently over Gian-Luca's and moved the brush backwards and forwards.

'Ecco!' she murmured. 'Now I think you understand. As they say here in England, "Let sleeping dogs lie!" And that proverb applies to our dust.'

'Thank you,' said Gian-Luca, very red in the face, and he quickly looked down at the floor. With a gentleness worthy of the Padrona he caressed the carpet with his brush.

The Padrona went behind the counter of the bar and busied herself with some bottles; from time to time she glanced at Gian-Luca, and her lips twitched into a smile. She began to notice his ash-blond head bent in an effort of attention. The back of his neck looked absurdly young, the hair grew down into a youthful hollow, and where it ended it turned suddenly sideways, forming a little comma.

'Have you not swept enough?' inquired the Padrona. 'I think you have swept enough.'

'As you will,' said Gian-Luca, getting to his feet, 'but I feel that the floor is not clean.'

'Come here,' said the Padrona. 'You shall help me with these bottles; you shall take this damp cloth and wipe them; but first, what is your name and how old are you? Mario brought you, did he not?'

He was staring at her now because he found her lovely;

his pleasure overcame his shyness. He said: 'I am called Gian-Luca, signora; I am nearly fifteen, I was fourteen last November, I came here with Mario this morning.'

'I see—Gian-Luca; but Gian-Luca what?'

'Boselli,' he told her, and flushed; then quickly, 'But I'd like to be called Gian-Luca, please; I have always been called just Gian-Luca.'

'Why not? It's a very nice name,' she smiled, surveying him calmly with experienced eyes, the colour of mountain gentians. 'You are tall, very tall for your age, Gian-Luca——' And she nearly added, 'and amazingly hand-some.' But instead she pointed to the row of bottles, which Gian-Luca proceeded to dust.

The Padrona was thirty; she was also a Venetian; she was also married to the Padrone; three facts which she found no cause to resent—she looked younger than thirty, she was proud of her birthright, and her husband was—well, just the usual husband—a thing it was always essential to possess and to pet into comparative good temper. Her nature was sceptical, sunny and placid; having never expected too much of life, she had never been disappointed. She was conscious of her beauty and in consequence of men, but her technical virtue was perfectly intact, and was always likely to remain so. With the clients she assumed that air of aloof-ness that had always impressed the good Mario. With her husband she was docile and unfailingly good-tempered, there was no necessity to be anything else; her beauty was the only weapon she needed to subjugate the Padrone. The Padrone was jealous, he adored and he suffered, and the more he suffered the more he adored. He lived in perpetual terror of losing the love of so beautiful a creature. Her docility never made him quite happy—he feared that it might be a cloak; yet so foolish was his love that he cringed to his wife and vented his anguish on the waiters.

But at moments the Padrona felt a little dull; she detested the English climate. It was weary work standing for hours behind the counter, serving out other people's drinks. There were times when her husband's ridiculous outpour-ings had begun to get on her nerves, when she noticed that little inclination to a paunch—it had not been there when they married. So when Gian-Luca turned to her with a smile, because he could not resist it, the Padrona smiled back and said:

'Splendid, Gian-Luca; you polish my bottles to perfection.'

And when he was once more busily at work she began to speculate about him, her speculations being principally concerned with what he would be like in a few years' time, and with what would happen when he first fell in love, and with whether the woman would be fair or dark, older than he was or younger. For of such fairly harmless but foolish romancing the mind of the Padrona was full. The more strictly virtuous the married woman, the more she will sometimes dally with fancies; and then Gian-Luca being almost a child, what could be the harm in her fancies?

Presently she said: 'Is your mother dead, Gian-Luca?'

'Sí, signora; she is dead.'

'And your father?'

A long pause and then: 'Sí, signora; my father is also dead.'

The Padrona sighed. 'I see, that is sad; but I also have lost both my parents. What part of Italy do you come from— from Rome?'

'My mother was born here in England, signora, and I too was born in England.'

He stood quite still with a bottle in his hand, dreading the Padrona's next question. Would she ask if his father had been born in England, too? And if she did, what would he say? The Padrona spared him this embarrassment, however; her mind had reverted to business; it was nearly one o'clock and she had suddenly discovered that she had only two siphons left.

'Go quickly, piccolo, and fetch me six more siphons and twelve small bottles of soda,' she ordered.

He flew to obey and went rushing downstairs, all but upsetting Mario in the process.

'Piano, piano!' cautioned Mario. 'You must walk with more repose; a waiter should never appear hurried.'

'Where are the siphons?' said Gian-Luca breathlessly.

'In the cellar at the end of the passage,' Mario told him; 'but, Gian-Luca, remember what I say and walk softly; a waiter must not be a whirlwind.'

By half-past one the Capo was crowded. The Padrona
took dish after dish from the lift that came up with a bump
at the back of the bar, and passed them across to Mario and
Schmidt, who grabbed quickly and disappeared. In between
times she served out whisky and brandy, filled glasses with
beer from the nickel-plated tap, produced cigarettes, cigars
and liqueurs, shouted orders down the lift shaft, opened
bottles, stacked up glasses, and surreptitiously powdered her
nose with a puff in a pink silk handkerchief.

Gian-Luca watched Mario with the bright, alert eyes of
a dog who expects an order; he was anxious to study the
celebrated manner that Mario employed to the clients.
Mario had said: 'You assert yourself, but with grace—
you expatiate on the food.' And Gian-Luca, who was there
on his first day to learn, waited, growing ever more anxious.
He remembered all the things that Mario had said about
tempting the appetite; his words regarding the handling of
dishes—only that morning he had spoken of a flourish, and
remarked that a plate should appear out of space, quickly
but without noise. He had begged Gian-Luca to watch all
his movements, and not only to watch but to copy—and
yet now Mario was doing none of these things, and moreover he was making a noise. Schmidt, on the other hand,
could carry four dishes and two plates with never a sound,
but when Mario did likewise the pyramid slipped; and once
a truly dreadful thing happened, for Mario upset a large
dish of salad right on to the shoulder of a client. Gian-Luca
dashed forward to the rescue with his napkin, but he only
rubbed in the mayonnaise; the client, a fat business man,
objected; the Padrone was called to apologize, and Mario,
pale, with goggling eyes, stood there doing nothing at all.
Of course after that Mario may have been nervous, for a
number of small things happened; an irate lady was given
a chop when her order had been for chicken; a coffee cup
was broken; some clients were kept waiting unduly long
for their food.

'I say, look here, waiter, we can't sit here all day; do
hurry up with that mutton!'

And Mario was dumb—that was what was so dreadful,
he neither protested nor cajoled. And he hobbled; the more

impatient they grew the more ostentatiously he hobbled.
There was peace at Schmidt's tables, comparative peace;
but Mario was having a bad day.

'Perhaps,' thought Gian-Luca, 'he watches the Padrone
too much, and that makes him careless.'

The Padrone was certainly well worth watching, for his
strange sign-language was now in full swing; he appeared
to be spelling things out on his fingers as though they were
all deaf and dumb. From time to time his sallow cheeks
would swell as though about to burst, and this happened
whenever Mario went near him, and yet he remained quite
speechless. The Padrone's silence was more terrifying than
the explosion of a bomb, for one felt that he must be gathering force for what was to come later on. Possibly Mario
was feeling this too, for his face looked worried and pale.

'Via! Do not get under my feet!' he kept hissing in Gian-
Luca's ear.

There were far too many plates and dishes for the lift,
and in consequence much running up and down to and from
the kitchen.

'Can you not help?' whispered Mario furiously, turning
to glare at Gian-Luca.

'What must I do?' Gian-Luca whispered back.

'Why, take all those dishes to the scullery, and on
your way up bring a basket of rolls, and I want some more
clean knives and forks.'

'Und I vant four coffee and fast!' ordered Schmidt. 'You
hurry und bring me at once.'

'Gian-Luca,' came the Padrona's soft voice, 'go and get
me a few clean glasses.'

It was almost as though as Mario's first protest, a spell
had been suddenly broken. Now the orders poured in on
Gian-Luca like hail; hitherto he had not been asked to assist,
being there on his first day to learn.

'Hallo, boy! Can you give me a match?' said a young man,
and proceeded to hold out a cigar.

'Send me that waiter; I've asked for my bill!' came a
voice from the opposite table.

Up and down stairs with armfuls of dishes, with glasses,
with coffee, with ices, went Gian-Luca. He had no time to
observe Mario's methods and he felt that this might be just

as well. His arms ached from the weight of the large metal trays, his legs ached from the steep kitchen stairs, his head ached from a super-human effort to remember, not one thing, but more like a dozen. In the kitchen Moscatone had returned to bad temper, and he almost threw the food at Gian-Luca. The man who washed up in the vault-like pantry would keep sending messages to the Padrone—of a kind that could not be repeated. Whenever this happened Gian-Luca snatched his plates and tried hard to pretend not to hear; then the man who washed up got offended with Gian-Luca and called him an insolent, bandy-legged puppy, and many less complimentary things.

At half-past three there were still people eating, just two little inconsiderate groups; or rather not eating, but chewing the cud, a habit that all waiters learn to dread very early in their careers. At half-past four Gian-Luca got his luncheon, which consisted of odds and ends; he shared them with Schmidt and the now sulky Mario who refused to speak or to look up. But the odds and ends were both plentiful and good, and Schmidt and Mario had each a glass of beer wherewith to enliven their spirits. After gobbling their food they all got up stiffly and went to the door for some air. Presently Mario decided to go home for a little, while Schmidt went out for a stroll; but Gian-Luca, feeling work-tired for the first time in his life, preferred to remain at the Capo.

5

That evening Mario acquitted himself better; Rosa had managed to cheer him up, and when he came back he was looking almost playful.

'Ah, Gian-Luca,' he said very brightly, as they washed their hands together at the sink, 'and what do you think of the Capo di Monte? Is it not rather fine?'

Gian-Luca was silent for a moment, then he said: 'I think that one must begin.'

'Jawohl,' agreed Schmidt, 'one must begin. I am nur here to learn English.'

The evening clients appeared more aristocratic, some of them had dressed for dinner. The Capo was occasionally patronized by people who were going on to the theatre. This amused Gian-Luca; he liked the women's clothes and the neat dress suits of the men.

'Some day I will have waistcoat buttons like his,' he decided, examining a smart young man out of the corner of his eye.

Once or twice Gian-Luca was actually able to get near to these elegant people.

'A match?' said Gian-Luca, striking one with a flourish and holding it to a fair lady's cigarette.

'Thank you,' said the fair lady with a small, fleeting smile.

'Niente, signora,' bowed Gian-Luca.

'That was very well done,' whispered generous Mario; 'that was done with distinction and grace.'

But the next time Gian-Luca offered a match his hand was pushed away with a curt refusal.

'If I want one I'll ask,' said a lonely male diner, beginning to study the menu.

The Padrone was very busy recommending wines to those who had dressed for dinner. A handful of bank clerks and such-like people he ignored completely, as did the Padrona, though some of them lifted their hats to her in passing and one youth openly admired her. Gian-Luca, of course, had no time to admire her, though he felt very conscious of her presence; when passing the bar he would look the other way because he so much wished to look at her. He hoped that she observed him with an armful of plates, quite as many as Schmidt could manage. When he felt her eyes on him, he assumed the grand air, he whisked out his napkin or made a remark with a shrug of the shoulders to Mario. If he had to approach her he became very stiff.

'A packet of Gold-Flakes, if you please, signora.'

'Ecco! How many packets?'

'Only one, please, signora.'

'Very well, there you are then, Gian-Luca.'

And off he would go without even a glance, convinced that the Padrona was smiling. He could feel that smile on the back of his head; it seemed to be singeing his hair.

They had had to abandon serving suppers at the Capo after a fortnight's trial. The Padrone was too experienced a slave-driver not to be able to gauge with some niceness the limits of endurance of his slaves. At half-past ten or a little after, the waiters found themselves free, and Mario, Gian-Luca, and the still cheerful Schmidt were jostled together in a last frantic effort to get out of and into their clothes. Mario appeared to have wilted again, his round face looked weary and drawn; from time to time he would glance through the door as though expecting something to happen. And it happened quite soon; downstairs came the Padrone, they could hear him talking to himself—he was muttering fiercely under his breath.

'He works himself up,' thought Gian-Luca.

The Padrone stood still in the doorway for a moment with his soft brown eyes fixed on Mario; then he opened his mouth and began to shout. All the while he was shouting his eyes remained gentle—dove's eyes in the face of a tiger. One by one he checked off the mistakes of the day, beginning with the horror of the salad:

'Scemo! Imbecille! Sporcaccione!' he shouted. 'How long am I going to endure you! You limp round my place like an old lame mule; no one else would engage you; very well you know that! If you did not come cheap, I myself would dismiss you; you bring shame on my Capo di Monte.'

And then, as though Heaven itself cast off Mario, Schmidt happened to move his foot—the toe of his boot struck full on that joint that had ached so intolerably all day. With a sharp yell of anguish Mario collapsed like a rag doll against the wall; his face grew red and, to Gian-Luca's horror, he suddenly burst into tears.

CHAPTER ELEVEN

I

'ON s'accoutume à tout,' said a wise French writer, and he might have added, 'Surtout quand on est jeune'; for youth in spite of its many small tragedies, its longings, its revolts, its uncertainties of spirit, has at least the blessing of adaptability, and no mean a blessing either. And so it was that by the end of eight months Gian-Luca had got used to the life of the Capo; his arms and his legs no longer ached acutely, his brain learnt to keep calm in moments of confusion, he seldom lost his temper and never lost his head; in fact, according to the watchful Padrone, Gian-Luca possessed that rarest of all gifts, the instinct for perfect service.

Mario's fall from grace as a super-waiter had somewhat disconcerted his pupil, who had honestly believed all that he had said regarding his position at the Capo. Mario was such a fine fellow at home, at times almost overbearing; but Mario at the Capo was a very different person; a cringing, servile, incompetent creature, who, far from being the Padrone's right hand, was obviously not even his left. It was evident therefore, that Mario had lied in a foolish spirit of bravado.

'Ma che!' thought Gian-Luca, making a grimace. 'Ma che! He is really a very bad waiter; if I were the Padrone I would not keep him even if he is cheap.'

But then would come memories of early childhood, of a Mario more active, more fierce, more light-hearted; a Mario who had insisted that a lonely little boy should always take part in his rare excursions; and Gian-Luca would be conscious of a tightening of his throat at times when he looked at Mario, of a vague regret, of an irritating pity for the great, limping, foolish fellow—a pity that was irksome and quite out of place in the busy life of the restaurant. All the same, it inclined him to neglect his own work in order to help his friend; and this worried Gian-Luca, who would tell himself sternly that a boy who had not even got so much as a name could ill afford to neglect his work, could indeed ill afford to pity. For Gian-Luca, now fifteen years old and a Latin, was quickly advancing towards manhood; more than ever he discerned the important difference that lay between substance and shadow. And somewhere in the region of unpractical shadows belonged this pity for Mario; it went with the pity for Rocca's small goats, a thing he sternly ignored.

Mario still bragged when Gian-Luca would listen—yes he actually still had the face to brag! Even after eight months of daily revelations, he continued to weave romances. Gian-Luca would stare incredulously at him, finding no adequate words; feeling hot and uncomfortable all down his spine, blushing with embarrassment for him. Then gradually a light began to dawn on Gian-Luca, though he tried to turn away his eyes; with a terribly clear vision he perceived the truth—Mario bragged from self-abasement; Mario had long ago realized himself, and he lied from the humility of failure.

'But a man should not fail,' thought Gian-Luca sternly. 'Who has got the time for failures?'

Meanwhile he could not help glowing a little with the knowledge of his own success. The Padrone was pleased; he could see that by his fingers which now seldom signalled to him. Poems were all very well, thought Gian-Luca, for those who wished to stay poor—he knew a poet now who fed at the Capo, that was when he fed at all. He was always hungry and he never washed his neck, and moreover, he seldom paid his bills.

'Sapristi!' the Padrone would grumble when he saw him. 'I am stupid to give that vile little worm credit; but he knows those of Chelsea, some that are famous, and they are the people I want. They shall come to the Capo and paint pictures on my walls, and eat foolish dry birds like peacocks. I shall make them believe that the peacocks strut in with their tails spread out: I shall say: "If only you had seen him, how he walked round the kitchen, so lovely, so elegant, only this morning!" And then they will think that he tastes all the better; I know them; they like a sensation.'

So the poet got credit from time to time, but from time to time he did not; and when he came back with some money in his pockets he would usually be looking rather thin. He said to Gian-Luca:

'You're a handsome boy, why don't you go as a model? I can get you taken on by Munster, if you like; he's looking for a sort of John the Baptist.'

'What would he pay me?' inquired Gian-Luca promptly.

'That depends on his circumstances. When he's flush he pays well; otherwise, my true Italian, he might pay you nothing at all.'

'Then I think I am better where I am,' smiled Gian-Luca, 'for some day I shall be a head-waiter.'

'Oh, summit of all ambition!' sighed the poet, who was picking a cutlet bone.

Gian-Luca surveyed him with patient eyes; he forgave much in one who was so hungry. There were not many people, for the luncheon hour was past, so he talked to the poet a little.

'You write poetry, do you not?' he said politely.

The young man looked up in feigned surprise. 'Is it possible that my fame gets abroad?' he inquired. 'Yes, I write, and I read *too* beautifully aloud—my own poems, of course; other people's are so dull. I'll send you my latest production, if you like, because I adore your profile. Only beautiful people are allowed to read my book; I've stated that clearly in the preface.'

But the book was never sent, for the poet went to Paris, owing ten pounds to the Padrone.

'No,' thought Gian-Luca, 'I do not think I will write poems; I do not think I will try any more.'

2

The Padrone liked Gian-Luca so well that he went in person to see Fabio. 'I hear that you are cheap,' was how he began. 'Now suppose I should give you an order?'

'We are cheaper than cheap,' said Fabio promptly, 'and we only sell of the best.'

'That remains to be seen,' said the Padrone suspiciously. 'I have heard that story before.'

Now Fabio was mild, but the mildest Italian responds like an old war-horse to a bugle when he senses the battle of a bargain. Fabio's eyes began to shine in anticipation, and he rubbed his plump hands on his apron.

'I am likely to require twelve dozen tins of tomatoes,' the Padrone announced with unction. 'On so large an order what discount do I get? My order depends on the discount.'

'Is that all?' exclaimed Fabio. 'So insignificant an order—will you not be requiring paste?'

'That is as it may be,' grinned the Padrone. 'Let us first come to terms for the tomatoes.'

'Shall we say two per cent. for cash?' inquired Fabio.

'Per Bacco! *No!*' shouted the Padrone.

'That is generous,' remarked Fabio in a rising crescendo.

'It is robbery!' retorted the Padrone.

They argued, they glared, they thumped on the counter, bringing strange but explicit accusations. One would have thought that blows were in the offing, so fierce were their faces and their gestures. As a matter of fact they were fast becoming friends, acquiring a mutual respect. In the end they retired to the room behind the shop and opened a bottle of wine.

'Salute!' smiled Fabio.

'Felicità!' bowed the Padrone, lifting his glass with an air.

'To-morrow we deliver without fail,' promised Fabio.

'Do not incommode yourself unduly, Signor Boselli; to-morrow will be good, but a day more or less——'

'I thank you for your courtesy,' beamed Fabio.

3

In the course of a week came the beautiful Padrona to pay her respects to Teresa. Teresa surveyed her with critical eyes, not at all allured by her beauty.

'She is Venetian, she is false, she is stupid,' said Teresa; 'and moreover she has a wanton eye on Gian-Luca.'

'Ma Dio!' gasped Fabio; 'he is yet but a child.'

'He will not remain always a child,' she reminded.

'But what of the husband? I am certain he is firm, I am sure he is a lion among men.'

'When the lion lies down with the lamb,' smiled Teresa, 'I have heard that he loses his strength.'

Fabio groaned loudly. 'Madonna!' he complained; 'and we have but now completed that large order.'

'That is why,' said Teresa. 'Her eye is on Gian-Luca, so she sends her lion here to spend money.'

'What must be done?' inquired Fabio weakly, beginning to fidget with the things about the room.

'Nothing,' said Teresa. 'If we take him away, we do but make him think the more.'

'But supposing——'

'We will not suppose,' she said firmly. 'He is handsome and young, but he is also ambitious; he will not stay long at the Capo di Monte. Meanwhile he will probably meet some young girls, one of whom he can marry later on—there is Berta, for instance; it is true she is plain, still, she will probably improve.'

'Alas!' exclaimed Fabio, wringing his hands. 'What a terrible danger is youth! When I think of our Olga——' But Teresa's face stopped him.

'I wish you would weigh up those hams,' she said quickly; 'I feel sure they are under weight again.'

4

A year slipped by uneventfully enough in all save one momentous happening; Gian-Luca experienced his first love of woman, and the woman he loved was the blue-eyed Padrona with her masses of red-gold hair.

A boy's first love is a love apart, and never again may he hope to recapture the glory and the anguish of it. It is heavy with portent and fearful with beauty, terrible as an army with banners; yet withal so tender and selfless a thing as to brush the very hem of the garment of God. Only once in a life comes such loving as this, and now it had come to Gian-Luca. In its train came all those quickening perceptions that go to the making of a lover; the acuteness of hearing, of seeing, of divining. A hitherto unsuspected capacity for joy; and an equal capacity for sorrow.

Gian-Luca felt himself taken unawares; yet when he thought it over he would feel quite convinced that he must have always loved the Padrona. Be this as it may, he now noticed things about her that had quite escaped him in the past; the lights in her hair; a dimple in her cheek, so faint as to be almost imperceptible; the fact that two of her pink finger-nails had little white marks upon them, and above all a tiny scar on her hand, a scar that filled him with the queerest emotion whenever his eyes beheld it. And what he now found so strange in his condition was his yearning over imperfections; he loved those two nails with the white marks the best, and the hand with the scar, and the whole of the Padrona when she looked tired, or ill, or fretful—or if her hair was untidy.

Alone in the night he would think mighty thoughts about goodness and greatness and valour; yet so humble was he that these thoughts would be detached. He longed to lay down his life for the Padrona, but that would be neither greatness nor valour, not even goodness—just something quite simple, like fetching cigarettes from the bar. This love of Gian-Luca's was a thing of pure giving, expecting nothing in return. Its motto was to serve, its desire to comfort, its ultimate ambition to worship. And as all that he now did was done unto Love, he polished the nickel more brightly; his tumblers and wine-glasses shone like the sun, his aprons were spotless, his hands red from washing, and he surreptitiously bought a pocket-comb with which he was always combing his hair when he found himself alone in the pantry.

If the Padrona noticed these things, she gave no sign that she did so. Her manner was gentle, her smile kind and sunny—though in this last respect she unbent just a little, she was always smiling at Gian-Luca. As time went on it was him she would call to fetch and carry for her bar.

'You go,' she would say, and her small front teeth would come gleaming out at him like pearls of great worth, 'you go—that old Mario is always so slow, and I cannot endure our fat Swiss.'

Occasionally too, she would send him on errands in the time between luncheon and dinner. This time belonged by rights to the waiters, in it they could usually do as they pleased; but the days when Gian-Luca was not sent on errands he would generally sit near the bar with a book, for among other things he wished to grow wise, in order to be worthy of the Padrona.

The Padrona would sometimes come into the bar. 'Reading, Gian-Luca?' she would say, smiling at him; and once she had asked him to show her his book. 'Dio Santo!' she had exclaimed, 'it looks very dull; as for me, I am not at all clever!'

At such moments Gian-Luca could only stare, all his self-assurance would leave him. In the hands of the Padrona he melted like wax; and once he had had to remember his motto: 'I have got myself', in order to be certain that his legs were not turning into fluid. But somehow these days the motto sounded wrong, nor could it restore his self-assurance. 'I have got Gemma!' he would catch himself repeating; Gemma being the name of the Padrona that nobody used but the Padrone.

The Padrone! a large, black-browed, insolent man who bullied the miserable Mario; a man whom the fierce Moscatone of the kitchen had threatened to split like a fowl. A man who had more lurid titles below stairs than hairs in his greasy black head; a man who owned the Capo and the food of the Capo and the slaves of the Capo and the mistress of the Capo.

'If only I too, were a man!' groaned Gian-Luca, writhing at the thought of the Padrone.

Yet he served him more devotedly than ever before, in mortal terror of offending. To offend the Padrone was to anger the Padrona—how strange were the ways of women!

At about this time Schmidt grew very friendly to Gian-Luca, anxious to curry favour, for everyone knew at the Capo di Monte that Gian-Luca was much liked by the Padrona. No doubt it was owing to her intercessions that he was given an evening now and then, and sometimes, on a Sunday, he would get the day off, an unusual proceeding at the Capo. She had once been heard telling the Padrone that Gian-Luca was young and still growing: 'If we work him too hard he may get ill,' she had said, 'and that would be very inconvenient.' Schmidt had winked heavily at Mario over this, but Mario had only frowned. Mario, outrageous old poacher that he was, had the makings of a fine gamekeeper.

To Gian-Luca, Schmidt said: 'You admire our Padrona? She is beautiful, wunderschön!'

Schmidt looked very sympathetic, he sighed once or twice, and just at that moment Gian-Luca's heart was full; so instead of snubbing Schmidt as he generally did he expanded ever so slightly. Schmidt was as sentimental as a schoolgirl and as lustful as any satyr, thus Gian-Luca's budding manhood began to amuse him.

'Ach Gott! They are dreadful, these women,' mourned Schmidt, 'they are surely put here to torment us.'

Mario, ever watchful, cautioned Schmidt severely. 'You be careful with Gian-Luca; I will not have you teach him to be a dirty dog like you are. I love him, he is clean, he knows nothing of life, my wife she was his foster-mother.'

Schmidt nodded and grinned wisely. 'I understand,' he said, 'but Gian-Luca is in love mit die Padrona.'

'You shut your face up quick,' Mario told him in a rage. 'If you do not, I make it shut up for you.'

In his methods with Gian-Luca, however, Mario was foolish for he jeered at the Holy of Holies. 'Caspita!' he laughed one afternoon that summer, 'you are growing as vain as any peacock. Now if all this fuss is about our Padrona, I advise you to stop being silly; for one thing you are young, for another she is old, I can see several wrinkles already—anyhow, it is silly, and if your Nonna knew she would certainly laugh at you as I do.'

Gian-Luca got up quickly from his chair in the pantry; he was pale, and his voice shook a little. 'She is young and she has not got one single wrinkle.' He turned to the door. 'I am going out with Schmidt,' he flung over his shoulder at Mario.

Now this was the last thing that Mario had wanted, so he hobbled after Gian-Luca. 'Piccino!' he called, 'do not stay out too long, and be a good boy, remember.'

Schmidt, who was standing on the pavement, sniggered: 'You are his little baby.'

Gian-Luca grew scarlet. 'I am sixteen,' he said hotly; 'at sixteen one is not a baby.'

Schmidt whistled and merrily twirled his cane. His hat

was too small for his head; he looked vulgar and foolish with a rose-bud in his coat, and an imitation diamond in his tie. Gian-Luca eyed him with disapproval, and decided that he could not endure him. But presently Schmidt said:

'I have heard the Padrona—she praised you to-day to that husband.'

'Did she?' breathed Gian-Luca, trying to keep calm. 'Do you think you could remember what she said?'

Schmidt pretended to think hard, and after a minute he invented a little conversation. He watched Gian-Luca from the corner of his eye; he was inwardly splitting with laughter. 'Did she *really* say that?' Gian-Luca kept repeating.

'Jawohl,' smiled the mendacious Schmidt. Then he suddenly got bored—'I shall follow that girl, look how pretty she is, she have got die small feet! You come on, Gian-Luca, perhaps we can speak—you make love, I let you this time, and that way you forget all about your Padrona for a while, and that do you good.'

Gian-Luca turned and left him in disgust, his soul had been deeply outraged. It was almost as though Schmidt had spat in the face of something very pure and sacred. He felt, too, as though he himself had been to blame, as though he had exposed her to this. 'Oh, forgive me!' he murmured. 'My very dear, forgive me. My beautiful—my good—my holy——'

CHAPTER TWELVE

I

Two DAYS later the Padrona said to Gian-Luca: 'Would you like to come upstairs and have tea with me? It is terribly hot down here.'

She was neither so sly, nor so stupid, nor so wanton as Teresa had proclaimed her to be; indeed at that moment she felt purely maternal—she was sorry for the pale-faced boy.

Gian-Luca hastily tore off his apron. 'Signora!' he murmured. 'Signora——'

'Come along then, you look tired—you work harder than them all, my husband was saying so this morning.'

He followed her upstairs and into a room that smelt of her favourite scent; it was crammed with the carved walnut furniture so dear to the Venetian heart. The chairs and the settee were upholstered in plush which stuck to your clothes as you sat. There were endless coloured photographs of Venice on the walls, and over the fireplace hung an oleograph depicting the Holy Family. A large tea-table was already set out, it was generously supplied with cakes; Gian-Luca had seen them in the process of baking—Moscatone liked the Padrona.

'Sit down,' she said, pointing to a little arm-chair. 'Will you have tea or coffee, Gian-Luca?'

'Whichever you prefer, signora——' he faltered.

She laughed and gave him some coffee. It was not very easy to make him talk, he kept flushing and paling by turns. To everything she said he replied:

'Sí, signora.' 'No, signora.' Or, 'Prego, signora.' Beyond this he seemed incapable of speech, nor was he enjoying his tea.

'Now do not be prim and shy,' she said smiling; 'at this moment we are just two friends. Downstairs you are a waiter and I am your Padrona; up here you are Gian-Luca and I am your friend. You think that is strange? But it is not strange at all, I have been to call on your Nonna.'

'*Have* you?' said Gian-Luca. 'Oh, but that was kind, signora!' He had not been told of the visit.

She waved this aside: 'We have business dealings, and in business it is always best to be friendly. Now tell me about yourself, Gian-Luca; are you happy with us at the Capo?'

'Signora——' he began, then stopped abruptly, unable to control his voice.

'Well, go on, my child.'

'I am more than happy—I—I am no longer lonely.'

She looked at him with interest in her large blue eyes, she had heard a little of his story. 'Were you lonely before, then, povero bambino?' she said softly. 'It is wrong that the young should be lonely.'

'I have always been very lonely,' he told her, suddenly not feeling shy any more; 'you see I had only got myself before I came here, signora.'

'And now, Gian-Luca?'

He hesitated, but only for a moment. 'Now I have got you,' he said quite simply; 'and so I no longer feel lonely.' His queer, limpid eyes were full upon her, innocent, ardent, unashamed. 'When one may see you every day, signora, and be near you, and hope to please you and serve you, then one is blessed—one grows and grows—something inside one blossoms.'

'You are a queer child!' she said, flushing slightly. 'You are a strange boy, Gian-Luca—yet if I had a son I would wish him to be like you.' And she suddenly took his hand.

His fingers closed quickly and strongly over hers, and stooping he kissed the little scar. 'I have so often wondered if it hurt—' he whispered. 'I have so often wondered if it hurt.'

She sat very still with her hand in his—for a long time she did not speak; then she said: 'No, it did not hurt very much, Gian-Luca—not as much as you are hurting me now.'

He started. 'I am hurting you now, signora?'

And she could not help smiling at the horror in his face; then she grew very grave. 'Yes, my child, you are hurting——

because I think you grow too fond. You are so young, Gian-Luca, and I am quite old, therefore you must not get angry. I am old enough to be your mother, remember—that is, very nearly,' she added.

'But can one ever be too fond?' he asked her; 'is it not beautiful to love?'

'It is beautiful,' she told him, 'but not always wise, especially for you who do all things intensely. I have watched you, piccino—as you work, so you would love, and life being what it is, that makes me fearful for you.' She let her gaze rest on his questioning face—she was strangely disturbed and sorry. She thought: 'Calf love: it is natural enough—it always begins for an older woman, but I must be more careful—yet what can it matter, he is perfectly safe with me.' Then she thought: 'If Cesare knew, what a fury! Ma che! That man is an imbecile. It is always the same, this thing we call love; it pretends, we pretend, but it is always the same——' Yet her sceptical thoughts did not quite reassure her. 'Gian-Luca,' she said, 'what will happen to you when you come face to face with real life? You are so quiet, so self-assured—you are old for your age, but if all the while you burn up inside, as I think you do, what will happen to the poor Gian-Luca?'

He smiled. 'Signora,' he said very gently, and his voice sounded suddenly mature; 'signora, I have never had anyone before, I have only had myself, just Gian-Luca. It had to be so—it could not be helped—I had not even a country. I was born all wrong—I had no name, signora; that is why they called me Boselli. I loved my grandmother when I was a child, but she did not want me—I wounded. That was not her fault—she hated my eyes, and also my hair, I remember. At first I was angry and then very sad, and then I wrote out a motto. I wrote: "I have got myself." For you see, everyone must have something——' He paused, still smiling, as though at his thoughts; then he said: 'But that is all over; now I no longer have such a motto, I have quite a new motto now.'

She could not resist it—she said: 'And your new one?'

'Must I tell you?' he asked, but quite calmly.

'I think so——' she faltered, a little ashamed.

' "I have got Gemma." It is that now,' he told her.

Once again she fell silent He still held her hand—he was stroking it softly with his fingers. His face was very pale, very quiet, very earnest; his arrogant mouth looked composed and gentle, and his eyes were dropped to the hand he was stroking, as though it needed vigilance and care. The Padrona stirred and the movement seemed to rouse him for he looked up into her face. As he did so she smiled a little questioning smile, slightly raising her eyebrows. Then all of a sudden his composure left him, he became very much a child.

'Oh!' he burst out; 'if the house would catch fire. If only the house would catch fire!'

'Madonna!' she exclaimed, and drew away her hand; 'I hope that it will not—but why?'

'So that I could save you,' he said, flushing deeply; 'so that I could rescue you, signora!'

Then she laughed, and he too laughed a little with embarrassment. 'Forgive, signora,' he said shyly. At that moment who should walk in but the Padrone; he was all affability and smiles.

'Ah, Gian-Luca, so here you are. Have you devoured many cakes?' He sat down and began unbuttoning his waistcoat. 'I have just come from seeing your Nonno,' he went on; 'he and I have affairs together. He inquired was I pleased. And I said that Gian-Luca would some day make a fine head-waiter. He is really an excellent fellow, your Nonno, and his shop is a joy to the eye.' The Padrone was now taking off his shoes—he had large and untidy stockinged feet.

'Shall I get you your slippers?' inquired the Padrona—and when she had fetched them she stooped and put them on.

He patted her head as one pats a dog, but his hand lingered over her hair.

'It is time that I go,' said Gian-Luca, getting up. 'I am deeply grateful for your kindness.' He brushed the Padrona's fingers with his lips, and bowed to the smiling Padrone.

'A fine boy,' said the Padrone, as the door closed on Gian-Luca; 'I hope we may some day have one like him.'

A great happiness came down like a luminous cloud, in which Gian-Luca moved and had his being. Every detail of that afternoon spent with the Padrona, lived vital and clear in his mind.

He remembered that her hand had lain passively in his, when he had bent and kissed the scar; that her smile had been gentle, her voice reassuring, her words full of kindness for him.

'Is it possible,' he thought, 'that she loves me—Gian-Luca?' And he all but decided that it was. So great was his joy that one day he said to Mario: 'Let me help you a bit more. I have plenty of time, I can quite well take on part service at your tables, and that way perhaps you can rest your poor foot.' For joy in the heart makes it kind.

Meanwhile the Padrone, observing his growth, ordered him to get a dress-suit. 'That short jacket is foolish now,' he told Gian-Luca; 'you look like a telegraph pole. How tall are you anyhow?' he inquired.

'I am nearly six foot,' said Gian-Luca.

'Dio mio, what a giant, and not quite seventeen—but when you are older you may then look less gawky.' And the Padrone laughed.

Fabio was told about the dress-suit, and he promptly consulted Mario. 'Where can one find it second-hand?' asked Fabio; 'he will only grow out of a new one.'

'And in any case,' said Mario, 'it is always the custom that a waiter's first dress-suit should be bought second-hand.'

'For what is the use of needlessly spending?' added Fabio.

'But a waste of good money,' agreed Mario.

It was not very easy to fit Gian-Luca, his arms and his legs were so long. In the end he looked like an elegant scarecrow, and he frowned at his own reflection in the glass, but Mario declared that he would do. His duties as piccolo now fell to the share of a new boy recently imported, and Gian-Luca became a fully-fledged waiter, sanctioned to open wine. The Capo was certainly rising in the world, the fame of its cooking was spreading. Moscatone had had his wages augmented.

'You see,' said the Padrone, in the privacy of bed; 'there

is no other chef in all England, Gemma, who could do what he does in such premises as these; the kitchen is unfit for a pig.'

'Will you be raising Gian-Luca as well?' his wife inquired.

'Gia, I think I will raise him, if I do not he may go, and I want him to stay on—I may shortly put him over Mario.'

The Padrona was silent; she was not quite certain that she wished Gian-Luca to stay on. It was not always easy to remember, these days, that the thin young giant was a child. Moreover, she had recently witnessed his temper; it had only been over the cat—Schmidt had hurled the cat through the pantry window because he had caught it lapping his tea. Everyone knew, except Gian-Luca, that a cat was possessed of nine lives—the Padrona herself did not care much for animals, she kept the cat to catch mice. But Gian-Luca had seized the Swiss by the collar and had shaken him until he yelled. The Padrona had had to go into the pantry and protest before he would let go; and even then he had looked reluctant, so much was he enjoying himself. The cat had survived—cats always survived; it was only a little bit lame —but the incident had thrown a new light on Gian-Luca, who could be very violent, it seemed. Yet whenever she thought of Gian-Luca leaving, she felt dull and a little depressed. After all, her existence was not a bed of roses—no bed could be that, that was shared with the Padrone.

These thoughts, however, remained hidden from Gian-Luca, who continued to see only kindness in her smile. And yet—with the infallible instinct of the lover, he began to feel strangely uneasy. For one thing, he had not been invited again to have tea in that room upstairs; for another, she seldom spoke to him now, unless it were to give orders. It was all very subtle, very hard to define, as elusive as a will-o'-the-wisp; but somehow the Padrona was withdrawing herself, was gradually slipping far away. He would look at her now with appeal in his eyes, standing tall and abashed in his ill-fitting clothes; waiting while she groped for a bottle of wine, or drew off the beer into glasses. Once she had noticed that look in his eyes and had frowned:

'Make haste!' she had said irrelevantly.

He had flushed and had stretched out a trembling hand for the glasses that were not ready.

The cloud of glory was certainly changing, becoming a damp, cold mist, through which Gian-Luca groped helplessly, unable to find his way. At times he would be stupid from sheer eagerness to please, bringing the Padrona the wrong thing; or he might grin at her familiarly, while his only desire was to be deferential. There were moments when his voice sounded sulky and gruff when he wished to be polite—and always his eyes held that dumb appeal, the appeal of a creature in a trap.

Schmidt, intensely attracted by the lure of emotion, felt obliged to forgive Gian-Luca. He could never resist discussing such matters, and so began sympathizing.

'You think she not like you so much as before? Never mind, Gian-Luca, it all come right. You bring her a small bunch of flowers one day——Ach! but she is wunderschön!' He oozed sentiment now from every pore, he was like a ridiculous maiden. 'I vill tell you about *my* girl,' he said sighing; 'she is all pink and white like raspberries and cream —she have lovely brown eyes and the big, round hips, what move all the time ven she walks——'

'Go to hell!' growled Gian-Luca, who could not endure this coupling of his love with Schmidt's.

'Very well then,' said Schmidt, as he turned away; 'you think yourself vunderful, very high up! But one efning you come and you say to me: "Schmidt, you show me some jolly, nice girls!"'

'Dio!' groaned Gian-Luca; 'will you leave me alone? I do not want any of your girls!'

3

The Padrone it was, and not the Padrona, who suddenly invited Gian-Luca to take part in a day's excursion on the river. This was in September when business was still slack, they would all lunch at Maidenhead. The Padrone was anxious to appear polite to Fabio, in order that he might drive harder bargains, so his ever fertile mind hit upon the idea of doing a small kindness to the grandson.

'Guarda,' Mario shrugged, 'you are getting very grand, you will soon not wish to come with me and Rosa.'

'Foolish words!' Gian-Luca told him. 'Do I not love you

and Rosa?' He was feeling far too happy to be cross.

The train was very crowded but this did not incommode them; the Padrone travelled grandly, first class. This had always been his way when things were going well; he drove hard and squeezed in business, but when on pleasure bent he spent his money freely, like a duke. The Padrona was most richly dressed in cherry-coloured foulard; her shady hat had three white ostrich feathers. Round her neck she wore a large, expensive, puffy feather boa, and her little hands were squeezed into new gloves. She was feeling tired, how-ever, and her face looked pale and fretful—she leant back and closed her eyes during the journey. From time to time Gian-Luca stole a surreptitious glance; her long lashes lay so softly—they were golden like her hair, but they darkened very slightly at their tips.

Arrived at Maidenhead, the Padrone hired a steam launch; they were very rich in everything to-day. They steamed up and down the river, the Padrone sprawling out with his greasy head supported by red cushions. He was smoking a cigar which he chewed from time to time, and then spat across his wife into the water. They went to lunch at Skindles' to amuse the tired Padrona, who liked gaiety, or so her husband said. Skindles' was very crowded and the service very slow; the Padrone made several little scenes.

'These English people!' he jeered to Gian-Luca: 'they eat roast beef and cabbage and pickled onions. Their waiters are vile and their cooks are still viler; and when they come out to enjoy themselves, one would think they were attending a funeral.'

The Padrone himself was growing rather noisy, he was drinking a good deal of wine. His morning had begun with several gins and bitters, and just before luncheon he had swallowed another in order to keep up his spirits. The Padrona was very quiet and aloof, she scarcely glanced at Gian-Luca; in his desperation he began making jokes at which the Padrone laughed boisterously—the Padrona did not laugh at all. Gian-Luca was filled with the bitter knowledge of doing and saying the wrong thing; he was thankful when at last the meal came to an end and his host was disputing the bill. The Padrona left them to go to the cloak-room and Gian-Luca strolled into the garden, but after him hurried the red-faced Padrone and seized the lapel of his coat. The Padrone was now feeling melodramatic, his brown eyes were swimming, his lips sagged a little.

'If you knew how that woman torments me!' he began; 'if you knew how she makes me suffer. I say: "Cesare, be careful, be very, very careful, she is young, any moment she may leave you!"'

'Ma no,' said Gian-Luca.

'Ma sí,' babbled the Padrone; 'I say; "She is young, she may leave you."'

Gian-Luca had perforce to stand there and listen, the Padrone was really very drunk.

'If you knew—if you knew——' he kept on repeating, and his eyes filled with idiotic tears.

'I do not wish to know,' Gian-Luca told him, hot with embarrassment and shame.

'You are so discreet——' gulped the tearful Padrone. 'I would not tell anyone but you——'

The Padrona came back, having powdered her nose, and they went for a walk by the river. She was still very silent, still very aloof; she walked primly between Gian-Luca and her husband, taking the latter's arm. On the feeble pretext of showing her a boat, Gian-Luca got her away. The Padrone, scarcely seeming to notice, strolled on down the tow-path alone.

'Signora, are you angry with me?' whispered Gian-Luca.

'Of course not,' she answered, smiling; but she looked straight passed him along the river, as one will look who is bored.

Words failed him. He suddenly seized her hand which he pressed and tried to retain; he felt that he must die of loving at that moment unless she would let him express it. He glanced at the unconscious back of the Padrone—the Padrone did not turn his head.

'I love you so terribly!' gasped Gian-Luca; 'I love you so terribly, signora!'

'Be quiet!' she said, wrenching her hand away; 'I will not tolerate this folly.' And turning, she hurried after her husband, leaving Gian-Luca to follow.

For the rest of the day they were all very silent, the

Padrone was growing sleepy. In the train going home he did fall asleep, and proceeded to snore quite loudly. Gian-Luca sat looking out of the window, not daring to look at the Padrona. His heart ached with a pain so intolerable and new that he wanted to protest, to cry out; but arrived at the station he helped them to alight—the Padrone as well as the Padrona.

'So,' thought Gian-Luca; 'so this is love!' And because of his heartache he felt a little frightened.

4

By the time that his seventeenth birthday arrived, Gian-Luca had decided that no one in the world was so utterly unhappy as he was. If all had not been well with the Padrona before, it was certainly less well now; if he had felt that she was slipping away, she was now so far off as to be quite inaccessible, for now she no longer singled him out to attend to her needs at the bar. She selected Schmidt—the plump Schmidt of all people—to polish and tidy and fetch and carry; Schmidt who would have a sly look in his eye whenever he passed Gian-Luca.

'Nun was!' grinned Schmidt; 'I do not wish it, you know —I have my own girl I like much better, and this gives me nur more work.'

Gian-Luca eyed him with open contempt; did he think, the fool, that the Padrona admired him? 'No, no, it cannot be that——' thought Gian-Luca; 'it is only that she now hates me.'

Yet why did she hate him? He had told her of his love, but surely she had known it long before he had spoken that day at Maidenhead? Then what was his transgression? A transgression of words? Yes, that must be it, he might love her it seemed, and she on her part might know that he loved her—only, he must not say so. This made him laugh a little it seemed so very foolish; then it made him frown a little, it seemed so very mean.

'While I spoke as a child, she could smile,' thought Gian-Luca; 'that day in her sitting-room I spoke as a child, I amused her perhaps; now I do not amuse her because she knows I am a man.'

For the quality of his love was gradually changing, the dew was no longer on the meadow. The knight-errant of youth was still in the saddle, but his armour was already slightly tarnished. Something deep down in Gian-Luca was conscious of this change and began to grow infinitely sad. It cried out because of the splendour that was passing— that particular splendour that could never come again, for no two dawns are alike in this world. Gian-Luca began to feel very angry because of the sadness that was in him; he would glare at the Padrona from the end of the room, and all that she did would seem mean and unlovely, yet this in itself would fill him with loving, and then he would almost hate her.

The poor Padrona would have many little tasks to perform in connexion with the bar. She might be mopping up the counter, for instance, removing the stale-smelling, beery foam, or rubbing the blurs left by whisky and brandy; or perhaps she might be wiping the sides of a bottle that had grown sticky sweet with liqueur. Her face would almost certainly be flushed by the exertion of providing other people with drinks; from time to time she would pause to draw a cork, bending ungracefully to the bottle which she held between her round feminine knees. 'Two mixed grill and mashed!' she might shout down the lift shaft, electing to speak in English; and when she did this her voice sounded Cockney, not soft and pleasing as when she spoke Italian.

The restaurant would smell stuffy, Schmidt's forehead would be beaded, and Mario's collar damp and creased; while downstairs in the kitchen, the sweating Moscatone might pause from time to time to pick his front teeth with a fork. And the beautiful Padrona with her fine Venetian hair, and her eyes the colour of gentians, would seem strangely out of place amid her surroundings, yet very much a part of them too.

5

'You grow sulky,' said Mario to his foster-son; 'what is the matter? You no longer work gladly.'

'I am tired of the Capo,' Gian-Luca told him; 'I think I must find a better job.'

'You are young and a fool,' snapped Mario crossly. 'I too have been foolish enough in my day, but never, no, never such a big fool as you are.'

'I am tired of the Capo,' Gian-Luca repeated, pretending not to understand.

It was all very lonely, more lonely by far than anything he had yet known. In the past he had been lonely but without the Padrona, whereas now he was utterly lonely with her; and to find oneself lonely with the creature one loves is to plumb the full depths of desolation. There was no one he could talk to, Mario did not sympathize and Schmidt was a low-minded fellow; as for Fabio and Teresa—at the mere thought of them Gian-Luca could not help laughing.

He still had his books, and long into the night he would read the 'Gioia della Luce.' All poetry hurt him a little it was true, but that poem could comfort while it hurt. There were many other poems which he re-read in that book, some of them spiritual and placid—they might have been written by a saint or a seer; but then would come others, crude out-pourings of passion that he had not understood as a child. Like the 'Gioia della Luce,' they partook of the greatness that, carnal or spiritual, belonged to the genius of their writer, Ugo Doria.

'A very curious book,' thought Gian-Luca; 'I must read some more of this poet's work.' So one day he made his way to Hatchard's, where he heard that they sold foreign books.

'Ugo Doria?' said the salesman, smiling at Gian-Luca. 'Oh, yes, he is getting quite famous. Will you have him in English or in Italian? We have all the translations of his earlier works, but his new book of essays has not been translated yet.'

' I can only afford one book,' said Gian-Luca; 'I will take the essays in Italian.' And he went to the Capo with the book in his pocket, in case he could read it between luncheon and dinnner.

Gian-Luca could not know that the technique was flawless, that each word had been tried and weighed and considered, that side by side with his vast inspiration the writer possessed the mind of an explorer—an explorer in the country of language. He could not know that all Italy was saying that Doria wrote with his pen dipped in gold dust, that never since Dante had there lived such a poet, and moreover, that his prose was even finer than his verse. But he did know that he, the sorrowful waiter, who could not write poems though his heart felt full to breaking, found solace and comparative comfort while he read, because of the beautiful lilt of the words. While he read he could almost forget the Padrona——

'And so,' thought Gian-Luca, 'he must be very great. I would like to see him, I would like to serve him, I myself would like to pour out his wine—I wish that he would come to the Capo.'

But Doria never came to the Capo—he happened to be living in Rome at that moment; and then, after all, he could only write—he might make one forget the Padrona for a while, but he could not soften her heart.

CHAPTER THIRTEEN

I

I<small>T WAS</small> just after Christmas when Signor Millo marched into Fabio's shop one day and handed his card across the counter.

'This way, signore, this way!' exclaimed Fabio, pink to the brow with pleasure and excitement. And he took him into Teresa's back parlour and pushed up the most propitious chair.

Signor Millo was a man of forty-five, of medium height and broad-shouldered. His brown hair curled close to his round, shapely head; there was something about him that suggested the antique—perhaps the Roman arena. But his brow was intellectual, and his mouth rather grave. His eyes, dark and set very wide apart, had a wonderfully wise and benign expression as though they neither questioned nor condemned. Seeing him thus, as he sat in the arm-chair with his hat held loosely between his knees, was to wonder what manner of man this was. An athlete? An author? A philosopher, perhaps? As a matter of fact he was none of these things; he was Francesco Millo, the director of the Doric, which, thanks to his skill, to his excellent judgment and elegant epicurean palate, had risen in the last few years to great fame among the restaurants of London.

That he should have come in person to the Casa Boselli was quite on a par with the rest of the man. He might have sent several intelligent people, all well up in their professional duties, but instead he had preferred to call on Fabio himself—such little excursions amused him. It is said that in each man there lurks the hunter; the hunter of money, the hunter of lions, the hunter of fame, the hunter of women; and Francesco Millo was also a hunter, as keen on the trail and as steadfast as any, indeed he was tireless, hence the fame of his restaurant, for Millo was a hunter of food.

He had said to himself at the beginning of his career; 'There are three very vital things; quality, variety and originality, and the last is perhaps the most vital of the three. A dinner should have, like a book or a picture, good workmanship, plenty of light and shade, and above all that individual touch, that original central idea.'

And so, whenever the spirit moved him—which was often, for he was a restless man—Millo went forth in search of strange viands. Just now he was after some special funghi that grew in the woods not far from Turin. As luck would have it he had heard from a confrère that the Casa Boselli had but lately imported a case of those special funghi.

'Ma sicuro,' said Fabio, 'we certainly keep them; they are fat, good funghi, you may see for yourself, you may smell them.' And he fetched a terrific looking toadstool for the great man's careful inspection.

Millo sniffed it. 'It is prime, as you say,' he remarked, and he promptly bought the whole case. 'And now I will look at your stock, if you please; I would also like to see your price-list.'

Fabio was trembling with excitement by now—the Casa Boselli and Millo. What a happening to make Nerone more jealous! What a snub for the Signora Rocca! He pottered about showing first this, then that, his paste, his hams, his tomatoes; then those elegant, more highly-specialized foods, caviare in jars, carciofini in oil, tunnyfish, fillets of anchovies with capers, and large, green, globular snails.

'All excellent, fresh, and quite inexpensive!' he kept chanting in a kind of litany. 'All excellent, fresh, and quite inexpensive—and we keep a great variety of foodstuffs.'

Signor Millo stood still, and surveyed him gravely. 'I would speak,' he said, holding up his hand.

'Prego!' bowed Fabio, trembling more than ever in case he had talked too much.

'I am rather disposed to give you some orders, your shop is so excellently kept; I think also that there must be some-one here who has an enterprising mind. If you get my custom, of course you are made, for I never stint recommendations; but, and this is important, so I beg that you listen, the first time you fail me I break you, signore. If ever you should send me a thing that is not fresh, a thing that could injure the stomach of a client, that day I write round to my con-frères and tell them—I cancel my recommendations, signore; and such is my system of management.'

Fabio bowed low; he was longing intensely for the reassuring presence of Teresa, but Teresa had unfortunately gone to the Capo to call on the Padrona that afternoon.

'It shall be as you say, I am honoured,' babbled Fabio. 'You shall have no cause for complaint.'

At that moment, Gian-Luca strolled in at the door, and seeing the stranger, paused. He looked very tall in the little shop as he towered over Fabio and Millo. His neat blue serge suit became him well—it had not been bought second-hand, for Gian-Luca was particular about his clothes, and when in mufti he dressed with great care, he was even a little foppish. Standing there young, fair-haired and alert, there was something incongruous about him, something that seemed to set him apart from the salumeria in Old Compton Street, from Fabio, from Millo even.

'This is my grandson,' Fabio explained; 'he is a waiter at the Capo di Monte.'

Millo bowed slightly. 'Piacere,' he murmured, as though he were thinking of something quite different; as a matter of fact he was all attention and his mind was working very quickly.

If Francesco Millo had a palate for good food, he had also an eye for a waiter; those who served were as carefully chosen by him as the dishes they were privileged to handle. Moreover, he prided himself on his flair. 'I know in a moment,' he was wont to say proudly; 'I know the moment my eye rests upon them. It amounts to a psychic faculty with me: I can pick the good waiter out of a thousand; the waiter is born and not made.' His eyes took in every line of Gian-Luca, without appearing to do so. 'He is mine!' he was thinking, with that thrill of satisfaction that belongs to the ardent collector. 'As it happens,' he said casually, turning to Fabio, 'I am wanting a waiter next month; now if your grandson is free I might try him—I suppose he has had some experience?'

'He has had three years at the Capo,' Fabio told him.

'That says nothing to me,' smiled Millo.

'The Capo di Monte in Dean Street, signore.'

'I have never heard of the place.' Then after a minute: 'But that need not matter, no doubt it serves some sort of meals. Perhaps you will give me the name of the Padrone so that I may take up your grandson's reference; he will get a good reference, I think.'

All this time Gian-Luca had not opened his mouth, nor had he once been consulted; now, however, Millo turned and addressed him directly.

'If your reference is good, as I think it will be, you may come on the morning of the twentieth, side-door, 9-30. I will let you know when I hear from your Padrone, so that you may order yourself a dress-suit.' He scribbled an address on a leaf from his notebook: 'This is the tailor who makes for the Doric, he will know how I wish your dress-suit to be made, he will also tell you what else is required. As for terms—they depend entirely on yourself; I pay high, but only for good service. You will not be dependent upon your tips, everyone at the Doric receives a salary—— I cannot stop to go into that now, I will speak to you when you come on the twentieth. If you prove satisfactory you will not complain of my terms; if you prove unsatisfactory there will not be any terms, for you go—we will try you and see. I think that is all—oh, do you speak English?'

'I do, Signore,' said Gian-Luca promptly, but before he could get in another word, the great one was leaving the shop.

'Dio mio!' breathed Fabio. 'Our Lady is good; she is patient in spite of Teresa.'

But Gian-Luca said nothing, he was thinking deeply— he was thinking about the Padrona.

2

A new idea came to Gian-Luca that night, and he sat up suddenly in bed. 'When I go she will miss me,' he thought triumphantly. 'She shall find out for herself what it means to be without me, how lonely it will feel not to have the Gian-Luca who was always so ready to serve her.'

He pictured the Padrona sitting behind the bar, with her face in her hands—weeping. 'Gian-Luca, Gian-Luca, I want you!' she wailed. 'I cannot get on without you!'

He would go there and see her, in a suit of fine clothes, they paid high for good service at the Doric. He would say: 'I have come!' And she would reply: 'Oh, but I am glad, Gian-Luca! I will meet you to-morrow between luncheon and dinner. Where can we go to be alone?'

'Gia,' thought Gian-Luca, nodding very wisely, 'that is the way with women; when they have you they despise you, but when they have you not, then it is they find out that they want you.' He was very near tears in this moment of triumph, but his fighting instinct held. 'I will go to the Doric,' he told himself bravely. 'I am glad that I have come to a decision.'

This of course was the purest make-believe, for he knew that he had no choice in the matter; Fabio might be weak, but he would not consent to the loss of a fine job like this. Moreover, there was Millo's custom to consider—that might mean fame for the Casa Boselli. And then there was Teresa, the ambitious, the strong-minded, the dominating woman of affairs.

Nevertheless, he went on repeating: 'I will certainly go to the Doric.' And he added: 'To-morrow I tell the Padrone, then we shall see what we shall see.'

3

The next morning he arrived at the Capo very early in order to tell the Padrone. By the greatest good fortune the Padrona was present, which was what Gian-Luca had hoped for. He did not look at the Padrone when he spoke, his eyes were on the Padrona.

The Padrone said wrathfully: 'So this is gratitude!' and his facial expression was appalling. Then he went out, banging the door behind him, and his voice could be heard coming up from the kitchen with a dash of Moscatone thrown in.

The Padrona said: 'This is very fine, Gian-Luca, I congratulate you, my child.' She was checking the accounts of the bar at the moment, and she went on checking her accounts.

Gian-Luca said uncertainly: 'I am going in four weeks—this means that I am going away——'

'It does,' said the Padrona; 'we must find another waiter, and that is always a bother. I shall not take a Swiss, I dislike them on the whole, though Schmidt is a very good fellow. By the way, we can give you an excellent reference, you have always been capable and quick.'

Gian-Luca left her without another word. His lip shot out, his eyes were very bright. He said to Mario later:

'I am lucky, my good Mario, I shall make my fortune now, you will see!'

4

The last four weeks at the Capo di Monte passed like an evil dream. For one thing there was Mario, very sorrowful and servile; he was going to miss Gian-Luca, and he said so. His manner to the boy had now completely changed, it was that of failure towards success. He bragged less about the Capo and not at all about himself.

'I am just an old lame mule,' he would say humbly, remembering that taunt of the Padrone's.

'He is not so lame as all that!' Gian-Luca would try to think; 'he puts it on in order to get pitied.' But he knew that this was not so; Mario's lameness was quite real, and moreover, it was often very painful.

Mario said: 'Since you were little and Rosa gave you milk, I have always been so fond of you, Gian-Luca—now you go out into the world with no old Mario near. You be careful; do not listen to people like this Schmidt, who are always thinking about women.'

'Women!' frowned Gian-Luca, 'I want no more of women!'

And at that Mario's mouth twitched a little; but he went on very gravely: 'You are angry with our Padrona, you have great unkindness in your heart towards her. Now that is what I fear, piccino, anger in the heart—I know, for I too have felt such anger. It is dangerous, it is stupid, it makes a man a beast; it makes him forget how strong he is. The Padrona is a woman and therefore you should pity, and moreover she is really very right. For one thing she is nearly old enough to be your mother, for another she considers her business, for another she remembers the Padrone no doubt

145

—a terrible man when in anger.' He paused, for Gian-Luca had turned his back, but presently he went on still more gravely: 'Forget her when you leave here, it would be better so—but if you must remember, do so kindly.'

'Is it I, then, who must show all the kindness?' exclaimed Gian-Luca.

'Precisely—that is so,' Mario told him. 'You have nothing to forgive, and if you had, remember the Padrona is only a woman.'

They were standing in the pantry. Gian-Luca glared at Mario; then he noticed that his hair had greyed a little. He looked old and sad and tired; the coarse texture of his sock was showing through the slits across his shoe. Nor was he very clean; his white shirt-front was spotted and the buttons of his coat were stained and frayed. He fidgeted self-consciously under Gian-Luca's eyes, and his hand went up to straighten his white necktie. They began collecting things; Mario could not find the napkins, he swore because the table-drawer had stuck; and presently he grumbled:

'It is hard, this life of ours, always standing, always running, always serving someone else. I feel at times as though I must go out and climb a mountain so as to look over something wide.'

Gian-Luca only grunted, and picking up a tray, he hurried off to set his luncheon tables.

Mario watched his youthful back disappearing through the door. 'He is very young,' thought Mario, 'he is very innocent—yet I think he grows a little proud.'

But Gian-Luca at that moment felt anything but proud; all he wanted was to get away from Mario. He did not want to pity, to see any cause for pity—and Mario was very pitiful.

5

Gian-Luca's worst times were in the afternoons, for he never quite knew whether to go home. If he sat beside the bar the Padrona did not come, but if he left the Capo he always thought that she might have come if he had remained. At home would be Teresa who detested the Padrona and said so between her rows of knitting. She would say it from the cash-desk, from the shop or from the parlour, whenever she could do so with discretion. In the shop there would be Fabio very jubilant and proud, relating for the hundredth time his interview with Millo. Rocca might look in a moment, slap Gian-Luca on the back and say; 'Ecco, you are grand now, Generale!' Then Nerone, who was genuinely pleased about Gian-Luca, was for ever stumping round to see his favourite. He loved the boy, and consequently only saw his virtues—by contrast he detested Rosa's children.

'You are lucky, you old brigand!' he said one day to Fabio. 'Now my Rosa's children are disgusting. That Geppe will not work and he steals my cigarettes, and when I leave he does not guard the shop. As for Berta, she is awful, she speaks only Cockney English and what she would have us think is French; our language is no longer good enough for her, it seems, and also she is very vain and ugly.'

He would ramble on and on, always cross, always complaining, and finally would try to pick a quarrel with his friend. 'Your prices are too high—you no longer sell good food—that is why you grow so proud and rich, no doubt.'

Sometimes Rosa appeared too, just to pass the time of day, and if it were a week-end she brought her Berta with her. Berta worked for Madame Germaine—née Smith and wedded Bulgin—who sold exclusive models in her shop near Wardour Street. Berta ran all the errands and took models home to clients—one in every dozen costumes might, with any luck, be French. Berta was temperamental and thought she loved Gian-Luca; she was always making eyes—enormous eyes. Her hair had grown more frizzy and, if possible, more black, and she wore it in a heavy pompadour. She refused to speak Italian, but had learnt a little French from the sisters at her convent school; this she tried hard to remember so that she could plague Nerone who loathed the French because about a hundred years before they had stolen those bronze stallions from St. Mark's. For the rest she spoke in English; not the rather stilted English of Gian-Luca who had never really learnt to clip his words, but in the English of the workrooms; and she spoke it without accent, that is, of course without a foreign accent.

Gian-Luca loathed and feared her; she was always edging close, and he lived in mortal terror that one day she would

kiss him. Her hand was always waiting to be squeezed or
stroked or cuddled; he felt sure of this whenever he observed it. And so, when Berta came, which was as often as
she could, Gian-Luca would rush back to the Capo. The bar
would be deserted until the dinner-hour, still, it was at least
a sanctuary from Berta.

6

Gian-Luca dressed one morning with almost painful care;
he was going to say good-bye to the Padrona. In two days'
time he would take up his new work, but this morning he
was going to say good-bye. It had all seemed so queer and
unreal the night before—the pantry, the kitchen with its
giant Moscatone, the long low restaurant, the chattering
diners, the clanking of the glasses and bottles in the bar;
and above all, he himself, in his shabby old dress-suit,
writing orders, serving dishes, fetching drinks, striking
matches. It had seemed as though his body did these duties
out of habit, while he stood aside and thought of the
Padrona.

The suit he wore this morning had been a present
from Fabio, and very smart it was, an immaculate grey
tweed.

Fabio had said: 'I would not have you shabby before
Millo. We wish him to observe that our little business
prospers. Is that not so, Teresa?'

And she had nodded: 'That is so.'

Gian-Luca stared at his reflection in the glass, and in
spite of his heartache he approved of what he saw. He gave
a final touch to his neck-tie and his hair, then, picking up
his hat, he went downstairs.

'Do not be long,' called Fabio from the shop. 'I must
consult you—I have certain business matters to discuss
regarding Millo.'

Old Compton Street was foggy, there was mud on the
pavement: Gian-Luca stooped and turned up his new
trousers, for one part of him remembered that he wore expensive clothes. At Nerone's door stood Rosa with her hair
still done in curlers; she was shaking out a very dusty mat.
She smiled broadly at Gian-Luca:

'How smart you look, piccino! What would Berta say, I wonder!' And she laughed.

Geppe peered across her shoulder, he looked spotty and unwashen. 'He is lucky, not like me who have to stop at home,' he grumbled.

'Continue with your sweeping!' said Rosa, turning quickly. 'You cannot have swept out half the shop.'

There were lights in Rocca's window because it was so foggy. Rocca himself was moving in and out among his corpses. As Gian-Luca passed he saw him neatly slicing off a shoulder with a quick, experienced sweep of his knife. The whole street was very busy preparing for its business, which consisted of supplying other people's daily needs.

'They need so much, so very much—how funny!' thought Gian-Luca, who himself was only conscious of needing the Padrona.

The Padrone was waiting for him when he reached the Capo; he was in a great hurry to go out.

'Here you are!' he said impatiently, glancing at his watch. 'Be good enough to sign the wages book.' Then he held out his hand, turning affable, it seemed: 'Well, I wish you good fortune. I am sorry to lose you, but when one is young one must think of oneself.' The Padrone did not wish to quarrel with Fabio, it was much too convenient to deal at his shop.

'May I see the Padrona?' faltered Gian-Luca.

'Sicuro, she will want to wish you luck. Gemma!' he called. 'Gian-Luca is here.'

'Let him come up,' came a voice.

'Go up,' said the Padrone, 'you know the way. I have to go to the City.' He shook hands once again and turned to the door. Gian-Luca went slowly up the stairs.

The Padrona was sitting on a low settee. The firelight fell on her thick coils of hair and slanted across her averted face, which was partially shielded by her hand. She did not look round, and Gian-Luca in the doorway stood watching her in silence for a moment, then he closed the door quietly and stepped into the room.

'It is I,' he said softly. 'Gian-Luca.'

She nodded; and now she was looking at him, smiling very kindly, he thought. 'I hope you will be happy, Gian-Luca,' she said, and then fell silent again.

A coal crashed into the grate and lay there smoking; the Padrona pushed it with her foot. Outside in the passage a cuckoo clock struck nine; the small, childish sound of it seemed to fill the room. Gian-Luca's strange eyes were very wide open, his breath came a little fast. As he stood there he could hear the beating of his heart, he could hear the Padrona's breathing. Then he drew himself up, he felt suddenly strong, he was filled with a knowledge of his manhood. He called her—standing there motionless, he called her. 'Gemma!' And then again, 'Gemma!'

She got up and stared blankly at him for a moment as though bewildered—uncertain. There was something very like appeal in her face—he saw it and his heart thumped with triumph.

'Gemma!' His voice was loud and compelling, and after he had called her he smiled. Then all of a sudden she was lying in his arms, giving him back his kisses.

As they stood there the years came down on the boy and dropped away from the woman; they were just two creatures welded into one by an impulse of mutual passion.

He began to speak hotly: 'My beautiful! My joy! I will never let you go any more. All my life I have waited, and now I have got you—I am all burning up with this loving.' Then his mood changed, his eyes filled with sudden tears. 'You are holy,' he whispered softly. 'I must treat you very gently—you are little and weak, and you need Gian-Luca because you are so little.'

But something, perhaps it was the sound of his whispering, made her stiffen as she lay in his arms. With a cry of anger she pushed him away.

'Stop!' she said shrilly. 'Stop!'

And then the Padrona sinned in her fear as she had not sinned in her passion. In her fear she struck out wildly like an animal at bay; she accused, she insulted, she degraded. She might have made an appeal to his goodness, to the chivalry that was in him, to that great, shy, virginal spirit of youth that was wrestling with him even now. But instead she confronted him, flushed and dishevelled, with the crude, ugly words on her lips.

'Go!' she said finally, pointing to the door. 'Go—or I tell my husband!'

And he went, without one more look at the Padrona. He was utterly bewildered, incredulous and outraged. Alone in her room the Padrona wept bitterly, but Gian-Luca's eyes were quite dry.

<h2 style="text-align:center">7</h2>

That night Gian-Luca returned to the Capo, but this time he did not go in. He hid like a thief in the opposite doorway, watching for the waiters to leave. Mario came first; that was good. He was glad. He shrank farther into the shadow, but Mario passed him with never a glance and went limping away down the street. Then came the new waiter accompanied by the boy; they said good-night and the waiter caught a bus. The boy looked round him then lit a cigarette —obviously one that he had stolen—after which he too walked away down the street, whistling softly between puffs.

In an upper window of the Capo a light showed—that was the Padrona's sitting-room. Gian-Luca watched it, and as he did so he was filled with a queer, ugly sense of pleasure. He was glad that the light should stream out between the curtains; it meant that the Padrona was near; and he thought of what he was about to do and felt glad that she should be near him. A door opened and shut, Schmidt came across the road—he was now all but touching Gian-Luca.

'Schmidt!'

'Nun was!' Schmidt jumped as though frightened. 'Oh, hallo! Is that you, Gian-Luca?'

Gian-Luca jingled the money in his pockets, then he slipped his arm into Schmidt's. 'Will you take me to see those girls?' said Gian-Luca, and he turned his face up to the lighted window.

'Ach so!' murmured Schmidt. 'You make up your mind —come along then, I understand.'

BOOK TWO

CHAPTER ONE

I

GREAT CHANGES had come to the Casa Boselli. It was now six years since that eventful day when Millo had ordered his first case of funghi. For six years now Gian-Luca had served him and meanwhile the Casa Boselli had prospered. A large plate-glass window had been recently added, and the lease of the next-door shop had been purchased. A green motor-van with the name in gold letters —'Casa Boselli'—painted large on its sides, might be seen any morning unloading its wares at the back doors of fashionable restaurants. Fabio was no longer permitted to serve; there were three young assistants for that. Obedient in all things to the wishes of Teresa, Fabio dressed himself neatly and wandered about in and out of the shop, empty-handed and foolish; sad too, missing his salami and cheeses, while Teresa sat in a business-like office in the basement of the new shop next door.

The years were dealing lightly with Teresa; she had scarcely changed at all in appearance, nor had she softened towards life in general; one thing only could bring a smile now to her lips, and that was the success of some new business venture, and of such a venture she was thinking one morning as she sat at her crowded desk. The May sunshine filtered down through the thick, greenish skylight and partially illumined the room, but Teresa switched on her reading-lamp and pulled a sheaf of papers towards her.

'Duecento cinquanta sterline,' she murmured, 'two hundred and fifty pounds——' then she stretched out a hand and groped for her pass-book, 'and five hundred pounds we have borrowed from the bank—that makes seven hundred and fifty.' She began making long calculations on the blotter. 'And we save on the freight?' She considered a moment, then she opened a drawer and looked over some bills. 'Ah,' she said smiling, 'it is just as I thought, I am scarcely a centesimo out.'

Teresa, who had saved money all her life, had begun to spend recklessly of late. Thrifty to a fault, there yet lurked within her the gambler's instinct—she was gambling in business, emboldened by recent successes. And now she was launching the greatest venture of her whole long business career, a venture hidden away out of sight in a room behind the new shop. It was nothing less than the making of pasta; the mixing and rolling and cutting and drying and tinting of excellent, freshly-made pasta, a thing that had never been attempted before in London, or indeed in England. On her latest price-list there appeared these words: 'The Casa Boselli will make your macaroni; no need to eat it many months old, we make it fresh every day!' And Teresa smiled gently whenever she read them; her smile was possessive, maternal even, for her heart that had gone so long empty and childless had taken to itself the Casa Boselli. The machinery required for the making of pasta had had to be imported from Milan; that was what had taken the extra money, so much money indeed that Fabio trembled whenever he thought about it.

'We spend!' he said faintly from time to time.

'And we earn,' his wife replied firmly. 'One must always strike while the iron is hot; our iron is hot so I strike.'

There were nights, however, when Fabio could not sleep for thinking of that debt to the bank.

'Are we not going to pay it off?' smiled Teresa. 'You grow old, my Fabio, you grow old and afraid. Now I am not young, yet I am not afraid; I drink little, I work hard, I am always on the watch, and above all my ears are open. Millo says: "The pasta is such a trouble, I would like them to eat it fresh; I am more than a little ashamed of my pasta. If only the English could make macaroni! But no doubt they would make it very badly." Then I say to Millo: "You shall have your fresh pasta; the Casa Boselli will make it." And that,' she would conclude, 'is the genius for business; that is why we now deliver our goods in a motor instead of with a horse and cart.'

And truly she possessed a great genius for business, as

her friends were all bound to admit. Nerone, Rocca, the Padrone of the Capo, Mario and Rosa were all lost in admiration; even Francesco Millo would smile and call her the Napoleon of the Salumeria. Only poor Fabio, in his stuffy black coat, would sigh a little for the past, when he had handled his salami and cheeses, when the money had all lain snugly in the bank instead of uneasily in plate-glass windows, new leases, and machinery brought from Milan.

'Sí, sí,' he would think, 'it was more peaceful then, and Teresa and I grow old.'

But on this May morning Teresa felt young as she got up briskly from her desk. 'I will go and inspect my little factory,' she murmured, and, climbing the stairs, she passed through the shop and into a room beyond.

She stood quite still just inside the doorway to enjoy this, her latest acquisition. Near the ceiling were purposeful, whirring wheels, and the sound of their whirring was as music to her ears. At a table in the corner a youth in white drill was mixing a mountain of flour. Sixty pounds he would mix, with an egg to each pound, and from time to time he must pause to wash his hands, a rule imposed by Teresa. The great, generous mixture came up to his elbows as he kneaded and stirred and pressed.

'Va bene,' said Teresa, and she smiled with approval. 'Va bene, but be careful of the egg-shells.'

As soon as a portion of the pasta was mixed it was fed to a rotund machine, and there it was pummelled and kneaded afresh until it was ready for the large, wooden rollers. This process of rolling fascinated Teresa; she would gladly have watched it for hours. In went a shapeless lump of the pasta, and out came a species of rubber sheeting, cool to the touch and flawless in texture. Then back it would go to be rolled yet again, with each fresh rolling to grow finer and thinner, until in the end it was almost transparent, so elegant had it become.

Teresa would sometimes whisper about it. 'One hundred times it must pass,' she would whisper; 'one hundred times it must pass through my rollers?' And then she would laugh a little to herself, thinking of this great new adventure.

There were other contrivances in that room, among them an uncannily intelligent machine for the cutting and moulding of pasta. What was your pleasure? Bircorni, Conchiglie, Stelline? Just touch a particular gadget and presto!—your etherealized rubber sheeting assumed any one of the fifty odd shapes that your need or your fancy had dictated. Upstairs would be waiting those new electric fans that sent out a stream of cold air, whereby your Bicorni, Conchiglie or Stelline would be hardened and rendered almost immortal—that is until they were eaten . . . .

Teresa's defiant black eyes were glowing; they had no need of glasses to help their sight. 'You have dropped in a trifle of egg-shell, Francesco!' she said suddenly, pointing an accusing finger at the youth with the mountain of flour.

Those who worked for Teresa were always Italian. 'The English do not work, they spend,' she would say; and her work-people feared her intensely, but respected. She was everywhere at once with her terrible black eyes, yet although her tongue lashed them they gave of their best. They said behind her back: 'Che donna maravigliosa!' A grand old woman they thought Teresa, and one who knew well how to drive a hard bargain, as they would have done in her place.

2

Nerone was less fortunate in his affairs, a fact for which he blamed Geppe. Geppe was a lazy and insolent young man with a predilection for philandering. He hated the shop though he liked its contents, to which he helped himself freely. This so much enraged the miserly Nerone that he would actually threaten to send for the police; then Rosa would weep and implore forgiveness for her plump and unsatisfactory offspring.

'I spare him this time, but the next time I send,' Nerone would babble in a fury. 'This is all Mario's fault; he was always a fool; he has spoilt the young, idling ruffian!'

Grandsire and grandson hated each other, and their feuds robbed the house of all peace; for Geppe could bellow much louder than Nerone—youth gave him a laryngeal advantage.

Geppe, who was now nearly nineteen years old, wished to be a commercial traveller. This struck him as a pleasant, safe way to see life, and one that would release him from the shop. He had met a young commercial traveller one day through a friend of Berta's at Madame Germaine's; a very smart fellow with plenty of money and a staggering knowledge of the world. Geppe of course had little to spend—only what Mario could give him—and being the grandson of Nerone, it was natural that he thought a great deal about money. But unlike Nerone, and herein lay the trouble, he liked it for what it could buy; to keep it in a till or to send it to a bank seemed to Geppe the height of all foolishness, and he said so when Nerone was listening.

Nerone had refused point-blank to pay him wages, and this was a very sore point. Geppe would have liked to run away to sea—he had read of such things in his paper-backed 'shockers'—but whenever he thought of the sea for too long he invariably felt rather sick. He had many wonderful adventures in his mind, but his body shrank weakly from hardships. He was soft; his skin was now colourless and flabby, his hands would easily blister; woollen vests made him itch; and now, when he shaved, the razor brought up little pimples. He was lazy with youth and would lie long abed; when he did appear at last it would be yawning. In the evening, however, he was as wakeful as an owl. In the evening he would go to a cinematograph, a form of entertainment which he liked above all others. He would sit in the darkness and watch desperate deeds, with a pleasant conviction of safety. And sometimes, if he found the heroine attractive, he would conjure up all sorts of amorous scenes in which he himself was the hero. Geppe was greedy, he still loved jam tartlets, he also loved chocolate creams; he would stroll about eating the latter while smoking, a perversion of the palate that disgusted Nerone.

'Che bestia!' he would mutter, unable to resist a morbid desire to look. And if Geppe noticed his grandfather looking, he would open his mouth and show chocolate creams in the process of mastication.

Nerone said that his grandson's place was behind the counter of the shop; as for wages, what was the good of wages? The shop might be Geppe's one day. He also said that cinemas were evil and encouraged immoral behaviour. Now Geppe was longing to be immoral, his difficulty was to find a partner in sin. He would often try to borrow money from Gian-Luca, who must obviously be very rich; but Gian-Luca would find an excuse for not lending.

'He is mean,' thought Geppe in bitterness of spirit. 'He himself is always after women.'

Mario was anxious, inadequate and pious, for he felt that his sins might be finding him out; he remembered those bygone halcyon days, when Rosa had had cause to be jealous of the barmaid—and many other things did Mario remember that Rosa had never known.

'He is like me and yet he is not,' mourned Mario, 'for I at least never feared hard work—and yet it is natural for a boy to want money—I think it is time the Babbo paid him something.'

But neither he nor Rosa dared anger Nerone, who still had to contribute towards their support, for Mario's wages at the Capo had not risen, though the Capo was rising every day. All sorts of great people now dined at the Capo and got drunk on its excellent liquor. There was Munster the painter, and Jenkins the sculptor, and their wives and their women and their models and their offspring, to say nothing of a certain broad-minded countess who had re-incarnated from a Babylonian suburb—there was also the poet who had once admired Gian-Luca and who, having lately married, had become very rich. He no longer wrote poems, his wife fed him too well—in the winter he wore a magnificent coat with a collar of Russian sable. But of him be it said that he was faithful to the Capo—grateful, let us hope, for past favours—for he brought many friends to eat costly dinners, and his wife always seemed to have his purse in her bag.

Oh, but many grand people now rejoiced the Padrone, who was somewhat less fierce than he had been. The best cure for bad temper is prosperity, of course—what a pity that we cannot all be prosperous! And then there was now something living upstairs, a tiny, red, bawling Padroncino; a thing with eyes the colour of gentians, and lungs that left no manner of doubt regarding its paternity. Whenever its father could spare a minute he would rush upstairs and yell: 'Bimbo!' Or perhaps he would tickle, when the small Padroncino would respond with such vigour that Munster would look up from his tumbler of brandy and smile a large smile. For if Munster loved women he also loved babies—which in his case was fortunate, perhaps.

There were now red silk curtains at the windows of the Capo, and Mario began to think himself a prophet, as indeed he had been in all but one thing, and that was his own promotion. The Padrone had now four waiters in all, but as yet he had no head waiter, so that Mario continued to live in hopes. But his present circumstances did not warrant interference with Nerone on behalf of his son.

'After all,' he told Rosa, 'the time is approaching when Geppe will have to go to Italy to serve. His military service will make a man of him, and when he returns we will then talk to Babbo—at the moment I think it unwise.'

And Rosa would often say to her son: 'It is splendid to think of my Geppe as a soldier—how I envy you, caro, to see Italy again! But then, I was forgetting, you have never yet seen it.'

Geppe would look sulky and mutter something vague about wanting to see a bit of life, not service; for the last thing on earth that poor Geppe wanted was to become a soldier. Rocca, who knew that the hour was approaching, added greatly to Geppe's torment. He would come to Nerone's and buy cigarettes for the pleasure he took in talking at Geppe and making him feel afraid. Rocca would jab at the air with his stick:

'It is thus, and thus, with the bayonet,' he would say, 'and the little, sharp twist in the pit of the stomach; one should always aim low for their bellies.'

Geppe's pale face would turn even paler, and his hand would instinctively grip at his middle. Then Rocca would laugh:

'Avanti, capitano! I can see you leading your men into battle. "Italia! Italia! Italia!" you shout, and then you give the small twist with your sword, for surely they will make you a captain!'

3

It was all most distressing, especially for Mario, who was more over-worked than ever at the Capo; and then there was Berta, not much of a comfort either, although she was now twenty-two. Berta no longer carried boxes and ran errands; she was now very smart and served in the shop. Madame Germaine thought the world of Berta, who could always persuade a woman of fifty that she looked like nineteen in a model.

'Oh, modom, you look charming!' Berta would lie, skilfully patting and tweaking. 'Too stout? Oh, no, modom, I cannot agree—this model gives such long lines.'

That was the way Berta talked in the shop; with her own special cronies it was different. 'Damned old fools, if you saw them!' giggled Berta. 'Heaving their stomachs up to their chins till they look like a lot of pouter pigeons!'

Berta herself had become quite slim owing to rigorous fasting; her fasts had nothing to do with the Lord, they were purely an offering to Venus. Berta had now many young lady friends who, like her, used lip-stick and giggled. Their Sundays were spent on the river in summer; they were usually accompanied by one or two 'boys'. Berta was young, she loved a good time, and she worked very hard all the week, so it soon came about that she missed Mass on Sundays—a new outrage to rouse up Nerone.

'Why you not go very early?' inquired Rosa. 'The Mass he go on from six.'

'Good heavens!' laughed Berta. 'I can't get up at five— I'm dog-tired, anyhow, by Sunday.'

Rosa sighed; she was racking her brain for words which never came correctly in English. But Berta refused point-blank to speak Italian; she declared that she had almost forgotten it. This placed her mother at a great disadvantage, as Berta was very well aware; she was fond of her mother, but she loved her own way, and she found it much easier to get it in English.

'You who were teached by the sisters and all, and you who are a child of Mary,' wailed Rosa.

'Well, I can't help that, it wasn't my fault,' said Berta with disrespect.

Nerone had decided to be dumb with Berta; he ignored her existence, for which everyone was thankful. She was sharper than Geppe, and just once or twice she had got the better of her grandsire. He and Rosa and Mario would go off to Mass, dragging the discontented Geppe. Geppe was terribly bored with his Church, but was fettered by a firm belief in Hell.

Mario said to his wife in their bedroom one night: 'I am thinking about our children.'

Rosa sighed: 'There is much need for thought, my Mario: they are very different from us.'

Mario scratched his head, then he looked very wise, and when he spoke he did so slowly. 'I was born in Milan, my Rosa. As for you, it was lucky that you came too soon, and so you got born in Siena. The baby drinks in the air at its birth, and the air it drinks goes all over. It touches the heart, it touches the brain, I think it gets into the blood. English air may agree with English babies, but it has not agreed with ours; our babies were Italian, they needed the air and the sun of their patria. And so,' he concluded a little sadly, 'no child should be born on strange soil. We think only of money and we sacrifice our children—yet some of us still remain poor!'

'If we lose our children we are very poor indeed, even when we become rich,' said Rosa.

CHAPTER TWO

I

I F TERESA had changed but little in six years, this
was not the case with Gian-Luca, for to him had come
the fullness of manhood. The touching lankiness of
adolescence had given place to a well-knit figure, he was
thin in proportion to his height, but his shoulders were
wide above his narrow flanks. His face was less gentle,
and his eyes less mysterious; they no longer seemed to be
searching the beyond. Their expression was keener and
more concentrated, so that now, when they rested on a
client or a waiter or a table or the most minute appointments
of the table, they took in at a glance significant details from
which their owner would draw his conclusions, conclusions
that were usually right. Very observant and prompt was
Gian-Luca, and those who worked under him found him a
hard master, one to whom constant small misdemeanours
meant more than occasional flagrant transgressions. Gian-
Luca had been known to forgive a subordinate who had
come to his work very drunk one morning, having merely
warned him of what would happen were the offence repeated; but a youth who habitually forgot to examine the
mustard-spoons for signs of verdigris, and who, moreover,
was careless of his nails, had been promptly reported to
Millo and dismissed on Gian-Luca's representations. And
so, although he controlled his hot temper, scarcely ever
raising his voice these days; although he was admitted to be
a fine waiter and one under whom a lad got a first-class
training; although they admired his arresting appearance
and the ability that had put him in charge of a room when
not yet quite twenty-four; although they worked hard,
because to work for Gian-Luca was to fall beneath the spell
of his mighty will to work, not a waiter that he ruled had the
least affection for him—they found him a little inhuman.

'I care nothing for what they may think,' said Gian-Luca. 'So long as they do their work well, I care nothing.'

And yet he did care, for with one part of him he wished very much to stand well with his fellows. A childish longing to be loved and praised, to be popular with his subordinates even, to be thought a good comrade, a boon companion, would come over him strongly at times. He would think of his school-days, when, try as he might, he had always been left just outside. In those days he had been a stranger to his mates, an alien among the English children; but here at the Doric he was not quite an alien, for all the waiters were Italians. And yet here also there stretched that little gulf, that sense of being just outside—that queer, empty feeling of having no real country and hence no real ties with those who had.

He would lie in bed at nights thinking only of himself and of life in connexion with himself; his babyhood, his boyhood, his painful adolescence—and then he would remember the Padrona. Looking back on the Padrona after nearly seven years Gian-Luca would feel almost kind; and that, he remembered, was what Mario had hoped for. Mario had said that anger in the heart could make a beast of a man. Oh, well, it had made a beast of him, Gian-Luca, who had tried to revenge himself on the Padrona, who had tried to insult her by insulting his love, or so he had thought at the time. Now he knew that it had not been only the Padrona, but his love on which he had wished to be revenged—that great, soft, foolish and selfless thing that had upset all his resolutions. For that was precisely what had happened; it had made him forget Gian-Luca. It had changed his motto—'I have got Gemma.' it had made him write—that was what it had done. And of course he had never had Gemma for a moment, never for a single moment. Poor Gemma! How he must have worried her with loving, just as he had worried old Teresa long ago. He must always have suffered from a kind of craze for giving—and people had not wanted what he had to give.

'It is now my turn to receive,' he would think, smiling a little. 'There must surely be someone who is ready to love *me*?'

For in spite of his success he would feel so very lonely,

so very much in need of being loved; he did not want to love, he wanted to be loved.

'It is wiser, and it leaves a man more free for his business. When one loves one is all misery, all body and no brain— one becomes a fool, one does and says nothing but foolish things,' he told himself, remembering those days with the Padrona. No, assuredly he did not want to love.

'I will go and buy a dog,' he suddenly decided. 'A good dog will give me his affection.' But then he reflected that a good dog never spoke, that a good dog could not tell him of its love.

There were Mario and Rosa of whom he was quite fond, and who gave him much fondness in return. There was cross old Nerone, who perhaps gave more than fondness— but then he was just cross old Nerone. There was Rocca, who thought him a very fine young fellow, and who winked and made jokes about women; and of course there was Fabio—Fabio said that he loved him, but Fabio's love was old and devitalized and weak; oh, not nearly enough for Gian-Luca. And then there were women. He considered the women that men in his position got to know. There were all Schmidt's 'jolly girls' and others too, less jolly but possibly a little more attractive. Poor devils all; one did not go their way expecting love, they were far too much underpaid for that. They never went on strike, they belonged to no trade-union—like Gian-Luca they had to fend entirely for themselves; and like him some few among them had not even got a name. Such people could ill afford to love.

'Ma che!' he would mutter after these reflections. 'It always comes down to the same; a man should try to be sufficient unto himself, and if he is not, well, then he deserves to fail. As for me, I do not intend to fail.' And then he would start thinking about his plans, his future, and his thoughts would be very gratifying. 'Already I have charge of a small room,' he would think, 'but soon I shall have charge of much more than just a room. I have my own ideas, I shall stay on at the Doric for a time—but some day I will be a second Millo.'

Yet, somehow this prospect, delightful though it was, would suddenly grow clouded and defaced; for in the very middle of his great self-satisfaction he would feel a little restless thing that stirred uneasily, and back there would come running the childish, young Gian-Luca—the Gian-Luca who wanted to be loved.

2

There were three verdant pastures for browsing at the Doric; the grill room which did not concern Gian-Luca, the large restaurant with its excellent band, and an octagon room which led off the restaurant and which had recently become Gian-Luca's province. To this smaller room came those of Millo's clients who preferred to be far from the music, either because they wished to talk business, or because they were lovers and therefore spoke softly, or because —and this was the most frequent reason—they were people who appreciated food.

Everyone knows that the true connoisseur prefers to savour in silence; that the thumping of a piano and the scraping of strings, however efficiently thumped or scraped, disturb a sensitive palate. No doubt there are dishes which, like certain poems, are rendered less effective by music; they must stand quite alone if their paramount merits would be fully appreciated. And so to Gian-Luca came mostly those clients who wished to do justice to their meals; there were also a few who came for Gian-Luca, because in his room they got promptly served; but these were only the busy people whom it did not pay very well to serve. However, he always greeted them politely as though they really mattered to the Doric. They would feel quite a little glow of self-importance:

'I always feed at the Doric,' they would tell you. 'I'm known there; I've got my special head-waiter.' For, say what you please, it is rather gratifying to feel that you have got your own special head-waiter—and with such harmless follies are the Dorics of life paved, and on them do the Millos of the world grow rich.

Gian-Luca would often unbend to his clients, as a father may unbend to his children. He would smile at them, chat with them, and always ask them gravely if their meal had been satisfactory. He would summon his subordinates to refill their glasses, to replenish their empty plates. If they ate less than usual he would grow almost anxious, he would

167

even inquire about their health. He studied their menus, and when he suspected that he might be dealing with a novice he would tell him politely but firmly what to eat, and then he would see that he ate it. In this way such people learnt the right things to order when they came to a place like the Doric. So also with their wines; Gian-Luca would whisper advice in the ear of Roberto, the wine-waiter, and Roberto, acting upon his advice, would point out the wine they must order. Gian-Luca did these things less from motives of gain than from a real pride in his profession. He aimed at raising the status of the palate via education, as some people aim at the raising of the working classes. It pained him to think that any client of the Doric might be lacking in true appreciation. He became a kind of elegant, soft-voiced tutor; if he spoke to them thus they had perforce to listen, and when the food arrived they would be glad that they had done so.

Men consecrate their lives to many different things, but truly it may be said that to each the object of his life will become an ideal—for otherwise how could we live? There are many ideals, some higher and some lower, but all real as long as they last. It is only when they cease to be our ideals, and descend with a rush to their natural levels, that we find ourselves suddenly outraged and debased by the thing we have lived to serve. And so to Gian-Luca the Doric and all it stood for were gradually becoming an ideal. For the most part he lived entirely for his work; and if it could not quite satisfy his soul, at least it was amply filling his pockets.

Whenever he had half an hour to spare he would wander down to the basement; to that vast, mysterious heart of the Doric, throbbing, bubbling, giving off steam like the crater of a busy volcano. He would try to absorb the spirit of the place, to learn all its complicated workings, to understand Millo, the heart of that heart—the life force that sat in a neat little office, thinking wise and profitable thoughts about food, making endless minute calculations. There would be the great kitchen with its many French ranges—long iron tables filled to bursting with fire. The pantries, the larders, the sculleries, the cellars, the store-rooms, the still-room, the airy refectory where presently the waiters themselves would go to eat. There would be the vast army of expert chefs with their scullions and kitchen-boys in attendance; seventy creatures all busily engaged in the sole occupation of preparing and cooking and garnishing and dishing those wise thoughts of Millo's which his clients upstairs would consume.

Gian-Luca would stand with his hands in his pockets, watchful but always admiring. 'How little the clients know,' he would think; 'how little they know about anything really; and as for the food they eat, they know nothing!'

And then he would smile a little to himself and think of a few favourite clients, devising new methods of making them happy for a while through the unfailing media of their stomachs.

3

In some respects life at the Doric was arduous, though the waiters all got a day off once a month, and the usual hours between meals. But their duties were endless; anxious, tiresome duties, very wearing to the nerves, very trying to the temper; for not the smallest detail must be neglected, since on details depended the perfection of the whole, and Millo believed in perfection. Of Millo it was said that he was lacking in compassion, that those of his staff who were stupid or ill would be promptly dismissed without a second thought. This was only partially true, for although he dismissed them, he often regretted having to do so, and sometimes he would help them with money. He was really a kind-hearted, tolerant man, but he knew how a restaurant ought to be run, and if a few people went down in the process that was not Millo's fault, but the fault of his times—of the age that demanded a Doric. Millo had his rules that must be obeyed, they were made entirely for the good of the clients; when clients came to feed they should never be disturbed by emotions other than their own. Thus no waiter dared intrude his personal feelings by so much as the ghost of a sigh. No waiter was allowed to have a headache or a backache or a legache, or even a heartache for that matter; such things ceased to exist when he came on duty, as Giovanni, the trancheur, found out.

Giovanni's young lady had married the hall porter under

his very nose, and Giovanni, from being a lighthearted fellow, had grown decidedly broody. He had slashed at a ham as though it were the porter, and when clients had sent messages regarding their beef—some preferring it well done, some pink, and others gory—Giovanni had been seen to scowl darkly at his knife as though he would have liked to carve the clients. Millo, walking softly through the restaurant one day, pausing now and then beside a table and bowing, had observed that his exellent trancheur, Giovanni, was not doing justice to his art; so that evening after dinner he had reasoned with Giovanni in the soft, deadly way that was Millo's. He had said, gently stroking the restaurant cat that was given the freedom of his office:

'Here we have no hearts and no emotions; no passions— no bodies except to serve. Am I not right, my good Giovanni? Is not that how we have built up the Doric? All such things as I speak of we leave to our clients; in clients they are good, they encourage much spending, but you and I cannot afford to indulge them—if we do, why, then we must go.'

Giovanni had bowed and murmured in agreement, feeling that Millo was right; feeling that a ham must be worth more to Millo than Anna who had heartlessly married the hall porter; knowing indeed that had he been Millo he would probably have shown less forbearance. For in this lies the great good fortune of the Latin, he can nearly always put himself in your place. An enviable trait, but one that in the long run spoils his fun in his budding revolutions. So Giovanni had gone back to his well-stocked cold buffet and had carved once more like an angel. If his heart was really broken—which was doubtful, let us hope—he managed to hide this fact while at the Doric. What happened when he left there at night to go home was a matter of little importance.

4

Gian-Luca still lived with Fabio and Teresa, still slept in Olga's old bedroom. He had had it repainted and papered a bright yellow, so that now there remained not even the scars as witnesses to what had once been. He could well have afforded to take a room nearer Piccadilly and the Doric, but the people among whom he had been brought up never left home except to get married, and not always then, for the family tie is a ten-ton chain to the Latin. No feelings of affection or duty, however, kept Gian-Luca at home; he remained where he was from a sense of habit—he was like that now, a creature of habit, after nearly seven years at the Doric. Young as he was, he was slightly pedantic, with a little crop of cut-and-dried ideas about life. He read much in his spare time, believing in culture, and had quite a good knowledge of all sorts of books, English as well as Italian. Perhaps the fact that he had so few friends had driven him back on books.

He was vain in a harmless, painstaking way, and would fold his clothes neatly every night. His trousers were stretched in a smart walnut press, his ties suspended from a tape in his wardrobe, his jackets from carefully selected hangers, and his boots and shoes always well treed. Apart from the Doric, his one ruling passion, he enjoyed his books, he admired astuteness, especially in matters connected with his business, and he found recreation in women—he was kinder to his books than he was to his women, perhaps because they cost him more. For Gian-Luca understood the value of money even as old Teresa understood it, even as Nerone and Rocca understood it, and Millo, the Lord of the Doric.

He was now in a position to buy all Doria's works, and he ordered each new volume as soon as it was published. These were the books that he loved above all others, and he kept them in a special little bookcase by themselves. A rebel among poets was Ugo Doria; a firebrand, an earth-quake, a disaster. And then suddenly, a saint, a peak of pure whiteness, a lake in the heart of the mountains. And this latter was the mood in which Gian-Luca liked him best; when he would feel that he was reading something more than Ugo Doria, when Gian-Luca—who did not believe in a soul—would know moments of joy and complete content-ment; moments when the Doric and Millo and food and money and success and even himself would seem just nothing at all. Whenever he was feeling particularly lonely, in spite of his astuteness and ability, he would take down the volume that contained his favourite poem, the immortal 'Gioia della Luce'. And sometimes, not often it is true, but sometimes, would come visions of wide, cool places; and of shadows, green because of their trees, and of all sorts of simple things. Then Gian-Luca would begin to grow younger and younger, but happier far than when he was a child; and perhaps he would go all the way out to Putney on his next free evening to visit the Librarian. For there he was always a welcome guest—not because he was successful but because he was himself. He would wander about among the old books, sniffing in their queer, musty smell.

'You ought to have been a librarian, Gian-Luca,' his friend would say, beaming at him.

But at that Gian-Luca would shake his head slowly: 'Ma no, I am very well content as I am. Books are for sometimes, my work is for always. I have chosen the safer part.'

'I wonder,' the Librarian would murmur softly. 'I very much wonder, Gian-Luca.'

They were excellent friends whenever they met, which naturally could not be often, and each Christmas Gian-Luca would send a large hamper to the red-brick villa in Putney. He would buy its contents from Fabio and Teresa, paying just as a stranger might have done. Teresa took the money as a matter of course, and she thanked Gian-Luca gravely, politely, much as she might have thanked a stranger. However, there were times now when she talked to her grandson, consulting him about her business. She was full of innumerable new ideas for the glorification of the Casa Boselli. Gian-Luca would listen and advise and quote Millo, his methods, his rules at the Doric.

'Sí, sí,' she would say, as she nodded with approval. 'I am glad to know what he feels about that—I am sure he is pleased with our macaroni factory.'

So now at last they had something in common, a ground upon which they could meet; the Casa Boselli, the Doric and Millo; Millo, the Doric, the Casa Boselli—and Gian-Luca, looking at her, would feel no resentment; indeed, he would think her a rather splendid figure with her hard eyes and clever, calculating brain that was more like a man's than a woman's.

No good telling Teresa that one sometimes felt lonely;

she would only have stared and stared. 'Nonna, I feel lonely!'
The childishness of it, for the smartest head-waiter at the
Doric. For that was what he was, their smartest head-
waiter—he had no doubt at all about that.

And Teresa knew it too: 'You do well, Gian-Luca, I
always knew you would do well.'

He would think: 'One cannot have everything, it seems—
and I have a great deal already.' Aloud he would say: 'We
all prosper, Nonna; we all work hard and we prosper.'

And she would reply: 'We work hard to grow rich.
Never forget that your money, Gian-Luca, is the best friend
you have, apart from yourself.'

CHAPTER THREE

I

THE SPRING is perhaps the time of all others when the lonely most realize their loneliness; and this had always been the case with Gian-Luca—he felt terribly lonely in the spring. His desire for companionship had been growing of late, becoming a kind of craving; even Fabio and Teresa saw more of him now; he would hang about the shop in his time off from the Doric; or if they were too busy he would go to Nerone's on the pretext of buying cigarettes. Schmidt had gone back to Switzerland, and Gian-Luca did not regret him. He hated Schmidt as one hates the creature who has helped one to gratify one's lower instincts; unjust, perhaps, since but for those instincts there would be no occasion to hate. He might have made friends of his fellow head-waiters, Riccardo, the head of the large restaurant, or Giuliano, who had charge of the grill-room. But he felt that they were jealous, as indeed they were, of the favour he stood in with Millo; and this knowledge made him stiff and a little awkward with them, while they on their part always eyed him with suspicion, as one who was waiting to jump into their shoes. Geppe, Gian-Luca could not endure, and besides he was more than four years his junior; Geppe, who was always asking him for money in order to run after girls. He still feared Berta with her flashing brown eyes, her temperamental moods and her affectations. He felt that Berta would have liked him to propose, and he thought her extremely unattractive. 'It is strange,' he would think, 'that I have so few friends.' And then he would wonder if the fault lay in himself, and this thought would make him unhappy.

But the spring that was thrusting the sap along the branches and filling the parks with flowers and lovers, and making Teresa's old heart feel young because of her new macaroni factory—the spring brought Maddalena to the Doric; and chance or the spring, both impulsive and freakish, took Gian-Luca down to the still-room one morning, and there he saw Maddalena.

Maddalena was standing by a mound of golden butter, with the large wooden pats just raised in her hands. She was looking towards the little square opening through which the waiters gave their orders. The still-room had the kindly innocent smell of butter and milk and fresh bread. On a table in a corner stood a huge bowl of salad, green and glistening with sunshine and water, and over by the fireplace a girl was grinding coffee; she was humming under her breath. There were several other young girls in the room, they were dressed in white and wore large white caps. A sense of cleanliness and youth hung about them, as about the cool little room itself; a sense of peace, pleasant, homely peace after the noise of the restaurant, and the hellish heat of the kitchens.

Maddalena was tall, strong-limbed and full-breasted; her face was oval and pale. Either side of her face curved her dark brown hair, covering her little ears. Her eyes were large and indulgent and soft, like the eyes of a mothering doe; and as she stood there in a patch of sunlight, she turned them full on Gian-Luca. There was nothing inviting in that gaze of hers, only it seemed to question; and his eyes questioned back—yet neither of them knew at that moment what they were asking.

Then he smiled. 'Buon giorno,' he said politely, 'you are new to the Doric, is it not so?'

'I came yesterday,' she told him, but she did not smile; 'I have taken Maria's place.'

He considered her a moment: 'Oh, yes, the Maria—was she a friend of yours?'

'No, a friend of my aunt's; I have just come from Rome— I have not got friends in England.' And then because she was feeling home-sick: 'Are you an Italian too? You speak our language as though you were—all the girls in the still-room are French except me.'

'I do not know what I am——' he said gravely, 'but I feel just like an Italian.' He was thinking: 'She is terribly home-sick, poor creature, they are always like that just at first.' Aloud, he went on kindly: 'You will like your work here; we all like our work at the Doric.' Then he gave an order to one of the maids and hurried upstairs to the restaurant.

Once or twice that afternoon he remembered Maddalena, and the next day he went back to see her; it was easy enough to visit the still-room on some slight pretext or another. The week that followed found him constantly there, when-ever he could get the chance, in fact.

'She is home-sick, poor soul,' he would say to himself; 'I am sure she is terribly home-sick.'

They spoke seldom; she seemed to be always patting butter, turning it into little rolls. Her large, competent hands held the pats very deftly. He liked to see her there by the clean, golden butter; the sight of her filled a void that was in him, she gave him a feeling of home.

Then one afternoon between luncheon and dinner, he met her crossing the street. On a sudden impulse he turned and walked beside her.

'Will you not come into the park?' he suggested. 'It is cool there under the trees.'

'Thank you,' she said simply; 'are you going to the park?'

He smiled and said: 'I am, if you are.'

They walked on in silence for quite a long time, then he found an empty seat and they rested. He noticed that Maddalena wore black and supposed that she must be in mourning.

'You come from Rome?' he inquired with interest.

She nodded. 'Yes, I come from Rome. I am very home-sick in England, signore; are you not home-sick too?'

And suddenly he knew that he was very home-sick, that he had been for years and years. He was home-sick for some place a long way away—much farther away than Rome. But he said:

'As for me, I was born here in London, so what right have I to be home-sick?'

'You have a look in your eyes——' she told him, then flushed, for she felt that she was being over-bold.

Gian-Luca turned, the better to see her; she filled him with a sense of peace; the curve of her bosom was kind and maternal. Her beauty was that of a vine-clad arbour, an arbour heavy with purple grapes, where a man might rest after toil.

'May I not know your name?' he said gently; 'I would like to know what I may call you.'

'My name is Maddalena Trevi,' she told him.

'And I am Gian-Luca,' he replied very gravely; 'Gian-Luca—just that, nothing else.'

He saw that she did not understand him, and his heart felt lonely and aggrieved. He wanted her to ask him about himself, to ask him why he was just Gian-Luca. For he knew that the telling would come as a balm, because he would be telling Maddalena. But her gentle brown eyes were on his face and he suddenly felt ashamed; ashamed of the impulse that possessed him so strongly to make this girl share his troubles.

'Tell me about yourself,' he said quickly, as though she might read his thoughts.

Then she told him all that there was to tell; speaking quietly, trying to remember back along the years of her innocent life—as though he had a right to know. She was twenty-six, and had lost both her parents within a year of each other. Her father had died only eight weeks ago; he had kept a small trattoria. She was quite alone now except for distant cousins, and her Aunt Ottavia who lived in London. Aunt Ottavia lived in 'Little Italy', and here Maddalena smiled at Gian-Luca. 'But it is not little at all,' she said; 'it is large and gloomy and very full of people—Italians who do not seem quite like Italians—nor is it the least like home.'

Aunt Ottavia let out her house in lodgings, and Maddalena must pay for her room—but Aunt Ottavia was kind, and asked little, later on she would pay her more. Maddalena was missing the big Campagna, where the sheep all wore little bells; and the sunshine and the hills, and the trattoria, which had been on the road to Domine Quo Vadis, where Our Lord had left His Footprint in the marble. Did not Gian-Luca think it gracious of Our Lord to leave us His sacred Footprint? There had been a good priest there, Father Battista, whom she had known ever since she was a child. She missed him, he had been such a kind, merry father— sometimes she had taken him a flask of Chianti, or a basket of oranges from her garden, or a loaf of home-made focaccia.

He had come to see her off at the station, and had warned her that most English people were not Christians, they were Protestants he had told her sadly, and had begged her to go to Mass every day. When she had been a girl of seventeen she had kissed a boy called Rubino—he had courted her for the space of a summer, and then he had gone to his military service. When he had come back he was changed, he was impudent, and Maddalena had not loved him any more. The grapes in the vineyards along the Via Appia had been unusually fine last year; the peasants had earned a great deal of money, but her father's mule had gone suddenly lame—a large white mule whose name was Umberto—a mule with a temper, and a passion for grapes—he would steal the grapes out of their baskets.

Gian-Luca listened with a little smile, while she told of these simple things. Of the faith that believed in that Footprint in stone, of the priest who ate oranges grown in her garden, of the tinkling sheep bells across the Campagna, of the mule who stole grapes and whose name was Umberto. And while she talked thus, she seemed very childish, and made Gian-Luca, nearly three years her junior, feel terribly cynical and old. But when he looked at her he felt very young, for her face was the face of a mother of men.

'I would like to know Aunt Ottavia,' he told her, 'for I want you and me to be friends.'

She smiled. 'I will give you her name and address.'

He wrote it down in his notebook. 'My grandmother will be glad to know her, too,' he went on; 'I will surely see that they meet, and then I can take you out sometimes—we might go into the country when we get our day off—I will try to arrange that we get it together.'

She said: 'I should like to go into the country, I should like to see fields and trees.'

'I hope you will like to see them with me,' he smiled.

She answered: 'Yes, I shall like that, too.'

He glanced at his watch. 'We must go,' he said reluctantly; 'to-morrow we will come here again. It is good in our life to get plenty of air—and you are so new to our life.'

She appeared to consider this for a moment, looking thoughtfully into his face; then she nodded, as though what she saw there reassured her. 'That is as you will, signore.'

Gian-Luca's courtship of Maddalena was tranquil and quite without pain, for this was not loving as he had loved the Padrona, but a gentle, kindly and grateful emotion, soothing rather than stimulating—for the rest, it was being loved. He made the acquaintance of Aunt Ottavia whose house was in Colbdath Square, and she in her turn went to call on Teresa, and was properly impressed by the salumeria, and properly respectful to its mistress. Teresa invited Maddalena to tea, and inspected her not unkindly. Old Compton Street getting wind of the event, in came Rosa, Nerone and Rocca. Presently Mario came in as well; and Maddalena, who was not yet affianced, blushed and smiled shyly beneath all those eyes, and prayed that the Virgin would tell her what to say, so that she might make a good impression.

Then Gian-Luca went to see Millo in his office and asked for an extra day's leave; he also asked that a girl in the still-room should be granted a holiday as well.

Millo smiled faintly: 'What is this, Gian-Luca? And who is this girl from the still-room?'

'Maddalena Trevi,' Gian-Luca told him; 'I wish to make her my wife.'

'I see. And so you are going to get married?'

'If she will have me, signore.'

Millo looked into Gian-Luca's face and noted the lines round his eyes—other things, too, he noted in that face.

'It is time you got married,' he told him with decision; 'and I hope it may mean that you are going to settle down.'

'What else can it mean, signore?' said Gian-Luca.

3

Gian-Luca took Maddalena to Hadley Woods—they are very lovely in June. Fabio had made up a luncheon basket, and as Gian-Luca carried it he smiled, remembering a day at Kew Gardens. Maddalena had dressed herself all in white, something had made her discard black that morning. She walked by Gian-Luca, very stately and tall, a true daughter of Rome the eternally fruitful—even so had her young virgins walked by their lovers for more than two thousand years.

They sat down together under the beech trees, and he lifted her hand and kissed it. 'Your hand is full of happiness,' he said, 'will it spare a little for me?'

'Whatever it holds is yours,' she told him, 'all that it holds, I give.'

'And yet I have not been a good man,' he said slowly, 'not as you understand goodness.'

'I do not know what you have been,' she answered; 'I only know what you are.'

'And that is enough for you, Maddalena?'

She smiled: 'It is more than enough.'

Then he said: 'I have no name to offer my wife, I was born in what men call sin.'

'If you are the fruit of sin,' she said softly, 'how great must be God's forgiveness.'

'Will you marry a man without a name?' he persisted.

She said: 'I will marry you. No name in the world has ever sounded so sweet to me as your name—Gian-Luca.'

Then he took her in his arms and kissed her on the mouth —but gently, for she did not stir his passion. And she kissed him back with slow, lingering kisses, as though she were groping for the soul of this man, with her tender, virginal lips. Presently she pressed his head down on her bosom and rocked him with her arms about his shoulders.

'You who have suffered so much,' she whispered; 'you who have suffered so much——'

'No one has ever loved me before,' he told her; and there was joy in his voice. 'I am glad that no one has loved me before—that you should be the first, Maddalena.'

'Yes,' she answered, 'for that is surely as it should be.' And now she was stroking his hair. 'Because of that, beloved, the others do not count: I have washed them away with my love.'

He said: 'Why are you so good to me, my woman?'

And at that she laughed to herself. 'If I told you, how could you understand—you who are so much a man?'

They got up and wandered together through the woods, arm-in arm like the other lovers; and Maddalena welcomed their presence—for although he was wishing that the woods might be empty, she saw those lovers through the eyes of her love, and beheld much glory about them.

Presently he said: 'These wide, green glades—they always make me feel strange; they make me feel as though I had come home—that is queer in a man like me——'

She pressed his arm. 'But you have come home, amore—you have come home to Maddalena. Wherever we two are together that is home.'

'Yes—it must be so——' he murmured. His eyes were searching the long, cool shadows, green because of their trees; the turf and the rustle of last year's leaves made him want to take off his shoes—— 'Let us get married very soon,' he said, as though his words were an answer to something. 'Since you will take me as I am, diletta, let us get married very soon.'

'As soon as you wish, we will marry,' she agreed. 'Why should we wait any longer?'

He withdrew his gaze from those long, cool shadows and let it rest on her face, and suddenly he wished to tell her of his childhood, knowing that she would understand.

'You are my woman—all my woman,' he repeated, 'and so I can tell you all. I have never had anyone to talk to like this—no one who cared to listen.'

While he talked she saw him less as a man than as a lonely little boy; and all her motherhood stretched out its arms, so that she could not speak for tears—so great was the heart within her. And something of her motherhood touched him, too, and he walked with her holding her hand.

He said: 'It is strange, but I think my mother must have been just like you Maddalena.'

They ate little of the meal that Fabio had prepared, and after a while it was evening. The voices of the other lovers came softly out of the dusk towards them. A large, yellow moon climbed up over the woods, and hung there opposite the sunset.

'Look!' said Gian-Luca, and his eyes were wide with the beauty and mystery of it.

But Maddalena's eyes were on him, seeing all mystery and beauty in his face, the beginnings and the noon-tides and the endings of all days—for such is the love of woman.

Maddalena took him down to the Italian church—St. Peter's in Hatton Garden. And there he must talk with old Father Antonio, Aunt Ottavia's confessor. For to please Maddalena, Gian-Luca had consented in the end to be married in a church. 'I would have a blessing on our love,' she had said. And because of the gratitude he felt towards her, he had been unwilling to grieve her. He had told her that he did not believe in God, and at that she had only smiled. 'You may not believe in Him yet,' she had said, 'but remember that He believes in you.'

'A man should believe in himself,' he had replied; 'he should not be dependent on his God.'

Gian-Luca had not disliked Father Antonio, a kindly old fellow, with very blue eyes, who on his part had not disliked Gian-Luca, in spite of the latter's lack of faith. Father Antonio was a fisher of men, and he sometimes cast his net in strange waters. 'One never knows whom one may catch,' he would argue; 'it is always worth taking a risk.' And so, when Gian-Luca had faithfully promised that his children should be given to the care of Mother Church, Father Antonio had consented to the marriage being performed at St. Peter's. Aunt Ottavia got very voluble and busy.

'I will go and light candles at once,' she told Gian-Luca; 'I will go and light candles for my nephew's conversion; I will also make a Novena to Saint Joseph.'

5

Maddalena would have liked them to live with Aunt Ottavia, who was willing to turn out all her lodgers, and to let Maddalena their rooms. But a closer acquaintance with Coldbath Square, and with Aunt Ottavia, kind though she was, had decided Gian-Luca against this plan. For Coldbath Square was anything but clean, in spite of its hopeful name; and as for Aunt Ottavia, she never stopped talking; failing an audience she would talk to herself, Gian-Luca had heard her at it. Aunt Ottavia was all blacks and whites like a magpie, and quite as voluble, it seemed. She was piously shrewd and shrewdly pious, she gave, as a rule, that she might receive. She contributed nothing to St. Anthony's Bread, for she liked to have something to show for her pennies, and this being so she would buy little candles. Three penny candles she would burn to the saint, and then proceed to tax his patience to the utmost by a long recital of her needs. She liked Gian-Luca and thought Maddalena lucky—a girl without a dot to secure so fine a husband! Yes, indeed, Maddalena was lucky!

Aunt Ottavia knew life, very thoroughly she knew it—for the most part it only made her laugh. She had come from a village in far-off Liguria, and there she had known what it was to be married to a cobbler who had liked to get drunk. He had been very funny on certain occasions, and had tried to lay her across his knees so that he might beat her with a newly-soled slipper; but as she had been agile and quick as a squirrel, he had fortunately never succeeded. Now she would laugh when she told of Pietrino; she would say: 'He was a kind man, he did it out of love—they are funny, these men, they have their little fancies.' And then she would cross herself, remembering that he was dead, and would mutter a prayer for his soul.

Gian-Luca took the basement and the ground floor of a house that he had found in Millman Street. It was not too far from the church for Maddalena, and the Russell Square tube was convenient for him. Maddalena was pleased at the thought of having her own kitchen, for she happened to be an expert cook.

Fabio insisted on helping to furnish this new abode for his grandson. 'Ma *si*,' he said firmly, when Gian-Luca demurred, 'I will do at least this much for Olga.' Aunt Ottavia, who always pretended to be poor, was evidently not quite so poor as she pretended, for she purchased a huge sideboard in the Tottenham Court Road—it had carving and a kind of overmantel. Rocca and his signora sent a silver-plated bread scoop, engraved with maiden-hair fern. Nerone broke all records and cashed a good-sized cheque; from him arrived a splendid parlour clock. Rosa bought two double sheets, and these she embroidered with a couple of large hearts entwined with flowers; she offered them with many words of love from her and Mario, and hopes that they would grace the bridal bed. The Padrone and Padrona of the Capo sent a cream-jug—solid silver with a suitable inscription. The Padrone said: 'I will not be outdone by that man, Millo, I send this for the honour of my Capo.' But Millo, as it happened, gave a cheque for fifteen pounds—hard lines, for the Padrone could not well take back his cream-jug.

<h1 style="text-align:center">6</h1>

Gian-Luca and Maddalena were married in July at St. Peter's, the Italian church; that queer old lump of Italy dumped down in Hatton Garden, its frescoes blurred and peeling from the horrid English climate, its heart grown chill from many English winters. As Gian-Luca was outside the flock, the Mass, perforce, was short, but everyone was there except Teresa. Teresa would not put her foot inside a Christian church, so Fabio went alone in a very tight black coat, and he it was who gave away the bride.

The Padrone, the Padrona, Millo and old Nerone, Rocca, Signora Rocca, Aunt Ottavia, Rosa, Mario, Berta, and the inquisitive Geppe, they all sat or knelt or stood along the dingy pews. And from Putney came the little Librarian with his wife—very strange they felt and awkward in the dim old Popish church, very anxious, too, to show all due respect. Maddalena, pale and lovely in her simple wedding dress, stood serene and undisturbed beside Gian-Luca. Her eyes were large and placid with the faith she had in God, and she prayed that He would grant her many children. Gian-Luca did not pray because he found no words, nor did he know of anyone to pray to. But he looked at Maddalena and his heart knew gratitude, and when he knelt, he knelt to Maddalena. So the two of them were married, while Rosa wept and wept, and Mario coughed and blew his nose to stop himself from weeping. In a pew beside his daughter Nerone scraped his wooden leg; while Rocca in the next pew puffed his chest to show his medals. Geppe's eyes bulged with excitement, and Berta lay back weakly in order to proclaim her broken heart. But Fabio, near the altar, wished Teresa had been there, and then put up a little prayer for Olga.

The service being over, Millo went back to the Doric, the Padrone and Padrona to the Capo. The Librarian and his wife had gently disappeared—but the rest of them all hurried off to Fabio's shop, where Teresa had prepared the wedding breakfast. A magnificent repast it was, quite worthy of the house, of the celebrated Casa Boselli. There was much Asti Spumante, and it went to Mario's head—he made reminiscent love to patient Rosa. Rocca drank so many toasts to the army and the bride that Signora Rocca had to interfere; Aunt Ottavia, very merry, as she always was with men, asked Nerone how he got his wooden leg. But Nerone was invariably sulky in his cups, and, moreover, he was thinking of that clock, so instead of being gallant to the little Aunt Ottavia, he stuffed his mouth with food and would not tell her.

They feasted, they made speeches, they sang patriotic songs: 'Avanti Bersagliere!' carolled Rocca with emotion, 'Avanti-vanti-vanti-Bersagliere!' Only the bride and bridegroom were shy and rather silent, not doing proper justice to their food. And presently the time came when the bride must change her dress, while the bridegroom waited for her in the hall. Young Geppe fetched a taxi, into which the victims hurried amid a shower of rice and confetti. They would go straight home to Millman Street; there would be no honeymoon, for Gian-Luca had not wished to worry Millo.

As they drove he leant towards her: 'You do not mind, my Maddalena? You do not mind about our honeymoon?'

She was silent for a moment and her eyes were rather wistful, but she said: 'I am contented. Let it be just as you wish—so long as you are happy, amore——'

CHAPTER FOUR

I

FOR THE first time in his life Gian-Luca knew what it meant to have a home; for home is a place in which we are wanted, in which there is someone to whom we matter more than anything else on earth. Of such an one's love are the four walls created—but to cover them with garlands we ourselves must love. Maddalena had built the walls that were home, and Gian-Luca rejoiced exceedingly; nor did he perceive in his first flush of pleasure that the walls she had built were bare. He would look at his wife very gratefully and gently; at her quiet beauty, her gracious body, her eyes of a mothering doe. He would think:

'Yes, I love this woman I have married—she loves me so much, and love begets love—a man could not well help loving Maddalena.'

And feeling his thoughtful gaze upon her, she would look up and meet his eyes; she would go to him, stroking and fondling his hair.

'Amore,' she would murmur, 'are you really happy?'

'Do I not love you?' he would answer, smiling.

Then Maddalena would be silent.

To the simple of the earth there comes deep wisdom; Maddalena was one of the simple of the earth and so she was very wise, and in her wisdom she read her man's heart, and she knew that he did not love her. But something else also Maddalena knew, and that was that he thought that he loved her, that he earnestly desired to think that he loved her, from an instinct of gratitude.

He said to her one day: 'I love you far more than when I married you, sweetheart—it must be because you love me so much; all my life I have wanted someone to love me—please go on loving me, Maddalena.'

He would often say artless things like this, trusting her to understand; overjoyed at having someone to whom he could speak freely—indulging himself in the blessed relief of putting his thoughts into words. She reassured him as though he were a child who might be afraid of the dark.

'You are all folded up in my love, Gian-Luca; you need never be afraid any more.'

And he wondered how she knew that he had been so much afraid, afraid of being alone.

No man could have been more kindly than he was during that first placid year of their marriage; he trusted her implicitly and would bring her all his money, asking her to keep what was needed for the house, and then to put what remained in the bank. She knew that he was saving from motives of ambition, trying to amass a little capital towards the day when he should start a restaurant of his own.

'Money is a man's best friend,' he would tell her very often, unconsciously quoting Teresa. And sometimes he would add: 'That is, next to himself.'

To please him Maddalena would go from shop to shop, bargaining, arguing, disputing. Consulting the penurious Aunt Ottavia as to where two sparrows might be bought for a farthing; rejoicing in his trust and his obvious contentment, caring very little for what she scraped and saved so long as she pleased Gian-Luca. There were times, however, when, sitting alone, Maddalena would look into her heart, and would know that even in their hours of passion, she never for one moment held the soul of this man. Her own soul leapt out to sanctify their kisses, but his remained cold and aloof, and gradually into her patient brown eyes there was creeping a look of resignation. Yet he clung to her, fearfully, desperately almost, for now less than ever could he bear solitude. If he found her from home in the afternoon, he would stand by the door, staring up and down the street, or perhaps he would hurry round to Aunt Ottavia.

'Where is Maddalena?' he would ask anxiously; 'she has gone out and left no message.'

When Maddalena came back he would be sure to reproach her. 'I have been here for a good half-hour,' he would grumble; 'I hate to find the house empty like this; why cannot you do your shopping in the morning?'

So she ended by never going out at all when he might be expected home from the Doric. She would sit in the window and watch for his coming—he had said that he liked to see her at the window. Yet sometimes she sat at the window in vain, for he would not come home between luncheon and dinner. He might have elected to go and see Fabio, or to potter about Charing Cross Road in search of a second-hand book; or perhaps he would have gone to visit the Padrona, for whom he now felt not the slightest attraction, but who, woman-like, regretted this fact, which secretly amused Gian-Luca. He would have to go hurrying back to the Doric with never a word to Maddalena; and if he was taking late duty at the restaurant, it might be two o'clock in the morning, or after, before he got home to bed. Maddalena would probably be fast asleep, and this would make him feel lonely—his legs might be aching from the long hours of standing; he would grumble to himself until she woke up, and then ask her to rub his legs. While she rubbed he liked to talk about the clients, about all the little happenings of the day. He would tell her in confidence things overheard, careful always to withhold the names, but criticizing freely and laughing a good deal, as though his clients amused him.

'They are funny,' he would say, 'they forget that their waiter has eyes and ears in his head. Millo hates eyes and ears except for his orders—so do I for that matter, in my under-waiters. But what can we do? They get mellow with food, and then they confide in each other!' Then he would pause as though considering his clients, and presently he would go on: 'I have one or two favourites whom it pleases me to humour—they do not tip particularly well, but they know how to order a dinner. For the rest, I serve them all, but I do not really like them, and they do not really like me. I am just a machine; if I broke down they would miss me, but only for a little while until they got another. I talk to them, they answer; I smile and they smile—and meanwhile, my Maddalena, I prosper. In spite of the fact that I have not got a name, I shall one day be famous as Millo is famous; and these greedy children whom I do not really like, they it is who shall make me famous. And after all, why should they not be greedy, and a little impatient, too, since they pay? It is often amusing to be a head-waiter; one orders and is ordered. I say: 'Go there, Alano!' And Alano goes. They say: 'Come here, Gian-Luca!' And Gian-Luca comes. One moment I am the master of Alano, the next I am the slave of a duke; but if he only knew it my duke is the slave— I make him a slave to his stomach!'

He would go on talking happily while Maddalena rubbed, but after a time he would remember his legs—legs are very important to a waiter. 'Not there!' he would say, 'rub lower down, mia donna, rub just here where my ankle is swollen —that is better—and now you might rub the other ankle.'

Perhaps she would look tired, as very well she might and then his conscience would smite him. ' Poverina,' he would murmur, 'I have kept you awake—I will try to come in very quietly to-morrow, you will see, I will creep in like a mouse.'

Yet although he intended to creep in like a mouse, he always managed to wake her. A hair-brush would drop or perhaps he would cough, and then there would be the electric light. Once she was awake it seemed natural to talk, Maddalena was an excellent listener; he had never had such a fine listener before, one to whom everything he said or did mattered. But long after Gian-Luca had talked himself to sleep, his wife would lie awake thinking. She would worry a little because of the English whom he served and flattered while secretly despising them. She would wonder if he bore them a grudge in his heart because of his long-ago school-days, those days when they had taunted him and left him out of things—he had told her about those days.

'But no,' she would think, 'he cannot be so childish—it is only that we Latins feel differently, think differently; they are good, we are good, but our goodness is different, we find it very hard to draw together.'

And then she would remember that Gian-Luca was English—English in the eyes of the law, and her simple, honest mind would grow puzzled and troubled, knowing that he owed so much to this England, that in fact they all owed so much.

2

She prayed a great deal, because Gian-Luca would not pray, so that she had to pray for them both; and her prayers, unlike Teresa's had once been, were quiet and utterly trustful. If she prayed very often that Gian-Luca might love God, she prayed still more often that he might love Maddalena; and doubtless her God who was one with His creature, listened and understood.

She felt very sure of the friendship of her Maker, and would tell Him about all sorts of everyday things. For instance she told Him how much it grieved her that she could not more often prepare her man's food. Gian-Luca had nearly all his meals at the Doric, and Maddalena longed to cook what he ate herself, to spend hours downstairs in her spotless kitchen making his favourite dishes. He was young and hungry, he liked good things to eat, his wife knew quite well what he liked. Fritto misto he liked, and ravioli, and her father had said that no woman in Rome could make ravioli as she could. When Gian-Luca had his day off once a month, then it was that Maddalena got her chance; she would plan the meals for that day a week ahead, but when the time came she herself could eat nothing for the joy of seeing him eating. He would settle down to be greedy like a schoolboy, praising her cooking between mouthfuls.

'Give me some more!' he would order, laughing. 'Millo and all his chefs can go to the devil when my Maddalena turns cook!'

Getting up she would eagerly serve her husband; and he, whose whole life was spent in serving others, would find it pleasant and rather amusing to be served in his turn by Maddalena. He would play with her, suddenly thumping the table in order to make her jump.

'Come along, waiter! I am starving!' he would thunder; 'send me the maître d'hotel!' And then he would grumble to a mythical Gian-Luca: 'Look here, Gian-Luca, what's the matter to-day? I've been waiting three minutes for that partridge!'

They would laugh, and in the middle of their laughter he would kiss her, and say that never was there such a waiter and such a splendid chef rolled into one as his wonderful Maddalena. After their dinner they would go for an airing; Maddalena loved Kensington Gardens. They would jump into a taxi on that one day a month, and be driven as far as the Serpentine Bridge; from there they would stroll through the gardens arm-in-arm, Maddalena watching the children. If it was wet he would go to his book-case and get a volume of Doria's poems; he would read Maddalena the 'Gioia della Luce,' she not understanding a word. He might look up and see her bewildered face, but still he would go on reading, not to please her but to please himself—for the joy he took in the rhythm. When he had finished he would probably relent and read her some simple poem, or to please her, the Latin hymn she loved best—the beautiful 'Te lucis ante terminum' from the quiet service of Compline. His voice would grow solemn and very sweet because he adored the sound of the Latin, not because he was moved by the meaning of the words. . . .

She would think that he looked like some mediaeval saint, so aesthetic were the hands that held the prayer-book, so thoughtful the line of his brow. But then he would laugh as he shut up the book.

'Well, there you are, piccina,' he would say, 'it is lovely because the language is lovely, but it is not the "Gioia della Luce." '

3

Everyone was anxious to be kind to Maddalena, and yet Maddalena was lonely. It was almost as though Gian-Luca's loneliness in leaving him had found harbourage in her, as though she had drawn it into herself, so that now she must bear it for him. Rosa came very often to see her and would talk of the infant Gian-Luca, telling of the time when he clung to her breast, telling of the day when he first said 'Nonno', and this made Maddalena feel lonelier than ever. Rosa was very maternal that autumn, for her Geppe had gone to do his military service; all the way to Italy he had gone— Geppe, who had seldom even been out of London. In the end he had actually wanted to go, glad of anything for the sake of a change, but Rosa was anxious because of those hands of his, which so easily blistered. The life would be hard, they might set him to digging, they might teach him how to dig trenches—two years he must serve in an infantry regiment. Poor Geppe, the life would be hard. Berta, whose heart had been caught on the rebound, wished to marry a young man called Albert Cole, the commercial traveller whom Geppe had once met and had longed to emulate. Nerone had disliked Albert Cole at sight—he had the misfortune to be English—Nerone was rude whenever he called, so Berta had decided to marry him at once; they were going to be married next month. And here Rosa's eyes welled over with tears, for Cole called himself an agnostic.

'I do not know what that means,' she said helplessly. 'It cannot be anything to do with Saint Agnes, for he does not believe in the saints, and my Berta wishes to give up her Church; they will marry at a register office.'

Berta said terrible things, it seemed—things connected with babies. They had made such a painful impression on Rosa that she knew most of them by heart. 'Me and Bert aren't going to be bothered with children, we know a thing or two, me and Bert!' That was one of the statements—oh, yes, but there were others—Rosa actually blushed while she told them, she could not even look at Maddalena.

And then there was Nerone who had suddenly grown home-sick, talking of nothing but Italy ever since his grandson's departure. 'I am old,' he would mutter; 'I feel I must go home. All my life I have saved in order to go home—I feel that the moment has arrived.'

Rosa expected him to sell up his business, which, however, he put off doing. From week to week he would put it off—they none of them knew where they were.

'He is so moody and queer,' complained Rosa. 'When Mario and I think he means to see about it, he will suddenly run off and start counting his money, and then he will come back to us shaking his head. He will say, "No, not yet, just a month or two longer—a few more little shillings must go home to Siena before their old papá can join them."'

Maddalena would listen and sympathize because Rosa had given her milk to Gian-Luca. She did not like Nerone or Geppe or Berta, but since they belonged to Gian-Luca's foster-mother she felt that they somehow belonged to her.

Fabio always made Maddalena welcome; he approved of the quiet young wife. The Signora Rocca was also quite friendly and would often invite herself to tea. But with her Maddalena found little in common; the Signora Rocca talked only of religion, a religion so alien to that of Maddalena as to form a kind of barrier between them. Perhaps the signora was conscious of this fact, for she sent Maddalena many hot little pamphlets regarding the climatic conditions in hell, and a good few on purgatorial fires.

The Padrona of the Capo would patronize; she would give much advice regarding Gian-Luca, and this with a gentleness hard to resent. 'As an old married woman——' she would usually begin, and then she would patronize.

The girls that Maddalena had known in the still-room were fond of coming to see her. 'Bon Dieu! It is you who are lucky——' they would say, 'to be married to Monsieur Boselli!'

They were all just a little in love with Gian-Luca, but they genuinely liked his wife. They were light-hearted creatures who were always laughing, and they teased Maddalena for being so solemn, and because of her funny, broken English. In the end she would have to laugh with them and be merry, for their youth and good spirits were infectious.

There were plenty of people who were glad to know her, to take her into their lives, and yet only one person in all the world who counted—that was how it was with Maddalena. Ah, but some day soon there would be another—surely there must be another? He would be very small and have strange, light eyes, and his hair when it grew would be ashen blond, and his name would be just Gian-Luca. A great welcome was always awaiting this other. A great welcome? Why, all the mothers of the ages were waiting in the mothering soul of Maddalena, crying out love within her.

'I shall never be lonely any more,' she would think; 'all day I can care for and play with the child, and then he will sit with me by the window, watching for his father, who will surely love me when I have given him a son.'

Once she spoke of these things to Gian-Luca, scanning his face for a light in his eyes—a light that did not come. 'Ma sí,' he smiled kindly, 'you shall tell me when it is so —for the rest, we are surely very well as we are. Children are a great expense, my Maddalena; now if Mario had not had Berta and Geppe he would certainly have felt more free to make his way—he might have left the Capo before he was too old.'

And Maddalena wondered exceedingly. Did not they

spring from a race who loved children? A race of eager, imperative fathers? And then, with a little sinking of the heart, she suddenly remembered that Gian-Luca was different—that Gian-Luca had never known a father.

4

She missed her own father very much these days, and sometimes she would go to see the old priest, for the sake of calling him 'Father'. All kindness and tolerance was Father Antonio, whose placid blue eyes could see into the heart—they had seen into so many hearts in their time that now they looked just a little sad. She never told him about her troubles, indeed, they were difficult to put into words; she and he would just sit there and talk of quiet things, like the flowers to be placed on the altar next Easter, or the picture of a saint that was said to bring healing, or the vineyards along the Via Appia. Father Antonio knew Rome very well, although he himself was a Tuscan, and while they talked thus, their faces would grow wistful; he would be thinking of the hills near Florence, and she of the friendly, wide Campagna, where all the sheep wore little bells. These visits could never be very long, for Father Antonio was busy. His work lay among the bedraggled little flock who had given the name of their country to the district—its name but none of its charm!

When she left him Maddalena would go into the church where she and Gian-Luca had been married, and there she would pray to the kindly Madonna who stood just inside the doorway. The Madonna had set her small Son on His feet, she had told Him to stretch out His arms; and in case He should fall—for He was so little—she supported Him gently with her hands. Maddalena would think that the Child looked very much as Gian-Luca must have looked when he too was a child, and then she would humbly beg God's pardon, for this was an impious thought born of love, of her poor human love; yet somehow the Madonna always managed to comfort Maddalena.

After praying for a while she would get up slowly and trudge off to see Aunt Ottavia. Aunt Ottavia was not sympathetic these days; Maddalena was thankful that her husband had been firm when it came to taking those rooms. Indeed, she had grown to look on these visits as a species of self-imposed penance—Father Antonio imposed such small penances that Maddalena sometimes added a few.

Aunt Ottavia would say: 'Well, and how is Gian-Luca?' in a voice that she made rather stern.

She was cross with Gian-Luca because of all those candles. As much as five shillings had she spent on blessed candles, and still he remained a pagan. She would ask many searching and personal questions as one who had every right to know. Was there going to be a baby? Was he after other women? At what hour did he get home at night from his work? At what hour did he usually get up in the morning? Was he tidy or untidy? How often was he angry, and what sort of things made him angry? In conclusion she would say:

'You are spoiling the creature, one has only to look at him to see it. He is vain, and like all men, of course he is selfish, and your foolishness makes him more selfish. Now I never spoilt that husband of mine; he certainly drank, and tried constantly to beat me, but for all that he knows well that I never spoilt him—he cannot blame me for his purgatory.'

One day she had suddenly laughed at her thoughts, a disconcerting habit of hers. 'If Gian-Luca were mine,' she had told Maddalena, 'he would surely by now have come into the Church—I would surely have compelled him to come in by now, and I never had your beauty, Maddalena——'

'How?' Maddalena had inquired falteringly.

But at that Aunt Ottavia had laughed again. 'If I told you you would only be shocked,' she had said, 'and so I prefer not to tell you.'

5

The months slipped by in prosperity. The following summer Gian-Luca took his wife for three weeks' holiday to Brighton; he had not wished to go too far afield, in case something should happen at the Doric in his absence. Nothing of any kind was likely to happen, but that was the way Gian-Luca took his work, he was always convinced that when his back was turned the prestige of his room would suffer. Millo had recently raised his wages, so that now he felt very well off; but this fact did not alter his way of living, the only difference that it made to Maddalena was that she had more money to put by.

The little band of exiles in Old Compton Street were feeling particularly satisfied with life; even Nerone, the least prosperous of them, had to admit that things were looking up. Geppe being abroad, he had engaged a young assistant who sold more tobacco than he stole, so Nerone continued to send home the shillings to breed little centesimi. Every evening he and Fabio played their game of dominoes—both of them peering hard at the dots because their eyesight was failing—and every evening Nerone told Fabio of his great home-sickness, his longing for Italy. He would soon be going back there, he said. But each morning would find him busy in the shop, and the business still unsold, because, in spite of that great home-sickness, that love of country and of all things Italian, there was still his love of the pretty silver shillings that bred little centesimi.

Berta was now living near Battersea Bridge, in a flat with her smart young husband; she came very seldom to see her mother, being much engaged with her friends. One fine day, however, Berta really could not come, nor was she prevented by social engagements—for God was not mocked, inasmuch as that Berta presented her husband with twins. Two lusty little daughters, both determined to live, came squealing into the world. Even Rosa was somewhat disconcerted, but Berta, after weeping over each of them in turn, and feeling a transitory aversion for Albert, decided that the world had much cause to applaud her, and proceeded to pose in the eyes of her neighbours as a kind of modern Cornelia.

6

A year passed, then another. Maddalena was still childless, and her heart was heavy with dread. She knew now that even her love for Gian-Luca could not make up for the longing that was in her. She never confided her fears to her husband, held back by a painful pride; he did not particularly want her child, he had said that children cost money. Yet since she had no little son to love, she must perforce love Gian-Luca for two, so Maddalena loved him for the man that was in him, but also for the child that is in every man—she loved him as a wife and as a mother. There had always been this dual element in her love, but now something new had begun to creep in—a kind of grave desperation. Gian-Luca would sometimes force his mind from the Doric in order to consider her more closely; the gravity of her love had begun to oppress him, it made him feel in a vague, uneasy way that his wife was no longer happy.

'What is the matter?' he would think to himself; 'am I not perfectly faithful to this woman? Do I not give her all?'

But Maddalena knew that he had never given all, and now in addition she feared that she might be childless; the little Gian-Luca who would make his father love her, held aloof and refused to be born. She tried to hide the ache in her heart from the world, yet everyone suspected it, it seemed.

'You spoil him! You spoil him!' chanted Aunt Ottavia; 'you are making a perfect fool of the man!'

'One should never let a husband feel too certain of one,' smiled the wise, blue-eyed Padrona.

'He was always a strange little boy——' Rosa told her. 'Always a strange, self-sufficient little boy; but at bottom he is all pure gold, the Gian-Luca. Do I not know it, who nursed him?'

To them all Maddalena would reply the same thing: 'I have nothing to complain of in my husband.'

And Gian-Luca often said: 'I have an excellent wife, I have nothing to complain of in my wife.'

Yet Maddalena had moments of sheer naked terror, when she fancied that they were drifting apart.

'What shall I do if I lose him?' she would think.

And then perhaps she would love him unwisely, so that even Gian-Luca who wanted to be loved would grow just a little impatient.

'Ma no!' he would say, 'I have not got a headache, I am very well indeed, and my shoes are not wet. Now run away, sweetheart, and leave me in peace—I would like to read for an hour.'

But she could not leave him. She could not let him go even for an hour to his book. While he read she would sit there stroking his knee, wishing with all her heart that he were small, so that she might carry him in her arms. In the end he would have to shut up his book and give himself over to her loving; and when he had done this he would feel less a man, and she would know that he felt less a man, and the knowledge would be anguish to her. Then, with the sudden inconsequence of woman, she herself would feel helpless and small; she would long to burst out crying in his arms, so that he might pet her and comfort. But no tears were ever permitted to fall, because she was patient and strong. Patient as peasant women are patient who have long submitted themselves to their men, asking little in return; strong as those bygone Legions were strong, who had flung the straight, white roads across the world, and had trodden them unafraid. No, Maddalena's eyes would be dry, but in her unhappiness she must needs push him from her—in the end she would have to let him go after all, till the pain of his nearness subsided.

'But what is the matter?' he would say, bewildered. 'What have I done, Maddalena?'

And she would not dare to answer that question, lest in the answering she should become weak—weak and unable to shield him. Finally he would feel aggrieved and unhappy; angry, too, as the blind may feel angry, who stumble and hurt themselves in their blindness. He would go back to work with the uncomfortable conviction that he did not understand his wife, that he did not quite understand himself either. Surely he had all that he had longed for in the past? Companionship, love—oh, a great deal of love—as for children, well, perhaps they would come along later; at present he was very well pleased to be free from the tax they would be on his purse.

His work would be waiting, there would be much to do, a hundred little duties to perform; and gradually, as the evening wore on, his mind would be gathered back into the Doric. He would pass to and fro among the diners, the distinguished-looking men, the beautiful women—all feeling just a little more brilliant than usual because of the good food and wine. Like a general and his chief of staff, he and Roberto would hurry their waiters to the kitchens and cellars, to those vast armouries that contained all the weapons wherewith to slay lassitude and boredom. Back they would come, the neat, black-and-white army, very well equipped to slay lassitude and boredom; very well equipped to slay other things, too, such as a passing scruple. Gian-Luca would watch with experienced eyes for a self-controlled face to relax; he would listen for the subtle change in a voice, in a laugh, for the voices and laughter to mingle; he would know just how long a time should elapse between the popping of a cork and the coming of the miracle. If all went well in his octagon room he would feel a glow of satisfaction; he would feel a passing affection for his diners, who were doing him credit, and via him the Doric, forgetting that they looked upon him as a machine, or not caring if he remembered. And when he got home there would be Maddalena ready to wake up and talk; a placid and gentle Maddalena again, whose beauty was that of a vine-clad arbour where a man might rest after toil.

'It was just a passing mood,' he would think, 'all women are like that, they have funny moods.' And as like as not he would go to sleep happy, holding on to her hand.

CHAPTER FIVE

I

GIAN-LUCA had been married for just three years when there came those mighty rumours of war in the July of 1914. Millo had expected an excellent season, but in June an Austrian archduke had been murdered—a grave, kindly man who deserved a better fate—and Millo had begun to feel uneasy. By the middle of July he felt still more uneasy, while to Old Compton Street came a wave of apprehension coupled with incredulous surprise.

'It cannot mean war,' said Teresa firmly, 'the financiers of Europe will never allow it. Is not the world ruled by money?'

'It cannot mean war,' repeated Fabio weakly. 'As you say, it cannot mean war.'

'If it comes it will ruin us all——' moaned Nerone; 'but then the English are such a calm people, England would never go plunging into war.' And at this thought he almost began to love England for breeding so calm a people.

'If only I had Geppe home!' fretted Rosa.

'He will come, he will come!' Mario told her cheerily. 'Why should he not come, donna mia? This would not be Italy's war.'

'Who knows, if they once start fighting——' she persisted; 'I wish that our Geppe were home. Suppose I should never see him again——'

'Dio! You women!' snapped Mario.

Rocca said: 'And so here is war at last, and it finds me a miserable butcher. All that I am fit for is to slice little goats, or to chop through the bones of a lamb!'

'You talk rubbish,' declared the Signora Rocca. 'Who says there will be war?'

'I do,' replied her husband, 'I, who once was a soldier.' Then he swore a great oath, and his eyes filled with tears. 'It is coming, it is coming, and I am too old—they will not allow me to fight.'

The Padrone of the Capo di Monte felt angry. 'Has the whole world gone mad?' he demanded. 'What is the meaning of all this great fuss? And over a dog of an Austrian too! Why do I read in my morning paper that stocks and shares are falling to pieces? Here have I worked for these English for years, and now they will not protect me. What has happened, has England fallen asleep? Why cannot England *do* something?'

By July the 25th they were really alarmed, for the bourse in Vienna had closed. Three days later there was war between Austria and Servia, and two days after that they saw in their papers that Russia was mobilizing. But worse was to come, for by the end of July the banks all over England had closed their doors.

'I cannot get a penny of my money,' said Teresa, and her voice was deeply shocked and surprised. 'Not a penny of my hard-earned money can I get—yet England is not at war.'

Disconcerting days for those who had lived so long in the most placid country on earth. They looked at each other with frightened eyes.

'What can it mean?' they kept on repeating.

England had stood to them all in the past less as a country than as bullion, and now the doors of her banks were closed —was she not quite so rich as they had imagined? Would she go bankrupt and all of them with her?'

'What have I always said!' stormed Nerone. 'Madonna! I am glad that my money is not here, I am glad that in my wisdom I have sent it all home; it is I who have shown great foresight!'

There were new lines now on Teresa's old face; she thought a great deal but spoke very little, for only she knew the exact amount that was owed by her firm to the bank. She had recently borrowed another small sum, just before the assassination—she had needed a more convenient counter and a range of larger glass cases. But her mouth was set in a hard, straight line, and her black eyes never wavered. When her shop was raided by people who feared that they might be asked to consume less food, Teresa stood firm as a rock in her cash-desk.

'I will not take five-pound notes,' she announced; 'I accept only silver and gold, if you please."

And they paid her in silver and gold if they had it—if they had not, then their motor-cars went away empty.

'We will save the Casa Boselli,' said Teresa. 'If Europe has gone mad, we at least remain sane; we will save the Casa Boselli.'

And Fabio, very old and thoroughly frightened, nodded and answered, 'Sí, sí.' But his heart misgave him when he looked round the shop. Denuded it was, as though by the passing of an impious swarm of locusts. 'Supposing we cannot renew our stock!' he thought. 'Supposing the transport is held up——'

2

Gian-Luca was taking late service at the Doric when the news came that England had joined in the war; like lightning it spread from table to table, and people suddenly stopped eating. Millo, rather pale but perfectly composed, whispered a word to his band; there was silence for a moment, and then through the restaurant sounded the National Anthem. A strange, new meaning the hymn had that night. So simple and yet so poignant a meaning, that something leapt into Gian-Luca's heart, a feeling of bitter resentment. The clients at his tables had forgotten their suppers, of one accord they stood up and sang.

'They are singing because they have a country!' thought Gian-Luca. And presently when the singing had ceased, he turned away from those people.

But in the large restaurant he ran into Riccardo, whose eyes were unusually bright. Riccardo's perfect manner had completely left him, he appeared to forget that he was a head-waiter, and seizing Gian-Luca's unwilling arm, he dragged him behind a screen.

'Dio! It is here?' exclaimed Riccardo. 'If only our Italy comes in! Surely our country will fight against Austria? Think of it, amico, we have waited so long, and now at last we get our chance!'

Gian-Luca was silent, and this angered Riccardo. 'Do you not feel for our country?' he demanded.

'It is not my country,' said Gian-Luca sullenly. 'I am told that it is not my country.'

3

Maddalena was waiting up for her husband; she came into the hall when she heard his latch-key. They stared at each other in silence for a moment, then she put her arms round him and kissed him.

'This is a terrible thing——' said Maddalena; 'a solemn and a terrible thing.'

'Terrible perhaps, but splendid for those who may fight for the country they spring from, mia donna—if Italy comes into the war——'

'Then Geppe will go,' she said thinking of Rosa.

He laughed bitterly: 'Già, then Geppe will go, and Riccardo who is still just young enough to fight, and Alano who is almost too young, and all the others—but not Gian-Luca; he will not be wanted, he may feel he is Italian, but who was his father? They will say: "You have not got a name, Gian-Luca, we are very much afraid that your mother became English, so as you are a bastard, you too became English." Dio!' he shouted, stamping like a child. 'Dio! I almost hate the English!'

She surveyed him very sorrowfully for a moment, then she said: 'This country has sheltered you, amore.' And as she said it she felt afraid, realizing the meaning of her words.

'No country has ever sheltered me,' he retorted; 'what I am I have made myself, Maddalena. I owe nothing to any man on earth but myself.' Then all of a sudden he wanted to cry. 'But I wish I were the little Alano——' he muttered.

'Italy may not come in,' she consoled.

'Oh, yes, she will surely come in,' he told her. 'There is something in my blood to-night that tells me that my people will fight—but it will not make any difference to me; I am English in the eyes of the law.'

'But what if this England should need you?' she faltered; and all her woman's weakness urged her to silence, for nothing was steadfast at that moment but her soul.

Gian-Luca's mouth grew arrogant and angry. 'If England needs me she can fetch me,' said Gian-Luca.

4

Six weeks later Geppe managed to get home, his military service having come to an end. He swaggered into the shop one evening; he had not let them know of his prospective arrival.

'Ah,' said Nerone, 'so you have returned!' But he could not quite keep the excitement from his voice. 'Rosa!' he called, 'here is someone to see us—a fine young soldier from home!'

Rosa came hurrying down the stairs. 'Is it my Geppe?' she almost screamed, and seeing that it was she burst into tears and wept in the arms of her son.

Geppe was very much what he had been, except that he now wore a miniature moustache and carried his shoulders better. His eyes were bloodshot from sun and wind, and his hands, which his mother examined anxiously, were covered with corns in the place of blisters; for the rest he was plump and still rather flabby in spite of two years in the army. But to Rosa, gazing at him through her tears, he seemed a thing of rare beauty.

Nerone said: 'I will put up the shutters, and then we can talk in peace.' And this from Nerone was a great concession, it meant that he welcomed his grandson home, that the hatchet was buried for the moment.

Geppe helped himself to a cigarette from an open box on the counter. 'Italy will not come in,' he announced, though so far no one had asked for his opinion.

However, Nerone paused for a moment in his task of putting up the shutters. 'It is surely you who must know,' he said agreeably, 'since you are just from the army.'

The shop closed for the night, they retired to the room that was full of Nerone's birds. Geppe promptly woke up the avadavats by puffing smoke into their cage.

'I think I will go and fetch Fabio,' remarked Nerone; 'also Rocca may like to come round.'

Alone with her son, Rosa stroked his large hand. 'Mio bimbo——' she murmured. 'Mio bimbo.'

'Where is papa?' inquired Geppe, feeling that his father ought to be among his admirers.

'At the Capo, tesoro. He works very hard, and they have not yet raised his wages——'

'As for that,' laughed Geppe, 'I know all about hard work! In the army we do not think waiters work hard—however, that is as it may be.' He crossed one leg manfully over the other, and groped for a fresh cigarette.

'I will go into the shop and buy you a packet,' said his mother, looking in her purse for a coin that she would afterwards give to Nerone.

Presently Nerone came stumping back, accompanied by Fabio and Rocca.

'Buona sera, Capitano!' said Rocca jovially, and he slapped Geppe's shoulder with tremendous vigour.

'This is splendid, splendid!' smiled Fabio.

'And now,' said Nerone, 'we would hear all the news How is our beloved country looking?'

'Very hot at the moment, very ugly and hot,' muttered Geppe, whose shoulder was aching.

'And what of the war?' inquired anxious Fabio. 'Do you think that Italy will fight?'

'Neanche per sogno!' Geppe answered promptly. 'There is no chance of such a thing.'

'What is that?' demanded Rocca. 'What is that you say? Perhaps I have not heard correctly.'

But Geppe, nothing daunted, repeated his words, and he added: 'Why should we fight?'

'Giurabbaccaccio!' began Rocca, very red.

'Now do let us have peace, here, at any rate,' pleaded Fabio.

'Peace!' thundered Rocca. 'You ask me for peace! I, who have known Garibaldi!'

'That will not make our country go to war,' remarked Geppe; 'I tell you that we remain neutral.'

'Per Bacco! You lie!' shouted outraged Rocca.

'Let us try to keep calm,' said Nerone unexpectedly; 'I would hear what the boy has to say.'

Rocca glared round the room. 'Must I sit here and listen?' he demanded; but as nobody troubled to answer, he was forced to listen or go.

Geppe, lounging grandly in his chair, began to give all of a hundred reasons why Italy would not come in. He talked loudly in order to cheer himself up. He kept racking his brain for convincing arguments that he himself could believe. Fabio was relieved, and even Nerone was gradually being persuaded, when Rocca got slowly on to his feet and held up his hand for silence. They all turned to stare in surprise at his face, which had suddenly grown very grave. His voice when he spoke was very grave too, not blustering as was its wont.

'I am only a miserable butcher,' said Rocca, 'and one who, alas, has grown old. To our young men the glory, to our old men the patience—because they are past the time for glory. But we who are old have heard many things, and some who are still alive have seen them; and those who have seen can never forget, and those who have heard remember. We have heard of the White Coats swarming in Milan; we have heard of our women flogged in the streets and our patriots hung from the lamp-posts. We have heard of the glorious Risorgimento—of Mazzini, and the martyr Menotti, and of many a youth much younger than Geppe who died that Italy might live. And this I say to you all this night, if my country stops out of the war, I disown her—I who have fought in the second Custozza, I who have seen the Austrian's blood, and the blood from my own three wounds; I who have known our father Garibaldi —yes, even I, Rocca, will cast off my country, I will take her no more for my mother. The ghosts of her patriots shall walk through her streets, wailing and wringing their hands; the spirits of her virgins whom the Austrians deflowered, shall come back and proclaim their deflowering; and Rocca will go in sorrow to his grave, because he will be as a man without a country. May the saints put a sword into Italy's hand, and may Italy use that sword!'

Then Nerone struck the floor with his wooden leg. 'Amen,' he said huskily. 'Amen.'

And Fabio, forgetting his naturalization, forgetting the debts of the Casa Boselli, stumbled over to Rocca and gripped his arm; and they both tried to stand very straight, like the young.

Rosa looked at her only son and through him and beyond

him at her country, and at all those mothers long since dead and gone, and at all their sons who had laid down their lives, whom she seemed to see living again in Geppe——

'Our country will use that sword,' she said quietly, 'and Geppe shall help her to use it. My Geppe is brave, he is anxious to fight.'

'Of course I am anxious to fight,' murmured Geppe, staring down at his cigarette.

5

That winter the nations settled in grimly to their struggle of life and death; while at home, in familiar, foggy old London—grown oddly unfamiliar somehow in those days—men and women struggled fiercely and almost as grimly to keep the business flag flying.

Millo, in his office, sat long into the night scheming, calculating, foreseeing. How to maintain the prestige of the Doric at a time when his world was falling to pieces, that was Millo's great problem. He sent for the heads of departments and addressed them as a field-marshal might address his generals.

'We are face to face with disaster——' said Millo, 'not financial disaster, for our company is rich, but something even worse, a total collapse of our splendid organization. Each of you will have many arduous new duties for which no money can pay. Already we have lost our most skilled French chefs, only old men and boys are left in the kitchen, but the boys must grow wise and the old men young, for it shall not be said that because there is war we no longer know how to cook. I foresee a coming shortage of food, yet somehow food we must find; if it is not precisely what we have been used to, we must aim at keeping this fact from our clients; we must coax it, disguise it, dress it up in fine clothes, so that they eat it gladly. I foresee a coming shortage of waiters —for Italy will soon be at war—but waiters we must have; I shall aim at getting Swiss, failing them we must do with the unfit English and the ageing—those rejected by the army. Several of you head-waiters will go; Riccardo, Giovanni, Roberto for instance; but you Giuliano, are well over age, I can count on you for the grill-room. The Swiss are a fairly hard-working people, your trouble will lie with the English, who, even when perfectly sound, make vile waiters; in my long experience I have only known one who was all that a waiter should be, but then he had lived among us for years—I remember we called him Luigi—you may have to put up with very many things, but do not come grumbling to me. Gian-Luca, here, will be able to help me; he is only Italian by blood it seems—he is English, he tells me, in the eyes of the law, but so far he does not feel called upon to enlist, and for this I cannot but be thankful. And now,' he concluded, 'just one last word; let there be no small jealousies among you. Away with such things! The times are too momentous; we must concentrate our energies entirely on our clients, and through them on the prestige of the Doric.'

Thus it was that the Doric buckled on its armour and girded its loins for battle; while Millo assured his Board of Directors, that if all Europe crumbled yet the Doric should stand as the emblem of perfection in restaurants.

6

Teresa, at the Casa Boselli, eyed her husband with open disfavour, for Fabio was growing more futile every day—he had taken to sitting about in the parlour holding his head in his hands.

'Already the transport is so slow,' he would mutter; 'what will it be like later on? Already the Germans are attacking the food ships—what can we do without food?'

And Fabio was right, there were many little luxuries that looked like disappearing from the price-list—those fat, green, globular snails for instance. No one had time to go hunting snails, they were too busy hunting Germans.

At moments now he gave way altogether. 'We are done, we are finished!' he wept.

Then Teresa remembered how much they owed the bank. The moratorium had saved them for a time, but now the bank was demanding higher interest, or failing that, repayment of the loan, and she did not blame the bank either. The Casa Boselli was dipped to the hilt, the leases of both shops had been pledged as security; if she could not meet the interest then the bank must take action, and all in a moment, in the twinkling of an eye, there might be no Casa Boselli. But Teresa had not fought against grief and shame, and even her God, for nothing.

'Coward!' she said, looking with scorn at her husband. 'You call yourself a man and you weep like a child! Have we not got our macaroni factory? Is not the Doric and many another restaurant clamouring more loudly than ever for our paste? To hear you one would think we were reduced to black-beetles; and suppose we were, I would pickle them with capers, I would surely contrive to make them the fashion, rather then let our business go bankrupt.' And her fierce eyes scorched up the old man's tears, so that he dared not go on weeping.

Nerone had a great consolation in life, since everyone was buying cigarettes for the soldiers; but his first kind impulse on Geppe's return was fast giving place to indignation, for Geppe was more useless than ever in the shop, in addition to which he now bragged.

'Here is no life for a soldier,' he would say; 'when I was in the army I could out-march them all, and as for my shooting there was nothing to beat it! A man smokes tobacco, he does not sell it.' And this when Nerone, persuaded at last, was actually paying him wages!

Once again their quarrels resounded through the house, more violent than ever, now that Geppe was older.

'I have got a dog for a grandson,' said Nerone; 'a lazy, insolent, lousy dog. What have I done to deserve it?'

And in the very middle of all the confusion, who should turn up but Berta with her twins.

'I'm going to make shells for Albert,' announced Berta. 'My Albert's enlisted, and the least I can do is to make ammunition for the poor old dear.' So she left the twins for her mother to look after, quite forgetting that *they* had been made for Albert, who much preferred them to shells.

Well, now there were babies again in the house, and rather fussy little babies. Poor Rosa, grown fat and a trifle breathless, found herself running up and down with bottles, trying first this patent mixture then that, in order to pander to their fancies. She who had come to the enviable age when the hips may grow larger and larger, she who had nursed Gian-Luca and reared him, then Geppe in addition to the

inconsiderate Berta, must now perforce rear a pair of outraged twins, who preferred death it seemed, to the bottle.
And Mario, who seldom protested these days, bore their
colic-rent nights without a murmur; while Nerone, after
storming and threatening to drown them, could never
resist playing with Berta's offspring, because in his heart
he adored all babies, whether they were English or Italian.

CHAPTER SIX

I

IN SPITE of many doubts and contradictory statements, of party politics for and against, Italy came into the war. Then it was that from the windows near Coldbath Square, and from Aunt Ottavia's windows in the square itself, there appeared as though by magic, strips of green, white and red; little flags, like humble hands stretched out towards the mother country from the poverty and squalor of her namesake. In Old Compton Street, however, might be seen two, splendid banners, one on Rocca's shop, the other on Nerone's; while the Casa Boselli, that displayed the Allied emblems, now added yet another to the group above the door. Teresa's heart leapt with a sudden, fierce pride, then sank with a dreadful sense of fear; for how could she hope to obtain provisions—all those strange, delicious things that had made her shop so famous—if the country that provided the bulk of her stock might itself be faced with starvation?

She was careful to hide these fears from Fabio, but Fabio had fears of his own; he knew quite as well as Teresa could know what this might mean to their business. But although his hands shook as he put up the flag, and his old cheeks were paler than usual, he lifted a fold of the flag and kissed it, for nature is stronger than naturalization.

Mario and Rosa looked at their son, and Mario said: 'It is hard to be a father—now if I were your brother we could fight together, we could share the hardship, the honour and the glory. If only I were not too old, Geppe!'

Nerone was like a creature possessed; Rosa became almost anxious about him.

'Guarda!' he exclaimed; 'my very matches march!'

He stumped around the shop and up and down the street, talking volubly and loudly to any who would listen, giving packets of Italian cigarettes to passing Tommies—yes, actually giving away his tobacco.

'Now you are safe, we are all safe,' he told them; 'Italy will win the war!'

'Papà, you are wearing yourself out,' protested Rosa; 'a man of your age to behave so—it is foolish!'

'To-day I am not an old man,' said Nerone; 'to-day I am Italy, the eternal.'

Only Geppe, of them all, was strangely pale and silent, moving as though in a dream. His loose-lipped mouth sagged a little at the corners; sagged as it had done when he was a baby, and Rosa had taken away her hand.

'Eat, tesoro, my pretty,' urged his mother at dinner noticing his untouched food; 'those who are going to protect us must eat, so that they may become strong.'

'I think that my stomach is upset,' muttered Geppe; 'I do not feel very hungry.'

Rosa was constantly forcing back her tears, trying to be Spartan and splendid; trying to rejoice that she had a son to give to her country in its need. Whenever his eyes were upon her she smiled, but her smile was not reassuring; it got on Geppe's nerves; as soon as he could he made an excuse and went out. He did not return until late that night, and when he came in at past twelve o'clock, Rosa, who was waiting up anxiously for him, knew that her son had been drinking.

2

Two days later Geppe received the order to rejoin his regiment at once. He sat staring helplessly down at the paper where it lay on the breakfast-table. Through his poor, shrinking mind surged a chaos of ideas. He would tell them all that he dared not go; he would rush to the docks and get aboard a ship bound for some neutral port; he would fling himself on his grandfather's mercy and beg and implore him to hide him; he would cling to his mother and surely she would help him, perhaps if he cried she would find a way to help him as she had done when he was little; he would go to the chemist and buy enough strychnine; he could say that it was needed to kill a wounded cat—anything, anything, anything but war! He had heard of the sort of things that happened in war on his journey home through France. That little, innocent bit of paper, how could it mean so much? If he tore it to pieces that would not help him, for the thing was possessed of life everlasting; destroy it and there was its damnable spirit waiting to drive and hound him. No good, no good, he must make a clean breast, he must speak now, revealing his shame, he must say to them all: 'For Christ's sake, help me! I am sick with the fear of going.'

He looked up, his mouth was already half open; then he met all those terrible eyes. Six terrible eyes in three terrible faces—terrible because so trustful, so gentle; so intolerably, pathetically proud. Nerone's old eyes almost patient and loving, because his grandson was a soldier; Mario's eyes very big, very round, and full to the brim with the pride of his manhood, because he had made a man; Rosa's eyes all swimming in tears, but with something like sunlight behind them—Rosa's motherhood looking out through the storm, making the beauty of a rainbow round her—a rainbow, the emblem of promise.

Geppe's own eyes dropped again to the paper which he folded and put in his pocket; and something of Rosa's glory reached him, so that when next he looked up at them all his trembling mouth was smiling. He nodded and managed to throw back his shoulders, managed to light a cigarette; not knowing in the least why he did these things, but suddenly feeling that they had to be done.

So that was how Geppe went to the war. In less than a week he was gone. Nerone could brag to Rocca of his grandson, and Mario could hold his head high at the Capo. Per Bacco! Why not? Was he not a proud father? Had he not every reason to be proud?

Only Rosa, bombarding the saints with her prayers, knew that her son was afraid. She did not implore them to give Geppe life, but courage in the face of death.

3

Italy was calling her children home; very soon three waiters had gone from the Capo and only Mario remained.

In the place of his waiters the Padrone put women, for men were increasingly difficult to come by, and those who had had a little experience could find work at the larger restaurants. These women were careless and inefficient and the wages they demanded were high; but someone must carry the food to the tables, and somehow the Capo must keep its doors open. The Padrone swore terrible oaths in his heart, but outwardly he submitted. So at last Mario found himself a head-waiter with his salary actually raised, for the harassed Padrone was almost reduced to looking upon Mario as a godsend.

'At least, I have you, my Mario,' he said; 'you at least know the ways of the Capo. Dio! These women are enough to drive one mad, but we two must work together like brothers.'

And Mario was so touched that he almost wept—such kindness, such praise from the Padrone!

'I always knew it must come in the end,' he told Nerone; 'to-day you behold in me the head-waiter of the Capo di Monte. Everything comes to him who has patience.'

4

Roberto, the wine-waiter, was the first to leave the Doric, and before he went he said to Gian-Luca: 'Now I may realize the dream of my life, now I may learn how to fly. As a child I would watch the birds in the air, I would think: "If only I too had wings."—Well, now my country shall provide me with wings; I shall ask to join the Air Service.'

Gian-Luca looked down at the little man with interest; so Roberto was longing to fly. Roberto had never shown signs of any longings; he had just been very neat, very skilful, very quick, with a most retentive memory for a vintage; and all the time he had been longing for wings, longing to conquer the air—perhaps he had longed to fly out of the Doric—what a curious thing was life.

A few weeks later went Giovanni, the trancheur, and he too confided in Gian-Luca. The war was loosening all tongues it seemed.

'I hope I may never come back——' said Giovanni. 'I shall try to get killed very soon.'

'Madonna! But why?' inquired Gian-Luca, startled. 'You are such a wonderful trancheur, Giovanni; Millo will certainly keep your place open—what have you got to complain of?'

Giovanni looked away: 'It is not that, my friend, I know I am an excellent trancheur—but when a man has a great pain in his heart——'

'Not that girl who married the porter, surely!'

'Ma sí, my Anna,' Giovanni nodded gravely.

Gian-Luca stared incredulously at him—all this sorrow it seemed, over Anna. Anna had not even been attractive, a red-haired girl with the eyes of a fox—and after the first not a sigh from Giovanni, not a tremor of that long, thin, accurate knife. What a curious thing was love.

5

One day soon after Giovanni's departure, Gian-Luca was sent for by Millo. Millo was looking both tired and worried.

'Now we are going to lose Riccardo,' he said; 'this is a fearful war!' He stared at Gian-Luca in silence for a moment, and then: 'It is you who shall take his place, I will make you the head of the restaurant, with an increase of salary, of course.'

Gian-Luca thought: 'The large restaurant—ah, so I get it at last!' And he knew that he had been hoping for this, ever since Italy had joined in the war.

It seemed like a kind of revenge on life, this sudden rise in his fortunes—a revenge on Riccardo, whom Italy wanted. His heart was beating with fierce resentment, for one by one they were all going home, these neat, quiet waiters of the Doric; and one by one they would cease to be waiters, they would look upon splendid, terrible things, with the eyes of men who were brothers.

'My God! If only I could go with them——' he thought, 'if only I too belonged——' But his face was impassive as he stood before Millo, and his voice when he spoke was quite calm. He said: 'And the octagon room, signore? Who will take charge of my octagon room? It is very important, I have my special clients, I am used to their little fads.'

'Do you mean that you want that too?' inquired Millo, and the corners of his mouth twitched slightly.

'That is what I should very much like,' smiled Gian-Luca. 'I should like to undertake both rooms.'

Millo considered him thoughtfully, and his tolerant eyes were a little puzzled. There was something he did not understand about Gian-Luca, something very angry yet coldly ambitious, he had only suspected it of late. He could feel the hard, calculating thing as he sat there, and the nearness of it oppressed him. For even to Millo, engrossed in the Doric, came a sudden, unexpected revulsion.

'You have your ambitions, I observe,' he said quietly; 'oh, well, it is an ill wind that blows no one any good!'

'As you say, signore, a very ill wind—you are right, I have my ambitions.'

'Sit down,' ordered Millo, 'we must talk this thing out, we must see if your idea will work. You would wish to retain your old salary of course, to which I am to add Riccardo's—for you know and I know just how valuable you are, but above all you know it—is not that so, Gian-Luca?'

'Magari——' murmured Gian-Luca softly.

'Very well. But have you considered what this will mean?' You will have a motley crew of waiters under you, not the well-trained men that you have been used to—and soon you may have a few irritable clients, for our food is already less good than it has been. At the same time I will not lower my flag one instant before I must, therefore you will have to be answerable to me for the standard of two rooms instead of one. I have known a long time that of all my head-waiters you are undoubtedly the most competent, but no man can do more than his best, Gian-Luca; are you sure that your best will content me?'

'If it does not, signore, you have only to speak——'

'Very well,' said Millo, 'we will try it and see. Riccardo is going in ten days' time.'

Riccardo smiled rather unpleasantly when Gian-Luca told him the news. 'So at last you jump into my shoes,' he remarked. 'It pays well to feel that one has no country.'

Gian-Luca was patient. 'Perhaps——' he replied. He could very well afford not to lose his temper.

'Oh, yes, but surely!' retorted Riccardo. 'However, I have

a feeling in my bones that I am not going to get killed.'

'In that case you may get your old job back again, unless I should prove to be the better man, Riccardo.'

'And if you should prove to be the better man?'

'Then it is Millo who will have to decide. One cannot have everything in this world—you have a country and I have your job, that seems to me perfectly fair.'

Riccardo turned on his heel and left him. 'He means to oust me if he can,' he thought bitterly. 'He means to make himself indispensable to Millo, he has always wanted to oust me.'

Gian-Luca was thinking: 'If I were Riccardo, I would not be caring so much about my job, but since I am Gian-Luca, then I care very much—a man must care about something——'

6

And now Gian-Luca worked as never before, for he felt himself second only to Millo. There was no assistant manager above him, for Millo had always preferred to stand alone. He was not unlike a certain type of statesman who abrogates office after office to himself, mistrustful of other people's abilities. Oh, yes, there were accountants and clerks and cashiers, but what did they know about the ways of clients? Oh, yes, there was all that vast army belowstairs, but who but Gian-Luca was responsible now for the standard of the dishes they served? Giuliano's grill-room counted for little compared with the two restaurants. Giuliano was gentle if dishes went wrong, as they sometimes did now that the best chefs were gone, but not so Gian-Luca—he was difficult to please.

'Take this outrage back to the kitchen,' he would order. 'I asked for pommes soufflées, not greasy goloshes—and get that Sauce Béarnaise re-made, and be quick! I have clients waiting to be fed.'

Gian-Luca was cordially hated these days by all save Millo and his clients; but he kept the flag flying against terrific odds—he had pity neither for himself nor for others. Through all the stress and anxiety of war the Doric still stood forth proudly supreme, so that men home on leave said:

'Let's go to the Doric; it's the only place now where the service is decent and where you still get decent food.'

And they came in their dozens, these men home on leave, most of them still very young; some of them whole but some of them maimed, with eyes that no longer saw very clearly, or a leg that dragged between crutches.

'Hallo, Gian-Luca! Still here?' they would say, glad to find an old friend. 'Well, thank the Lord, no one's grabbed you yet—yes, all right, if you say so—it sounds jolly good—and bring us a bottle of champagne.' For they thought of him always as an Italian who was waiting to be called to his class.

Then Gian-Luca would see that they got food and wine, would see that they feasted on the fat of the Doric, for even against his will he must like them—they had seemed very different from this in the old days. Sometimes he would want to hurry away as he had that night when war was declared, but now it would be because he liked them too well. All the manhood that was in him would leap out towards them, towards the thing that they stood for. He would feel a sudden, imperative impulse to seize some brown-faced young soldier by the hand, to say:

'Take me along; I too want to fight.' But then he would remember himself and smile bitterly: 'These English are not my people,' he would think. 'Why should I go until I am taken? Here I am quickly making my fortune—well, why not? I am surely poorer than they are, for I have not even got a country.'

7

Another seven months of the war dragged by, and then came conscription in England. At first they took only the unmarried men which, however, did not deceive Millo. That February he said to Gian-Luca:

'I am going to lose you quite soon—the question is, how shall I replace you when it happens?'

Gian-Luca answered. 'I will stay until they fetch me.' And his mouth looked arrogant and stubborn.

'You have served me faithfully and well,' Millo told him. 'I do not forget good service. You have worked like ten men to keep your rooms going, and for that I want to say that I am grateful—well, I think that is all, Gian-Luca.'

That March came the news that Riccardo had been killed. Riccardo would never come back to the Doric, in spite of that feeling in his bones.

'So now I am sure of his place,' thought Gian-Luca. He felt no particular pity for Riccardo—after all, Riccardo had died for his country, and could there be a better way to die?

But Millo was secretly grieved in his heart, for the little Alano was also dead. Oh, but many who had faithfully served the Doric would never serve it again. Day after day alone in his office sat Millo, thinking always of food; struggling with problems of luncheons and dinners, of dwindling provisions and a dwindling staff. Secretly grieved in his heart, yes, perhaps; but doggedly determined to see the thing through; for war or no war, there were people to feed, people who still expected to be fed very much as they always had been.

8

When Gian-Luca was conscripted in the June of that year he was conscious of a great relief; thankful that the moment had arrived at last when he no longer had any choice in the matter.

He said to Maddalena: 'I am ready to go, I am ready to fight side by side with the English. There have been days lately when I have felt that I must fight. As a woman you may not understand; it is something that lies hidden in all men, I think—a kind of primitive instinct.'

And she answered: 'I am only a woman, amore, and my heart is terribly afraid—and yet I am glad to think that you go—so perhaps I do understand.'

Then his mind became practical again from long habit, and he smiled contentedly at her: 'I have managed to make certain of my job before going, my job will be waiting for me when I come back. I am lucky, for now I can go to the war with Millo tucked away in my pocket; he will never forget the work I have done, what the Doric owes to Gian-Luca.'

But a few days later he was greatly disturbed to find himself placed in the Army Service Corps. They said that with so much experience as a waiter, he might prove very useful to them.

'This is not what I want at all,' he protested. 'I wish to go out and fight.'

'Everyone must go where they are most useful now,' was all the reply he got.

'If you had your little fancies why didn't you enlist in the early days?' inquired a comrade-in-arms. 'In the early days a man could pick and choose, now it's just: "Do as you're told."' And he added, 'But you're not an Englishman, are you? Aren't you an Italian or something?'

'Whatever I am, I am good enough to fight,' said Gian-Luca, flushing darkly.

'Well, don't lose your shirt!' advised his acquaintance. 'When we're all out in France you can get yourself transferred.'

'Can I?' inquired Gian-Luca eagerly.

'Yes, of course, it's easy enough out there.'

Gian-Luca's spirits began to revive, and he made a joke of the thing to Maddalena. 'Of course it is all nonsense!' he told her laughing; 'I shall get transferred quite easily, they say. I am young and strong, they have only to see me.' And then he surveyed himself gravely in the glass, passing his hands down his slim, wiry flanks, thumping his broad, deep chest.

Maddalena hid the joy in her heart—her heart that had been so terribly afraid—and because she was a woman who loved very greatly, she sent up a quick little prayer to the Madonna that Gian-Luca might never get transferred. For most of that night she prayed to the Madonna and now every morning and evening she would pray, for this seemed like a sign of God's infinite mercy.

Gian-Luca went off to his training in high spirits, so sure did he feel of his transfer. As the camp was near London he got home fairly often, and Maddalena marvelled at the new gayness of him, he seemed to have grown so much younger. He would stroll about smoking the traditional Gold Flake, making fun of his duties in the Army Service Corps.

'It is not precisely the Doric!' he told her, and then he

laughed, remembering the food, 'and yet it is rather like, too——,' he added, 'and that is what makes it so funny. However, I shall not remain long at this job, there is other work waiting out there in France.'

He was thoughtful and gentle with her at this time, considering her plans in his absence. 'You had better stay here where you are,' he advised. 'You will have the separation allowance, but in any case there is plenty of money tucked away for you at the bank.'

'But that is for your future,' she protested, astonished. 'That is our nest-egg for your restaurant.'

'The future will take care of itself,' he said glibly. 'Be saving, of course, but meanwhile you must live; I do not want to think of your going without things—there is plenty of money at the bank.'

One day he strolled into the public library and there he found the Librarian. He had not seen him now for nearly a year.

'Hallo!' said Gian-Luca, then he stopped abruptly—the Librarian's hair was quite white.

The Librarian said: 'So you are in khaki? Have you made up your mind to go?'

'The Government made it up for me,' smiled Gian-Luca.

'Oh, of course,' said the Librarian. 'Conscription—I forgot.'

He looked very small as he stood at his desk, the more so as he now stooped badly.

'What news of your sons?' Gian-Luca inquired.

'No news——' said the Librarian. 'They can't send me news now.'

'Why not?'

'Because they were killed six months ago within a week of each other.'

There ensued a painful interval of silence, then Gian-Luca stammered: 'I am sorry.'

'Oh, yes—and I am sorry too,' said his friend. 'After all, I did love them better than books—does that surprise you, Gian-Luca?' He did not seem to expect an answer, for he went on to talk about the war. He discussed it as though it were some curious volume whose contents had left him bewildered. 'I do try, but I can't understand it——' he said. 'Why must human beings do such things? A lovely world—a wonderful world—and all broken up and trodden to pieces—yet when my two boys said they wished to enlist, it was I who encouraged them to go. It was I who felt a deep hatred of the Germans—a far deeper hatred than either of my sons—my sons went out from a sense of duty, but I would have gone to kill—and that's funny too, in a man of my sort who has spent all his life among peaceful things like books.'

'But I feel as you do!' Gian-Luca said quickly. 'Surely we must all feel as you do.'

'Yet now I don't hate any more——' said the Librarian, 'because they have killed both my sons, I can't hate—that seems very queer to me——'

'It is queer,' thought Gian-Luca. 'He is suffering from shock.' And as soon as he could he made his escape; that white hair had begun to depress him. 'I must go,' he said suddenly, holding out his hand. 'I am only on very short leave.'

'Well, God bless you——' muttered the little Librarian, and he turned again to his books.

9

There came an afternoon a few months later when the real good-byes must be said. Gian-Luca and his wife went to Old Compton Street, where the clan had gathered itself together as it did on all momentous occasions.

Fabio wept as he kissed Gian-Luca, remembering that night many years ago when his cheek had been pressed against an unwanted child—'Little Gian-Luca come to Nonno,' he had said. So now, because he was growing very old, he must needs shed a few facile tears. Rosa was there with Berta's twins whom she had not dared to leave at home, for like the other young things whom Rosa had cared for, the twins had become unruly. Nerone was there, with twenty-four packets of good Macedonia which he pressed upon Gian-Luca; and after a little Mario came in, then Rocca with his signora.

Nerone grumbled: 'The English are slow, and as for the French, they are slower. Moreover the French stole those horses from St. Mark's—I consider it a pity that we fight for the French. However,' he added, 'it cannot be helped, and thank God we have Italy now; Italy will quickly finish up the war. Ma che! What a wonderful country!' And then he produced a snapshot of Geppe, which he carried about in his pocket. 'Here is young Italy!' said Nerone proudly. 'Does not the boy look magnificent?'

Rocca said: 'Give them a thrust from me, a good thrust in the belly, Gian-Luca, and remember to say as your bayonet goes in: "This is a present from Rocca!"'

Mario, whose eyes were moist with emotion, dared not speak because of the lump in his throat. Teresa was silent because, since the war, she so seldom spoke at all.

In the end Rosa threw her arms round Gian-Luca and her tears splashed on his tunic, just as they had splashed long ago on to his head, spoiling his appetite for breakfast. Everyone promised to be at the station to see the troop train depart; everyone kissed Gian-Luca on both cheeks, then seized both his hands and kissed him again—all save Teresa who kissed him on the forehead, coldly, as though she kissed because she must. And at that Maddalena's heart swelled with anger, and finding Gian-Luca's hand she pressed it. She, who was so gentle, hated old Teresa at that moment for a woman of iron and steel, for a woman without the bowels of compassion, who all through Gian-Luca's life had denied him.

But as they walked home together that evening, Gian-Luca said: 'Listen, my Maddalena, she grows old, the Padrona of the Casa Boselli—they are very short-handed in the shop, I notice. Will you not go and help Nonna sometimes? I think she would be very glad.'

Maddalena marvelled at his infinite patience, the patience that could keep him loyal to Teresa.

'I admire her so much,' he was saying thoughtfully, 'she is rather a splendid old woman, I think—and what a fine head she still has for business!'

Who could deny him so simple a request? Certainly not Maddalena at that moment. 'All that you wish I will do,' she promised, glancing at his calm, happy face in the lamplight—so calm, so happy, in spite of the fact that in three days' time he would leave her.

CHAPTER SEVEN

I

ALTHOUGH GIAN-LUCA had noticed before his departure that Teresa was very short-handed, the exigencies of his work at the Doric, and later on of his military training, had prevented his suspecting the full depths of the disaster that threatened the Casa Boselli. Even Maddalena who now went there daily, only vaguely suspected the truthat first; for how could she know the amounts that were owing? Teresa never spoke of these things; the deeper her trouble the less it became vocal—that was Teresa's way.

It was not a dearth of customers that was killing the business, but a dearth of commodities to sell them; a stoppage of nearly all the supplies that should have come from Italy or France. Italy was producing less and less, while daily requiring more and more for home consumption; one after another her exports were failing, and with them the tiny, struggling atom known as the Casa Boselli. Those fine new glass cases that had cost so much money, and that should have been harbouring delicious things to eat, now harboured nothing but mendacious tins—mendacious, because they were all completely empty. Fabio had scrubbed them and soldered down their tops, then set them along the shelves, for anything was better than the heart-breaking void in those acquisitive glass cases.

One by one the men employed by Teresa had been consumed by the war; like the food—the salami, prosciutto, mortadella, parmesan cheeses and decadent tomatoes—they had ceased to contribute to individual stomachs. For now there was only a universal stomach, whose size and capacity no man could gauge; the stomach of a horribly greedy modern Moloch, for whom the armies must be fattened.

The new shop was now almost entirely deserted, there being no Italians to tend it. Two young English girls who had stayed for a fortnight had left to work in an aeroplane factory; Teresa's eyes had got on their nerves—always watching, always spying, they had said. There had followed a series of young girls and men, all most unsatisfactory, according to Teresa; the English did not like her imperious ways, and she on her part thought them lazy, and said so. No doubt they were trying, but then so was Teresa, who spoke little, it is true, but those words when they came, were as hard and as sharp as her eyes. And then there had been those Zeppelins over London, which, while failing to strike real terror to the heart, had succeeded in laying a fuse to all tempers. People felt peppery after a raid, and Teresa's employees had proved no exception.

Maddalena was ordered to serve in the old shop, in which were now gathered together all the forces that remained to the Casa Boselli, that is, all save the last adventurous stronghold that still stood to Teresa as the symbol of success, her unique macaroni factory.

The macaroni factory! All night long she lay awake, as straight and as stiff as a corpse, beside Fabio; scarcely twitching a muscle in case she should rouse him, in case he might talk, disturbing her thoughts. All night the thoughts whirred like wheels in her head—like the wheels of the macaroni factory—wheels made of steel that turned faster and faster, stretching their leather bands tighter and tighter —and the bands were somehow a part of her head. All night those wheels whirred out first this thought then that, frightening thoughts because of the darkness. Not a German and Austrian invasion combined, not a sky full of Zeppelins, not a world full of fire, could have equalled in terror those whirring thoughts that came as she lay beside her husband.

For the macaroni factory was threatened on all sides, the forces of disruption were closing in upon it. There was now no expert left to attend to the machines, or to mix that enormous mountain of flour—sixty pounds with an egg to each pound. Francesco had been called up and with him the others, and in their stead, one poor, bewildered Anglo-Saxon struggled resentfully to cope with the pasta; and the longer he struggled the less apt he became in its delicate fabrication. And then there was the flour—a dreadful, grey mixture of wheat, barley, maize, and Heaven alone knew what other disgusting adulteration; a gravelly, husky, unpalatable outrage. Why, the very machines spewed it forth. You could turn it into something resembling dough, you could stir it and knead it and put it through the rollers—one hundred times you could roll it and more—and when you had finished, your fine rubber sheeting would be lumpy and harsh and vile to the touch as a hand that is covered with corns. Who could cut pasta from such stuff as this? Who could produce the simple Lasagne, let alone the ornate Bicorni?

'And yet,' Teresa would think in the darkness, 'I will *never* abandon my beautiful factory! Life itself has not beaten Teresa Boselli, then shall it be said that she is beaten by flour—so flimsy a thing, so foolish a thing, that a puff of breath can disperse it? I will master this accursed new filth they call flour—yes, but how? But how? But how?'

Every morning she would get up looking gaunter than ever, and would hurry down to her factory. There she would gaze with something like despair at the untidy traces of yesterday's failures. When the poor Anglo-Saxon arrived she would point with an angry, accusing finger.

'So much waste!' she would exclaim. 'You must make the flour go further.'

'Cawn't be done!' he would assure her, loudly sucking his teeth.

'It has got to be done,' Teresa would say coldly. 'If you cannot do it there are others who can.'

One day he had retorted: 'Very well then, you find 'em.' After which he had demanded his wages and had left.

'Imbecile! I am glad that he has gone,' frowned Teresa. 'I am glad to be rid of the untidy pig. I must find a younger man to take over this work.' But no one whom she found gave satisfaction.

2

That Christmas the pains in Fabio's back were rather more violent than usual, and in consequence he thought a great deal about God and much less about the Casa Boselli.

It was now his duty to help Maddalena to price their diminishing stock; his the task of watching a fluctuating market that bucked up and down like a turbulent bronco, thoroughly out of hand. But somehow those pains in his poor old back, together with his thoughts about God, made such trifles as customers, food and money, seem very far off and unimportant, so that sometimes now he would make mistakes, on the wrong side, too, for the Casa Boselli. Then it was that Teresa would undress him and rub him and swathe him in yards of red flannel; after which she would push him back again between the shafts, like an antiquated horse that only stands up because it is strapped to its toil. He would hobble about consulting his price list and dolefully shaking his head.

'Is it the bacon that has risen?' he would ask, 'or is it the last of those imported hams?' And Teresa would have to desert her cash-desk and reprice the stock herself.

Maddalena did all in her power to help them, but she had her own trouble to bear, for Gian-Luca's letters from France were very brief. He had not yet got his transfer, it seemed, and was working as a sergeant in charge of a Mess somewhere far back at the Base. He said very little because of the censor, but his wife could read between the lines, and what she read there was a great discontent. Those were dreary little letters that Gian-Luca wrote home from the Officers' Mess at the Base. And yet she was thankful, oh, deeply thankful to know that her man was safe; and now she redoubled her prayers to the Madonna, begging that the transfer might never be granted, begging that the creature she loved might come home unharmed when the war was ended. But sometimes while she prayed she would feel strangely guilty as though she were betraying Gian-Luca; as though she were plotting behind his back, as though she and the Madonna were plotting.

'It is only my fancy——' she would try to tell herself. 'Every poor woman, all over Europe, is praying for her husband's safety.' Yet so anxious was she that she went to St. Peter's to consult old Father Antonio.

Father Antonio smiled at her confession and proceeded to reassure her. 'Your prayers will be answered as God thinks best. He knows that you pray for your husband's conversion, and He knows that you must pray for his safe return, for is it not He who puts love in the heart, and who knows the way of that love? I would not worry about it, my daughter, I would just confide in the Madonna, and she, through God's grace, will do what is best—I think I would leave it all to her.'

After that Maddalena felt a little more happy, but she wished that Gian-Luca could get leave. His letters said nothing about coming home; perhaps he was afraid of losing his transfer—perhaps he was staying out there by choice, hoping to get sent into the trenches if he stayed—could he do that? She wondered.

Meanwhile Teresa now sat long into the night, trying to balance her accounts. She would have to go upstairs to rub Fabio's lumbago, but when she had done this she would go down again to her office and get out her ledgers. Perhaps a letter would have come that evening—a letter from the bank, requesting payment of the interest that was overdue; a letter that she dared not ignore for a moment, while not knowing how to answer. Alone in her office sat hard old Teresa facing defeat and disgrace; facing an incredibly empty world as she had done nearly thirty years ago. Then she had lost the fruit of her womb, Olga, the belovèd; and now she might lose the fruit of her brain, the fruit of a lifetime of unceasing toil—the belovèd Casa Boselli.

'Cento, duecento cinquanta——' she would mutter, staring down at the figures; and then she would get up to pace her small office, and then she would sit down again. She would think: 'If only we could get our supplies, if *only* we could get our supplies!' There were moments now when she would have walked to Rome in order to fetch a tin of tomatoes. Then her thoughts would begin to spin round and round like the wheels in the macaroni factory; 'My pasta— my wonderful pasta——' she would murmur, and her voice would be almost tremulous with sadness. 'Who can I find who will make me my pasta, now that Francesco has gone?

3

After Christmas Fabio felt a little better, and so he thought less about God. Indeed, by the New Year he had almost recovered, and this was to the good, for the factory machines were crying out loudly for attention. Fabio, so his wife had discovered since the war, had a very cunning hand with machines; he could make fine adjustments with accuracy, oiling and coaxing the while.

'Sii buono, sii bravo; suvvia!' he would coax; and then, strange to say, the machines would run smoothly, as though they wished to pleased Fabio.

That January Fabio adjusted the machines, after which they gave much less trouble; but by March there was no one in the factory to run them, for the latest acquisition had thrown up his job, preferring to make munitions. Now indeed Teresa had her back against the wall, for she could not replace the man. There was plenty of good work going those days, and better wages than she paid to be earned. Then week by week the flour was growing worse, becoming more difficult to mix; she would gladly have taken on the factory herself but that she must needs be always in the cash desk; and as for Maddalena, she was wanted in the shop, besides which she had never learnt how to make pasta. Yes, but old Fabio had—he might try to deny it, but Teresa knew that he lied. As a lad he had worked in a macaroni factory, he had told her so many times in the past, it was therefore quite useless to lie. And, moreover, it was being a deserter, a traitor to the Casa Boselli in its need.

'It is you who must make the pasta,' she told him, 'it is you who must run the machines, it is you who must help me to save our business. Ma che! You are old, but you are still a man, and you know how the pasta should be made.'

'No, no,' he whimpered, 'I do not know, Teresa. If I once knew, then I have forgotten—and my arms have grown weak for the kneading of flour, and my back is weak too from those horrible pains. As God is my witness I cannot do it! I am old—very old, Teresa.'

'Yes, and I too am old,' she answered harshly, 'but I do not whine like a cur. I say: "No, I am not yet utterly defeated, and while I have breath I fight." '

'But my back, my miserable back——' he pleaded, peering at her face with dim eyes.

'A little work will limber your back; a little work hurts no man,' said Teresa.

And knowing that further resistance was useless, Fabio muttered 'Sí, sí.'

So all through that war-racked, agonizing spring Fabio tried to make pasta; tried to lift and carry and knead and roll the strange-coloured flour, till his agèd arms were corded with hard, blue veins. It was pitiable how little he made, considering his long hours of toil—not enough to throw to a coop of chickens, according to Teresa—but Fabio worked on in an anguish of spirit; dumb, too, because when a man had grown old what was the use of complaining? The sweat would go pouring down both his cheeks and drip into the dough unperceived; and sometimes there would come a queer singing in his ears, and long, floating black things in front of his eyes, so that he must needs stop and take off his glasses, in order to brush away those black things. But the black things would remain, and now in addition some flour would have got into his eye; and when this happened he would go to Maddalena, who would make him wet his handkerchief with the tip of his tongue, after which she would wipe out the flour.

'Poverino!' she would think as he turned to leave her. 'Poverino! He grows very feeble. It is cruel to make him do such heavy work—but then Teresa is cruel.'

Yet in spite of herself she was forced to admire this woman of steel and iron, this gallant old pilot who clung to the wheel while the storm increased in fury; this woman who did not spare Fabio, it was true, but who did not spare herself either. When Maddalena wrote to Gian-Luca these days, she wrote with admiration of Teresa; but she did not tell him what she herself suspected, namely, that the Casa Boselli must go under in spite of those hands on the wheel. Not for all the world, much less for Teresa, would she have worried her man; nor would she have touched one penny of his savings for fifty Casa Bosellis. Now Maddalena also had her back to the wall, but she was fighting for Gian-Luca. He had little enough cause to be grateful, she felt, to this woman who would not love him. He had worked ungrudgingly all his young life, and what he had earned he should keep. Yes, he should keep it, though the Casa Boselli were split to bits on the rocks. For though neither Teresa nor Fabio mentioned money, Maddalena had eyes in her head, and what she was never told of she guessed—and then there was Nerone, who began to talk freely about Teresa's large debts. Teresa's speculations were now an open secret, as most secrets were in Old Compton Street.

'Dio! That Fabio is a fool!' said Nerone. 'Any man is who is ruled by a woman, but then Fabio was always a poor fool.'

4

That summer came a series of rather bad air raids, and Fabio was openly afraid. He would sit in the office under the pavement, praying, with his fingers stuffed in his ears, or begging Teresa to take him to the Tube, where Rosa had gone with the twins. Teresa, however, despised such precautions.

'If we die, we die,' was her motto. 'The Tube is for mothers with little children, not for old men like you and old women like me. No, I will not let you go to the Tube,' she would say. Then Fabio would begin to cry.

The raids added much to his misery, for now he could never go to sleep. 'Do you think they will come to-night?' he would enquire, peering anxiously up at the sky.

Nor could he be sure that they would not come by day—there had been a bad daylight raid—and sometimes now, while he kneaded his dough, he would pause to listen, mistaking the whirr of the wheels for an aeroplane. He began to suffer from stupefying headaches and a full, tight feeling in his head; the dough he was kneading would go round and round, and with it the machines and the room. If he stood in a draught he would feel his lumbago, that terrifying pain across his back—supposing a raid should come at that moment and catch him unable to move——

But one day in October, the God of his lumbago drew nearer, becoming the God of his soul; and Fabio's old knees gave under him, and his head fell forward and lay upon the table, and his cheek lay buried deep in the flour that his weak hands had failed to mix.

That was how they found him two hours later—just a little, old bundle that had once been a man, with flour on its clothes, on its hands, on its face; flour, too, on its halo of white hair. All foolish weakness he had been, that Fabio,

and very often afraid; afraid of Teresa, afraid of God, and
latterly terribly afraid of the Germans. He had little enough
to tell of himself, now that he must face St. Peter at the
Gate—but perhaps he said: 'I tried to make pasta—I did
try very hard to make pasta——'

5

Now that he was dead and gone, everyone knew how
much they had liked poor Fabio. They missed the mild-eyed,
deprecatory figure that had wandered about Old Compton
Street for more years than they cared to remember. But
Nerone knew how much he had loved Fabio, and that was a
very different thing. Nerone mourned the friend of his youth,
and with him the passing of his own generation.

'I suppose it will be my turn next,' said Nerone. 'I
am not so very much younger than he was; but God grant
that I die in Italy—when this war is ended Nerone goes
home.'

'So you shall, papa,' comforted Rosa.

'Ma sicuro!' Mario said kindly.

After the funeral Nerone spoke little, but he went to the
cupboard and found his dominoes. He turned them out
on to the sitting-room table, where he dusted them one by
one; from time to time he spat on his finger and rubbed
some dirt off an ivory face, then, he laid them back gently,
reverently even, as though they were poor little corpses. He
made Rosa go out and buy him some striped ribbon—the
green, white and red that they were selling in the shops—
and with this he carefully tied up the box, then put it at the
back of the cupboard. Thus, the dominoes had a small
military funeral, being laid to rest in the colours of their
country; and all this for the love and honour of Fabio, who
had not had a military funeral.

Teresa was alone now at the Casa Boselli, alone, too, at
night in her bed. No need to lie stiffly not twitching a muscle,
for now there was no old husband to wake—Fabio was sleeping
very soundly. All night long she could think undisturbed.
Oh, and Teresa had very many thoughts, some of them
coming unbidden to her mind—queer, far-away thoughts
about sunshine and youth at a time of the gathering-in of

the grapes. And the thoughts would paint pictures for old Teresa, and then she would begin to remember. Into these pictures that worried and perplexed her would come walking a quiet, unimportant little man; a man with the eyes of a patient dog whose importunate loving wearies the master, who, nevertheless, must keep it to guard him. Then, less dimly, would come the figure of that other—so gallant, so merry, so passionately young, so anxious to drink youth down to the dregs—ay, and to make her drink with him. And face to face they would stand, those two men, as perhaps they were standing now—who could tell? For she was the debt that had lain between them, the debt that Fabio had paid for that other, who had been unwilling to pay.

How futile a thing was this so-called life, which always ended in death—the death of Olga, the death of Fabio, the approaching death of the Casa Boselli. Struggle and sweat and sweat and struggle to make fine good pasta in the turmoil of war—that was what Fabio had done, and had failed, for down he had dropped like a little old bundle, beside his huge mountain of flour—Fabio the patient, the timid, the foolish—Fabio, the father of Olga.

Thoughts, always thoughts, intolerable thoughts; but not pity, no, for pity was weakness—weakness that might lead you to pray for the dead; you, who had long since done with prayers.

Teresa would sit up stiffly in the darkness, with her thin hands clenched on the bedspread. Her hard black eyes would be staring at nothing, now that she had them wide open. Then one night she must suddenly speak to the Madonna to whom she had not spoken for years.

'You think I am beaten!' she told her fiercely. 'You are glad to think that Teresa is beaten, Teresa who will not serve you. But no, you are wrong, for Teresa is not beaten—she will never be beaten while she lives! If she has to sell matches as a beggar in the streets she will not be beaten by you to her knees.'

And then she listened as though for an answer, an answer that did not come. For not in poor, faltering human speech could the Mother of God reply to Teresa.

'Ah!' said Teresa. 'You answer me nothing, you wish me

to think that you are angry. The foolishness of it! You are a thing of plaster that my hands destroyed easily many years ago. Less than a minute it took to destroy you—of course you can answer me nothing!'

CHAPTER EIGHT

I

I N THE days that followed after Fabio's death, the members of the clan showed their metal; and their metal, at bottom, was pure gold it seemed, for one and all they rallied to Teresa, rallied to the Casa Boselli. Nerone sent Rosa to help in the shop, preparing his own midday meal. Every morning at nine she arrived with the twins, who were shut up to play in Olga's old bedroom. The afternoon frequently brought kind Mario who was anxious to do odd jobs; he might be seen dusting, or polishing brass, or even cleaning a window. Rocca discovered a club-footed boy who happened to be an Italian, and Teresa engaged him to sweep and run errands—only he could not run. Rocca would sometimes send round a small present, the tongue of an ox, the feet of a pig, or even a couple of kidneys; and these, considering the shortage of meat, were tokens of very real friendship. The Signora Rocca put on her old clothes and over them a large apron, then she went to Teresa and said abruptly:

'I am here to wash down and tidy those shelves. "Gold begets gold, but dust begets dust," as my mother would say when I was a child.'

And Teresa replied with another true proverb: ' "To find a staunch friend you must dig deep in trouble." ' Then she added: 'I thank you, signora.'

Sometimes Nerone would come in the evenings to drink a glass of Amarena, and he and Maddalena would talk to Teresa while she sat silently knitting. Maddalena would tell her the little she knew of Gian-Luca's life out in France, hoping that now Teresa might soften, might even express some interest.

'So he is still working in the mess, the Gian-Luca——' Teresa would say. 'Oh well, and why not? All our lives we have studied the art of feeding; no doubt he is better suited for that job than for firing off guns at the Germans.' And then she would appear to forget Gian-Luca, frowning a little at her knitting, murmuring softly over her stitches: 'Knit one, purl two, knit one.'

Even Aunt Ottavia, who was not of the clan, felt called upon to assist; she it was who could teach Teresa new patterns, she it was who discovered a fine book on knitting, which she promptly bought for Teresa. Berta turned up, a little through kindness, and a great deal through wishing to talk about Albert. Albert had received the Military Cross, and just after that—which was more to the point—a 'blighty,' which was likely to keep him in London for many a day to come. Berta would soon have to take the twins home in order to pacify Albert.

There was someone, however, as high above them all as the Lord is above little fleas, and this person was Millo, who sat in his office and considered the Casa Boselli. Millo was omnipotent and so he knew all things, at least he knew all things connected with food, and one fine day he put on his hat and went forth to call on Teresa.

He said: 'I would like to have a few words, suppose we go into the parlour.' And after a minute when they were alone: 'Suppose you show me your ledgers.'

Teresa stood tall and defiant before him, but Millo divined the anguish in her heart. He smiled very kindly at the gallant old woman—she was well worth saving because of her business, but above all because of her courage.

She said: 'My ledgers are private, signore; I do not show my accounts.'

'And yet you will show them to me,' he told her, 'for the Casa Boselli is about to go bankrupt—and that would be a great pity, signora; we need the Casa Boselli.'

'I will save it yet,' Teresa answered without a tremor in her voice. 'You may have heard rumours, and perhaps they are true, but the Casa Boselli will be saved.'

'Sicuro!' said Millo; 'I have come here to save it. Now suppose you bring me those ledgers.'

For one awful moment she stared at him speechless,

236

while the great tears welled in her eyes. For one awful moment she thought that she must weep, standing there before Millo. But the moment passed, and once more Teresa could look him squarely in the face.

'Why should you trouble about me, signore—about the Casa Boselli?'

'That,' he said gently, 'is quite beside the point—I am rich enough, say, to pay for my fancies, and I have a fancy to offer you a partner—one Francesco Millo, signora.'

Then Teresa turned without another word and brought him those miserable ledgers; brought him the accounts that she could not balance, and the copies of the deeds that she had signed for the bank, pledging her two long leases. He spread them out on the parlour table and made her sit down at his side; and presently he and Teresa were scheming, putting their business heads together, forgetful of all save the Casa Boselli and of how it might best be served. When at last he got up to go he was courteous, but a number of papers were reposing in his pocket, papers that Teresa had wished to keep secret for the prestige of the Casa Boselli.

'Our solicitors shall meet not later than next week, and meanwhile I must send you some help,' he said gravely; then he added: 'I thank you for accepting this partner,' and stooping he kissed her hand.

Alone, Teresa sat very still, she was staring down at the table. Millo had saved the Casa Boselli, its debts would be paid, its credit restored, its future secured and cared for. Never again need she lie awake at night tormented by fears for her factory, never again need she worry about money, pacing up and down in her office. True, but never again would the Casa Boselli be all hers, all her own; never again would she unsheath her sword to do battle in its dear defence. She saw herself surrendering that sword. All battered and bent it was —for love of the Casa Boselli she surrendered; so now in the moment of great salvation, she laid down her head and wept bitterly. She who had faced life with hard, dry eyes, she who had shed no tears over Fabio, now wept for love of the Casa Boselli as she had not wept since the death of Olga, thirty long years ago.

The great news spread quickly, Such wonderful news! Everyone congratulated Teresa.

'If only Fabio could know!' sighed Nerone. 'He would surely have been so proud.'

An engineer arrived from the Doric, to grease and lay up the factory machines, for Millo advised no more making of pasta until the war came to an end. He had managed to find three Italian women, whom he sent with orders to help in the shop; and many other things he did for Teresa, setting the Casa Boselli in order to withstand the siege of the war.

Maddalena stayed on at Teresa's side, as head of the new assistants; but Rosa went home again to Nerone, and Mario could rest in the afternoons, for now there were others to polish the brass, to dust, and to clean the windows. Teresa purchased a new black dress; grimmer than ever she stood in her cash-desk—a tall old woman with the face of an eagle, and hair that refused to turn grey.

Now that the storm had been safely weathered, Maddalena wrote of these things to Gian-Luca. She wrote guardedly, however, to spare his feelings; that was how she had written of Fabio's death, careful to omit the details.

And Gian-Luca sighed as he read her long letters, because he had taken to sighing lately; and his sighs would come from a weariness of spirit, from a sense of futility born of his boredom; for a transfer had not yet been granted Gian-Luca who was such an efficient mess-sergeant.

3

Death, that was striking at heart after heart, now struck at the hearts of Mario and Rosa; for that December Geppe was killed in the twelfth great battle of the Isonzo. Geppe had gone through those weeks of hell without so much as a scratch, and then, *zipp!* a large splinter of shrapnel in the stomach, and presently no more Geppe!

Mario was unexpectedly quiet, saying little, not weeping at all. He just gathered Rosa into his arms: 'Povera, povera donna,' he murmured, rhythmically patting her shoulder.

Rosa's tears came gushing up from her heart in a great, irresistible flood; she was all dissolving with love and pity, weeping less for the death of her only son than for what she knew must have been his fear in those last few agonizing hours.

Nerone sat silently staring at his birds and rubbing his wooden leg. When at last he did speak his voice was solemn. 'A hero has died,' said Nerone slowly; 'my daughter Rosa is the mother of a hero. Let it be always remembered among us how nobly our Geppe died.'

There had been nothing noble in poor Geppe's death, unless death itself be noble—he had died as hundreds of others had done, because there was no escape. Scourged and tormented by vile engines of war, by terrible, nerve-breaking, soul-sickening noise, by the smell and the sight and the slime of blood—crowding, thrusting, yelling, retreating, in a welter of maimed, half-demented men—that was how Geppe had died. But now he must needs be a hero to Nerone, and Rosa must mourn him as a hero, and Mario must speak of 'My brave son Geppe', as though Geppe had been willing and glad to die in that awful retreat of Caporetto.

Nerone went out with his snapshot the next day, and two weeks later there arrived an enlargement—an enormous affair in a wide gilt frame—showing Geppe's weak face beneath a steel helmet, and a little blurred at that. Nerone hung the picture in the shop, above a low shelf just opposite the door, where all who came in must see it; he draped an Italian flag round the frame, a silk one, befitting a hero. Mario wrote out a little inscription which he stuck at the bottom of the picture: 'Of your charity pray for the soul of Giuseppe Varese, who died that Italy might live.' Then he made the sign of the Cross on himself and muttered: 'God grant that he rest in peace.' After which he hurried away to the Capo, for the living would be wanting their dinners. But Rosa came later and cleared from that shelf all the tins of tobacco and cigarettes, and in their place she set flowers before Geppe, so that now he looked more like a warrior-saint than the poor, frightened soldier he had been— Geppe, who had always liked cigarettes infinitely better than flowers!

Whenever a customer glanced at the picture, Nerone would tell him about it. 'Ecco! My grandson, Geppe!' he would say; 'as gallant a lad as ever went to war. Ma che! The boy was a veritable tiger, but what will you, he was young, and the young are too reckless——' And then he would spin out those long romances that his mind had woven around Geppe.

Rosa would hear him and shake her head sadly, thinking that her father had aged a great deal, thinking that the customer looked a little bored, a little anxious for his change. But not for the world would she have told old Nerone that he grew too voluble these days, that his yarns about Geppe were quite without foundation.

'After all, I believe he was fond of the boy,' she would think, and the thought would bring comfort with it; for nothing is so sweet a consolation in grief as the affection of others for our dead.

4

Meanwhile there was no one who was quite without their troubles; the Padrone, for instance, had troubles and to spare, for not only must he cope with inadequate service, but he could not afford a band at the Capo, in addition to which there was no room for dancing. Yet never before in the history of England had there been such a craze for movement; such a gliding and hopping, such a swaying and clinging; such a stamping and clapping and grabbing of food. Two mouthfuls and then: 'Come on, let's have a turn!' After which more grabbing of food.

Millo, wise man, had foreseen what was coming, and now there was dancing every night at the Doric. The supper-tables had been carefully arranged to leave a large space in the restaurant.

The New Year brought with it a couple of air raids, for six hours on end the bombs banged about London. 'Play louder,' Millo murmured to his band; and pale but determined the band played its loudest: 'Honey bee, give us a kiss!'

Sometimes Millo would linger to watch his dancers, and the smile on his lips would grow rather grim, then after a little he would shrug his broad shoulders. In Berlin they were cursing, in Paris they were praying, and in London they were dancing—oh, well, such was war. . . .

But Death was in nowise daunted, it seemed, for the spring came in on a great tide of blood. Yet this was not nearly enough for the glutton, who must needs go seeking out peaceable people who neither danced nor made war. Humble civilians just lay down and died from this cause or that, or from no cause at all except that they felt very weary. It was strange how many such people were dying; strange too, that as often as not they were those who had no one to lose in battle, and among them was talkative, small Aunt Ottavia, who caught cold in May and died early in June, leaving all that she possessed to Maddalena.

Who could have thought that the small Aunt Ottavia would have had so much money to leave? Four thousand pounds, securely invested in first-class American railroads. She had flatly refused to sell her good shares to the English Government or to anyone else; she had lent them to the Government for the time being only, receiving a tip in the process. But in spite of all her astuteness she had died, and her shares had remained behind her, to say nothing of the house in Coldbath Square, its contents, and one or two boarders.

Maddalena felt suddenly rather helpless, missing the tactless Aunt Ottavia. She longed intensely for her husband's return, almost frightened by so much money. Gian-Luca wrote advising that the house should be sold, as he did not wish to live in Coldbath Square, and fortunately a purchaser turned up, who bought the house, boarders and all. Maddalena added the proceeds of the sale to Gian-Luca's deposit at the bank; and now all her letters to him were full of new plans regarding the future.

'We can sell out the stocks,' she wrote happily, 'and then you can buy your restaurant; only think of all that this means to us, caro! I am grateful to Aunt Ottavia.'

His answers were kind but curiously vague; it was almost as though he had scarcely grasped the extent of his own good fortune. And why did he never come home on leave? Surely he might have got home once on leave? But his answers were vague upon this point also.

He wrote: 'I have not yet obtained my transfer.' As thoughthat could explain his not getting leave to a woman who loved as she did.

Maddalena was praying more earnestly than ever that the transfer might not be granted. How could she well do otherwise, when Fabio was dead and Geppe was dead, and now the poor Aunt Ottavia? The thought of so much death had struck terror to her heart, terror because of one life.

'Give me his life, dear Mother of God!' she entreated; and surely her prayers were being answered, for was he not working in comparative safety at the Officers' Mess at the Base?

5

Yes, and that was where the Armistice found him, at the Officers' Mess at the Base. All of a sudden the guns stopped firing; a stillness so intense that men clasped their heads, bewildered, came down on the blood-drenched pastures of France. Gian-Luca stared round him at the Officers' Mess, and knew that the war was over.

He thought: 'It is gallant, this record of mine, it is something that a man can be proud of! All my battles have been fought with the peasants over chickens. A fine victory the capture of a couple of fowls, a splendid victory! And what a defeat to return to the Mess empty-handed!'

From the Doric to the Officers' Mess at the Base, there had only been a difference in degree. Food, always food, the thing they had lived by, Fabio and Teresa, Rocca and Millo, and he himself who had planned to grow rich via the media of people's stomachs—oh, well, it had followed him out to the war, certain, no doubt of his allegiance: and now that the war was ended, more food—for Gian-Luca must prepare a very fine dinner in honour of victory and peace.

6

Three months later his train steamed into Victoria, and there on the platform stood Maddalena, scanning the passing windows. The train stopped and she had him safe in her arms, all the bigness and the manhood of him. Her cheek was pressed tightly against his shoulder; and because she could feel the roughness of his coat, and the strong, even beat of his living heart, her gratitude leapt to her lips in words.

'Blessèd be God!' said Maddalena.

He kissed her, then pushed her gently from him, as though in some way he rebuked her; but her joy was too great to feel his rebuke.

'Amore, amore, you are safe——' she whispered.

'Yes, I am quite safe,' he answered.

That evening she urged him to talk about himself, to tell her about his life out in France: 'Your letters told nothing at all, caro mio, why did you tell me so little?'

'Because there was so little to tell——' said Gian-Luca; 'they never gave me my transfer.'

'Oh, I am glad, I am glad!' she murmured. 'Day and night I have prayed to the Virgin.'

But at that he smiled, and seeing the smile she must get up and kiss his mouth.

Then he took her in his arms, for was she not a woman made more lovely through her love of him? And he kissed her again and again on the lips, until she must needs believe that he loved her—that at last he had come to love her.

'Amore mio—amore,' she whispered, filled with the joy of his nearness.

And he answered: 'Amore mio, amore,' while he strove to find peace and contentment of spirit, even as she had found it.

All night they lay in each other's arms, and her cup of happiness was full, for she thought that all night he came nearer and nearer—yet all night he was slipping farther away from the arms that she fancied held him.

The next day he was gentle but strangely silent, and she studied his face more closely. Then it was that she knew that her husband had aged.

'Can it be that he has fretted himself, my Gian-Luca, because they would not transfer him?' she mused. 'But why should he fret?—he was doing his duty, he was doing all that they asked.'

But now she discovered yet another thing about him; he preferred not to talk of the war.

He said: 'It is over, let us try to forget it; the English did not wish me to fight—va bene, and now I must think of Millo and the Doric, I must go and see Millo to-morrow.'

As the weeks went on Maddalena was puzzled by a curious change in Gian-Luca. 'They worked him too hard out in France,' she would think; but this explanation was unsatisfactory, for he did not seem physically tired.

To interest him she talked of Aunt Ottavia, and of all the money she had left them: 'You will soon be the head of your own restaurant,' she told him, smiling proudly.

'Yes, I know, but not just yet,' he answered; 'I cannot leave Millo in the lurch—I shall stay at the Doric for a few years longer—at least, I think I shall stay.' And then he quite suddenly changed the subject, as though it actually bored him.

His place had been waiting for him at the Doric, he was Millo's chief head-waiter, and far more important than Riccardo had been, who had only had charge of the restaurant. Everything was just as he had wished it to be; he had four very excellent aides-de-camp, to say nothing of a large, well-trained staff of waiters, now that the war was over. Yet he seldom discussed his work with Maddalena, and this made her anxious and unhappy. He had grown very careful these nights not to wake her, he would steal through the hall and into their bedroom, having first taken off his shoes. And suspecting this, she would keep herself awake, feeling lonely at sleeping without him.

'Is that you, Gian-Luca?' she would say, sitting up.

And then he would frown: 'Go to sleep, Maddalena, it is past two o'clock in the morning.'

Then Maddalena would talk to the Madonna: 'Blessèd Mary, help me with Gian-Luca,' she would whisper; 'you who so mercifully kept him out of danger, show me what I must do. He is changed, he no longer wants to tell me about things—he is not like a child any more—how can I make him grow younger again—I who have no other child?'

And perhaps she might pause as though expecting an answer, an answer that did not come—for not in poor, faltering human speech could the Mother of God reply to Maddalena.

BOOK THREE

CHAPTER ONE

I

THERE HAD never been such a season at the Doric as the season that followed the Armistice; everyone was flocking to the restaurants now, in a kind of hilarious reaction. Millo was in the seventh heaven of delight, and so were most of his waiters, for people were recklessly spending their money, eating up banknotes with every mouthful, and washing them down with champagne or spirits, so that, naturally, when they got up to go, they left a fat tip behind them.

Millo had long since had to duplicate his band, for a supper without dancing was unheard of. It was said that among other excellent things, he possessed the best jazz-bands in London. The craze for dancing was on the increase, and now there was no age limit; the white-haired, the portly, the withered, the ailing, young or old, maid or matron, they must get up and dance; while a decadent Pan—discarding his reed-pipe—turned sobriety to bibbing and dignity to folly, with the help of a water-whistle.

Gian-Luca inspected his rooms one May morning and quietly nodded his head. Everything was perfect, from the vases of flowers to the well-polished plate and glass.

'Va bene,' he murmured, 'it is all as it should be; that Daniele is a competent fellow.' And then he observed a fork out of place and hastily put it straight.

A man in a baize apron, with a dust-pan and brush, was stalking a couple of waiters; every few minutes he would suddenly swoop at some microscopic speck on the carpet. At a long side-table a person in shirt-sleeves opened endless packets of matches; he filled the match-stands with infinite care so that each little red head stood neatly in its place awaiting its coming cremation. Daniele was giving a last expert touch to the wicks of the spirit-lamps, pinching them firmly between finger and thumb, then spreading out their tips as though they were petals; for these wicks were important, since they would assist in the making of the temperamental Crêpe Suzette!

At last all was in order for the business of the day—and what a momentous business! The Doric would feed many hundred stomachs, post-war stomachs too, long deprived of their fill and now determined to get it.

The telephone began to ring every few minutes—people calling up to book tables; Gian-Luca must consult that complicated list which stood on a desk by the door.

'What name do you say is asking, Daniele? No, I do not know that name, we have not got a table.' Or: 'The Duchess of Sussex? Yes, of course; how many, five? She can have her usual table in the window; and see that you put some flowers by each plate—say a couple of those pink roses.'

And now Gian-Luca was much in request, for the clients were calling in person. 'Good morning, signore, a table for three——' 'Certainly, Milady, a table in the corner—will you take that one over there?' 'Ah, scusi, signorina, have you been waiting long? Yes, yes, I have seen to everything for supper, it shall be exactly as you wish.'

Gian-Luca was all ingratiating smiles, he seemed so anxious to please you. To see him was to think that he liked you for yourself—not for what you would eat for the good of the Doric; no, he liked you because you were just yourself—that was what was so charming about him. It made you feel genial, you glanced round the room in the hopes of finding someone to nod to, and there stood Roberto, that capital waiter with the really good knowledge of wine.

'Good morning, Roberto. So you're back again. That's splendid; I'm jolly glad to see you!'

And Roberto grinned shyly and bowed from the waist as though you had done him an honour—that was what was so nice about Roberto, he made you feel like a sultan. And there was Giovanni, and he too was smiling, smiling and rubbing his hands—Giovanni who knew how you liked your cold beef, not too underdone, just pink.

'Good morning, Giovanni! So you're safe and sound. Glad to get back here, aren't you?'

And Giovanni looked flattered: 'I thank you, signore. I hope the signore is well?'

Oh, and there was Millo himself, also bowing, waiting to catch your eye—that was what was so nice about Millo, he never forgot the face of a client; a wonderful gift, and it went a long way towards making you feed at the Doric.

2

This then was the atmosphere of well-being that Millo had managed to create. He believed in giving people exactly what they wanted, for someone was certain to gain in the process, and as a rule it was the giver. Millo might sometimes smile rather wryly, he might even shake his wise head, but then he would murmur: 'Le monde est ainsi fait.' And remember that he had not made it.

Of his vast staff whose duty it was to see that everyone got what they wanted, none so deft, so proficient, so agreeable as Gian-Luca, whose lips had acquired an automatic smile which he kept expressly for the clients. Millo, watching his clever head-waiter, would consider him wellnigh perfect. He would think:

'After all he was right to be ambitious; the man knows the worth of his talent, and why not? I am lucky to have him in days like these, when everyone feels so hungry!' And then he would chuckle a little to himself, thinking of the people who felt hungry.

But sometimes, if nobody happened to be looking, Gian-Luca's face altered completely; it grew sullen and tired, it was quite a different face from the one that he showed to the clients. Backwards and forwards superintending the service went Millo's clever head-waiter, and all that he did was supremely well done, for so many years had gone to his making that now he must work like a perfect machine, without hitch, without flaw, without hurry. There had been many days during that time in France when Gian-Luca had tried to work badly, to be inefficient, clumsy, forgetful of orders; hoping against hope to get sent to the Front if he ceased to give satisfaction. But then, even as now, his long training held, and he could not be other than himself, the perfect mess-sergeant, the perfect head-waiter, the master and slave of innumerable details, the man who could not see a fork out of place but that he must put it straight. He had slipped back into his groove at the Doric as though he had never been away, taking up his work just where he had left it; ordering his waiters, humouring his clients; with a watchful eye, too, for his master's interests, which he served whenever he might.

Yet all the while, and herein lay the change, Gian-Luca cared nothing at all. If the Doric had suddenly fallen to pieces, and he himself with it, he would not have cared; a curious indifference had begun to possess him, he worked without interest or pleasure or ambition, because he had the habit of working. Now he would try not to think of his work, because if he thought about it too much he was filled with a sense of smallness. Everything he did now seemed infinitely small, and he himself seemed small in the doing; Millo, the Doric, Gian-Luca, all small—the servants of poor Lilliputians. And yet he could never stop doing small things, he would pause to pick up a pin; a badly-drawn curtain would worry his eyes until he must go and arrange it. A crumb on the carpet, a chair out of place, would cause him acute discomfort; but after he had spoken pretty sharply to Daniele, he would think: 'Dio Santo! what does it matter? What do all these trifles matter?'

He began to grow anxious about himself, because of this curious indifference. He who had all but reached the height of his ambition, and could buy his own restaurant now if he chose, or if he preferred it get a manager's job and work up in time to be a rival to Millo; he who had achieved so much single-handed in the face of unpropitious fate, what had he got to complain of? Nothing—and yet, somehow, the thought of his days lay heavy, like a cold, hard stone on his brain. The clashing of music, the clattering of dishes, the incessant talking and laughing; the perpetual movement of knives and forks, the perpetual chewing of food.

'Maître d'hotel!'

'Sí, signore?'

'I want the wine-waiter.'

'Sí, signore, I will send him at once!'

'Gian-Luca——'

'Sí, signore?'

'I'd like some more hors d'œuvres.'

'Sí, signore, I will send you your waiter.'

Food, food, food—all those dozens of people thinking of it, talking of it, eating. His business in life just to see that they got it, just to see that they ate more and more. His head would feel dizzy with the fumes of the food, until he would grow almost stupid; but then he would suddenly pull himself up, while a kind of terror seized him.

'This is my life, my whole life,' he would mutter, 'and I like it—I like my work.'

To assure himself how much he liked his work, he took to going down to the basement again, in the time between luncheon and dinner. He would stand on the steps that led into the great kitchen, and listen to the pulsing of that mighty heart; he would think of Millo, the heart of that heart, while he tried to recapture the lure of the place that had held him before the war. Food, food, food—great cauldrons of food. Food on the tables of wood and of iron; splashes of food on the walls, on the floor, on the clothes and the hands of men. The vastness of the thing would begin to oppress him—grotesque that it should be so vast—the vastness of the Doric and all that it stood for, the vastness of the appetites that it must appease, the vastness of that long vista of jaws. Yet the larger the Doric grew in his imagination, the smaller it seemed to become; so small that now it was crushing and squeezing; a prison, a press that closed in and in until he could scarcely breathe. But how could a thing be vast and yet small? Surely that way lay madness.

His hand would go up to his throat. He would think: 'It is awful—it suffocates!' And then he would hurry away to the larders, afraid of these fantastic fancies.

In the principal larder there would be much to see, the chopping and slicing of meat, for instance; great chunks of raw meat, which a chef called Henri was for ever dividing with his knife. There were also those long rows of newly-plucked chickens, with their necks swinging over the shelves, and those deep, white dishes of quaking entrails, and those slabs full of slow-moving, beady-eyed lobsters, who protested that they were alive. Henri would look up from his work with a smile, and perhaps he would say:

'Good morning, Gian-Luca. Would you like to select a

nice, fat lobster for your pretty Milady? You are always so fussy, and no wonder, for she is extremely gourmande, she will eat it up shell and all!'

And Gian-Luca might answer: 'She is little and lovely—they are always the greediest kind.' But he would not select the fat lobster for Milady, instead he would just stand staring at Henri, and one day he said: 'Do you like what you do? Do you like the feeling of food?'

'Ma foi! But why not?' laughed Henri, surprised. 'Do I not live by their food?'

3

Gian-Luca still found consolation in his books, he still read the 'Gioia della Luce', and now Ugo Doria had written a new poem, an epic of peace and of peaceful things, of vineyards and hill-sides and valleys. It had come to Gian-Luca like a breath of sweet air, like a cool hand laid on the forehead. He said to Maddalena:

'When I read Doria's words I can almost believe in the Spirit—I can almost believe in your God, Maddalena, for that is how Doria writes sometimes—as though he wrote with his spirit.'

One day he went off to see the Librarian, taking the poem in his pocket. 'Have you read it?' he demanded. 'It is wonderful, sublime—it is equal to the "Gioia della Luce." '

The Librarian shook his head. 'No,' he said slowly; 'I am sick unto death of books.'

Gian-Luca stared: 'You are tired of your books? But I thought you loved books as I do.'

'A man may change——' the Librarian said softly, 'perhaps every man must change.'

Then Gian-Luca was silent because he felt frightened, terribly frightened of change. But presently he said:

'A man must not change, he might lose himself in the process!'

'Would that matter very much?' inquired the Librarian. 'Suppose he should find something better.'

'He is mad!' thought Gian-Luca. 'He is obviously mad!' And he wished that he had not come. 'It must be the shock of those boys getting killed within a week of each other.'

'Do you still care for books and food and stomachs?' the Librarian asked him gravely. 'I am disappointed in books myself, such a lot of them seem to suggest indigestion —a kind of deranged mental stomach.'

'I care very much indeed,' said Gian-Luca, and his voice was loud and aggresive; 'I care for the things that I know to be real; I cannot afford to be a dreamer like you. I am just a head-waiter at the Doric.'

'I know nothing so inexpensive as dreams——' said the little Librarian, smiling.

But Gian-Luca did not smile: 'He is quite mad,' he mused; 'I suppose they keep him on out of pity!'

4

That summer Teresa said to Maddalena: 'What is the matter with Gian-Luca?' For even Teresa, immersed in her business, had noticed a change in her grandson.

And then it was Rosa and Mario who spoke, and they both looked hard at Maddalena. 'What is the matter with Gian-Luca?' they demanded, as though Maddalena were to blame.

Two days later Nerone called on Maddalena, and there he found the Padrona. The Padrona had just been giving advice as to how one should manage a husband.

'One should never allow him to sulk,' she was saying; 'now I think your Gian-Luca is sulking.'

'Per Bacco, he is not!' Nerone protested; 'the boy is doing nothing of the kind. I think he is probably ill, our Gian-Luca, I think you should send for a doctor.'

Rocca waylaid Maddalena one morning and beckoned her into the shop: 'I do not much like the look of Gian-Luca, his face has grown dull and he speaks very little—I hope you take care of our child, Maddalena? He was born in our midst—such a queer little boy, with a positive terror of goats. You must not mind an old fellow like me speaking frankly: I think he is ill; he works very hard, and he needs his small comforts, and I hope you see that he gets them.'

Maddalena reassured them all as best as she could, but her own heart was deeply anxious. Gian-Luca looked weary and discontented; he was sleeping very badly, and when he got up his eyes would be vague and unhappy.

'What is the matter, amore?' she would say. 'Try to tell me what is the matter.'

But he always replied: 'There is nothing the matter; leave me in peace, donna mia.'

He was growing coldly unkind to Maddalena; never angry, just coldly unkind. At times he would treat her as though she were a stranger, preferring his books to her company, it seemed, and that summer he refused to go out of London when the time for their holiday arrived.

'I do not want people,' he told her firmly; 'wherever one goes there are too many people.' So he sat at the open window and read, sometimes he would not speak for hours. Once he looked up and noticed her eyes: 'You are always watching,' he said sharply; 'stop staring, Maddalena, I do not like your eyes—they are frightened, they remind me of a rabbit in a trap; I wish you would look more cheerful.'

There were days when he found fault with everything she cooked. 'How can I eat this mess!' he would grumble. 'It is all greasy butter, you use too much butter. Dio Santo! I get enough grease at the Doric; cannot you cook more simply?' But then he would proceed to finish the whole dish. 'I must eat, a man must eat,' he would mutter. And the watchful Maddalena would know that he was not hungry—would know that he forced himself to eat.

At moments her self-control would desert her, and then she would go down on her knees: 'I love you so——' she would tell him wildly. 'I am childless, Gian-Luca, I have no one but you; all these long years I have waited for a child— be kind to me—kiss me, Gian-Luca!'

He would look at her dumbly as though trying to be kind, and after a moment he would kiss her. 'There, there, mia donna,' he would say, getting up; 'there, there, mia donna, you are tired.'

Oh, indeed Maddalena had need of her prayers, had need of the kindly Madonna at St. Peter's, had need of the Child who stood at her knee, and of Father Antonio, their priest. Father Antonio counselled much patience, it would surely come right, he told Maddalena. God worked in strange ways, but He knew His own business, and His business might well be a prodigal son—Maddalena must leave it to God.

And she honestly did try to leave it to God, try to have courage and patience, but her great faithful heart was failing a little. She would think:

'He came home to me safely from the war, but was it for this that he came home safely—so that he might grow to hate me?' Then she would remember her prayers for his safety, and something within her would tremble, and something within her would start to ask a question, over and over again it would ask it. 'My God!' she would answer in a kind of desperation, 'I was right to pray for my husband's safety, every poor wife all over Europe was praying for her husband's safety!'

5

Gian-Luca worked better than ever in the autumn, determined to slay this thing that possessed him, this spirit of indifference and depression. People were hurrying back from the country, and the Doric was full to overflowing once more; then one morning the telephone rang loud and long, it was someone demanding the head-waiter.

Gian-Luca put the receiver to his ear: 'Yes, I am the head-waiter—the restaurant, yes——'

'I want a table for two,' came a voice, 'it must be a small little table and quiet—for two, yes, next Thursday for lunch, half-past one—I want a quiet little table for two. Are you an Italian? Then for God's sake talk Italian!' And the voice proceeded to order a luncheon that spoke well for its owner's palate.

'What name, signore?' inquired Gian-Luca when at last the order was completed.

'Doria—have you got it?' came the voice less distinctly. 'A table for Ugo Doria.'

Then Gian-Luca suddenly ceased to be a waiter. 'Ugo Doria, the poet?' he babbled.

'Ma sí, I am the poet—never mind about that, have you got it all down about the luncheon?'

Gian-Luca walked straight into Millo's office. 'Ugo Doria is lunching here next Thursday, signore; I have come to ask if I may serve him myself——'

Millo looked up from a bundle of papers. 'Doria the poet?' he inquired.

'Sí, signore, Ugo Doria, and coming to the Doric—I have just written down his order.'

Gian-Luca's voice sounded young with excitement. Millo glanced at him in surprise. 'You are fond of poetry then, Gian-Luca? Doria is certainly a great writer, but I did not know that you were a great reader. Have you read his new epic, "The Sowing of Peace"? It is very lovely, I think.'

'Yes, but have I your permission to serve him myself, signore?'

'Certainly, Gian-Luca, why not? Let Daniele take your place in the restaurant during luncheon, I would wish you to serve Ugo Doria.'

'Thank you,' said Gian-Luca, 'you have made me very happy.' And his eyes were actually shining.

'How curious; he reads Ugo Doria's poems,' thought Millo as his head-waiter left him. 'How little one knows about other men's minds, and as for their hearts—well, nothing.'

That afternoon Gian-Luca went back to Maddalena. 'Maddalena! Where are you?' he shouted.

'I am here,' she answered, coming quickly towards him. 'I am waiting for you, piccino.'

Then he hugged her, and laughed, and told her the great news—Ugo Doria was coming to the Doric. 'And I shall serve him myself, Maddalena; my hands only shall serve him!' Presently he said: 'When I was very young—before I left the Capo, Maddalena—I used to long for this thing to happen, I used to long to serve Doria. I used to see myself pouring out his wine and passing his food with a flourish; I used to wish to impress him, I remember—I distinctly remember that I wished to impress him—but he never came to the Capo.'

'And now you can do it all!' she said gladly; 'you, who are a head-waiter! I hope he will know who it is who serves him, but of course he will see by your neck-tie.'

Gian-Luca teased her: 'He will know by my appearance; he will know by my splendid appearance! He will say: "Why here comes the great Gian-Luca!" And then no doubt he will write me a poem, inspired by my exquisite waiting.'

She scarcely dared to believe her own eyes, Gian-Luca was laughing with pleasure. He was young and gay and affectionate again, and all because Doria was coming to the Doric! But what did that matter, so long as he was happy, happy and kind to Maddalena?

She said: 'I will bless this man Ugo Doria, because he has made you smile.'

Then Gian-Luca kissed her: 'It is foolish perhaps, but yes, I feel as excited as a schoolboy.' After which he must needs get out Doria's poems, and read her the 'Gioia della Luce.'

CHAPTER TWO

I

ON THE following Thursday Gian-Luca arrived at the Doric an hour before his time. He must interview the head chef regarding certain dishes that Doria had specially ordered; he must speak to Roberto about the champagne; he must give the final directions to Daniele; in fact he must rouse the whole staff of the Doric by announcing Doria's prospective visit.

Doria's table would be in the octagon room, in a quiet corner by the window, and at each of the plates there should be a red carnation made up as a button-hole, for Gian-Luca felt sure in his own mind, somehow, that Doria's friend would be a man. He might be bringing a well-known statesman, or a soldier famous in war, or perhaps a poet less great than himself, to whom he was doing a kindness. But whoever he brought was sure to be important, if not now, then at some future date, for the man who had written the 'Gioia della Luce' was not likely to cast his pearls before swine—and then greatness attracted greatness.

Gian-Luca, who was now nearly thirty-two years old, was weaving romances like a boy; he pictured Doria as slender and tall, with the strong, lean flanks of a race-horse; his eyes would be inspired, the eyes of a poet, but above all the man would convey a sense of bigness, bigness of mind, bigness of spirit; oh, yes, and bigness of sin when he sinned —for nothing small or despicable or mean could have written the 'Gioia della Luce', nor could it have conceived those many other poems that burnt with the fires of the flesh. Serene and enduring he must be, this Doria, in spite of those outbursts of passion—a pasture swept by occasional storms, a valley that harboured a mountain torrent, a mountain whose peak was covered in snow, and illumined by swift crude lightning.

To everyone he met at the Doric that morning, Gian-Luca said: 'Doria is coming here to-day.'

And they answered: 'Ugo Doria the poet?' Then Gian-Luca nodded and smiled.

Monsieur Martin, the head of the army of chefs, was inclined to be short in his manner, however. For no war stop-gap was Monsieur Pierre Martin, but a culinary king returned to his kingdom, and now on his coat showed a green and red ribbon which stood for the Croix de Guerre.

'Parbleu, is he God?' inquired Monsieur Martin. 'Is he God, this poet you speak of? I have never so much as heard his name; now if it could have been Rostand—but Rostand is dead, a very great pity, for only the French can write verses.'

'As you please,' said Gian-Luca; 'let us not discuss writers, I am here to discuss their food.'

'Why not cook it yourself!' suggested Monsieur Martin.

Gian-Luca smiled: 'I should do it so badly; it is you who are the poet of the kitchen!'

After which Monsieur Martin had himself to smile, remembering his exquisite dishes.

'You may leave it to me,' he said, graciously enough; 'I will care for your poet's digestion.'

2

At ten o'clock Gian-Luca put on his dress-suit, taking quite a long time in the process; he was almost as fussy about this ritual as he had been about all his other arrangements. But once dressed, there was nothing left for him to do, and more than two hours must elapse before luncheon; so he said to Roberto:

'*I* will open the wine, I wish to serve everything myself.'

'You have told me that three times already, signore,' Roberto replied, somewhat nettled.

'Very well then, I tell you again!' snapped Gian-Luca, who was feeling like an overwrought piccolo.

He sat down and anxiously studied his lists; nearly all the tables were booked. He said to Daniele:

'Can you manage, do you think? For God's sake do not disturb me.'

'I can surely manage, Signor Gian-Luca,' Daniele replied, much aggrieved.

'Very well, then, remember all the things that I have told you,' warned Gian-Luca in an ominous voice.

They said to each other behind his back: 'He is not like this as a rule—to-day one would think he was new to the work. And why must he wait on Doria himself? That is not a head-waiter's business.'

Gian-Luca could feel their covert disapproval, but it left him entirely unmoved. To-morrow he would be their head-waiter again, the implacable Gian-Luca with the all-seeing eyes, and the method of a ruthless machine. But to-day he was going to be human for once, he was going to be a creature of feeling; to-day he would serve for the joy of serving, and his service should be a thing to remember, because it would have come from his heart.

3

It was one o'clock, clients were beginning to arrive, Daniele was ready and smiling. Gian-Luca stood silently waiting near the table by the window in his octagon room. It was ten past one, then a quarter-past one, then all of a sudden it was half-past; the room had filled up, all the tables were occupied except that one by the window. It was twenty to two; Gian-Luca stiffened, Doria and his friend were late. Stooping down, he fingered the red carnations, very slightly changing their angle. Then someone was coming in at the door, a woman, the little Milady; and after her followed a white-haired man who was taking off pale grey gloves.

All in a moment Gian-Luca perceived him; every detail struck through to his brain; a bulky, elderly man of sixty with a self-willed mouth that had weakened and coarsened, with pale eyes that looked small because of the skin that was gathered in bladders beneath them. A man with a face that looked foolish at that moment because it was close to Milady, or rather to Milady's elegant back which preceded it into the room.

Gian-Luca stepped forward and bowed very low. 'Signor Doria's table?' he inquired.

'Ma sí, I have booked a table,' said Doria, 'I have booked a table for two.'

'It is ready, signore,' Gian-Luca murmured. 'It is ready —this way please, Milady.'

They sat down, and Doria smiled at his companion and she smiled back at Doria, and Gian-Luca served them with artichokes in oil and other delectable things.

Doria was talking in broken English, making gestures with his long white hands; every few minutes Milady laughed softly, and whenever she laughed Ugo Doria stopped talking, and his eyes looked sheepish, but old and tired—too tired to do justice to Milady.

'Open the champagne, waiter,' he ordered.

And Gian-Luca opened the champagne. He filled their glasses, while Milady said, still laughing, that she really preferred ginger-beer.

Presently they were comfortably launched, and Doria nodded with approval. 'Buonissimo, quel poulet Maryland!' he murmured, spearing a piece with his fork.

And now he must drink very much champagne, because he was tired and ageing, and because Milady, who was little and lovely, was as greedy in passion as in food. Doria's eyes grew bolder, ridiculously bold for a man who was tired and ageing, while over his face spread a deep red flush that was less of virility than wine.

He said softly: 'You are beautiful like morning, bellezza, you are like my "Gioia della Luce." Have you read my "Gioia della Luce," bellezza?'

'Of course I have read it,' Milady lied; 'everyone has read the "Gioia".'

Gian-Luca smiled coldly as he poured the champagne: 'Un'altra bottiglia?' he whispered.

Doria nodded: 'Sí, un'altra bottiglia!'

Then Gian-Luca opened a fresh bottle.

As he drank, Ugo Doria felt younger and younger, but his face remained terribly old. Milady's eyes wandered away at moments to someone who sat near the door. And seeing this, Doria must work for her favours, smiling, and trying to be gay; trying to look clear-eyed and fair-haired and twenty, like the person who sat near the door. He talked of his poems, of his literary triumphs, laughing as though he were amused.

'A ridiculous success it have been, my new epic; what you call it?—a bumper success!'

He bragged like a child who covers its bragging with a flimsy pretence of humility; while his eyes, those lustful, miserable eyes, demanded and cringed and worshipped by turns whenever they dwelt on Milady.

Tall and silent, but terribly watchful, stood Gian-Luca, always at his elbow. From time to time he refilled Doria's glass, and whenever he did this his lips would smile coldly; a queer, cruel smile that distorted his features, twisting the corners of his mouth.

Forgetting the presence of this soft-moving waiter, Doria expanded more and more; dragging his exquisite art in the mire, using his immortality as a cloak for a brainless woman to tread on. A large, foolish, love-sick viveur of sixty, greasy with food and wine; hot with the passing caprice of the moment—a triumph of a poet, a disaster of a man; this then was Ugo Doria.

Gian-Luca calmly brought in his coffee and poured out his liqueur brandy; very calmly, too, he presented the bill, which Doria paid with scarcely a glance. Then Milady got up, and as she did so, she smiled and nodded at Gian-Luca. Then Doria got up, but heavily, slowly; and he handed Gian-Luca a tip of two pounds in order to impress Milady. Not that he was rich, Ugo Doria, far from it—it costs money to make the beau geste; and all his life he had made the beau geste, whenever it seemed worth while.

He said to Gian-Luca: 'It have been a fine meal,' and his voice was a little husky.

Gian-Luca bowed and held open the door: 'Buon giorno, signore, e grazie.'

When Doria looked back, Gian-Luca was still standing with his hand on the open door.

And that was how Gian-Luca served his father; and that was how Doria was served by his son—neither of them any the wiser.

That night, while Maddalena slept, Gian-Luca burnt
Doria's books. He burnt them deliberately, one by one, and
the pound notes that Doria had given him he burnt also;
and the flames that consumed these things were less searing
than the anger within his heart.

Now he no longer felt weary and indifferent, he was
terribly alive with this anger. It shone in his eyes, it tightened
his muscles; he felt young with the will that he had to hate,
and as he watched Doria's verses burning he leant forward
and spat into the fire.

He talked to the shrinking, shrivelling things: 'You
hypocrites! You impostors! You liars! Here is Gian-Luca
who believed you all these years, who went to you for comfort when he was so lonely, who went to you for courage
when he was afraid, who set you apart as though you were
worthy to live all alone in your grandeur; and all the while
you were nothing but lies. He is small, small, small, the man
who conceived you; his vanities are small and his lusts and
his sins. His sins are the sins of an over-charged belly, he
must drink in order to sin. I must fill up his glass many
times while he sits there in order that your Doria may be
sinful! Dio buono, if I could not sin better than that I would
call myself less than a man!'

All the years of his lonely, outraged childhood, of his
painful adolescence, his maturity of toil with its bitter will
to succeed; all the dull resentment of that period in France,
and the weariness of spirit that had followed after; yea, and
strangely enough, that occasional yearning towards the
ideal that had come to the son from the father who had
written the 'Gioia della Luce'—all these things now struck
with the blows of a hammer on nerves too long sternly
repressed; a hammer in the hand of Ugo Doria, who struck
and struck and struck. Fantastically enormous he loomed,
that poor creature, by very reason of his smallness; a monster, an outrage, an idol in ruins, a god with feet of coarse clay.

The flames that had destroyed the 'Gioia della Luce'
illumined Gian-Luca's face, a face that seen thus in the
gleaming firelight came perilously near to madness. And
now he turned, as though Doria were present, and began to
revile him also:

'You beast, you fool, you ridiculous bladder! You say to Gian-Luca: "Quick, open the champagne!" You say to Gian-Luca: "It is excellent, this chicken!" You say to the woman: "You are beautiful like morning, you are like my 'Gioia della Luce'!" And all the while she is splitting with laughter. Do you hear? She is splitting her sides with laughter! And her eyes are on someone who is stronger and younger, because she is greedy; I know her, the Milady—and all the while your eyes are on her, and your eyes make Gian-Luca go mad with anger, because of the "Gioia della Luce." But you are not alone, there are many more like you, the Doric is full of you, the whole world is full of you, eating and drinking and moving your jaws, pouring the wine down your gullets. You say to Gian-Luca: "Come here, my good fellow, and tell me what I must eat." He is such an obliging head-waiter, the Gian-Luca; he bows, he smiles, he produces his menu, he recommends this, he recommends that, he feeds you up like a lot of stud cattle. Damn you!' he shouted, shaking his fists, suddenly beside himself with anger; 'damn you and your children and your children's children! May you all eat and drink yourselves to hell.'

Upstairs, Maddalena moaned in her sleep as if she were suffering with him; and as though he heard her, Gian-Luca fell silent, while his face took on a brooding expression.

'I must be very careful with Maddalena, or else she will think I have gone mad,' he muttered. 'What shall I say about all this burnt paper? I think I will get it out of the house, I can dump it somewhere in the street. And if she asks me about Doria's books, I will say that I have lent them to Roberto; and if she says that they were all there this evening, I will say that she has made a mistake; and if she asks me about Ugo Doria, I will say that he is all and more than I thought him—it is lucky that I found her asleep when I got home, it is very lucky indeed!'

And stooping, he began to collect the burnt paper, which he presently threw into the street.

CHAPTER THREE

I

IN THE months that followed on the meeting with Doria,
Gian-Luca acquired the habit of watching. Never before
had he watched like this, with eyes that weighed and
appraised and condemned; with an anger that glowed all
the more intensely because it was kept beneath the surface. For after that one wild night of destruction, Gian-
Luca had found his self-control again; the next morning he
had actually smiled at Maddalena, had actually assured her
that Ugo Doria was as great as, if not greater than, his
genius. Oh, yes, he was wonderfully self-controlled, and
more attentive than ever to his clients; he was everywhere
at once with his low-voiced suggestions regarding their
food and drink.

He would say to Roberto: 'They are drinking too little,
go quickly, my friend, and make them drink some more,
but do it with tact or else they may suspect you—never
irritate, always persuade.'

And Roberto would sometimes stare, almost frightened
at the look in Gian-Luca's eyes; a brooding, cruel, inhuman
expression. 'They have ordered a bottle of champagne,' he
would mutter; 'that lot always drink a good deal.'

Then Gian-Luca would laugh: 'Not enough, not enough!
Go and try them with some Napoleon brandy; but always
take care that they do not get *quite* drunk, for that would be
bad for the Doric.'

Roberto would think: 'What is the matter with the
fellow? It is almost as though he hated our clients, it is
almost as though he took pleasure in their weakness—ma
che, we are all weak at times!'

In spite of his constant service on the clients, Gian-Luca
found time to watch them, and the more he watched them the
more he hated, and the deeper his hatred the greater his zeal.

And now there was plenty of eating and drinking and dancing and lusting to the tunes of the band; but never enough to content Gian-Luca, who, distrusting Roberto, would tempt them in person, with soft-voiced praise for this vintage or that. He would think of Giovanni who had gone to the war, but had come back to slice up their meats; Giovanni who had wished so much to get killed because of his faithless Anna. There would be Giovanni, very quiet, very pale, with his long knife always so busy—a patient, resigned, rather stupid sort of man who had said to Gian-Luca:

'I am back after all. Oh, well, I suppose it was fate!'

And Gian-Luca's anger would flame into his eyes, because Giovanni must still slice meat. Yet Giovanni was quite unfit to rule empires, whereas he was an excellent trancheur. . . .

Gian-Luca would think of Roberto, the wine-waiter, so humble, in spite of those years at the war—Roberto who would tolerate stupid impatience with a smile and a plea for forgiveness. 'Scusi, signore, I am very sorry; the cocktails will not be long coming.' And then he would remember Roberto's fine record, for Roberto had been an 'Ace.' Oh, yes, and he had flown with the gallant d'Annunzio, the dreamer who had known how to turn dreams into actions, and of whom it was told that in moments of peril, it had not been his way with the men to say: '*You* go!' But instead, 'I am going, come with me.' Roberto had done many wonderful things, he had played many times with death. Like a fearless eagle he had soared in the air, swooping, destroying, then up, up and up, while something went spinning earthward! Roberto seldom spoke of these deeds, but one day he had said to Gian-Luca:

'I will never keep birds in a cage any more, for now I know what it means to have wings.'

Gian-Luca's anger would wellnigh choke him, because this Roberto must open their wine; and then he would urge him to open still more, eager for their undoing. Yet all wars must end and with them brave deeds, while the Dorics go on for ever, and Roberto had a mother to keep in Rapallo, so perhaps it was well that he understood wines, and was such a polite little waiter. And indeed he was marvellous, little Roberto, considering all he had done—a quiet, sober man with a great sense of duty; contented too, or so he appeared, as he opened those innumerable bottles. And if he was less contented than he seemed he took care that you should not see it, arguing no doubt that the longings of your waiter would make bad seasoning for supper.

2

Gian-Luca discovered that on certain days there would be more to watch than on others; on certain days interesting people would arrive, people whose faces appeared in the papers, together with their outlandish doings. Perhaps Jane Coram would come in with her friends, satellites surrounding the star—a generous star too, who provided them with money, and invariably paid for their meals. Gian-Luca would hasten to find them a table, for such people were always welcome at the Doric; they amused other clients, who could go home and say: 'I saw Jane Coram at luncheon.'

She was still very young, the famous Jane Coram, and on rare occasions quite sober; but Gian-Luca knew the lure that would catch her, and almost before she could ask he would bring it; then she would sometimes look up with a grin, possessing a great sense of humour. She would sit lolling loosely back in her chair, with her long legs sprawled beneath the table; and as like as not she would have some grievance, a grievance with its tongue in its cheek.

'I'm a most unfortunate woman,' she would say, 'everyone seems to be down on Jane—if I try to help people there's sure to be a row, I'm always misunderstood. Got my brandy-and-soda, Gian-Luca? All right, now get us something to eat.' And then all the satellites called for brandy, just to show that they were satellites.

After a time they would get very loving, loving and jealous of each other. Their eyes would grow veiled and mysterious and pensive; but Jane's eyes never changed, they were always the same, the eyes of a home-sick monkey. There she would sprawl, this darling of the people, this plaything of the gallery and pit, with her body of an athlete and her mind of a buffoon and her soul of a Solitary. And now it would be the turn of Roberto to bring her those double-brandies,

267

Roberto who had been such a fine man in the war, Roberto who had flown with d'Annunzio. While Gian-Luca, always watchful, would be thinking to himself:

'She cannot last very long at this rate.' But never a twinge of pity would he feel for those eyes of a home-sick monkey.

Perhaps a pair of young lovers would arrive, temperate children who drank little as a rule, but because they wished to appear worldly, they must now order cocktails and wine. And gradually the fine ardour of their love would be superseded by something less fine, by something that made them look flushed and coarsened—a stupid, fictitious, unworthy thing, that sat ill on their fresh young faces. They would eat the rich food of the restaurant and their skins would look hot and even rather greasy; then the girl must get out her powderpuff to correct the effects of eating. And now their perceptions would have grown a little blurred, and their sense of values a little untrue, so that they felt much richer than they were, felt that the world was made for their buying, with all its delightful baubles. When they looked across the table at each other and smiled, they were looking through a mist of illusion. Not so Gian-Luca, the quietly observant, he had no illusions about them. He saw them precisely as they were at that moment, when the beauty and the glory of their youth had left them, and into its place had crept something ugly, something that reminded him of Doria.

He would think: 'What fools, what intolerable fools! They need neither food nor wine for their loving, and yet they must do as the others are doing—as Ugo Doria did.'

Compassion? He had none; let them eat, let them drink, the more they consumed the better! 'A generation of fools,' he would mutter; and then his anger would flare up afresh. So much splendour of suffering and sacrifice and death, and now this, a generation of fools!

Oh, but the agèd who must needs feed alone, having neither lover nor friend—the people who drank their lonely champagne and ordered long, lonely meals! Sometimes a woman and sometimes a man, and how carefully they studied their menus; they would have the food-expression in their eyes, in their hands, in their backs, in their whole intent persons. They had come to an age when all other things failing, their meals must provide their diversion, when the garden of Kama must give place to the Doric, and passion to the lusts of the palate. Poor old pitiful, greedy babies, with their unreliable teeth; with their receding gums and their gouty knuckles; with their aches and their pains and their Continental Cures. Four weeks of strict diet then back at the Doric—but dear God! they had to do something for Old Age, he was really terribly insistent. . . .

Gian-Luca detested these senile gourmets, they made him feel physically sick; and yet he would watch them as he watched all the others, in order the better to hate.

3

With each day that passed, Gian-Luca's vision was becoming more cruelly acute, so that now he observed the minutest details that accompanied the ritual of feeding. Nothing was too trifling to strike at his nerves, and via them to arouse his anger; he saw something to condemn in harmless people even, for if they were temperate in eating and drinking, then his mind would seize on their unconscious habits. There would be the crumbling of bread, for instance, and the making of small bread pills; the cleanest of hands would leave the pills dirty, and there they would lie on the spotless linen, an indictment against human skin. Then the habit of preparing a fork full of food so that it comprised a little of all things; a bit of potato, a couple of beans, a section of mushroom, a smear of tomato, a portion of veal— and how maddening the gesture that finally got it to the mouth! There was also the habit of relieving the teeth with the tip of a surreptitious tongue, it not being considered polite in this England to disengage food with a toothpick. Quite nice people would sometimes leave blurs on their tumblers, which they tried to wipe off with their thumbs; while others might leave little stains on their lips, and even after they had rubbed them with the napkin, the stains would remain in the corners. And then there were the people who peered at their food because they were very short-sighted, and the people who sat well back in their chairs because they were the other way round. There were people who made their plates rather untidy, and others who ate in a pattern; a trifle of this, a trifle of that, and keep it all nicely trimmed up and in order like a kind of suburban garden.

And then the chewing! There were so many methods of chewing, since everyone came there to chew. Gian-Luca would watch with a kind of fascination, and their busy moving jaws would make him want to scream for the ugly absurdity of it. Some people would chew with their mouths slightly open; if you faced them you knew the condition of a cutlet about to enter Nirvana. Some people would chew with their lips firmly closed, and this kind occasionally made a small noise, a rhythmical clicking connected with saliva, or their tongues, or perhaps their false teeth. Some chewed with a thoughtful, circular motion that suggested an aftermath of grazing, while others nibbled their food very quickly, like rabbits devouring a lettuce. But the thing that Gian-Luca detested most was a species of ball-bearing jaw-bone, you could see it rotating inside the cheek with the effort of mastication. The more his mind dwelt on this problem of chewing, the more he marvelled that they did it in public; hundreds of good-looking people all chewing, openly chewing in front of each other—that was what amazed Gian-Luca.

One day he felt a violent distaste for the pleasant, white-tiled refectory, where he himself would begin to chew, and Roberto, and all the others. He tried to swallow his own food down quickly, tried not to look at Roberto, but Roberto was picking the leg of a chicken and Gian-Luca had to look.

'Do not do that!' he shouted suddenly; and Roberto dropped his bone in surprise.

But then Gian-Luca smiled blandly at him: 'Scusa, Roberto, I was thinking aloud, please take up that bone again and pick it.'

Roberto obeyed, but that afternoon he whispered a little with Giovanni: 'He is strange, very strange, our Signor Gian-Luca—and I do not much like the look on his face, it reminds me of men I have seen after battle—but then he was never near a battle.'

It was in March that her husband said to Maddalena: 'It is horrible, all this eating. I hate them for it, they are pigs at a trough, they wallow, they make horrid noises.'

Maddalena looked up with fear in her eyes, a fear that had been growing lately. She said: 'But, Gian-Luca, of course they must eat, otherwise you would not be a waiter.'

He scowled at her, then he began talking quickly: 'Do you know the meaning of hatred? Of a hatred so enormous that it chokes a man's breath and jerks the heart out of his body?'

'No—no——' she faltered. 'I have never felt hatred——' And now she was very much afraid.

He saw it and smiled grimly: 'Because, Maddalena, that is what I feel for those beasts at the Doric, I hate them; and now I am going to tell you something: that is how I hated Ugo Doria.'

She got up and tried to take him in her arms, feeling an overwhelming need to protect him against this thing that menaced. 'Tell me, my blessing, tell me——' she pleaded. 'Tell Maddalena what has happened.'

Then he laughed: 'What has happened? Why, this has happened; I see them exactly as they are, pigs at a trough with their noses in food, and when they are not gorging they are swilling! Perhaps you will wonder why I stay at the Doric? Well listen, mia donna, I will tell you. I stay at the Doric to make them eat more, to make them drink more; I coax, I persuade. I am all soft cajoling and smiles and politeness, for no one must know how intensely I hate them —oh, I do my work well—I am crafty, Maddalena, I do my work better than ever.'

She stared at him aghast: 'You are ill,' she whispered. 'You are surely very ill, Gian-Luca.'

But he pushed her away: 'I am well, I tell you, I never felt better in my life. I am working like ten men; you ask them at the Doric, they will tell you I am working like ten men.'

At that moment he caught sight of his untasted breakfast —and all of a sudden he was violently sick.

Nothing that Maddalena could say would persuade him to see a doctor.

'You want me to lose my position,' he told her. 'No doubt you pity those pigs of the Doric for having Gian-Luca to tempt them.' He refused to see Teresa, or Mario, or Rosa, or indeed any member of the clan. 'I am well, I tell you,' he kept on repeating. 'Millo has not complained of my work—I forbid you to go and discuss me with Rosa, or with anyone else, for that matter.'

And Maddalena, afraid to enrage him, must needs keep her great fear hidden in her heart. But now he was eating less and less, complaining again about the richness of her cooking.

'For the love of God, cook things simply!' he would say. 'You disgust me with all your grease.'

Then Maddalena would try to cook simply, boiling his vegetables in water like the English; but even so he would always complain: 'It is horrible, all this food!'

At the Doric he was finding it hard to eat a mouthful, for there the head-waiters must finish the remains of all those expensive dishes. They might help themselves freely from the buffet or wagons, feasting like kings, if they felt so disposed, on the very fat of the land. Gian-Luca would scrape off the rich yellow sauces and the soft white billows of cream, but everything he ate would have too strong a flavour; his nostrils would be full of the smell of the cooking and his ears of the sizzling and hissing and bubbling that came from the kitchens near by. But in case they suspected, he must try hard to eat, and this was a veritable torture; his throat would close up when he wanted to swallow; he would not know how to get rid of the food with which he had filled his mouth.

Daniele, who was still young, enjoyed the fine fare. 'U—m,' he would gurgle, 'é molto buono! É buono, non é vero, signore?'

Then Gian-Luca must nod and reply: 'Buonissimo!' in case Daniele suspected.

And then there was Roberto who picked every bone, spitting out little bits of gristle; and he watched Gian-Luca with large, anxious eyes—Roberto was always watching.

He would say: 'Will you not eat your chicken, signore? Shall I go and fetch you some mousse—or perhaps you would like a little "sole Mornay"? It is good, the "sole Mornay" to-day!'

So terribly watchful he was, this Roberto, almost as watchful as Gian-Luca; almost as anxious to feed him, it seemed, as Gian-Luca was to feed the clients. Yes, but that was another terrible thing; it was not so easy any more to feed the clients, for whenever Gian-Luca must talk about food his stomach would heave and his head would grow dizzy—God! how he loathed them, those hungry clients who would force him to talk about food! But he must talk. Oh, more than ever he must talk, in case any client suspected; in case Millo suspected, or Giovanni or Roberto—did Roberto suspect already?

Night after night he would lie in bed sleepless, wondering if Roberto suspected. What should he do if Roberto told Millo? What should he do if Millo dismissed him? Ruined, he was ruined if Millo dismissed him, no one would give him a manager's job—perhaps no one would come to his restaurant if he bought it; they would all know that Millo had dismissed him. And his money; he would lie there and count up his money—a good sum by now, but not nearly enough for him and Maddalena to live on; one of them might live on it perhaps, but not both—two could never live in comfort on that money. He would hear Maddalena whispering her prayers, prayers to the Madonna, and one special prayer that began with: 'Blessèd be God.'

He would shake her: 'Stop praying like that, Maddalena! Why must you always be whispering something? I can hear you, it gets on my nerves; do stop praying, I am tired, I want to go to sleep.'

Maddalena would lie there obediently silent, but Gian-Luca would know that she was praying in her heart. What was she praying about in her heart? Her silent prayers would begin to torment him, he would try to imagine those prayers in her heart and would want her to whisper again. In the mornings he would get up angry and weary, and there would be Maddalena. Then she too would watch him as Roberto watched him, following him round the room with her eyes;

urging him to let her send for the doctor, urging him to eat his breakfast.

'Eat, amore!' she was always saying. 'Try to eat something, amore.'

And one day his hand shot out and he struck her. Full in the face he struck Maddalena, then he struck her again because she said nothing but just stood there dumb like an animal who loves and is wounded unto death by its master.

6

Terrible days indeed for Maddalena, but even more terrible days for Gian-Luca, who must struggle through his work at the Doric with a smile—especially if Millo was watching. And now he felt certain that everyone watched him: Millo, Giovanni, Roberto, the clients. It came down like an avalanche on him, their watching; their watching was a *thing*, an intolerable presence that stood between him and his own will to watch, so that he could not see clearly.

'Dio!' he would groan, 'will they never stop watching? Do they think I am drunk, or crazy or what, that they follow me about with their eyes?'

CHAPTER FOUR

I

ONE EVENING that June the Signora Rocca looked up from her sewing and said: 'What a deplorable thing is pride, and how right I was when I warned the Bosellis not to send Gian-Luca to that heathenish Board School.'

Rocca took off his spectacles and swore, beyond which he vouchsafed no comment, so his wife continued: 'I am sorry for Gian-Luca, as a Christian that is my duty—but as the English say, and it is a good saying, "Pride cometh before a fall." I do not see what he has to be proud of, considering his unfortunate birth; however, it is clear that he sets himself above us; does he ever come here to see us these days? He does not, he treats us as though we were dirt, he is getting too big for his breeches!'

Rocca, for once, sympathized with his wife. Her words had opened the vials of his wrath so that he thumped the table; large angry thumps he inflicted on the table, as though he were thumping Gian-Luca.

'Giurabaccaccio! you speak truly,' said Rocca, 'we are not good enough any more! Imagine it, a fellow that I dandled as an infant, a fellow to whom I had to give fruit-drops because he so feared my small goats! It is impudent indeed the way Gian-Luca treats me, I who fought at Custozza. I did not play waiter in an Officers' Mess! No, no, I was only a poor, common soldier; I killed men in those days, not scraggy French chickens—but then I was only a soldier!'

Rocca spoke in great bitterness of heart, not for nearly five months had Gian-Luca been near him, and now, Maddalena would never come either—grown proud, no doubt, like her husband.

Rocca was so angry that he went to see Teresa in order to tell her about it: 'That grandson of yours has become

275

swollen-headed, he ignores his old friends, he gives himself airs, he is what the English call "snob." My wife is offended and I am offended at the manner in which he treats us. We are humble but proud. I am only a butcher, but I fought in the battle of Custozza!'

Teresa shrugged her shoulders: 'My excellent Rocca, I am not the keeper of my grandson—he never comes here, I know nothing about him, and now his wife does not come either. Perhaps he has become what the English call "snob," or perhaps he is just very busy—Millo tells me they are all very busy at the Doric—but whatever it is I am busy myself, much too busy to run after Gian-Luca.'

'Only a fool throws away his old friends,' muttered Rocca as he turned to leave her. 'As for you, I consider that he owes you a duty; in our country the family tie is sacred, and only a fool would copy these English, who care nothing for family ties.'

'That is so,' she agreed, 'but on the other hand, only a fool would allow sentiment to stand in the way of his business. I do not resent the fact that my grandson is too proud or too busy to bother about me—since I am too busy to bother about him, why should I feel resentment?'

But if Rocca was angry and Teresa indifferent, Mario and Rosa were wounded; so deeply wounded that they looked at each other and their kindly brown eyes filled with tears.

'He does not love us any more,' sighed Rosa, while Mario shook his head sadly.

'Yet he drank of your milk—it is strange, my Rosa, for they say that much love flows in with the milk that is drawn from a woman's breast——'

Poor Mario was deeply depressed this summer, and he had good cause for depression, for now he was no longer the head-waiter of the Capo; his triumph had been short-lived, and his fall the more bitter because of that short-lived triumph.

The Padrone had said quite pleasantly one morning: 'I have just engaged a head-waiter. Now that we have our full staff back again, and no more lazy, imbecile women, the Padrona and I think the time has arrived to have a head-waiter at the Capo. I shall have to reduce your wages, of course—that will be only fair—but even so you will be getting more money than you dreamt of before the war. Then again, there is always the question of your lameness, my wife was speaking of it only last week: "It is dreadful to see how old Mario limps, we must get a head-waiter," she said.'

Mario had stood with his mouth slightly open and his napkin drooping from his hand, for whenever the Padrone mentioned his lameness he certainly felt very old. He had been quite unable to trust himself to speak, so had hobbled away to the pantry; and there he had started biting his nails—what could he do but start biting his nails? Give notice? Ma che! who else would engage him? He was only an old lame mule.

It was terribly hard when it came to telling Rosa, who naturally shed a few tears; 'Geppe dead, and Gian-Luca so proud and now this——' she whimpered, mopping her eyes. But then she noticed her husband's grey hair, nearly white it had gone at the temples, and all that was brave in her leapt to his defence, the kind, patient creature that he was! 'It is scandalous, you look younger than ever!' she lied. 'And as for your grey hair, I like it; it is very becoming, it gives you distinction, a head-waiter looks better with grey hair.'

And this obvious falsehood really consoled him, at all events for the moment, since the hearts of some men are the hearts of small children—especially when they ache badly.

Nerone, however, was not nearly so tactful. 'It is all that infernal bunion!' he shouted. 'Why do you not get the damned thing cut off? Are there no hospitals in England?' But at such a terrific suggestion as this, Mario turned very pale: 'I do not like operations,' he babbled, 'one cannot know what they will do to one's body; one is helpless like a pig about to be slaughtered. I have heard that they wish to experiment on one, I have heard the most terrible things——'
In his fear he began to plead for his bunion; 'No, no, Babbo; no, no, I have had him for years—I will paint him with iodine night and morning, I will get some new boots many sizes too big, I will try to limp less—it is only a habit, one gets into the habit of limping——'

'Fool!' bawled Nerone. 'They cut off my leg, and the students amused themselves with it! Did I care if the students played football with my leg? Well then, why need you care what they do with your bunion? Sacramento! one would think you were proud of the thing! Perhaps they would put it to float in a bottle, and then you could keep it in your bedroom!'

After which Nerone must mourn his own fate; he would have to stay in England, he declared. How could he give up his miserable business when his daughter would obviously starve? In vain did they both try to reassure him; Mario was not so ill-paid, there were no children now—why, Berta was quite rich, with her Albert promoted to buyer—there was no need to worry, there was no need to stay, Nerone could go when he pleased. Of course he must go if he still felt so home-sick—poor Babbo, of course he must go! But Nerone shook his head and glared hotly at Mario, which was certainly rather unfair, for it was not the thought of his daughter that held him, but those pretty silver shillings that winked back from the till; prolific past all expectations they were being, because of the Italian exchange.

There was someone, however, who could never do wrong, according to old Nerone, and this was Gian-Luca, whom he loved more than ever for the sake of his dead friend Fabio. He said to Rosa: 'You make a great fuss, always snivelling and dabbing your eyes—Dio Santo! One would think that Gian-Luca had been hanged, whereas he is only trying to make money. He is making good money, and so he has no time to come paying you foolish visits. But apart from all this, he is not well, I think, that is why I called on Maddalena. As for Rocca, I have told him quite plainly that he lies when he says that Gian-Luca has grown proud. That Rocca is making me sick with his talk of his courage, and his wounds, and his battles. Custozza, ma che! that was all very well, but my grandson died on the Isonzo! Leave Gian-Luca alone, he will come home to roost, he will want to see his old Nerone. Did he not call me "Nonno" that day, and make Fabio so terribly angry?'

'Magari——' murmured Rosa, which meant nothing or all things, according as you chose to interpret.

Meanwhile Gian-Luca still held aloof, feeling strangely unwilling to see them. They would talk, about eating and food and the Doric. Oh, he knew them, they thought about nothing but food, they were almost as bad as Millo. When he got his day off at the end of June, he wanted to spend it alone, but of course Maddalena must begin about Rosa— she was always reproaching him now about Rosa whom he had forbidden her to visit.

She said precisely what he had expected: 'Do let us go and see Rosa—she is very sad, caro, she misses her Geppe, and you are her foster-son.'

'Dio!' he complained, 'must I never forget that I drank of that good woman's milk? I do not wish to see Rosa or the others. I am tired, I am not getting up at all this morning, do leave me in peace, mia donna.'

She left him, and he lay in bed trying to doze; he was feeling very weak, he discovered. He had noticed lately that when he stopped working, his body ran down like a clock. At half-past one Maddalena brought his dinner all neatly arranged on a tray. He sat up in bed and glared at it frowning.

'Is it not good?' she inquired with a sigh. 'I have tried to cook everything simply.'

'Ma sí!' he muttered, 'it is probably good, but do not stand watching, Maddalena. How can a man eat his food when you watch every morsel he puts into his mouth?'

So she went down again to her own lonely meal, which was little enough to her liking, being cooked as the English cook most things, in water, and never a touch of good butter with the beans or the dreary-faced boiled potatoes. And as she sat eating the unappetizing fare she remembered her father's trattoria, and from this her thoughts strayed to the far-off Campagna, and then she felt home-sick, terribly home-sick—very lonely she felt and unhappy. For the longing to live among her own people had been growing in Maddalena lately, the longing for blue sky and wide, quiet places, where the sheep all wore little bells. She would think of that wonderful day when Our Lord had left His Footprint in stone, and would wonder if He too had loved the Campagna—if indeed that might not well have been

Our Lord's reason for blessing the humble stone. Then her heart would begin to yearn over Gian-Luca, who laughed when she spoke of such things—perhaps if she got him away to the sunshine he too might receive the blessing of faith. Some day she would show him that Footprint in stone, after which he must surely believe.

3

Late that afternoon Gian-Luca got up and went for a walk alone. He could feel Maddalena watching from the window, and for just a moment he paused on the pavement, but he did not turn his head. He wished that she would not stand there at the window, with her questioning desolate eyes— the eyes of a woman who was doomed to be childless— why must she always reproach him with her eyes, was it his fault that she was childless? His feet dragged a little as he walked on slowly, not caring much where he went. And now he was passing the Foundling Hospital—queer to be living so near that place; why had he chosen to live near that place? The thought had never occurred to him before— yes, it certainly was rather queer.

The foundlings appeared to be happy enough; they were playing out in the garden, not troubling at all about the problems of fate. At their age he had troubled very much about such problems—oh, very much he had troubled! He looked through the tall iron gates, and marvelled at the noisy, shouting children, remembering the pain of his own lonely childhood; remembering bitterly, cruelly even, wounding himself in the process.

'Go on, go on!' he said, staring at the foundlings. 'Go on, go on—but you will not escape it, it is waiting for you round the corner!' But when he would have liked to tell them what was waiting, he found that he did not know. 'Ma che!' he thought dully, 'what does it all matter; they play, they shout, they think they are happy—oh, well, and why not? It will come soon enough, that thing that is waiting round the corner.' Shrugging his shoulders he went on his way, and quite soon he forgot about the foundlings; forgot about everything except Gian-Luca, for whom he was deeply concerned. 'I am ill,' he muttered, 'I think I am ill.' He laid his fingers on his pulse, and then he felt frightened and walked more quickly, just to prove that he was not ill.

One or two women glanced at him in passing, struck by the expression of his face; a pale, handsome face with its arrogant mouth and its queer, inscrutable eyes. And presently a woman came up and touched him, murmuring something in his ear.

'Go to hell!' he said roughly, and pushed her with his arm so that she fell back frightened.

The noise of the traffic began to grow louder; he was suddenly conscious of the noise; he found himself walking in New Oxford Street without knowing how he had got there. All around him were shabby, insufferable people, and they jostled him as he walked. He felt sick with disgust at the contact with their bodies, and squaring his shoulders he thrust them aside; he would gladly have trampled on them. The stench of the traffic was heavy in his nostrils, the hot, greasy smell of engines; of monstrous engines, all spewing and belching up oil and petrol, and poisonous fumes from the pipes of their filthy exhausts. He hated these engines as though they had life, as though his hatred could harm them. They were foul, greedy feeders, and they stank of their food like creatures with rotting stomachs.

Oh, but he was tired! He had gone much too far; he had not intended to go far. His legs were trembling, and his hands, and his lips—— Wait, he would smoke, that would steady the trembling—he groped for a cigarette. He found one, but now he could not find his matches—what had he done with his matches? He began to ransack all his pockets in a panic, so intent on this process that he passed a tobacconist's without having noticed the shop. Now the urge to smoke was becoming a torment, he must stop that trembling of his hands. The cruelty of it, to have come without his matches! So harmless a longing, just to light a cigarette, and yet he had come without his matches! He stood still, staring round him in a kind of despair, with the cigarette lolling from his mouth; then he started to run forward; he had seen a woman who was selling matches at the corner.

'Give me a box of matches!' he panted. 'Quick, give me a box of matches!' Without waiting, he snatched what he wanted from her tray and started to light his cigarette.

The woman was battered and dirty and dejected; her face looked humble yet sly; for hers was the face of the intolerably poor, of those who must cringe to the lash of Fate and fool him behind his back. But by her side stood a thin little boy who clung to her threadbare jacket, and his face, unlike hers, was wonderfully quiet. Resigned, too, it seemed, as only the faces of very young children can be. Something was terribly wrong with his eyes—what was it that was wrong with his eyes? The closed lids were shrunken and flat and disfigured—so woe-begone somehow, they looked, those closed lids, in spite of that quiet expression. And Gian-Luca, who cared not at all for children, must gaze and gaze at this child as though he were suddenly suffering with him, as though in some curious way he belonged to those woe-begone, sightless eyes.

He said: 'That child—who is he, what is he?'

And the woman answered: "E's mine.'

And the child stood very still as though listening, with his head a little on one side.

Then Gian-Luca said: 'But his eyes, his poor eyes——'

And the woman answered: 'They're gone. 'E ain't got no eyes, they was both taken out, they was all diseased like, 'is eyes.'

She lifted the lids one after the other, showing the empty sockets; and the child never spoke, and neither did he flinch, nor indeed show any resentment.

Down the street came a jolting coster's barrow, and the barrow was full of spring flowers. All the colours of heaven seemed to be passing, drawn by a mangy donkey. The sun came out from behind a cloud, making the flowers more lovely: and because of a child who could not see, Gian-Luca realized the flowers. Then he looked again at the face of the child, at that face of dreadful resignation, and all in a moment he had pulled out his purse and was emptying it into the tray. Something rose up in his throat and choked him, and suddenly he was weeping; the great tears went trickling down his cheeks and splashed on his coat unheeded.

The woman mumbled her words of thanks: 'Thank yer, mister; God bless yer, mister.' She thought he was mad, but what did that matter, he had given her nearly five pounds! She pushed the child forward: 'Just look at 'im, mister—ain't he a poor little feller!' For she hoped that this soft-hearted, weeping madman might be tempted to still further madness.

But Gian-Luca had turned and was rushing away; away and away from the sightless child, away and away from suffering and affliction, and the great, blind sadness of the world. And even as he ran something ran beside him, he could feel it close at his elbow. A quiet, persistent, intangible presence —the great, blind sadness of the world.

4

When at last he got home he went to Maddalena, and he laid his head down on her knee, and he told her about the child without eyes, and all the while he was talking he wept; and over and over again he must tell her about the child without eyes.

She sat there gently stroking his hair, murmuring her pity for the little blind creature, murmuring her pity for the desolate man who crouched there sobbing at her knee. And when he had cried for more than an hour he looked up into Maddalena's face.

'I struck you——' he whispered. 'I struck you, Maddalena.' And his tearful eyes were amazed.

She shook her head slowly: 'It was only your hand— you have never struck me, Gian-Luca.' And stooping, she kissed the guilty hand and forgave it and pressed it to her cheek.

Then he said: 'I am very tired, Maddalena, and tomorrow I must go to the Doric; I think I should like to sleep for a little, only—sit by me, Maddalena.'

5

That night he dreamt about the beggar who sold matches, and about the child without eyes. And in his dream he thought that they looked different; curiously different, for although they were beggars, there was something noble about them. The face of the child was serene in its suffering, and wise—oh, intensely wise; and the face of his mother was no longer as it had been; now it seemed to Gian-Luca to be full of high courage, a steadfast, enduring face.

She said: 'This is my little son, Gian-Luca, who must bear so much for the world. Will you not see for my little son who must bear the blindness of the world?'

Then Gian-Luca wept afresh, in his sleep, for the eyes that were not there to weep. And hearing him, Maddalena woke him:

'You are dreaming, Gian-Luca—wake up, amore, and tell me what you have been dreaming.'

He tried to tell her but somehow he could not—he could not remember his dream.

'There, there,' she soothed, 'it is all right, piccino.' And as though he himself were a child, she rocked him till he fell asleep again in her arms.

CHAPTER FIVE

I

GIAN-LUCA was ill on the following morning, too ill to go to the Doric.

'I think you have caught a chill,' said Maddalena.

And he nodded: 'Sí, sí—it is a chill.'

He was patient, letting her minister to him, letting her wash his hands and face, letting her give him those simple old remedies so dear to her peasant's soul. His pale eyes followed her round the room, wherever she went they followed; and always they held a look of surprise, as though they were seeing this grave, simple woman for the first time, and seeing her, marvelled. And this poignant new seeing had little in common with the stately beauty of her body; her gracious body was only a cloak beneath which lay the suffering heart of Maddalena—that was what he seemed to be seeing.

He said: 'You are very unhappy, Maddalena. Is it I who have made you unhappy?'

'If you would only get well——' she murmured. 'If you would only try to eat——'

Then Gian-Luca shook his head: 'Come here, Maddalena; come here and stand by the bed.'

And she went to him slowly, turning her face, for she could not steady her lips.

He caught hold of her hand: 'It is not that, Maddalena, it cannot be only my illness—your heart feels so empty, so horribly empty—you are lonely because of our unborn children, and because there is something lacking in me, something that I cannot give you.'

'No, no!' she protested. 'No, no, Gian-Luca.' But her voice was heavy with tears.

And hearing that voice he sighed to himself and stared down at her trustful hand.

'It has always been that, Maddalena,' he said slowly. 'I laid my loneliness on you; from the first day we met I have forced you to bear it—and yet that was not quite enough, it seems, for I have remained very lonely.' Then he said: 'You were made for great loving, Maddalena—for great simple primitive loving; for the kind of love that knows no ambition, no anger, no bitterness, no doubts and no fears, that is selfless because of itself. Such a great love as that would have filled up your heart, so that if you had had no children, you would still have possessed the most complete fulfilment that life is capable of giving——'

He paused, for now she was kissing his forehead, and her arms were around his shoulders.

'Get well—get well, my belovèd,' she whispered. 'You are my only fulfilment, Gian-Luca, my little child and my husband.'

But Gian-Luca looked into Maddalena's eyes, so faithful they were but so hopeless; the desolate eyes of a mothering doe whose young has been slain by the hunter.

'You have very much to forgive,' he said gravely. 'Can you forgive, Maddalena?'

And she answered: 'If I have much to forgive, then may God forgive me as I forgive you, and love me as I love you, Gian-Luca.'

2

To please her he drank up the good beef tea, and the milk and wine that she brought him; and when she took him his simple meals, he made her stand by him and watch while he ate, hoping to reassure her.

'Give me a little more fish,' he would say, then look up quickly at her face; and because of her smile he would praise the fish: 'It is good, I must be getting much better, Maddalena, already I feel much better.'

By the fourth day of nursing he was certainly stronger; he was able to get up and dress. He was able to smoke too, an excellent sign, as he pointed out to his wife. And by the next morning he had grown rather restless, he wished to go out, he told her, he wanted to find that woman again, and the child who had lost his eyes.

'But why, amore?' Maddalena protested. 'But why, when they made you so sad?'

'I must find out much more about them,' he answered. 'Do not worry, I shall not be long.'

And something told her that he had better go, so she sighed and nodded her head.

In Theobald's Road he got into a taxi and drove to New Oxford Street, stopping the cab when it came to the corner where the woman had sold him matches. He paid off the driver and stood looking about him, but the woman and her child were not there; and this gave him a little shock for some reason, so that he felt afraid. He went up and spoke to the policeman on point duty, describing the pair to him minutely.

But the policeman shook his head: 'I've not seen them, sir, I don't ever remember having seen them.'

Then Gian-Luca began to urge him to remember. 'The child had no eyes,' he repeated. 'Of course you have seen them—a child with no eyes—there cannot be many such children?'

'Well,' said the policeman, 'maybe I have seen them, we've a good many beggars round here—they don't always stop in the same place for long—but I can't recall them at the moment.'

Then Gian-Luca inquired at a shop on the corner, but there also they could not remember. The street was so crowded, there were so many people—a woman selling matches with a little blind boy? Yes, they thought they had seen her; or was it a man? They were sorry, they could not remember. Still intent on his search, Gian-Luca walked on until he came to High Holborn. There were several other beggars, one or two who sold matches, but not the beggars he wanted.

'If I could only find them,' he muttered, 'if I could only find them!' Not that he knew what he would say if he found them—what could anyone say?

And strangely now he had turned in the direction of home, still feeling afraid; for his eyes were full of that awful new seeing, so that he must pity the straining horses, and the men who crouched by their dingy loads, urging those straining horses. The stench of the traffic seemed more horrible than ever, and the throb and the roar of engines. In and out of the turmoil dashed tired, anxious people—across the road limped a foolhardy cripple, swinging a perilous crutch. There were babies with incredibly old, suffering faces, bearing the sins of their fathers; there were women with blemished, disease-stricken bodies, bearing the sins of their men; there were men with blotched skins and small, hating eyes, eyes that were looking for vengeance; there were children who were full of a crude, horrid wisdom, learnt in the school of degradation. And then there were all the more prosperous citizens, wearing their liveries of business. Grey clothes, grey faces, grey minds, grey spirits; that blank, grey stare of preoccupation with the unrelieved greyness of the office. Such excellent, hard-working people these latter, such neat little wheels in the machine; so proud of the order to which they belonged, so contented—yes, that was the worst of it, so contented to be neat little wheels in the machine. And then there were the idle who passed in their motors, which were constantly checked by the traffic. Inquiring faces would look through the windows; what a bore it all was, they wanted to get on! They wanted to go quickly, to go more and more quickly; they had nothing to do so they wanted to go quickly, in order the better to do it. And then there was Gian-Luca, seeing sadness in these things, disintegrating with pity, so that the years swept backwards to childhood, so that he muttered the words of a child: 'Oh poor, oh poor, oh poor!'

What did it matter if the things that he saw were the work and the will of these people; all the hideous folly the work of their hands, all the hideous injustice the will of their brains; it was there, they had done it, they had built up the monster, and had called him Civilization. And now they were sweating great gouts of blood, or so it seemed to Gian-Luca—rich and poor, idlers, workers, they were all sweating blood. Ay, and the patient beasts that must serve them, all sweating great gouts of blood.

He quickened his steps because of Maddalena, who would surely be watching and waiting; a quiet, patient woman, herself so much a victim; and his pity overflowed when he thought of Maddalena to whom he could never give love. If he could have realized anything to pray to he would surely have prayed at that moment; he would surely have prayed that he might love Maddalena, but his mind and his lips were both strangers to prayer. He could not find God in this anguish of pity, he could not find himself, he was utterly lost; he could not find high-sounding, resonant phrases, for only the words of his childhood came to him: 'Oh poor, oh poor, oh poor!'

3

By the end of a week he was back at the Doric, a thin, grave man who now stooped slightly, and whose hands were not quite steady.

Roberto exclaimed in surprise when he saw him: 'Ma, signore, have you been very ill?'

And Gian-Luca was silent; had he been very ill? Perhaps —he was not quite sure. As he stood there looking at the anxious Roberto, he forgot all about his wine-waiter's brave deeds; he could think of nothing but the little man's eyes; such round, bright eyes like those of a bird, like the eyes of Nerone's caged skylarks. But Gian-Luca must turn away to his duties, he must superintend all the preparations for the day, so that when the clients began to arrive he would be in his place by the door. The business of his life had begun for him again, the interminable business of feeding.

'Gian-Luca!'

'Sí, signore——'

'Do send me Roberto.'

'Subito, signore, I will tell him.'

'Maître d'hotel!'

'Permesso——'

'I don't like this salad!'

'I will change it at once, signore.'

And now there was no need to watch his clients, for he saw too much without watching; and all that he saw he seemed to see clearly, with a ruthless but pitiful vision. He saw Jane Coram, with her body of an athlete, and her eyes of a home-sick monkey; a monkey that must prance to the tunes of the band, that must take off its cap and grimace and gibber so that fools might find pleasure in its antics. Her face looked sallow and slightly thickened as she sat in a patch of sunlight; and as though the presence of the sun-light confused her, she called for Gian-Luca to draw the silk curtains in order to shut it away. She was rather untidy to-day, Jane Coram, and her mouth was a little awry, for her uncertain hand had slipped with the lip-stick, marring the shape of her lips. Behind those eyes of a home-sick monkey Gian-Luca perceived something cowering; something that feared and hated the crowds, something that shrank from noise and applause, something that wanted to be all alone—the soul of a Solitary. And seeing, he could not order the brandy

He said to Roberto: 'She has drunk much already, they all have, that lot, poor devils! Go slowly.'

And Roberto answered: 'I will do what I can, but you know what they are, they must have their brandy, other-wise they will go somewhere else.'

Then Gian-Luca grew infinitely sorrowful and humble as he looked about him at his clients. He had set himself up as their tempter and their judge, he who was surely the least among them, for had he not grabbed at their money with both hands, seeking to grow rich through their weak-ness? And now he must serve them in anguish of spirit, a dreadful, unwilling serving.

'Gian-Luca!'

'Signorina?'

'Another double-brandy!'

Then that horrible: 'Sí, signorina——'

4

The season dragged on, and whenever he could Gian-Luca went home to Maddalena. He clung to her now like a frightened child, eating without complaint the food that she prepared, in order to keep up his strength. Sometimes he would try to express his great sadness but his words would be inadequate and vague.

'I saw something horrible to-day,' he might begin, 'a poor wretch in khaki grinding an organ——'

'They are often frauds,' Maddalena would tell him.

Then he would stammer and would want to explain that this in itself was a reason for pity, only the words would fail him. He wanted to tell her about Jane Coram and the thing that cowered behind her eyes.

'Maddalena, it is lonely because of the crowds——'

'But why must she drink as she does?' she would ask him.

Why indeed? He would stare at his wife, bewildered; somewhere deep down, he thought he knew the answer, but it always seemed to evade him.

There were days when his sadness infected Maddalena, descending upon her like a cloud, when all that she did seemed futile and useless; her very prayers lacked conviction at such times, as though there was no one to hear her. Then it was that in a kind of self-preservation she would speak to Gian-Luca of her Church.

'If only you belonged to the Church,' she would tell him, 'you would know peace, amore, you would come to know God.' And the sound of her own words would comfort a little. 'You would surely come to know God!'

He always listened patiently to her while she praised and glorified her faith, listened because of the burden he inflicted in making her share his sadness. But when she had finished he would shake his head:

'I cannot find God, Maddalena.'

'You have never looked for Him,' she would say reproachfully.

'Ma sí——' he would tell her. 'I have looked for Him lately, only I cannot find Him, and if I should find Him, Maddalena, I should have many questions to ask.'

'The Church would answer your questions, Gian-Luca, is it not God's own mouthpiece?'

Then Gian-Luca would smile: 'I do not feel God as needing a mouthpiece in that sense, piccina—I feel Him as being too vast and aloof—perhaps that is the trouble; your God is too aloof to notice poor, everyday things.'

But Gian-Luca was beginning to notice more and more those pitiful everyday things, so that now he could not pass one of the afflicted without a strong thought of pity. Sometimes it would be a long-suffering beggar who must earn a living by displaying the shame of a wretched, misshapen body; sometimes one of those dwarfed, consequential creatures who elbowed their way through the crowded streets with a kind of pathetic and impudent defiance, born of a conscious grotesqueness; sometimes it would be a man out of work, bearing military ribbons on his coat, or another performing some mean, dreary labour in the remnants of glorious khaki. And Gian-Luca would want to comfort such people, not weakly, but with the whole strength of his being, only he did not know how to set about it; he would feel inadequate, self-conscious and shy, and when he stopped to give money to a beggar he would flush with a curious feeling of shame, and as like as not would speak brusquely: 'Be quiet, do not thank me!'—for the thanks of the poor filled him with a sense of outrage. He had not yet learnt that Compassion, the divine, has a sister whose name is Gratitude, and that each must form part of the perfect whole that alone is capable of healing.

5

Gian-Luca made his peace with the clan very simply, by going one day to see them. And because of the deep sadness that they saw in his eyes, their warm hearts forgave him those months of neglect—only Teresa's heart held aloof, for her heart remembered his mother. Looking at Teresa, so stern, so much alone, Gian-Luca made one more effort to win her, returning in spirit to the days of his childhood, but offering now the pity of a man to this arrogant, defiant old woman.

He said: 'I would so much like you to love me—is it impossible, Nonna? I would like you to want me, to need me a little—not because of my advice about the Casa Boselli, you have Millo to help you with that now—but because I am your grandson, the only living creature upon whom you have any real claim.'

Then Teresa stood up and confronted her grandson, and they looked at each other eye to eye: 'I have only loved once in my life, Gian-Luca. Only one creature have I loved in my life, and that was my daughter Olga.'

His arrogant underlip shot out a little, and he felt a quick impulse to break her: 'I am the child of your child,' he said hotly; 'I am the flesh and blood of that Olga for whose sake you always hate me.'

'I do not hate you,' she answered quietly; ' I neither love you nor hate you; but to me you have been as alien flesh; can I help that, Gian-Luca? I respect you, I am even proud of your success, but to me you are alien flesh. I saw your mother agonize and die in order that you might have life.'

Then Gian-Luca nodded slowly, and his arrogant mouth grew gentle as he silently accepted her decision, for the unassuageable grief of the old stared at him out of those hard black eyes. He seemed to be seeing the heart of Teresa, a bitter, unforgiving but desolate heart—all bleeding it was, with the sorrow and shame that his life had called into being.

'It must be as you wish,' he said very gravely, and turning away he left her; but it seemed to Gian-Luca that her sorrow went with him and followed him into the street.

6

It was a very good thing that Gian-Luca's under-waiters were a well-trained lot of young men, that indeed he had trained most of them himself to the standard required by the Doric. For the eyes of a head-waiter must only be all-seeing in purely material matters, and once they begin to see beneath the surface their owner is no longer really proficient, and this was what had happened to Gian-Luca. Gian-Luca the implacable, the perfect machine, with those long years of training behind him, was gradually becoming a mere obstruction. His voice would sound vague when he gave his orders, and the orders themselves would be uncertain, so that Daniele must ask him to repeat them, while Roberto the watchful would whisper to Giovanni:

'He is stranger than ever today, amico; we had better look out for trouble.'

And trouble there was on more than one occasion, especially with the Milady who was little and lovely and who liked her good food, and whose table Gian-Luca might forget to reserve, because he was worrying over Jane Coram or some other unfortunate creature.

'What is the matter?' the waiters asked each other. 'He is going to pieces, our Signor Gian-Luca. He no longer takes command; a man cannot be certain of receiving an order correctly.'

But because of the spendid head-waiter that he had been, they rallied in something like pity. They who had borne his hard yoke for so long, whose smallest misdeeds had been severely censured, who had never expected mercy from Gian-Luca, must now show mercy and hide him from Millo; and in this they were led by the little Roberto—he was loyal, the little Roberto. But it could not go on, and one day in September, Millo sent for Gian-Luca.

'Deceive Signor Millo? Ma che!' sighed Roberto, 'he has eyes in the back of his head!'

'In the back of his head, do you say!' snapped Giovanni, who remembered his own short period of transgression; 'he has even more eyes than a peacock's tail! I am sorry for Signor Gian-Luca.'

Millo said: 'Will you please to sit down, Gian-Luca, so that we can have a little talk? It appears to me that you work badly lately, indeed I may say that you do not work at all. For the most part you stand about doing nothing, and when you do make some sort of an effort you only confuse your waiters. Moreover, I have noticed a strange thing about you—you look at our clients with pity. Now nobody comes to the Doric to be pitied; for the most part they come to amuse their stomachs, they come to forget the necessity to pity themselves or anyone else. Your waiters have been trying to shield you, I know, hoping that Millo would not see; but Millo sees all things pertaining to the Doric, and he sees that the restaurant is not what it was, and that clients grow angry because their orders are neglected—is not that so, Gian-Luca?'

Gian-Luca bowed slightly, and Millo went on to check off a list of complaints. Milady's table, it had twice been forgotten; the Duchess's supper, she had ordered oysters and had been given smoked salmon instead; Jane Coram's brandy—moderation in all things, but Jane had not yet signed the pledge—Gian-Luca omitted to order her brandy if Roberto was busy, and this made her fretful, and when she was fretful she was like a spoilt child, complaining of all sorts of things. And then there was Gian-Luca's uncontrolled face, which looked pitiful and gloomy by turns. He no longer smiled, and all clients expected a perpetual smile from their waiter.

'Dio Santo!' exclaimed Millo, 'they pay for our smiles, and we make them pay high at the Doric! A smile will often cover an omission, a smile will often make good food taste better, a smile is the best appetizer in the world, and do not forget that, Gian-Luca.'

Gian-Luca nodded but found nothing to reply, for Millo was speaking the truth.

'Here we have no time for moods,' he was saying; 'the man who feels moody is a nuisance at the Doric; you have been a fine waiter, but now you are a nuisance. What is the reason, Gian-Luca?'

Gian-Luca said slowly: 'It is something, signore, that I find it hard to explain—a kind of great sadness has come over me lately——' And he looked at Millo with his strange light eyes as though he felt sorry for him also.

Millo frowned and tapped on the desk with his fingers: 'Your nerves are out of order,' he said firmly. 'What you need is a rest; you have worked hard for years, you worked like ten men before you went to France, while possessing only one body.' He paused, then went on: 'I have seen Maddalena. I went to see her last week, and I want you to go to my doctor at once; you will please go not later than to-morrow. I have spoken to Daniele, he can manage quite well, at all events he must manage,' and he scribbled something on a half-sheet of paper. 'Here is the doctor's address, Gian-Luca; I have made an appointment for to-morrow at eleven. In the evening I will come and see you and Maddalena—I shall not expect you to come back to work until I have seen you again.'

7

The next morning Gian-Luca went to see the doctor, who pronounced him to be suffering from a bad nervous breakdown. He was much too thin for a man of his height, his pulse was thready and unduly fast, he must eat nourishing food—plenty of it, said the doctor—the more he could eat the better. As for his depression, that was easily explained, it was simply the outcome of weakness. But overstrained nerves were not things to ignore, Gian-Luca must try to get some months of rest; a thorough change of air and scene was what he needed, but above all he must not worry.

'You know what I mean,' said the doctor soothingly; 'get your mind off troubles, and don't worry about life. Go somewhere jolly, but don't overdo things, and rest in the middle of the day.'

Gian-Luca thanked him, and received a prescription containing valerian and bromide. After which he was able to go home to Maddalena and assure her that he was quite sound.

8

In the evening Millo arrived as he had promised.

'Nerves—all nerves—as I told you,' he said kindly. 'The doctor says that you need a long rest, at least three or four months, and I think he is right. While you are away I propose to pay your salary, you can look upon that as a retaining fee, Gian-Luca. And now I want to know where you two will go, have you made up your minds?' It seemed that they had not, so Millo continued: 'Well I have a suggestion to make; you should go to Italy with Maddalena, you should give the blue sky and the sunshine a chance. After all, Gian-Luca, you are an Italian, and yet you have never seen our fine sunshine." Then he laughed, 'I too must try to have a break-down, I have not been home for ten years!'

Gian-Luca thanked him, and Millo talked on in order to cheer Maddalena. It was not his way to do anything by halves, and once having made up his mind to be generous, he spared neither money nor kindness. 'You will see, he will come back a lion, Maddalena!' he said cheerfully, patting her shoulder.

After he had gone they looked at each other: 'Italy!' murmured Maddalena; and all the ineffable longing of the exile was in that name as she spoke it. Her anxious brown eyes were pleading with Gian-Luca, asking him to take her home.

He nodded: 'Yes, we will go, Maddalena——'

'Blessèd be God!' she whispered.

They sat on discussing ways and means. It was nearly the

end of September. Maddalena said they could be ready in two weeks, they would board with her cousins who lived near the coast on the Riviera di Levante. Her cousins were always writing, these days, urging her to go out and see them; they were anxious, it seemed, to know Gian-Luca, of whom she herself wrote so often. It would not be Rome and the wonderful Campagna, but then, it would be cheaper than Rome; if they went to her cousins they could live very cheaply, especially with the exchange.

'I would like to go to your cousins,' said Gian-Luca, 'they live in the country away from people; that is what I long for, to get away from people, there are too many people in the world.'

Then Maddalena told him about her cousins; he had heard it all many times before, but he let her talk on because it made her happy, since it was talking of home. Her cousins lived in a good-sized farmhouse on the hills behind Levanto. Sisto was a person of some importance, fattore, he was, to Marchese Sabelli. An excellent position to be fattore to such a noble estate. Lidia his wife was a simple creature, but kind, oh! intensely kind. They had a fine son in the Bersaglieri, and a younger son who must now be sixteen, and who helped his mother on the farm. They would get there in time for part of the vendemmia; the Marchese owned most of the neighbouring vineyards—all day they would sit on the hill-side in the sunshine—they would hear the peasants laughing and singing as they stooped to gather the grapes. She talked on and on, and Gian-Luca, as he listened, began to catch something of her joy, so that his eyes grew as bright as Maddalena's.

'I have not yet seen our country,' he said thoughtfully, and as he said this he felt suddenly hopeful. 'A man might find peace in Italy,' he murmured; 'do you think that I shall find peace?'

Then Maddalena laughed in her infinite contentment; 'Is it not your own soil, Gian-Luca? You are homesick for the sunshine and the big blue sky; long ago I told you that your eyes looked home-sick; that was when I first met you, amore——'

'Yes,' he answered, 'I think you are right—I think I have always been home-sick; only——' he hesitated a moment, 'only I have never felt perfectly certain where I am home-sick for, Maddalena.'

Then she kissed him and began to play with his hair, twisting it as though he were a child: 'For us there is only one home that we long for, and that is the home of our people, belovèd.'

And because he so very much wished to believe her, he kissed her too, acquiescing.

CHAPTER SIX

I

THERE ARE some experiences that remain in the mind as possessing a charm all their own, so that no matter what may follow after, they stand forth unblemished as something to remember with a sense of deep gratitude. And of these, the first glimpse of that lovely coast-line that curves like a sickle round the Genoese Gulf is surely not the least, for nothing more perfect could ever be wedded to sunshine.

The train had steamed out of Genoa station and was moving slowly by the side of the water, now into a long dark rumbling tunnel, now out into the glorious sunshine again, the rich, orange sunshine of mid-October. The sea and the sky were incredibly blue, and the peace of the sky stooped down to the sea, and the peace of the sea reached up to the sky, and the drowsy, motherly peace of autumn encircled them both, as with arms.

Gian-Luca stood in the corridor of the train with Maddalena at his side; they were holding each other's hands, and their faces were steadfastly turned to the window. The peace had got into Maddalena's eyes so that they were full of contentment; from time to time they rested on her husband, and then she must murmur in a voice of rapture: 'Com' è bella, la nostra Italia!'

Gian-Luca silently pressed her hand, his heart was too full for speech at that moment. All the beauty and the wonder of this first home-coming had filled him with a kind of reverential awe. He was conscious of a queer sense of things familiar, he felt that he knew the little white houses with bright-coloured garments flapping from their windows, and the pergolas covered with strong green vines, and the jars of rioting red carnations that stood along the sides of the roofs. There were people, too, in the tiny gardens, women with handkerchiefs bound round their heads; men lolling back on chairs in the sunshine; children who played on the hot, virile soil, and whose bare arms and legs were the colour of copper, so that they seemed to be part of the soil, part of the eternally patient Mother from whom sprang all fruitful things. And Gian-Luca felt that he too was a child, but one who had grown very weary; and he wanted to lay his cheek close to this earth and let all the strength of it go throbbing through him, and all the joy of it make him feel young, until he forgot about suffering and sorrow, and cared for nothing at all but the sunshine and the glory of being alive.

Presently he said: 'This will make me quite well, this is the thing I have been needing.'

And hearing him, Maddalena rejoiced, and she praised the Mother of God in her heart.

All the way, curving gently southward, the splendid blue water went with them; and the sun and the warm air came in at the window, touching Gian-Luca as though they felt happy to welcome this tired son home. And every few miles the leisurely train would stop at a wayside station, and the names of such places would be soft on the tongue, so that Gian-Luca must speak them aloud for the pleasure he took in their beauty. There were Nervi, Rapallo, Zoagli, Chiavari, Sestri Levant, Moneglia; and all these small hamlets were bathed in sunshine which the walls of their houses caught and gave back, and the vines and the flowers that clung to the walls, and the eyes and the faces of the children.

Very soon Maddalena was waving from the window, for the train was coming into Levanto, and there on the platform stood Cousin Sisto patiently waiting for the train.

'Eccoci! Here we are!' called Maddalena.

The Cousin Sisto waved too: 'Maddalena, but this is splendid!' he shouted. 'And Gian-Luca, but this is splendid!'

Cousin Sisto was a broad, squat person of fifty. His grey hair was cut en brosse, giving to his large head a square appearance, and the hair itself was very stiff in texture; you felt, indeed, that if you held him upside down, it would polish your parquet floors. His clothes were suggestive of Sundays or funerals, and belonged by rights to the latter;

for Cousin Sisto had lost his Mamma a year ago at the age of eighty; and now, although he had gone out of mourning, his best suit survived, so he wore it for galas, enlivened by a bright yellow neck-tie. Cousin Sisto's watch-chain was a thing to remember; it was made of an opulent red gold. The links were enormous and unusual in pattern; they ended in a species of curtain ring, which was clipped through his button-hole. And now Cousin Sisto took out his watch, and the watch was of tarnished white metal; it was rather a shock after seeing that chain, but then, as its owner was wont to say, smiling: 'Non importa, *he* lives in a pocket!'

'It is late, this train,' remarked Cousin Sisto, in a voice of incredulous surprise; 'nearly one hour and a half of delay!' And he hurried them off to retrieve their luggage which was being hurled out of the van.

Then he gave an order to Carlo, the porter, who groaned and sighed loudly as he heaved the small trunks on to his antiquated truck. At the entrance to the station stood Sisto's conveyance, a species of market-wagon. A lean, white mare was drooping in the shafts, too languid to twitch the flies off her ears, where they clustered in blue-black blotches.

'Sacramento!' swore Sisto, 'I forgot about the chickens and now the train has departed! Oh, well, never mind, they must wait until the morning. Carlo, come here and help me!'

Carlo looked even more languid than the mare, and considerably less sweet-tempered. He dropped the handle of his truck with a frown, and together he and Sisto disinterred the chickens, banging their crate on the pavement. The crate appeared to be filled to bursting, judging by the heads that protruded, and those that could not find an opening to protrude from were firmly pressed against the slats. The fowls shuffled and squatted on top of each other in a futile effort to get ease; from time to time they clucked rather weakly, and tried to shake out their feathers.

Carlo examined the address on the label: 'No train before ten o'clock to-morrow morning,' he announced, staring crossly at the crate.

'Allora? And what then?' demanded Cousin Sisto.

'It is big, it will take up much room in the station.' muttered Carlo, ignoring any inconvenience that might accrue to the chickens.

Sisto waved his objection away. 'Climb up beside me,' he said to Maddalena, 'Gian-Luca will not mind if he sits on the luggage? He knows that we are only simple country folk. Get in, Gian-Luca; are you ready? Va bene, and now we will make for home.'

He found his imitation panama hat, and pressed it down on his head. 'Ee-yup!' he encouraged, cracking his whip, and the mare moved stiffly forward.

Gian-Luca refrained from looking at the crate, but he wondered if Maddalena had noticed. Perhaps she had not; now, at all events, her eyes were turned to the sea. He followed the direction of her gaze, determined to think of nothing but the sunshine; before him there stretched a calm little bay in a semicircle of hills. The sun had begun to drop down westward, and whatever it touched it gilded; the half-furled sail of a skiff in the harbour looked as though cut out of cloth of gold, while the windows of the villas that lay back from the water were all afire with the sunset.

Sisto turned inland and drove through the town, where people sat outside the café; some of these people were drinking Amarena, and Gian-Luca thought of Nerone. And now they were out on a white country road, a long straight road that sloped upwards; and down the road came the tinkling of bells and the sharp clip, clip of home-going mules, laden with loads of herbage. On their right lay a very ancient smithy where a youth was working the bellows; with each downward sweep of the rough, wooden pole, the fire glowed softly through the gathering dusk, and the blacksmith's hammer clanged on the anvil in harmony with the mule-bells. They passed a pair of tall iron gates, above each gate was a crown.

'Guarda!' said Sisto, pointing with his whip; 'the estate of my master, the Marchese.'

Gian-Luca could just glimpse a big, untidy garden from which came a mixture of sweet scents, and sweetest of all, the scent of hot earth, steaming a little under dew.

'He is rich, very rich,' Cousin Sisto was saying; 'I will show you his villa, Maddalena. Just now he has gone to Milan on business, and it is I who must see to all things in his absence; I have very much to do at this time of the vendemmia, they are terrible robbers, our peasants.'

The road had begun to climb upwards in good earnest, and the mare was stumbling and straining. Her sides were going in and out like the bellows at the blacksmith's down in the village.

'Ee-yup! Ee-yup!' commanded Cousin Sisto, in the voice of him who must be obeyed.

But the mare, unable for the moment to go farther, stood still, ignoring Cousin Sisto.

And now Gian-Luca forgot about the sunset, and could think of nothing but the mare. 'We are much too heavy for her,' he protested, 'she looks as though she would drop between the shafts; if you wait for a minute, I will get out and walk.'

'Neanche per sogno!' laughed Cousin Sisto, 'she would never understand it; you will see, she can go very well when she wishes.'

'But her flanks are all dripping with sweat,' said Gian-Luca, 'her flanks are quite grey with sweat!'

Then Sisto heaved a sympathetic sigh and glanced over his shoulder at Gian-Luca. 'She is old, very old, poverina,' he said sadly, and proceeded to lash her with the whip.

'Stop!' shouted Gian-Luca, 'my wife and I will walk. Come down, Maddalena, we will walk!' And he jumped out and held up his hand to Maddalena, where she sat beside Cousin Sisto.

Obedient as always, she climbed down from her seat and stood beside her husband in the road. Then Gian-Luca went to the back of the cart and tried to ease the wheels forward. Meanwhile Cousin Sisto stared round in amazement.

'But what is the matter?' he demanded. 'Ma guarda, she is twenty years old the good mare, do you expect her to fly?'

The cart had begun to move slowly again, but nothing would induce Gian-Luca to get in; so he and Maddalena tramped on through the dust, which sprayed up over their ankles.

Cousin Sisto felt annoyed. 'He is mad!' he was thinking. 'He makes his wife walk for a horse!' and he looked down on Maddalena with pity, 'Povera disgraziata!' he muttered.

Still walking, they arrived at the gates of the farm, where Lidia was standing to receive them; a plump, comely woman with wavy brown hair, and small, very even white teeth. But seeing Maddalena tramping through the dust, she held up her hands and exclaimed:

'Madonna! What has happened?' she inquired in agitation. 'Has there been an accident, Sisto?'

'It was only our Giuseppina,' said Sisto; 'she pretended that the cart was too heavy.'

'The Giuseppina is sly,' smiled Lidia; 'she is old, and the old grow crafty. But to walk, that is too bad, and on your first evening! However, you are safely arrived, God be thanked; and now do come in, I must get to know Gian-Luca, I am happy in having a new cousin.'

2

Early the next morning they went out on the hills, and Gian-Luca saw the vendemmia. He was walking through a region of wide, green vineyards in which worked an army of peasants; their strong, slim bodies arched over the vines as they stooped to gather in the grapes. Here and there stood huge baskets overflowing with fruit that glowed purple-red in the heat; for the sun was already gathering power, pushing the mist away from the hill-tops, pushing the light clouds away from the sky that stretched widely, fervently blue. The paths between the vines were strewn with crushed grapes, and the air was heavy with a queer, intense odour of fermentation and sweating human bodies; it smelt of fertility, virility and women, all steaming together in the sunshine.

The peasants were quick to observe a stranger; they glanced at Gian-Luca from under their lids, and whenever they stood up to ease their backs, they stared quite openly at him. Their eyes were the eyes of curious children, of the very young of the earth; they were not the eyes of those bygone Legions who had flung out the straight, white roads. For some reason Gian-Luca appeared to amuse them, perhaps it was his English clothes; but whatever it was, no sooner had he passed than they started laughing and talking loudly, calling him 'forestiere.' Once or twice he spoke to them in Italian, but at this they seemed rather nonplussed, as though something in the fact of his knowing their language struck them as embarrassing. He observed that with Maddalena, however, these people were perfectly at ease; and quite soon her sleeves were rolled up to her elbows, and there she was, one of them, gathering grapes. Then Lidia followed suit, and Gian-Luca was alone with Sisto and his son Leone.

Leone was a lumping lad of sixteen, his expression was bovine and surly. Like his father, he wore his hair en brosse, but in his case, the top of his pate was so black that it looked like a monster pen-wiper. His thick throat was bare, he was wearing no collar, and his shirt was unfastened for coolness; round his neck hung a little gilt crucifix and a medal of the Virgin Mary. He spoke seldom, eyeing Gian-Luca with suspicion, but his voice when he did speak was gruff; his voice was already that of a man, and his lip was well shadowed with down. He appeared to be curiously un-observant except in regard to beetles; butterflies also attracted his attention, which was rather unfortunate for them. The little, round beetles crept out of the vines, dis-turbed by the busy peasants, and whenever a beetle came the way of Leone, Leone crushed it with his foot. His hand would swoop out to afflict flying things, a game at which he was unusually dexterous, and the palm of his hand would be covered with powder from the wings of his unfortunate victims. Gian-Luca looked once or twice at Sisto, who however, seemed to be quite unperturbed by the unpleasant pastime of his offspring, and presently Leone wandered away, muttering something about chickens.

Then his father turned to Gian-Luca with a smile. 'A fine fellow, no? He is useful on the farm; my Claudio is a soldier in the Bersaglieri, but this one shall be a fattore.'

Sisto was making a great effort to be friendly, despite the unfortunate incident of the mare; he was very disap-pointed in Maddalena's husband; however, they must make the best of him. He had said to his wife on the previous night: 'He is queer, Maddalena's husband. Imagine it, making a poor woman walk because of a beast—and then our Giuseppina—I remarked: "She is twenty years old, Giuseppina, do you expect her to fly?" '

'He is very handsome,' his wife had replied; 'a fine figure he has, but too thin; and how little he eats—such an excellent supper, such good ravioli, and the melanzane ripiene. All that I could lay my two hands on I cooked, and then he must come and eat nothing!'

Sisto had shrugged his shoulders in disgust: 'He is hardly a man, my Lidia; and as for not eating, he ate many grapes, and figs, and much bread; but such stuff is for children, I think he is hardly a man!'

However, he had always been fond of Maddalena, so that now he was trying to be friendly. 'Are you feeling the heat?' he inquired of Gian-Luca. 'You English are not used to the heat.'

Gian-Luca looked surprised: 'But I am not English; I thought you knew I was Italian.'

'Ma no, you are English,' laughed Sisto, amused. 'You speak fine Italian, but your manners are English, and then, who but an Englishman pushes a cart that has a good horse to draw it?'

Gian-Luca was silent, this was quite unexpected. So Sisto regarded him as English! But at last he said firmly: 'You are quite wrong, Sisto, I consider myself an Italian—there are many Italians living in England.'

'All the same, you are English,' smiled Sisto. His round, brown face looked incredibly stubborn. 'One can see that you are English,' he persisted; 'your clothes, your behaviour, your manner of eating——' Then he hastened to add: 'They are nice folk, the English, we like them, they bring us much money.'

How many times in his life had Gian-Luca listened to similar words: 'The English are rich, they bring us much money.' Yes, and how many times had he himself said them! He stared at Cousin Sisto in exasperation.

'One gets sick of this talk of their money,' he muttered.

'Caspita, I do not!' chuckled Sisto.

And now Cousin Sisto wished to hear about London, and above all about the Doric. Did it pay? Was the food good? What sort of a man was Millo? Had Gian-Luca grown rich? His Nonna must be rich; it paid well, a salumeria! Gian-Luca tried to answer all these questions politely, and after a little, to his infinite relief, Sisto began to talk of the Marchese, who he said was a person of vast importance, owing to his very great wealth. Now Sisto must puff himself out and grow pompous; was he not the fattore? And the watch-chain protruded on his round little stomach, and a long coral horn, worn against the evil-eye, swung to and fro from the watch-chain.

'It is I who do all things,' he told Gian-Luca, 'a very responsible position. The Marchese is merry, he admires pretty women, and he has a dull wife. She is good, poverina —too good; it is said that she longs to be a nun. The Marchese says: "Sisto, I leave all to you, take care of my grapes, and see that you weigh them." And I answer: "You may trust me, Signor Marchese, not the pip of a grape shall be stolen." Which reminds me,' went on Sisto, glancing at his watch, 'that the hour has arrived for the weighing of the grapes; it is time that we hurry home!'

They turned and went back to the court-yard of the farm, in which had been set up an immense pair of scales. The peasants had begun to arrive with full baskets balanced on their heads or their shoulders. Sisto eyed them with open suspicion and made notes in a thick black notebook.

'Avanti!' he ordered peremptorily, and the weighing of the grapes began.

Each peasant in turn must empty his burden on to the giant scales; Sisto weighed it, then the grapes were tipped back into the basket, and off went the basket down the steep little track that led to the Villa Sabelli.

Sisto rumbled a good deal under his breath: 'Due cento sessanta kili,' he rumbled, and presently: 'Cinquecento ottantatrè e mezzo—va bene!' And he made some fresh entries in his notebook.

And now the whole court-yard was redolent of grapes, the rough stones were slippery with them. The hands of the peasants were stained and sticky, while the sweat from their labour stood out on their arms, beading the coarse, black hairs of the men, and the smooth, olive skins of the women. Gian-Luca was rather surprised to notice that several large baskets made their way into the farmhouse, the others, he knew, had gone down to the villa to await the treading of the grapes. But Sisto waved a nonchalant hand in the direction of his cellar; then he made some very elaborate calculations, called for Leone to take away the scales,

hummed the 'Marcia Reale,' winked once at Gian-Luca—
and that was the end of the weighing for the morning.

3

That afternoon Sisto took them to the villa. 'You will
like to see how we make our good wine,' he said pleasantly
to Gian-Luca. 'The Marchese is very fond of good wine,
and why not? He is young and merry!'

The Villa Sabelli was a low, white building with a large
coat-of-arms above its door. The paint on this door had once
been bright green, but now it was faded to a soft bluish-grey,
and its surface was webbed with many little lines, owing to
the heat of the summers. An old stone court with a marble
fountain stretched to the right of the entrance; but the
fountain was usually tongue-tied and dry, because of the
shortage of water. At each corner of this crumbling, silent
fountain, grew a splendid cypress tree, thrusting its roots far
under the flagstones, digging in the dark with relentless
fingers and lifting the stones in the process. Wherever a
stone had been slightly dislodged, something humble had
found an asylum; for all things might prosper to repletion
in this garden, and the will to grow was a positive frenzy;
weed or flower they all throve very much alike, and remained
undisturbed for the most part. Everything needed thinning
out or pruning, everything was arrogantly fruitful, and
everything was indiscriminately watered from the three deep
vasche near the lodge. But the glory of the garden was its
grove of orange trees, already beginning to colour very
faintly; a grove that was planted in symmetrical lines that
stretched for more than a mile. Sisto pointed it out with great
pride, as well he might, thought Gian-Luca, for this was a
miniature forest of fruit, in which presently every green
globe would turn golden.

'This is where our Marchesa walks reading her prayers,
the poverina,' whispered Sisto; 'just now she is making a
retreat near Rome. She is doubtless praying for the soul of
the Marchese; she is good, very good, but Santa Madonna,
our Marchese is only young!'

He led them round to the back of the villa and down a
wide flight of stone steps; then he knocked on a massive oak

door with his stick. Through the chinks of the door came the same acrid odour that Gian-Luca had noticed in the vineyards. The door was opened by a very old man.

'Beppo!' announced Sisto grandly. 'He is old, you will say, but he still treads more grapes than anyone in the paese.'

Beppo was wearing a dingy cotton shirt that clung to his body with sweat; his trousers were rolled back over his thighs, and the flesh of his hairy old legs had shrivelled, leaving a cordage of sinews. His legs and his broad gnarled feet were stained and moist from the juice and skins of the grapes; his toes were beaded all over with grape pips, and soiled with dirt from the floor. He was toothless, and so he spoke very little, preferring to nod and grin, and after he had carefully closed the oak door, he climbed back into his vat.

There were three outside cellars at the Villa Sabelli, that were connected with each other by arches. Their ceilings were vaulted, their floors and walls of stone, and just now they conveyed a strong impression of a church given over to some pagan ritual. The vats were a species of glorified barrel standing on a rough wooden platform; they were high, they were wide, four of them to a cellar; and in each vat a man was prancing and stamping, raising his knees with a rhythmical motion grotesquely suggestive of dancing. The cellars were full of the soft, slushing sound made by the grapes in dying; a sound half solid, half liquid, that mingled with the grunts and the heavy breathing of the men, and the creaking of the age-old barrels. The fumes in these cellars were wellnigh overpowering, for Beppo was frightened of chills; all that he would allow was a half-open lattice high up in the farthest wall. It was said that a man could get drunk on such fumes; there was something wicked about them. Wicked but merry, no doubt—like the Marchese, whose excellent wine was in the making.

From time to time someone crawled out of his vat in order to stretch his legs; and his toes would be stuck with grape pips like Beppo's, and after he had padded about for a little, with the dust and refuse of the floor. Then someone must pause to have a good spit—for habit will defy most conventions—and if he was dexterous he spat clear of his barrel, but if not—oh, well, then the juices of the body would be mingled with the juices of the vine!

Sisto looked on in apparent satisfaction, and after a while it was time to go home. 'Come, Maddalena,' said Sisto smiling; 'to you this is nothing, you have seen it all before; we came for your husband—in England, of course, one could not see such a fine sight. When he gets back he can tell them about it; he can tell them how we make our good wine.'

And Gian-Luca said politely: 'I will certainly tell them, it has been very interesting, Sisto.' But his head felt heavy with the fumes of the cellars, and he longed to get back into the clean, open air and the health-giving blessing of the sunshine.

Maddalena took his arm as they walked through the garden: 'It is better than this in Romagna,' she whispered; 'this vendemmia is so small; but I would not tell Sisto, he wishes very much to impress his new cousin, he is proud of his little paese.'

CHAPTER SEVEN

I

SISTO CONTINUED trying to be friendly because of Gian-Luca's wife. Lidia was friendly because of Gian-Luca; she liked Maddalena's tall, quiet husband; but even Lidia was not at ease with him, he struck her—indeed, he seemed to strike them all—as being a 'forestiere.'

The Englishman's home may well be his castle, but the home of the Latin is his fortress, and seldom may the stranger hope to penetrate beyond its outermost portal. Thus Gian-Luca, while sharing their family life, had a sense of being always just outside; they were never completely natural with him, he suspected a number of subtle reserves, and this made him stiff and shy in his turn, shy of asserting his claim.

Moreover, he resented their superior air, their complacent conviction that every alien was either a madman or a fool; he had met such convictions before, it was true, but in Old Compton Street they had not affected him, whereas here they appeared to affect him directly, and the injustice of this made him restive. Then these people differed very much from the clan in one all-important respect; these people had no need to assert themselves, they were in their own country and could afford to be generous, they were not compelled to keep memories green in the constant fear of absorption. What had been excusable in Nerone and the others—a kind of virtue in a way—was irritating in Lidia and Sisto, and more irritating still in Leone. And then there was the question of veracity; poor Mario was not strictly truthful, of course; he must always say, for instance, that the little round tins were entirely unknown at the Capo; as for Nerone, he would swear by his gods that his Macedonias were fresher than fresh, and this in spite of the fact that the tobacco poured out of their ends like dry chaff. Oh, un-

doubtedly lies were told by the clan, and the clan was grasping over money; but its lies were pure white in comparison
to Sisto's, and if its members loved money they worked hard
to get it, whereas Sisto was both grasping and lazy.

Sisto was quite a new type to Gian-Luca, a man devoid
of any ideal as far as his work was concerned. The ambition
of the exiles was completely lacking in him; he cared not
at all how he ran the estate, provided that he ran it to his
personal advantage with as little trouble as might be. His
pride of office never went beyond words, and even in words
it could not be maintained, for at one moment he would
brag of the trust imposed in him, and the next he would
wink a large eye at Gian-Luca, explaining at great length
and with many a chuckle some underhand piece of sharp
dealing. Nothing was too mean or too puerile for Sisto, so
long as it brought him gain.

'Ma guarda,' he would laugh, 'a man has to live! What
do you say, Gian-Luca?' And Gian-Luca, finding nothing
appropriate to say, would observe that Sisto looked offended.

Very unwilling indeed was Gian-Luca to become the
confidant of Sisto, but Sisto could never resist for long the
pleasure of expounding his cunning. Yet after having
poured out these revelations, he would usually assume the
grand air, becoming very pompous and rather distant; then
Lidia and Leone would also become distant, and Gian-Luca
would be given to understand once again that he was only a
stranger. He realized more and more every day how little
he had in common with these people, how little they had in
common with him, and this realization came as a shock;
he had journeyed a very long way to discover that a man
could feel foreign to his country.

Maddalena, who saw what was happening, grew anxious:
'They are still rather shy, give them time,' she would plead,
and then she would add: 'But you are so much better, therefore what does anything matter!'

And this was quite true, he was certainly better, beginning
to feel almost strong. But he would think: 'It is queer, I am
always a stranger—I felt like a stranger among the English,
and out here I feel even more like a stranger——' And then
he would try not to mind very much, because he had been
warned against worry.

Yet all the same, he must say to Maddalena: 'I have come home too late, donna mia—a man may come home too late to his country——'

And she, in her turn, could find nothing to reply; she could only gaze at him sadly.

2

The gulf had widened when Gian-Luca's new cousins discovered that he never went to church. Sisto and his household were excessively pious, and their chagrin was great when they found that their guest refused to accompany them to Mass. Sisto had so many sins to confess that he needed the Church very badly; indeed, he used it as a spiritual lifebuoy to keep his soul from total immersion. Lidia, who had very few conscious sins, had a great many superstitions—so many, in fact, that her life was a torment —and these she must deluge with much Holy Water, in order, conversely, to submerge them. As for Leone, he was made to serve Mass—every Sunday morning he must serve it. His thoughts on the subject were not inquired into, but he had so few thoughts about anything at all that this was of small importance. What was of importance, and very grave importance, was Gian-Luca's unorthodox behaviour; he claimed to be Italian, yet refused to go to Mass. Very well, then he must be a secret Freemason, or if he was not a Freemason he was worse, he belonged to the Socialisti, and this for Sisto, who served a Marchese, was a matter of no small moment.

'But is he not even baptized?' inquired Lidia.

'He has been baptized——' Maddalena admitted.

'That makes it far worse,' announced Sisto firmly, 'the insult to our faith is the greater.'

And all this made Maddalena unhappy; unhappy and a little ashamed, so that she said to Gian-Luca one Sunday: 'They cannot understand why you never go to Mass.'

And he knew from her voice that she felt ashamed, and then he too felt unhappy.

Sisto, returning newly shriven from confession, would often look askance at Gian-Luca, for at such times he suffered from much pride of spirit; then Leone would quickly emulate his father, and he too would try to look prim and disapproving, while Gian-Luca, considerably better now in health, would be longing to kick them both. A nice frame of mind, indeed, for a man who had just been restored to his people.

Maddalena, however, felt at home with her cousins, for hers was not an analytical mind. She accepted their faults as things familiar; she had seen them all before, and while she deplored them, she could not find it in her to be over-critical. Moreover, she was growing very fond of Lidia; it was pleasant to have another woman to talk to, and the everyday duties of the household were pleasant, performed as they were in bright sunshine. Maddalena loved also to talk to the peasants, because then she could play with their babies. She enjoyed the red wine and the rich peasant cooking, but above all the blue sky and glorious weather— she expanded, growing younger and less careworn every day, a fact not lost on Gian-Luca. For Maddalena's sake he endured her cousins—the last thing he wanted in the world was a quarrel—he had promised to remain at the farm for four months, and Sisto's disapproval of his lack of religion had not been extended to his money. So Gian-Luca took to being much alone and would wander for hours in the mountains. His muscles grew firm and his cheeks less sunken, while the sun tanned his skin and nourished his body. As for food, he need eat only simple things—bread and cheese and much fruit, with occasional pasta, when Lidia had not drenched it in butter.

Yes, his body responded readily enough, for his body was young and strong; but his soul still doomed his eyes to their seeing, and now they must see yet a new cause for pity—on all sides they must see it, wherever man dwelt and compelled the dumb beasts to serve him. Never before had Gian-Luca realized the helplessness of those who cannot speak, for the English, on the whole, are too just to be cruel—a quiet, unemotional people, it is true, but possessed of a great sense of fairness. And Gian-Luca decided that by living among them, this sense of fairness was unconsciously acquired, for he could not conceive of any member of the clan doing what these peasants did. Rocca had hung his small goats upside-down, but at least his goats

314

had been dead, whereas here they were carried bleating to slaughter with their legs tied together over a pole, and their heads all but bumping against the pathway—a brutal, unnecessary torment. Nerone kept his birds in small cages it was true, and believed that his skylarks were happy; but at least he gave them clean food and fresh water, and their cages were as palaces compared to those that Gian-Luca now saw in the paese. Horrible, punishing, heart-break cages, filthy with excrement and slime; their water green and stinking from neglect, their one narrow perch encrusted with droppings, their inmates dishevelled and bare in places from the constant rubbing of the bars.

Wherever he went he saw the same thing, an absolute disregard of dumb creatures, a curious lack of human understanding, of the realization of pain. But more than anywhere else, perhaps, he saw it on Lidia's farm; for Lidia was a pleasant and kindly woman, and yet she had taken Leone to help her, and Leone did not lack understanding of pain—on the contrary he liked to inflict it. The farm consisted principally of chickens, and these Leone could crowd into crates, or better still, he could wring their necks slowly, taking a long time about it. He could pluck out their feathers before they were dead, or swing them about by their claws—there was no end to what he could do to the chickens, and no end it seemed to Lidia's indifference; that was what so amazed Gian-Luca.

In addition to the chickens, there was one doleful cow, a half-grown calf, and a few lousy sheep; these lived all together in a species of damp cavern, hollowed out of the rock near the farm. A slatted oak door had been fixed at the entrance, admitting a modicum of light and air; but the beasts very seldom got a glimpse of the sky, and practically never of the grass, it appeared, for as Lidia explained to Gian-Luca one morning: 'If our cow saw the grass, she would be so delighted that she might well forget to give milk!' The cavern reeked of filth and ammonia, causing the beasts' eyes to stream; when they came into the light they must half-close their eyes—especially the calf, who was young and unaccustomed, and who suffered from conjunctivitis. Gian-Luca would lie in bed sick with pity for the patient, enduring creatures.

'Can you not sleep?' Maddalena would ask him.

And then he must tell her about the cattle.

'I know, I know——' she would answer, sighing, 'but thank God, they do not suffer as we do!'

Gian-Luca would sit up and stare into the darkness. 'How do you know?' he would ask her.

And one night she answered quite naturally and simply: 'Perché non sono Cristiana.'

Then Gian-Luca felt that his wife was slipping back in mind and in spirit to her people; that her country was luring her, drawing her away, since she, who was all tender mercy and compassion, could repeat this crude blasphemy of the peasants.

'Inasmuch as your Christ had pity,' he cried hotly, 'so must every poor beast be Christian!'

But Maddalena hid her face on his shoulder. 'No, no, Gian-Luca!' she protested. 'God is good, He would not allow them to suffer—I have asked the Parroco, and he says the same; the beasts do not suffer as we do.'

Gian-Luca sighed, and taking her hand, he tried to explain more gently: 'The priest is a peasant himself,' he told her; 'and he thinks and speaks very much as they do—but listen, mia donna: the dumb things do suffer, if you look you will see it in their eyes.' He could not go to sleep, and she had perforce to listen while he pleaded the cause of the dumb: 'They cannot tell us,' he kept on repeating; 'they can only trust us, Maddalena.'

And now Maddalena was almost weeping, yet he knew that she was only half convinced.

'God is good, God has always been good!' she pleaded.

'He is merciful, then,' said Gian-Luca.

3

The creature Leone loved best to torment was a little Sardinian donkey; in size it was not much bigger than a dog, and its hoofs were easily avoided. A favourite pastime was twisting its tongue, and one day he kicked it in the stomach— just by way of letting it know that he was there—and the donkey stood still and shivered. But Leone was as cruel as death to all beasts, and all beasts knew it and feared him, and he it was who helped on the farm—yet Lidia was a kindly woman . . . Gian-Luca's eyes sometimes blazed fury at Leone; Leone would see this and snigger.

'Non sono Cristiani!' he was always saying, because this tormented Gian-Luca.

And Gian-Luca would have to walk away quickly in case he should be tempted to strike, for he too was a Latin, in spite of his pity, in spite of his new-found seeing. But where could he turn to be rid of this seeing? There were days when he knew despair: 'A country as lovely as Paradise and as cruel as Hell!' he would mutter.

Under the very window of his bedroom hung Marchese Sabelli's richiami—ortolans used to decoy their fellows— there were eight of them, each in a tiny cage not much more than six inches long. They were fairly large birds, so that only with an effort could they stand half upright or turn round; and their calling would wake Gian-Luca every morning: 'Dio!' he would think, 'those miserable creatures!' And perhaps he would bury his head in the bedclothes so as to shut away their calling.

At last he spoke to Lidia about them. 'I will buy you much larger cages,' he told her.

But she answered: 'They are wild, the wildest of all birds —in a larger cage they would beat themselves to pieces, one must always keep ortolans in a small cage. These belong to our padrone the Marchese.'

Then Gian-Luca lifted up his voice in protest, and his protest was far from polite. He said: 'May your damned Marchese go to hell, and may he be kept there in a cage as small for him as these cages are for his poor tormented birds, and may he remain there for ever and ever; I hope he will never get out!' After which, Cousin Lidia was naturally offended, and she went and complained to Maddalena.

One morning Gian-Luca could bear it no longer; he stole out of bed at dawn, and his long arm shot out to each cage in turn, and he opened their doors, and the birds flew away, too astonished to thank Gian-Luca.

Oh, what a hubbub when a couple of hours later Sisto saw all those empty cages! His oaths far exceeded Rocca's at their best, he attacked the Madonna from every point of view, nor did he omit to mention the Mass, which he lingered over in great detail.

'Who has committed this outrage?' yelled Sisto. 'They are gone! The Marchese's richiami!' His voice sounded almost tearful with rage, he was literally dancing with passion.

Gian-Luca unfastened the window and looked down. 'Of course they have gone,' he said, smiling serenely; 'of course they have gone; I opened their cages—the birds were not fools, you can tell your Marchese!'

'You—you——?' stammered Sisto. 'Che vergogna! What an outrage! They were specially trained richiami— you are mad, mad, mad—you behave like a madman——'

'I like being mad,' said Gian-Luca, quite gravely, after which he closed the window.

Maddalena had risen from her bed and was staring at her husband in horror: 'What *have* you done, Gian-Luca?' she exclaimed. 'They were trained richiami. The Marchese will be furious, he will surely punish our miserable Sisto—he will surely make Sisto pay for the birds!'

'I hope so, indeed,' said Gian-Luca.

Then Maddalena's eyes filled with tears. 'Yes, but what shall I say?' she demanded.

'Tell them that your husband is mad but harmless.' And Gian-Luca laughed softly, thinking of the birds away by now in the mountains.

What his wife really said Gian-Luca never knew, but nothing could have made any difference, for Sisto and Lidia were firmly convinced that they harboured a lunatic. When Gian-Luca went down to breakfast that morning, they eyed him timidly a moment without speaking; then Lidia inquired if he would not prefer to have his breakfast upstairs. He thanked her, but said that he would go for a walk in order to ease his poor head; his head had been paining him lately, he told her, and at that she glanced quickly across at Sisto, and Sisto looked at Maddalena. But Gian-Luca's enjoyment was somewhat damped when he saw Maddalena's face; it was red with shame and embarrassment.

'It is all right,' he whispered,' I will pay them for the birds.' But his wife turned suddenly away.

The weeks passed, and still they stayed on at the farm; Maddalena was loath to go, for Gian-Luca seemed almost well again, cured by the fine air and sunshine. Her cousins quite openly said that he was mad, but because of his affliction they forgave his behaviour.

'If he is not mad, then he is English,' declared Sisto, 'and, that after all, is very much the same thing!'

His solitary habits lent colour to the rumour that Gian-Luca was one of God's afflicted; he would wander all over the countryside, never speaking to the peasants, unless it were to urge them to show some mercy to their beasts. Those days spent out in the open air had given new life to his body; but his compassionate mind was weary unto death, and his heart was filled with a great loneliness, and his soul had begun to long intolerably for something—only, he could not tell for what. He would look into the eyes of the saddle-galled mules, and the stumbling, ill-cared for horses; for he felt that they held a message, those eyes, and he tried very hard to understand that message, talking to the dumb things gently. But one day he must look into the eyes of cattle that were being driven to slaughter.

He had wandered a very long way from the farm and was climbing a steep salita; and there at the summit of the pathway stood a cross, and the Christ on the cross looked straight down the pathway. Then over the sharp, loose stones came stumbling those terrified driven cattle: their eyes were filled with a knowledge of disaster, for their sensitive nostrils had scented death from the slaughter-house half-way up the hill. Long festoons of slime were swinging from their lips, and they tried to turn back into safety; then their drover struck them on their anxious faces, and on their bowed heads and their quivering flanks; and he cursed them, while the blows fell heavy in his fury, so that they had to go forward.

On they must stumble to Calvary as Another had stumbled before them; poor, lowly, uncomprehending disciples, following dumbly in the footsteps of God who had surely created all things for joy, yet had died for the blindness of the world. And because the sky was so radiantly blue His cross stood out darkly defined. Looking up, the drover suddenly perceived it, and he signed his breast with the emblem of compassion; then he struck yet again at his bullocks. But Gian-Luca saw neither the cross nor the sky, he saw only a creature's eyes—for he thought that a poor beast looked at him in passing, seeming to accuse him as he stood there helpless, so that he too bowed his head.

Nor was this all that he must witness that day, for going home in the evening he heard a bird singing at the door of the cobbler in the village, near Sisto's farm. He had never heard such singing before, it was indescribably lovely, and behind the song was a spirit of hope so poignant that it seemed to be racking the bird's body. The bird was singing in an agony of hope that came very near to despair.

The cobbler nodded and smiled at Gian-Luca: 'Buona sera,' he said politely, 'you admire him? He is new—he has a fine song.'

'A marvellous song!' said Gian-Luca. And then he must make his eternal request: 'Let me buy him a larger cage.'

But the cobbler shook his head: 'If you did, signore, he would not find his food, he is blind.''

'Blind?' said Gian-Luca, incredulously.

'Sí, signore, that is why he sings so finely; we often blind them to make them sing, it seems to give sweetness to their notes.'

His voice was neither pitiful nor cruel, only lacking in understanding; he chirruped to the blind bird as though he liked it, and going into the house he fetched some lettuce, which he pushed between the bars of its cage. The bird felt the cool, green stuff against its wing, and burst into a torrent of song; as it sang it shuffled its claws on its perch, swaying from side to side. Then Gian-Luca put his hands up to his ears and started to run down the street, and as he ran he remembered the beggar and her child who had lost his eyes. The child and the bird seemed to merge together, no longer two separate creatures; the suffering of the one was the suffering of the other, and the suffering of both was the suffering of Gian-Luca. And although he had covered his ears with his hands, he thought that he could still hear that singing.

It was February when the crisis was reached; they were
nearing the end of their stay, and Gian-Luca's resentment
towards Leone had got wellnigh beyond his control. As
for the boy, he hated Gian-Luca and went out of his way
to enrage him; the weapon he used was the little brown
donkey, who must suffer accordingly. Yet as sometimes
happens, a very small incident led to the final explosion;
Gian-Luca came on Leone one morning thoughtfully
tweaking out the donkey's mane—a painful proceeding, but
as heavenly balm when compared with the other torments.
For one long minute Gian-Luca stood quite still while
Leone looked up and grinned:

'Sai che non sentono niente——' he began. Then he
stopped abruptly, for Gian-Luca had swooped forward and
seized the discarded whip.

It was all so sudden that Leone knew nothing until he
was swung off his feet and the whip was crashing down on
his shoulders; over and over again it crashed down and, with
every fresh blow Gian-Luca recited the woes of the little
donkey.

'Take that for twitching out his mane!' he shouted; 'and
that for twisting his tongue; and that for prodding the sore
on his shoulder; and that for the kick you gave him in
the stomach; and that for keeping him all day without
water; and that for working him when he was lame. Take
that! and that! and that, you young swine! And now you
know what it feels like!'

But Leone was yelling as though half-demented, and
fighting to get away. The sound of his yells and Gian-Luca's
shouting brought Lidia running with Maddalena, and when
Lidia saw the plight of her last-born, she too must start
yelling as though she would go mad, and even Maddalena
had to lift up her voice: 'Gian-Luca! Gian-Luca! Santa
Madonna, what are you doing, Gian-Luca?' Lidia was
tearing at Gian-Luca's arm, which was taut and as hard as
steel, then she started to thump with inadequate fists, and
finally buried her small teeth in the hand that was gripping
Leone's collar. For this comely-faced woman was like something possessed in her fierce defence of her offspring; a
primitive thing, a tigress at bay, driven crazy by the howls

of her cub. And now Maddalena was reaching for the whip, and she got in the way of the blows; Gian-Luca must either strike her or stop beating, so he had to release Leone.

'Oh, oh! Oh, oh! Oh, oh!' wailed Leone as he dropped in a blubbering heap.

'Well, I am glad that you know what it feels like.' said Gian-Luca; and he turned on his heel and left them.

Lidia knelt down by her cowering son and gathered him into her arms, then her eyes blazed up at the silent Maddalena. 'The pig! the devil! the madman!' shrieked Lidia. 'To beat my Leone because of a donkey!' And many other things she said in her wrath that are not, as a rule, recorded. When Leone had stopped sobbing and had got to his feet, Lidia pointed to the gates: 'Take that madman out of my house!' she babbled. 'Go quickly before Sisto comes home to kill him—the outrage, the scandal, to lay hands on our son because of a miserable donkey!'

What could the poor Maddalena answer? It was true that Leone had been thoroughly thrashed, it was also true that the cause of the thrashing had been a Sardinian donkey. And who should know better than Maddalena the pride of the Latins in their children? Gian-Luca's sin could never be forgiven—he had sinned against the deep-rooted, primitive instinct of personal reproduction.

'My husband and I will go——' she faltered, then her loyalty suddenly came to her aid. 'But,' said Maddalena, 'we are not afraid of Sisto or of anyone else on earth!' And now she was full of her old, quiet courage, and she looked very straight at her cousin: 'Before I go, Lidia, I will tell you what I think: if my husband speaks truly and the beasts feel as we do, then your son is more cruel than the devil himself, and Gian-Luca was right to defend the small donkey who cannot complain when he suffers.'

She turned and went slowly into the house, regardless of Lidia's abuse. In their bedroom she found a placid Gian-Luca—he was quietly packing their clothes.

He looked up with a smile: 'We will go, Maddalena, but I wish we could take the little donkey!'

'We cannot do that,' she told him gravely, 'but I am glad that you beat Leone.'

When they came downstairs half an hour later, dragging

their trunks behind them, there was Cousin Sisto waiting in the hall—presumably to kill Gian-Luca. But Cousin Sisto was not very large and moreover he dreaded a scandal; the whole village was talking already, it seemed, for a passing peasant had heard the uproar: the news had reached Levanto no doubt by now, to say nothing of the Villa Sabelli. The Marchese was coming home the next day, and he was almost as queer as Gian-Luca, he protested quite freely—when he was not too lazy—about horses and mules and all sorts of creatures; he had even forbidden the caging of richiami, which Sisto had caged all the same. No, Sisto was not particularly anxious for his master to visit the farm— he was merry and he loved pretty women, the Marchese; but once he had stopped to talk to the donkey, and had pointed out the sore on its shoulder, speaking quite sharply to Sisto. So Sisto forbore to slay Gian-Luca, and merely puffed out his cheeks.

'Go!' he said haughtily. 'You have outraged my house; you reward hospitality by beating my son. I give you all, all that my poor house can offer, you take it and then beat my son!'

But at that Maddalena became purely a peasant, and a peasant's memory is long. 'And very well we have paid you,' she told him. Then she checked off their numerous payments on her fingers, and, declaimed with much fervour as Maddalena declaimed them, they sounded extremely impressive.

Sisto had ordered a fly from Levanto, anxious to be rid of his boarders, so Gian-Luca got the driver to help him with the luggage; then he and Maddalena were driven to the station, where they waited for the Genoa train.

6

Maddalena was very silent on the journey, and Gian-Luca knew that she grieved, so he too was silent, for how could he console her for this unhappy ending to their visit?

When they came near the frontier at Modane the next day Gian-Luca looked at his wife; Maddalena was gazing out of the window and he saw that the tears were rolling down her cheeks—she, who so seldom wept. Then he took

323

her hand and stroked it with his fingers, while the other passengers pretended to read—they were all English people who were fond of Italians, and they thought this a quarrel between lovers.

Gian-Luca said gently: 'Listen, donna mia, I know that this thing had to be—I came as a man who longed for a country, but I go as a man who no longer needs a country, for no country on earth could give me what I need—what I must some day find.' He did not know what he meant by the words, did not know, indeed, why he spoke them; but he went on gently stroking her hand, and now he heard himself speaking again: 'It is you that I pity, you are patient and loving, and always you share my misfortunes—but try not to cry; you will go back, I know, you will go back to the Campagna——' and he added: 'Just think of the white mule, Umberto, who was such an old robber of grapes!'

Then Maddalena must smile through her tears, remembering the wicked Umberto. 'And the sheep all wear little bells,' said Maddalena.

'Sí, sí,' he consoled, 'they all wear little bells—and your Christ left the print of His foot in the stone—and at sunrise the mists look purple and golden—you have often told me about it.'

She said: 'But will you come with me, Gian-Luca?'

And he answered: 'Rome is the cradle of your faith—would you not like to see St. Peter's again, after all these years, Maddalena?'

'Yes, yes—but you will come with me?' she persisted.

And he answered: 'It is very wonderful, St. Peter's—all night and all day they burn eighty-nine lamps, and the faithful kneel down and pray at the tomb—you have often told me about it.'

Then her eyes grew reminiscent, and she started to tell him many things about the churches of Rome: San Pietro in Vincoli—old, very old, and containing the chains of St. Peter; Santa Prassède with its bones of the martyr; Santa Bibiana, with its stump of a column at which the good saint had been scourged. And as she talked on he nodded and smiled and continued to fondle her hand.

'Ma sí,' he murmured, 'I am glad that you are Roman—it must feel very fine to be Roman, I think—so many brave deeds behind you, Maddalena—and you too are brave, one can see it in your face; and now, look, you have quite stopped crying!'

The train had jolted itself into Modane, and all was noise and confusion. Shouting officials running backwards and forwards, dignified English folk talking Italian learnt from inadequate handbooks. There were people snatching a hasty sandwich or an orange, or an apple, or a bun—not a fat currant bun, but its thin Latin cousin containing no currants at all. Presently the train was ready to start: 'In vagone! In vagone! Partenza!'

And that was how Gian-Luca left the land of his fathers, taking Maddalena with him.

CHAPTER EIGHT

I

O N his return Gian-Luca went to Millo and tendered his resignation. This he did very simply, giving no excuse, for indeed he had none to offer. 'I cannot come back to the Doric,' he told Millo. 'I cannot any longer be a waiter—all I can do is to thank you from my heart for your very great kindness and patience.'

Millo, who had long since ceased to be surprised at any queer happening in this queerest of worlds, said: 'Allora— and what then?'

And Gian-Luca answered: 'I myself am waiting to know.'

Then he handed Millo those four months' wages that had been his retaining fee, but at this Millo made a sound of impatience: 'Do not be such an imbecile, Gian-Luca! You can give the money to Maddalena—at all events I do not want it.'

'I have not earned it,' Gian-Luca persisted, 'for I cannot return to your service.'

'Well, never mind all that——' grunted Millo; then he added curiously: 'You have left my service—whose service will you be in next, I wonder?' And he stared with interest at Gian-Luca.

Gian-Luca shook his head, and his strange, pale eyes looked past Millo and out beyond. 'That I cannot tell you——' he said very gravely. 'I must try to find myself first, signore—I am utterly lost—I must find myself again— and something else that I need.'

Millo sighed; he was going to sustain a great loss, he was losing his finest head-waiter. He had hoped against hope that Gian-Luca would come home quite cured of his curious condition. And then he was genuinely fond of this man who had served him faithfully for years, genuinely worried regarding his future—for Millo knew life even as Teresa knew it, a ruthless, intolerant business this life, in which there was no room for dreamers; so he said:

'You must do what you think best, Gian-Luca, but for God's sake get rid of your illusions! Remember that the world is a very greedy place—it is only an extension of the Doric. To keep pace with the world one must wink at its follies and if necessary pander a little; there is no room for those who want to dig beneath the surface, we are too over-crowded, we are too civilized, we object to the disturbance and the dirt of excavations—and in any case, no one has time for much spade work, our everyday needs are too numerous.' Then he suddenly held out his hand to Gian-Luca, for he himself was very busy: 'Well—I think that is all—take care of yourself, and remember I am here, if you need me.'

Gian-Luca grasped the strong, friendly hand: 'I cannot find anything to say——' he faltered.

'No need,' Millo told him. 'We part as good friends—and I hope you will prosper, Gian-Luca.'

Gian-Luca left him and went to the restaurant, where the early morning work was in progress; and there he found little Roberto and Giovanni and Daniele, and several of the others. He said to them all:

'I am leaving the Doric, I have come here to say good-bye.' And the words sounded ominous and sad to his ears, so that his heart misgave him.

But now they all gathered round talking at once: 'Ma, Signor Gian-Luca! you are leaving the Doric? No, no, it cannot be possible!'

And seeing their surprised and incredulous faces, he realized that his faults had been forgotten, and only his virtues remembered. Then it was that he knew that he was fond of these men, especially of little Roberto; and he let his gaze rest on each of them in turn as though he wanted to remember their features—as though they were worthy of being remembered, these patient, uncomplaining servers. After he had drawn them all into his mind, his eyes wandered round the room, the room in which he too had patiently served—and the room seemed full of his own past emotions, of his longing for money, his restless ambition, his ruthless will to succeed. And all these things came at him gibing, deriding, tormenting, so that he trembled a little; for now they were striking as enemies, whereas once he had thought of them as friends. A shaft of pallid February sunshine was touching a table that stood just through the archway—the table at which Ugo Doria had feasted beside the little Milady. But all that seemed a long time ago, and the pain and the anger of it—and there near the door was Jane Coram's table; someone had decked it with large hot-house roses, while the table itself had been widened and extended —perhaps she was giving a party.

Roberto was speaking: 'We shall miss you, signore, it will not be the same here without you.' And his eyes of a skylark looking through bars were dim with something very like tears.

Gian-Luca pressed the little man's hand: 'I must thank you all——' he said slowly. 'I must thank you for what you did when I was ill—and if I have sometimes been over-severe, I must ask you all to forgive me.'

But at this there arose a great hubbub of protest: 'Ma no, ma no, Signor Gian-Luca!'

'You have always been perfectly just,' said Daniele.

'Davvero, that is true!' they agreed.

When at last he had said good-bye to his waiters, he made his way to the basement; for he wished to seek out the good-natured Henri and the dignified Monsieur Pierre Martin. As he went down the tortuous steel-rimmed stair-case, he was met by a blast of hot air, for the great, greedy monster was stirring to action, and its breath was already heavy with the food that fumed on its tables of fire. He found the culinary King very quickly, but the King seemed preoccupied; he glanced up from a sizzling copper saucepan as though impatient of distraction. His eyes held the brooding, inward expression of a poet pregnant with song, and his white linen crown, which was slightly awry, had slipped to the back of his head. For Monsieur Pierre Martin was in the throes of a very real inspiration, he was busily inventing a dish of his own that would some day be called: '——à la Martin.'

However, the French are proverbially polite, so he bowed as he greeted Gian-Luca: 'Ah, Monsieur Gian-Luca, you are better, I hope?' But his gaze returned to the saucepan. 'Encore de la crème, vite, vite!' he called sharply. 'Bon Dieu! must I stand here all day?' And now he was frowning, and breathing quite hard, as a man breathes in moments of peril.

'I am leaving the Doric for good,' said Gian-Luca. 'I have come to wish you good-bye.'

'Tiens——' murmured Monsieur Martin; and then again: 'Tiens!' as he stirred with a delicate motion.

But now a young chef had returned with the cream, and the air was heavy with portent. 'Excuse if I do not offer my hand——' said the great man, seizing the cream.

Henri was in his pantry as usual, and to-day he was cutting up veal. 'Blanquette de Veau' would appear on the menu as one of the *plats du jour*.

'Ah! so you have returned,' he said, smiling at Gian-Luca, and he offered a greasy paw; then he tried the blade of his knife on his thumb and continued to cut up the veal.

'Yes,' said Gian-Luca, 'I have returned—but only to say good-bye.' And he told the good Henri that he was leaving, that he was no longer a waiter.

But at that Henri laughed and looked very wise. 'Once a waiter always a waiter,' said Henri, 'and once a chef always a chef, mon ami—we can never get away from food. By the way,' he added, 'our storeman leaves too, he is going back to Como to run a hotel. I for one am not sorry, a disagreeable fellow—I never could support Agostino!'

They talked on for a little about Agostino, then Gian-Luca bade Henri good-bye.

'This is only au revoir,' said Henri, smiling. 'We shall soon have you back at the Doric.'

Gian-Luca went thoughtfully up the stone staircase and passed through the wide entrance hall. He pushed the swing door that led out into the street, and the door closed noiselessly behind him. He stood quite still on the pavement for a moment, staring down at his shoes; then he raised bewildered eyes to the Doric, sighed, and turned towards home.

2

That evening Gian-Luca told Maddalena that he could not go back to the Doric. She accepted his decision quite quietly, uttering no word of complaint.

'You are good to me, Maddalena,' he said. 'You do not reproach me for what I have done.'

'Why should I reproach you?' said Maddalena. 'All I want is that you should be happy.'

He gave her the money that Millo had refused, and together they went into accounts, while he tried to explain their simple finances in a way that she could understand. All this he did with great care and patience, making her answer questions like a schoolgirl, making her add up long rows of figures, then pointing out her mistakes.

'You will soon understand about it,' he told her, 'for you have the sound money-sense of our peasants. I shall never buy that restaurant now, Maddalena, so my savings had better be invested.'

At the back of his mind an idea had been forming, but as yet it was nebulous and vague; it had come to him first that day in the train when he had tried to console Maddalena. And because of this vague and nebulous idea he was thinking now of her future.

'Are you listening, piccina?' he said almost sharply when he thought her attention was straying.

'But why should I know all about these things?' she asked him. 'It is you who decide such matters.'

'One can never be certain, Maddalena,' he answered. 'I prefer you to understand.'

So to please him she tried to be more attentive, frowning and biting her pencil.

He stared at her thoughtfully; she was not looking well, and her eyes had grown dull and weary, and all this he knew was because of his burdens—too heavy for her to bear. He pictured her back on the wide Campagna in the sunshine among her own people.

He muttered: 'Where the sheep all wear little bells ——' And half hearing, she looked up and smiled. Then he said: 'if you go home again, Maddalena, it is you who must help the poor beasts, for the peasants do not look upon you as a stranger, they will listen to you who are one of themselves— you will try to help, Maddalena?'

She put down her pencil and looked at him closely: 'Why do you speak so, Gian-Luca?'

'I was thinking of your Campagna,' he told her, 'that is where you seem to belong.'

'I belong to you,' she said gently but firmly, 'wherever you are is home.'

But he shook his head: 'I belong nowhere, piccina——'

'You belong in my heart,' said Maddalena.

After that they were silent for quite a long time, while she went on doing her sums; and all the while he was staring at her thoughtfully, thinking of the wide Campagna. Presently he made her put away the books, and they drew their chairs close to the fire.

'I must get work,' he told her.

And she asked him what work, but he seemed at a loss how to answer.

Then he said: 'I have such a strange feeling lately—as though something were calling me away, as though something were waiting for me to find it, something very splendid, Maddalena.'

She did not understand, and her eyes looked frightened. 'Calling you, Gian-Luca?' she said slowly.

He nodded: 'It is something that is waiting to be found——' Then because he could see that her eyes were frightened he tried to reassure her: 'It is nothing, cara mia, it is only my fancy—— Now come, go to bed, it must be getting late.' And he kissed her and patted her arm. But as she turned away his heart ached with pity. 'Do not be afraid,' he comforted.

3

But Maddalena felt terribly afraid, and now she would never leave her husband; when he went out she must always go with him. He had not the heart to oppose her in this, yet he knew that he needed solitude, for he who had always so feared loneliness now craved it with all his being. He tried to make some sort of plans for their future, but somehow he could not think clearly. The noise of the traffic, the presence of people, the constant presence of Maddalena, these things bewildered; so the weeks slipped by and still he had come to no decision. He would walk about the streets with his wife at his side, or sit gazing out of the window;

and a great urge would rise in him, filling him with longing
—an urge so insistent that he wanted to cry out——

'I am coming!' he would mutter, and then grow afraid,
not understanding his own words.

He was filled with an intolerable, homeless feeling—he
felt like an atom cast into space—he wanted to stretch out
his hand and grasp something that was infinitely stronger
than he was.

He would think: 'There is something greater than life—
perhaps even greater than death——'

And then he would wonder if this thing might be God,
and then he would wonder how a man might find God who
was greater than life and death. But when he tried to think
of God in this way, he would always grow appalled by God's
vastness, for his heart was aching for simple things; yet the
simple things were terribly finite, or so it seemed to Gian-Luca.

There were days when his mind would be clouded and
numbed by a deep sense of personal failure; when he saw
his past life as a road that had led nowhere, when he saw
his present as a kind of chaos in which he was involving
Maddalena; and even more hopeless did he feel about the
future, for when he looked forward he could not find the
future, and this made him terribly afraid.

'What must I do?' he would sometimes mutter; and then
again: 'What must I do?'

He grew anxious about money and would sit for hours
poring over his account books; yet all the while he would
feel strangely detached, as though none of this mattered to
him. Maddalena, it was, that was always in his mind, and
how best he could provide for her; even his savings were
not his, he felt, nothing was his any more. His clothes were
growing shabby, the time had arrived when he usually
ordered a new suit, but nothing would induce him to go to
his tailor's, for in all sorts of personal ways he was saving,
depriving himself of the small luxuries to which he had been
accustomed. And seeing this, Maddalena protested almost
crossly.

'You cannot wear that suit, Gian-Luca!' For she took a
great pride in her husband's appearance, and she felt like
weeping to see him these days, so disheartened and hopeless
and shabby.

Gian-Luca would be thinking: 'It is Maddalena's money, I must spend as little as I can.' But to her he would pretend to take the thing lightly: 'Ma guarda, mia donna, this suit is almost new—there are years of wear in it yet.'

But quite apart from the question of money, he felt bored when he thought of his tailor; bored too when he looked at his personal possessions—quite a number they were, he found to his surprise—for such barnacles collect on the keels of most ships as they plough through the sea of life. 'Too many useless trifles,' he would think. And one day he started giving them away to beggars that he met in the street, avoiding Maddalena and slipping out alone, intent on this unusual proceeding.

Maddalena might exclaim: 'Your silver cigarette case—I cannot find it, Gian-Luca!' Or: 'Those little gold cuff-links, where have they gone? I see that you are wearing your mother-of-pearl ones.'

And then he would look sheepish and would have to confess this new folly that he had committed, wondering as he did so why he had not sold the things and given the money to his wife.

She would say: 'But, amore, what are you doing?'

And he would not know how to answer, for when he saw the surprise on her face he would suddenly grow very shy.

One possession, however, he still clung to firmly, and that was his collection of books; for he felt that his books should be able to help him—they were so wise, his books, and their range of subjects was so varied, so wide and so learned. He began to turn more and more to these friends, asking them to solve his problems, yet somehow the problems remained unsolved—a new cause for fear in Gian-Luca.

'I cannot find it——' he would say, bewildered, staring up at Maddalena.

'Find what?' she would ask sharply, and then she would sigh, knowing that he could not answer.

He said that he must see the Librarian again, because he would tell him what to read; so one day they walked to the public library, but when they got there Maddalena stayed outside.

'I do not want to come in,' she remarked firmly; 'you

333

will talk about things that I cannot understand—I would only be in the way!'

The Librarian was sitting with his arms on his desk; the library was quiet and empty.

'So you have come,' he said rather gravely. 'I have waited a long time, Gian-Luca.'

And Gian-Luca remembered that he had not been near him or written for more than two years.

They talked for a little, then Gian-Luca said: 'I want you to tell me what to read—there must be some books that explain our existence, that explain all the sorrow and the suffering around us—I cannot be the only creature who sees it, others must have seen it before me.'

'So you have seen it at last!' said his friend.

'Too much I have seen it,' frowned Gian-Luca.

'It was bound to happen,' the Librarian told him. 'I have known that for a long time past. Why, I knew it when you were quite a little boy——' Then he smiled at his recollections. 'You were rather a greedy little boy, I remember—Swiss roll with apricot jam——' Then he said more gravely: 'You ask me for books that will help you to face your life; well, the world is literally snowed under with books, and nearly all books are written about life—but not one of them can help you with *your* life, Gian-Luca; that book you'll have to write for yourself.' He saw something very like terror in the eyes that were eagerly searching his face. 'Why are you so much afraid?' he inquired.

And Gian-Luca answered irrelevantly: 'Because I am feeling so terribly lonely—and yet I want to be alone.'

'No one is ever alone,' said the Librarian, 'but of course it needs solitude to prove it.' He got up stiffly, for now he was old, and he found a few well-worn volumes. 'Take these,' he said; and Gian-Luca stared at them—he had given him fairy tales. The Librarian laughed softly: 'The wisdom of belief—the wisdom of children——' he murmured, 'learn to believe in a fairy tale and the rest will certainly follow.'

But Gian-Luca had laid the books down on the desk and was turning slowly away.

'You don't believe me?' the Librarian said gently.

'No,' answered Gian-Luca. 'I do not believe you.'

'Oh, well,' sighed the Librarian, 'perhaps you're too young—or not yet young enough, Gian-Luca.'

Then Gian-Luca held out his hand with a smile, for he thought that his friend might really be in earnest; but he could not help wondering whether the Librarian was approaching his second childhood.

CHAPTER NINE

I

THERE WAS consternation in Old Compton Street when the clan learnt that Gian-Luca had left the Doric, even Nerone's firm faith in him was shaken. 'Dio! he must have gone crazy!' he exclaimed chewing the ends of his moustache.

Rosa and Mario were almost speechless for the moment, so great was their horrified amazement. 'The Doric—the Doric—the Doric——' murmured Mario, and then he could get no further.

Rocca shook his head as he sharpened his knives with a long, slow, experienced movement. 'Mad!' he muttered, 'completely mad!'

'Well, what did I tell you?' broke in his signora. 'This is all the fault of that Board School!'

But old Teresa said nothing at all, as was often her way when very angry, and this reticence greatly annoyed the clan, who could talk of nothing but Gian-Luca.

'I do not wish to discuss him,' she told them; 'my grandson is no longer a child—if he wants to ruin himself and his wife that concerns neither you nor me.'

'But I love him!' wailed Rosa, whose tongue had to wag in defiance of old Teresa. 'Our little Gian-Luca, I love him, I tell you! And so elegant and handsome he looked in his fine clothes. He had such an air as a piccolo even; Mario remembers when he lit his first match for a young lady's cigarette—tell her, Mario, how Gian-Luca lit his first match for that young lady's cigarette.'

Then Mario, nothing loath, and with many wide gestures, told how the youthful Gian-Luca had lighted his first match, and from that he must go on to tell other glories concerning Gian-Luca's career.

'A marvellous waiter he was,' declared Mario. 'He had

336

all that a waiter should possess—alacrity, dignity, persuasiveness and charm; and his smile was enough to turn sour cream to sweet, and his wonderful eyes when they rested upon you would convince you that old cat was chicken.'

'Ma, per carità, leave me in peace,' snapped Teresa, who was struggling to pick up a difficult stitch; after which she just sat and said nothing at all, so what was the good of their talking?

However, when Millo arrived it was different, for even Teresa could not disregard Millo. 'I have come to discuss your grandson,' he announced, so Teresa was forced to discuss him. 'This nonsense has got to stop,' declared Millo. 'Gian-Luca has a bee in his bonnet. Now you, cara signora, must chase out that bee; you must send for him at once and find out what is wrong, and the sooner you do so the better, I think; it is April, and Gian-Luca left me in February, and ever since that the man has been idle—something is terribly wrong.'

Teresa's defiant black eyes met his wise ones, and those wise, kindly eyes looked quite stern. 'He is your grandson, after all,' he said firmly; 'Maddalena is weak, she cannot control him, it is time that you took a hand.'

'As you will,' she replied, smoothing her knitting; 'but my grandson is not easy to manage—he has always been strangely unlike my people—I do not suppose he will listen to reason. However, I will certainly see him.'

'You too have a will of your own, signora——' Millo told her, smiling slightly. 'But when you have seen him,' he continued more gravely, 'I should like to hear about his plans for the future—I am anxious about him, he has served me too well for me not to feel a certain affection——' Then he laughed, for Millo always laughed at himself when he heard his heart talking to him.

After he had gone, Teresa's mouth hardened, and her hand shot out for her stick—a constant humiliation, this stick; but the winter had brought her bad pains in her knees, rheumatism according to the doctor. She got up slowly, grunting a little as she did so, and made her way into the shop. Standing quite still, she surveyed those possessions which she now shared with Francesco Millo.

The Casa Boselli was crowded that morning, people must wait to be served, and this in spite of the eight smart assistants who ran hither and thither dressed in white. Beside the cashier stood a stern-faced young person in a golf coat, and the young person's locks had been shorn. In the top button-hole of her knitted jacket showed one or two tiny war ribbons. This young person was very proficient in all things; she could add up long rows of complicated figures by merely flicking her pen, she could type with a speed that made you feel giddy—she had shorthand, Italian, French and some German, and just now she was keeping an eye on the cashier who had only been recently engaged. She was hard, she was clever, and Millo had secured her, scenting a valuable find.

As Teresa surveyed this importation of Millo's, her lips grew exceedingly grim, and she forced her old knees to assume a straight angle, and she swung the offending stick under her arm—just to show that she did not need it. But down it must come, that accursed stick, because of the weak left knee, and the capable young person left the cash desk— for among other things she had nursed in the war—

'You shouldn't stand more than you can help,' she remarked, fetching a chair for Teresa.

Teresa thanked her coldly, refusing the chair; and Teresa must thank her in English—for she would not admit that this capable young person could really understand good Italian.

'You are now doing, what?' inquired Teresa abruptly.

And the young person slightly raised her eyebrows: 'I'm showing Miss Gibson the ropes at the moment—don't forget your medicine, will you, signora? And I'm quite sure the doctor would want you to rest——' That was how she answered Teresa.

The Casa Boselli! The dear Casa Boselli! The belovéd Casa Boselli! with its hams and its paste and its cheeses and its olives and its coils and bolsters of salame! The friendly, dark, odorous Casa Boselli, smelling of Chianti and oil; smelling of sawdust and pickles and garlic, of sour brown bread and newly-ground coffee; of split peas and lentils and pods of vanilla—of people and Fabio's boot-blacking. Who would have known the old Casa Boselli in this large, overlighted, over-ventilated store; this brass-bound, marble-faced, red-tiled emporium—three shops it was now, that had been turned into one, the top floors supported by green marble columns in place of the party walls. Why, Fabio would have gasped at his resurrection, had he happened to wander in mistaking it for Heaven, and perhaps he would have turned tail and hurried out again, preferring his purgatory.

Teresa surveyed the fruition of her dreams, leaning on that hateful black stick. Her dreams? Oh, no, the realities of Millo, aided and abetted by the clever young person, who received a large salary for whisking her pen over figures that could just as well be added on the fingers! And every Saturday this clever young person must play hockey or lacrosse or squash rackets, and—Santa Madonna! she proposed to play football dressed like a man, in short breeches! When Teresa had asked her abruptly one day why women were doing these things, the young person had laughed:

'We've got to keep hard, we're not just breeding cattle, signora.'

Teresa Boselli went back into her parlour, at the door of which progress had stood still. Like Moses of old she had rolled back the waves, and the hot little parlour was just as it had been—it smelt of the years as dried herbs will smell of the dust and sun of past summers. Teresa Boselli sat down in her parlour, resting her head on her hand; and the bitterness of old age was heavy upon her, the bitterness of those who no longer belong, who have outlived the thoughts and the feelings of their time, and their bodily strength as well. And when she had closed her defiant black eyes for a moment, in order to rest them, what must she see but a low-ceilinged bedroom with a figure stretched out on the crazy wooden bed, and over the figure a bright patchwork quilt, the work of Teresa's hands. In her ears was a shrilly protesting sound, the sound of an infant wailing; and across the room on the opposite wall, the smiling face of the Mother of God . . .

Teresa sprang up with a low cry of anger, then she groaned because of her knee. Nevertheless she ignored its stabbing and started to pace the floor. Shame and sorrow?

Change? Progress? Old age and its ailments? Away with them all! they could not break the strong.

'Miss Dobell!' she called loudly to the clever young person, 'be good enough to bring me that invoice!'

2

Two days later Teresa sent for her grandson, and he went the same afternoon, but he would not allow Maddalena to go with him, suspecting why he had been sent for.

Even Teresa must exclaim when she saw him standing in his shabby old clothes. 'You are not yet a pauper,' she began sharply, then she shrugged her shoulders. 'But why do I talk? You will do as you please, Gian-Luca.'

He drew up a chair, then he noticed her stick: 'What is that?' he inquired, surprised.

'It is nothing,' lied Teresa. 'I have sprained my left knee.' And she threw the stick on to the sofa. Then she said: 'I have sent for you to come here, Gian-Luca, because Millo asked me to do so; as for me, I do not want to see you at all, you are idle and I have no patience with the idle. But that is beside the point, I suppose, since Millo wishes to know of your plans for the future.'

Gian-Luca said calmly: 'I have not got any plans, so far I have not made any.' And his mouth looked wilful, as when long ago a small boy had confronted Teresa.

'Then do you propose to let Maddalena starve?' inquired old Teresa, quite as calmly.

He smiled: 'She will never do that, I think, Nonna—she has Aunt Ottavia's money to fall back on, and besides, there are all my savings.'

'I see,' said Teresa, 'and what of yourself? You propose to live on your wife?'

He shook his head: 'No, I am spending very little, as little as I can of my savings.'

'So I observe from your clothes,' she said dryly; 'you are obviously spending nothing.'

Then he suddenly wanted to stop this useless fencing, and he tried to explain his situation; but try as he would he explained it very badly, because put into words it sounded foolish.

As Teresa listened she tightened her lips, and her black brows met in a line: 'It is not I who will tell all this nonsense to Millo, you had better write yourself, and not later than to-night.'

He nodded: 'Va bene, I will write to him, Nonna——' he told her, 'and now you would like me to go——'

'It is true that I have nothing more to say,' she answered grimly, 'and all that I have said has been wasted.'

She tried to get up but her weak knee gave way because of that discarded stick; and going to Teresa Gian-Luca raised her gently, but as soon as she could stand she leant on the table, unwilling to let him support her.

Yet he thought: 'She is gallant indeed this old woman, see how she tries to stand alone!' For nothing she did could make him resent her, and this had been so all his life.

But before he went he must pause in the doorway, and take a last look at Teresa, and she looked back at him with deep scorn in her eyes, and Gian-Luca saw that scorn. Then all of a sudden the light of her scorn had kindled a lamp in his mind; and his mind grew clear and calm and illumined, for his vision stretched far beyond old Teresa, and he knew the thing that he must do.

'Remember, you have always got Maddalena, that is if you need her,' he said gravely.

After he had gone she stared at the wall as she had done many years ago, and now as then, she was thinking of his hair, and his curious, alien eyes.

Gian-Luca walked down the street to Nerone's, and there he saw Mario and Rosa. Nerone he saw, and Berta's twin daughters who were paying a visit to their Nonna. Albert had gone to Paris, it seemed, and Berta had wanted to go with him: 'Look after the kids, there's a dear!' she had said—so Rosa looked after the kids.

The twins were as alike as twins ought to be, it amused Gian-Luca to see them, for not contented with looking like each other, they were also the dead spit of Albert. They had greasy, blond hair, which however was bobbed, and they spoke with a strong Cockney accent. Of Italian they knew nothing, for Albert despised it, and Berta had not bothered to teach them. They most unexpectedly hated each other, and this always shocked the poor Rosa, for as Rosa would say: 'What can God do more? He makes them as one, yet they wish to be as two—they hit and they kick, and if one of them says "yes," then the other will say "no." It cannot be right, I am sure our dear Lord is offended.'

But on this particular afternoon the twins were comparatively peaceful. They eyed Gian-Luca with china-blue eyes, then one of them said: 'Please give me sixpence,' but the other said: 'Give me a shilling.'

'Now, now,' protested Rosa, 'you run up di sopra—up the stairs you go quickly!' she translated.

'I will give you some sweeties if you do,' bribed Nerone, an inveterate old spoiler of children.

The twins disappeared, and presently Mario must hobble away to the Capo; then Rosa unburdened her heart to Gian-Luca, while Nerone listened and grunted.

It was terrible now at the Capo, it seemed, for the new head-waiter was a devil. He was infinitely worse than the Padrone, said Rosa, and his oaths and his tantrums all fell on poor Mario, because he was lame and ageing. He yelled names at Mario in front of other waiters, and hissed them in front of the clients, until Mario had threatened to stick a knife in him, so unspeakable were those names. Rosa was sure that the low-minded 'porco' meant to get her husband dismissed.

'He is only waiting his chance,' snivelled Rosa, wiping her eyes with her finger.

So full was Rosa of Mario's troubles that she forgot to cross-question Gian-Luca, and for this her foster-son felt very thankful—he did not want any discussion. As for Nerone, he only grunted, thinking of all his own grievances, and when he suddenly remembered Gian-Luca, and began to look stern and rather aggressive, Gian-Luca saw what was coming in his eye, and hastily got up to go.

He said to Rosa: 'I will not forget Mario, I am going to see what I can do.' And he called her 'Mother' for the first time in his life, and at that she burst out crying on his shoulder.

'Mio bimbo!' she murmured into his coat, as though he were her little baby.

And now he kissed her fondly on both cheeks, and told her to cheer up and stop crying; then he went to Nerone and kissed him on both cheeks, according to the custom of their country.

When he had left them, Nerone said to Rosa: 'Why did he kiss me as he did?'

'It was strange,' said Rosa, 'it was certainly strange—just as if he were going on a journey.'

3

That evening Gian-Luca wrote the letter to Millo, but he wrote for the old lame mule. Of himself he said little, having little to say, beyond thanking Millo yet again for his kindness.

'If you could try Mario Varese,' he wrote, 'I think he would give you satisfaction. He would make an excellent storeroom keeper, for there his lameness would not affect him, and, moreover, he knows a great deal about food, its price, and how to select it. He is honest and sober, and a very hard worker; he has had to work hard all his life, and although he is not as young as he was, he must be as young as Agostino.'

Gian-Luca went out and slipped the letter in the post-box, after which he returned to Maddalena. For a moment he looked at her without speaking—she was darning his socks by the fire. Then he called her and made her sit down beside him, and he took the darning from her hand, while she stared at him silent and always fearful, wondering what he would say. As gently as he could he told Maddalena the thing that he knew he must do. He must go right away all alone, he told her, he must try to find God in great solitude—he must try to understand this thing she called God; for only in that way would he ever understand the reason and the meaning of life, and only in that way could he find Gian-Luca, the man who had lost himself. He wanted to understand pity, he told her, and the suffering that had called it into being, and why the beggar had lost his eyes, and why the singing bird had been blinded. He wanted to think out the problem of death and where it must ultimately lead, but above all the problem of God concerned him.

343

'Because,' he said slowly, 'if your God does exist and is good, as you think Him, Maddalena, then all these big problems must come right in the end—but supposing you are wrong and God does not exist, is there any hope for the world?' Then he said: 'I have always been a good fighter, and now I am fighting again. I am fighting to get to your God, Maddalena; I am like a poor sailor who looks for a light that will get him to port in a storm. I have never uttered a prayer in my life, for I felt that I had nothing to pray to. All my life I have depended entirely on myself, but now I have not got myself to depend on—because I have lost myself.'

And all this time she had sat there quite silent, speaking never a word, and Gian-Luca appeared not to notice her strange silence, for he went on to tell her of his plans. He would take very little with him, he told her; whatever he needed he could buy on his journey—but then he would need scarcely anything at all, for he meant to live very simply. At the end of his journey he would send her an address to which she could always write, and he too would write, but their letters must be brief: 'I am well, Maddalena,' 'I am well, Gian-Luca,'—though if either of them were in sore need they must say so; only, he begged her to wait for that need before she summoned him home. And now he made yet another condition: she must not let anyone know his address, nor must she come herself, trying to find him, for he wanted to be quite alone.

He said: 'I shall not forget you, Maddalena, and I promise that I will come back—while I am gone I shall think out our future, and what I must do to earn my living, and if I find God it will all be so simple, for of course He will show me the way.'

Then he groped for her hand and tried to hold it, but she wrenched it free with a cry; and now she had risen, and he too had risen, staring at her aghast. For Maddalena's face was white to the lips, and her gentle, mothering eyes were on fire, and all of her shook with a kind of fury, and her voice when it came was choked with passion, so that he scarcely knew it.

'You will never come back, Gian-Luca,' she said wildly, 'you will never come back any more—and as God is my witness I will not let you go—you belong to me only, and God gave you to me, therefore He cannot take you away—not like this, not while you still live, Gian-Luca. I need you, I need you far more than God does. He has got the whole world, I have only got you——'

'It is I who need Him,' said Gian-Luca.

'The Church——' she began.

But he held up his hand, and a strange, new authority looked from his eyes: 'I am told to find God in my own way, Maddalena. I am told to go now and find Him.'

'You are told?' she said loudly. 'Who has told you, Gian-Luca?'

And he answered: 'I do not know; but I mean to obey that summons, Maddalena—I will not ignore it any longer.'

Then all that lies dormant in the heart of woman rose up and gripped Maddalena. The long years of civilization slipped from her, and she stood forth a naked, primitive thing, and she crushed down her spirit and she called on her body to help her in her fight for this man.

'I love you, I love you!' she whispered fiercely, and her arms were around his neck. Her soft, ample body was pressed against him, so that he could feel the warmth of her body; all that was gracious in it he felt, and the deep, happy comfort of her breasts. Her lips were on his, insistent, compelling, while she murmured the words of her love; and her love swept the years away from Maddalena, so that she seemed like the splendid young virgin who had walked that day by the side of her lover into the woods at Hadley.

'Stay with me—stay with me, amore,' she pleaded, 'you cannot leave Maddalena—you have so often slept with your head on her breast——' and she lifted her hand and pressed down his head, as she had done long ago in the woods.

For one moment he let his cheek rest on her shoulder, kissing her strong, white throat—for was not this wife of his a woman made more lovely through her love for him? But then he must push her away very gently—pitiful and almost ashamed.

He said: 'If you love me, have mercy, Maddalena.' And he knelt down before her and prayed for her mercy—prayed her to let him go forth in peace on this journey in quest of God.

Then the passion died out of Maddalena's eyes, and the motherhood came back and possessed them entirely—and her eyes filled with gentle and most blessèd tears, to see him kneeling before her. She stooped, and he grasped at her outstretched hands as she drew him up from his knees.

'May God go each step of the way beside you, and may you feel Him and know Him, Gian-Luca, and may He give you the thing you most need, which is surely peace,' she murmured.

Then they kissed each other very gravely and sadly and they looked into each other's eyes, and Gian-Luca said: 'God must exist somewhere, since you exist, Maddalena.'

CHAPTER TEN

I

THE GREATEST adventures in the lives of men will sometimes be embarked on very simply, and that was how Gian-Luca set out on his journey—taking no heed for the morrow. To please Maddalena he must carry a suit-case in which she had managed to pack some warm flannels, and his raincoat she had strapped to the side of the suitcase, adding thereby to its bulk. For the rest he would take nothing but what he stood up in, and this for a very good reason; he intended to tramp to his destination, wherever that might ultimately be. A great longing for freedom of movement possessed him; he wanted to be quite untrammelled; he would not be restricted by so much as a map, far less by time-tables and trains. He felt blessedly vague regarding his plans, though he meant to reach Staines by the evening; after that his road should be left to fate.

'Some place must be waiting for me,' he thought, 'some place is always waiting——'

His clothes were quite as vague as his plans; he was wearing what had first come to hand—an old tweed suit, some well-worn brown shoes, and a shabby grey Homburg hat. To all Maddalena's protests he had answered firmly: 'I can buy what I need on the journey'; so what could she do but put up a prayer that the fine warm weather would hold?

He wandered along New Oxford Street, carrying that tiresome suit-case, a ridiculous encumbrance for a very long walk; he must buy himself something more practical, a knapsack—but he felt rather tender towards the suit-case, thinking of Maddalena.

'Just for a little I will keep it,' he mused, filled with his gratitude towards her, and filled with a certain sense of guilt also; he had not told her that he meant to tramp: 'I will let you know where I am when I get there,' he had said, allowing his wife to suppose that he meant to get there by train.

The first part of his journey was dull and uninspiring, Bayswater, Shepherd's Bush, and then Chiswick High Road; mile upon dreary mile of London—he felt as though the city were stretching out its coils, trying to trip him, to impede him.

'It will not let me get out!' he muttered, gripping his suit-case more firmly.

But now he was passing Kew Bridge Station, and this reassured him a little; he paused and stood gazing towards the bridge, with his eyes filled with recollection.

'Such a very long time ago,' he was thinking; 'It was all such a long time ago——'

Mario and Rosa, Berta and Geppe, and the little Gian-Luca with his hamper—the sudden blue and coolness of bluebells, a child who had pushed them roughly with his foot because they had made him unhappy, because for some inexplicable reason they had taken the comfort from his motto. A gallant motto it had been in its way, so simple, too: 'I have got myself——' 'Yes, but no one has really got himself, that is the trouble,' thought Gian-Luca. 'Come on, avanti! There is not much time!' Mario limping with his bunion—— 'Come on, avanti! There is not much time!' and yet Mario was still at the Capo di Monte, and there he would remain unless Millo took pity and rescued the old lame mule——. Mario had never had time to admire things that lay right under his nose, such as a flowering magnolia tree, or prunias in blossom, or a patch of cool bluebells—he had only had time for enormous longings that had stretched to Land's End and beyond. And supposing he should ultimately reach his Land's End—why then he would still say: 'Avanti! Come on, avanti! There is not much time, we have no time to look at the sea! . . . '

Gian-Luca began to walk forward again, and quite soon he had come to Brentford, a detestable place always smelling of gasworks, its streets always fouled by its grimy, black wharves and the grimy boots of its workers. Yet in Brentford it was that the first romance of his pilgrimage touched Gian-Luca; for a steep little hill led down to the water, and there on the water lay a battered old barge, and that barge with a blue swirl of smoke from its chimney was Romance—yes, even in Brentford. But just past the canal he saw a wonderful thing, a tiny orchard in blossom. In spite of the grime and the squalor, it was blooming—a brave little remnant of that army of orchards that must once have marched almost through Brentford itself, filling the air with their good scent of growth and the eye with their heavenly whiteness. Gian-Luca suddenly caught his breath, for a deep new craving was upon him—the craving to bless because of that orchard.

'Not God,' thought Gian-Luca, 'for I have not yet found Him——' so his grateful heart blessed the orchard.

Hounslow he passed, and then Neals' Corner, after which the tram-lines ended. Sturdy quick-hedges began to guard fields, real fields that looked placid and consciously green in the pale April sunlight of the morning. Now he was coming to the open country, and meadows with streams and willows he came to, and a widening stream that spread as it rippled brown over last year's leaves. A great number of birds were piping and singing—blackbirds and thrushes, with here and there a robin; many other birds also, whose songs were unfamiliar to this man for whom England had meant London.

He thought: 'It is like a very kind garden where everything goes unmolested.' And he marvelled at how little he knew this garden. 'I must always have been too busy,' he mused, beginning to loiter a little.

He walked down a pathway that led to the stream, and, undoing his suit-case, he got out some food. Maddalena had included hard-boiled eggs in the menu: she had rolled them up carefully in a grey flannel shirt-sleeve, and this made him laugh when he found them. But when he discovered what else she had done, his eyes grew pitiful and tender, for lavender sprigs had been laid among his flannels —two little bunches tied up with blue ribbon—and although his bread and butter had a lavender flavour, he consumed it gladly for her sake.

It was pleasant under the trees by the water, and he stayed there resting for quite a long time; and as he rested what should he hear but the first insistent call of the cuckoo, that strangely alluring, mysterious call to something that lies always just beyond.

Presently he got up and trudged on again, passing through Bedfont, and loitering once more to look at the church, with its tall clipped yew and its curious, squat wooden steeple. By now he was beginning to feel very tired indeed, and the suit-case grew heavier and heavier. Seeing him, one or two people wondered, for the stigma of the city was still upon him in the cut of his suit, in the lightness of his shoes, but above all, perhaps, in his pale, thin face that had lost its Italian sunburn. Footsore and weary, he trudged into Staines and stared dully about him for an inn. He must lodge very cheaply, having brought little money; every penny he had belonged to Maddalena. But he finally selected an inn quite at random, because he liked the look of its signboard—a friendly white lion with the face of a sheep-dog.

And that was the end of the first day.

2

Next morning he bought a capacious knapsack with wide webbing straps for the shoulders. His suit-case he left with the landlord of the inn: 'I will call for it on my way back,' he promised, not considering where that might lead him.

For that matter he did not know his way forward, but he took the road to Egham. He felt rested, he was stepping out quite briskly with his knapsack, and, after a little, Virginia Water was lying on his right, through the trees. Now he was passing small woods and parklands; there was bracken, too, with its questioning fronds like green marks of interrogation. The sun was turning the water to silver, as though it lay bathed in moonlight; but all these fair things were behind iron fences, and none of them seemed quite happy or free.

'I have not yet found what I need,' thought Gian-Luca, slowly shaking his head.

The road grew more thickly wooded beyond Virginia Water, and he fancied that the trees were tramping beside him—beech tree and ash tree, holly and chestnut; and their branches swept forward a little in the wind as though pointing the way to Gian-Luca.

'Where are you taking me to?' he asked them, and for answer the trees swept forward again.

All day he tramped on, forgetting his luncheon, and the trees never left him for long. Sometimes he would pass through a town or a village, but the trees would be waiting on the far side to meet him, while the gentle, green pastures with their gentle-eyed cattle would be drowsing beyond the trees. This was the day on which he saw his first lambs; quite new they were, and unbelievably clean. Being strong little lambs, they played a great deal, but without any sense of direction. On their stiff, hoop-stick legs they wore fluffy black gaiters; their faces were black, too, so the rest of their fleece seemed exceedingly white by contrast. After their babes walked the careful old ewes, nuzzling, pushing, calling. From time to time a lamb stopped abruptly, ducking its head for the comfort of its mother, and the ewe would stand patiently gazing into space while the lamb drank in life from her body.

How pleasant they were, these wide English meadows, happy with flocks and herds. The sky and the green grass belonged to their creatures, but Gian-Luca, remembering Lidia's poor beasts, must turn his eyes away from these meadows, filled with a reminiscent pity.

Towards evening he came to a quiet inn standing at the end of a village, a low black-and-white building with timbers and gables; and because a huge elm tree guarded its entrance, he decided to stay there for the night. He ate his supper at a rough wooden table that stood just under the tree; he could hear the perpetual talking of leaves, and, whatever it was that they talked of, it soothed him, for their sibilant words sounded patient and hopeful.

And so ended his second day.

3

Gian-Luca fell in with a tramp the next morning who was going in his direction, a dusty fellow with a hole in his shoe, and the restless eyes and shuffling gait that belong to the Brothers of the Road. Gian-Luca himself looked scarcely less dusty, and he too was shuffling a little, for those who walk far must economize force—they very soon drop their goose-step. A two days' growth was on Gian-Luca's chin, for he had not troubled to shave.

'I will let my beard grow,' he had said to himself, and now it was obviously growing.

But this unkempt appearance did not deceive the tramp, who had taken in Gian-Luca's clothes. 'A toff,' thought the tramp, 'and 'e's tryin' to look shabby. Lordy, ain't people amazin'!'

'Good morning!' said Gian-Luca on a sudden impulse; 'it looks like being a fine day.'

'Yus,' grunted the tramp noncommittally, and proceeded to scratch his head.

After that there was silence for several minutes while he eyed Gian-Luca with suspicion; he had certainly met this type before, he decided—swells, and loonies, and suchlike, doing the simple; they generally tried to find out all about you, then wrote a lot of rubbish to the papers.

'Are you going very far?' inquired Gian-Luca, breaking the awkward pause.

'Middlin',' he was told, and again there was silence as they trudged along side by side.

'This road leads to Basingstoke, I think,' remarked Gian-Luca.

' 'Ook comes fust,' growled his Brother.

'Oh, does it?' said Gian-Luca.

'Yus, it do,' snapped the tramp; 'ain't yer looked at the sign-posts? Don't yer know where yer goin'?'

Gian-Luca smiled at him: 'Well, no, not exactly, but every road must lead somewhere in the end.'

And now the tramp felt thoroughly suspicious: 'I suppose yer've come walkin' out 'ere for fun; yer one of them crack-brains wot wants ter live simple. Blimey! you try it! It ain't so darned simple to live no'ow, to my way of thinkin'.' Then he added quickly: 'Or maybe yer a writer, one of them as writes for the papers.'

But Gian-Luca informed him that he had once been a waiter, and at this his companion looked a little more friendly: 'A waiter, was yer? That sounds all right ter me—so nice and 'andy to the food.'

'I suppose so. I have thrown up my job quite lately. I used to be at the Doric.'

'Gawd!' muttered the tramp, 'that swell plyce in Piccadilly? Yer spoilt, that's wot you are; some folks never knows their blessin's, not till they've lost 'em.'

Gian-Luca examined the man's face more closely, noticing the restless eyes. He said: 'You would never tolerate four walls——'

'Now then, wotch'yer gettin' at!' scowled the tramp, glancing at Gian-Luca with annoyance.

At Hook the tramp bethought him of food, and he paused beside a shop window. The window was full of cold meats and pork pies, interlarded with rock cakes and apples.

But the tramp shook his head: 'No, thanks,' he remarked. 'I ain't got the price of the Doric terdye, nor yet of the Berkeley neither——'

'You may choose!' said Gian-Luca.

'Go on!' said the tramp.

'You may choose; I mean it,' laughed Gian-Luca.

The tramp chose a couple of large pork pies and a goodly portion of beef. Gian-Luca chose bread and cheese and some apples.

'Well, I never!' scoffed his companion.

Farther on down the street Gian-Luca bought beer, then they hurried along through the town.

'Come on!' urged the tramp. 'I knows a nice spot fer a picnic!' and he grinned with amusement.

Out beyond the town they came to a meadow; a large board was affixed to its gate: 'Trespassers will be prosecuted,' read the board, but the tramp wormed his way through a gap in the hedge, and after him went Gian-Luca.

The tramp was soon mellow with pork pies and beer, his eyes grew more steady and friendly; and now he was talking of the life of the road as though he were talking to a Brother. Gian-Luca heard about the hard law of trespass, and how it might best be evaded; he learnt how a man could find comfort at night, in what type of barn it was safe to take refuge, what formation of hay-rick provided good shelter, what species of watch-dog was most to be feared, and what words were most likely to calm him. All these things he learnt and a great deal besides, including the right houses to beg at, for mystical signs would be found on gate-posts, chalked there by considerate Brethren in passing; some were danger signals, some the other way round; every tramp understood these signals. Then just as his guest grew most eloquent down came a sharp April shower; Gian-Luca completely forgot his rain-coat, as his wife might have guessed that he would do. When the shower had passed over, the tramp collected sticks from the sheltered side of the hedge, and choosing a nicely secluded corner, he proceeded to light a fire.

'Got to be careful of fires,' he said gravely; 'getch yer into trouble, they does. Alwers let yer smoke blow away from the 'igh road, that is if yer can—see, mate?'

But Gian-Luca was not attending to the words; he was watching the creating of the fire from three paper bags, and a few dryish sticks collected on the lee-side of the hedge. There in that rain-soaked English meadow the prehistoric ritual was performed—the ageless ritual of the calling of fire to the help and service of man. Like a priest of old, the tramp stretched forth his hands in a gesture of command and benediction, and the flames leapt up to the summons of those hands.

'Kind of attrac's it, flesh do,' he explained, looking up at Gian-Luca.

Then they crouched beside the fire and let themselves steam, glad enough of the warmth and comfort; and the clouds broke apart, leaving rifts of blue sky, while the fire did its best to dry them.

Presently they sidled out through the hedge, having carefully stamped on the glowing ashes, and they walked as far as Basingstoke together, where the tramp said good-bye to Gian-Luca. He was going to pick up some work at a farm that lay two miles away down a lane.

'Just enough to keep me goin' fer a bit, so I'll 'ave to wish yer good afternoon, mister.' He had suddenly grown suspicious again, too suspicious to call this man 'mate'.

Gian-Luca said: 'If I keep to the high road, where shall I come to in the end?'

The tramp considered: 'If yer keeps right on this way, yer'll be bound to come to the Noo Forest.'

'The trees were right, then,' murmured Gian-Luca; 'I felt that they were trying to lead me——'

'Gawd!' laughed the tramp, 'you are balmy, aren't yer? Well, good-bye, mister, and thank yer.'

Gian-Luca strode forward along the road, while the afternoon passed and the shadows lengthened; but still he strode forward, not pausing to rest, for his thoughts ran before him to the forest. At King's Watney, however, he must stay the night, for his feet were aching and swollen; indeed, he was aching a little all over, having tramped that day for twenty-five miles. Securing a room at the 'Horse and Ploughman', he gingerly took off his shoes and socks, only to discover that his heels were both blistered and the skin of his feet very tender. He bathed them, remembering old Fabio in the process. Fabio would have recommended rubbing with soap, and since he did not know what else to do, Gian-Luca tried his prescription. He finally rolled into bed with a sigh, and was lying between sleeping and waking; then his mind saw a picture quite clearly in the darkness, a thing that had not happened for years. There were wide, placid spaces and running water; but something more lovely than this he saw—a quiet and very beautiful gloom, green from the leaves that made it.

'They have come to me again, my pictures,' he murmured.

And that was the end of the third day.

4

Gian-Luca was up betimes the next morning, and his feet—thanks perhaps to Fabio's prescription—were certainly much less painful. In Winchester he stopped to buy provisions, which he stuffed away in his knapsack; then he started to tramp again in good earnest, lured on by the thought of the forest. He had never been in this part of the country, and he noticed many pleasant things about it; all the cottages, for instance, were heavily thatched, and one cottage that he passed had a queer little window shaped like an eye, just under its hair, which gave it an inquisitive appearance. The walls, too, were thatched, the thatch sitting astride them, jauntily riding their tops.

The road became increasingly lovely; it was bordered once more with trees. 'They look strong and proud and

happy!' thought Gian-Luca, and he wondered if they felt
the nearness of the forest, and if that was what made them
look so happy.

He came to the sleepy town of Romsey, which he left by
way of the old stone bridge that spans the River Test; the
water was chuckling softly to itself, swollen by April rains.
At the top of a steep hill he sat down to rest, eating his food
by the roadside. A gipsy caravan crawled up towards him,
and its inmates nodded and smiled at Gian-Luca; they had
very bright eyes, like Nerone's skylarks, only their eyes
looked free. Smoke was coming from the chimney of their
small house on wheels; no doubt they were cooking their
breakfast. A whiff of fried bacon reached Gian-Luca, and
two lean lurcher dogs dashed backwards and forwards,
barking in anticipation.

'Where are you going to?' shouted Gian-Luca.

And the driver waved a brown hand: 'To the forest,' he
shouted loudly in his turn, in order to be heard above the
barking.

Gian-Luca lay back and smiled in the sunshine, repeating
the happy words; then he thought: 'They will not have it
all to themselves, for Gian-Luca is going there too.'

He got up quickly and shouldered his knapsack, following in the wake of the gipsies. The aspect of the country
was very subtly changing, though the change was not easy
to define. The trees grew no thicker, nor were there more of
them, yet the whole landscape seemed suggestive of trees—
for the strange, mysterious spirit of the forest hung over it
like a spell. Past the village of Ower, plantations of young
firs stood ankle deep in heather that was waiting to purple;
and just about here Gian-Luca first saw the little wild New
Forest ponies.

Brothers of the Road were passing him now, a tattered
and feckless army; aye, and Sisters of the Road, looking
even more tattered—one sallow-faced Sister held an infant
to her breast, suckling it as she walked. Some of the Brethren pushed improvised hand-carts—sugar-boxes lashed to
old perambulator wheels—and these vehicles contained a
variety of oddments, from babies to worn boots and rusty
tin cans; while in one lay a bundle of decomposing rags
upon which sat a blear-eyed puppy. Here and there a

Brother, more fearless than his mates, had kindled a fire by the road-side.

'He will surely get into trouble,' thought Gian-Luca, remembering the warning of his tramp.

But such fires smelt pleasantly of dry leaves and pine wood, and their soft, smoky glow was alluring, so Gian-Luca must toss one old sinner a shilling, feeling like an outlaw himself.

Cadnam! The name of an unimportant village, having neither interest nor beauty, yet for those who pass through it in search of dreams the name of a deeply-enchanted gateway, for just beyond lies the softly-breathing forest—still dreaming after eight hundred years.

Gian-Luca went through that enchanted gateway, and even as he did so, it seemed to close behind him, and he looked at the forest, and the forest looked back out of drowsy, thoughtful green eyes. The road still led forward so Gian-Luca still followed, curbing his eagerness, tasting anticipation like a lover on the eve of ultimate fulfilment. But when he had passed the little town of Lyndhurst the greenness clamoured more loudly; he could hear that clamour in the beating of his heart, in the strong, anxious beating of his pulses. The damp, pure smell of the earth in spring travail—the moss smell, the leaf smell—laid hold on his senses; while those drowsy, thoughtful green eyes of the forest followed him down the high road.

Then suddenly Gian-Luca could resist it no longer, and he turned and plunged into the forest, stumbling against the trees in his haste to thrust farther and farther inward. Now he had left the road far behind him and had come to a wide green glade. The glade was full of the singing of birds, the grass was dappled with sunshine and flowers—clumps of anemones. He sat down under a gracious beech tree, pressing his cheek against its smooth bark; he was tired, and he suddenly felt rather drowsy, sitting there under the beech tree. He stretched his long legs with a sigh of contentment, then his head nodded forward on his breast—that night Gian-Luca slept out in the forest.

And that was the end of the fourth day.

357

CHAPTER ELEVEN

I

JUST AS the world had once possessed Gian-Luca, the world of the Doric and all that it stood for, so now the forest had begun to possess him. The simple, innocent life of the earth, upon which he wandered or rested or slept, became a part of this man's life also, until gradually, when he looked about him, he could not conceive of any other. He was faithful to his promise to his wife, however, and once every week he sent her a letter, at the same time calling for her letter to him, addressed: 'G.L., The Post Office, Lyndhurst,' in accordance with his written instructions.

He wrote always the same thing: 'I am well, Maddalena.'

And she answered: 'I am well, Gian-Luca.'

They got to know him by sight in Lyndhurst—a tall, thin man, with a little cleft beard—some said he was an artist, some a writer, some a crank, and some thought him mad but harmless. But nobody really knew anything about him, except that he was living in the forest; and since he apparently did no damage, they allowed him to live there in peace. Apart from that weekly visit to the Post Office, he only went into the town to buy food; and just at first for another reason also, in order to get his hair cut. But after a little he began to feel shy, for his clothes very soon grew worn and earth-stained, so he chopped at his own hair as best he could, sitting with a small looking-glass on his knees.

He had dropped all set rules and all method in his life, shedding them as easily as threadbare garments. He wandered about when and where he listed, sleeping out in the forest, like the beasts and the birds, he got up at dawn, and lay down to rest when the light failed. He washed his body in some secluded stream at sunrise, and again at nightfall;

there were many such streams in the forest, he discovered, where a man could bathe unmolested. The washing of his clothes was a far greater problem, yet he managed to accomplish this also; he would soap and then rub them on a smooth stone or boulder, rinsing out the soap in the clear running water, as the peasants in Italy had done. He dried his clothes in the sun when he could, but sometimes it was necessary to kindle a fire, and after the first few abortive efforts he became quite an expert fire-builder. Very crafty he grew in judging the wind, its direction, and where it would carry his smoke—there were woodmen and keepers patrolling the forest, and the lighting of fires was forbidden. Nevertheless it was done pretty often by the passing Brothers of the Road, and from such folk Gian-Luca learnt many harmless ruses for evading the arm of the law. The forest itself was his staunchest ally—so vast that a man might escape detection; and one day he discovered a charcoal-burner, who was kindly and willing to befriend him.

The charcoal-burner was the last of his kind to carry on that very ancient craft; from father to son it had been handed down, but this man was the last of a long line of burners who had earned their living in the forest.

'Me brothers don't seem to fancy it somehow—looks as though this job would die out with me,' he told Gian-Luca, who was thankfully drying a flannel shirt by his fire. But when Gian-Luca inquired with interest whether it was love of the forest that held him, the charcoal-burner looked rather bewildered. 'Maybe,' he answered; 'who knows?'

He was always as black as a chimney-sweep, but black with the sweet, pure ashes of the wood; his grey eyes looked out of his round, dusky face like kind lamps shining in darkness. There was skill in his work, very great skill indeed, as Gian-Luca discovered when he watched him. A huge mound of faggots he must build, this small man, and the mound must be dome-topped, and ten feet in height; at its base it must be at least twenty feet wide—no mean funeral pyre for the trees. The whole must be covered with dry forest litter, then thickly powdered with charcoal dust; many hours would be spent in this careful preparation for the ultimate sacrifice. The dome had a deep depression in the middle, like a monster navel in the stomach of a giant, and here it was that the fire would be started, to burn slowly into the entrails. Up and down his old ladder climbed the little black adept, spacing his faggots to admit of a draught; and last, but not least, came the large iron shovel filled with red crematory embers. Then the air would grow fragrant and cloudy with wood smoke, the scent of it reminding the homeless of home—the dear, warm, ingratiating scent of logs burning, so companionable always to man.

Sometimes Gian-Luca would sit watching for hours, lending a helping hand when it was needed; and the charcoal-burner would welcome this stranger, for his was a solitary life. Sometimes he would tell Gian-Luca old legends, old tales of the forest and its pioneer squatters, never forgetting to mention William Rufus, whose body had been carried in a charcoal-burner's cart.

2

Gian-Luca adopted the glade where he had rested on his first day of entering the forest; he made it his own, a kind of head-quarters, shared only with the beasts and the birds. A spring of clear water bubbled up close at hand, and this was the spring that he drank from. His knapsack he would hide in the hollow of an oak tree, and since he had no other worldly possessions, the glade made a charming hostel.

During his first few weeks in the forest he was always losing his way, but as time went on he developed new senses—an acuteness of instinct rather than of sight, and much other subtle, inexplicable wisdom that he shared with the lower creation. Thus, he knew when a woodman was somewhere about, feeling the presence of a man before he heard it; the coming of rain or of wind he knew also, though the sky might be cloudless at the moment. And now he was very seldom lost in his wanderings; he would find himself walking back into his glade without quite knowing how he had got there; with the homing instinct of a bird or a rabbit, Gian-Luca would return to his home. The humbler creatures got used to his presence—they began to eye him with interest; while he, in his turn, would offer them friendship, moving gently among them with a kind of politeness.

'You were here before me,' he would say very often; 'it is kind of you to make me feel welcome.'

His desire for the beautiful had grown into a craving which the forest constantly augmented, for the great trees were lovely in rain as in sunshine, especially the beeches with their small pointed leaves—glossy leaves, surrounded by a gossamer down which Gian-Luca liked to touch with his finger. One splendid old beech tree he took as his friend, and every morning he would stand close against it, with his back to its trunk and his arms extended on either side of his body. His hands would be held very still, palms upwards, for morsels of food would be lying on his palms, and presently he would whistle softly to the birds that were watching from the branches. So it happened that Gian-Luca, who had served all his life, continued to serve in the forest, waiting upon the simplicity of birds as he had upon Milady's caprices. One by one the birds would come flying down, blackcap and greenfinch, goldcrest and linnet; and with many small twitters and flutterings and circlings the birds would feed from his hands. Then Gian-Luca's pale eyes would look out and beyond, seeming to see all things clearly; for all that he saw at such moments as these would be lit by a deep sense of love.

'Is this God's love or mine?' he would wonder, conscious of the quiet whirring of those wings.

But quite soon the birds would have finished their feasting, and Gian-Luca's empty hands must drop to his sides; then the light would die out and his vision become darkened.

'I have not found God,' he would mutter sadly, 'and yet I came here to find Him.'

He took to talking to the beasts and the birds, not as good St. Francis who had preached them the Word, but rather as a fellow-creature, who must suffer because of their suffering. For even here, in the quiet green forest, suffering and sorrow had pursued him; he had come on a tortured rabbit in a trap, its neck deeply wounded from the wire snare that held it. Sick and sorry, he had stooped down and killed it with his hands, releasing it from its pain; but its pain had lived on in Gian-Luca's spirit, a shadow on the glory of the forest. One night he had heard the sound of a shot, and the next day he had found the traces of that shooting; a hare with a gun-shattered leg had passed him, trailing the leg behind it. Gian-Luca had started to follow the hare, bent on his errand of mercy, and the wild thing had hidden itself from his pity—knowing him for a man.

But the rabbits and the hares played fearlessly at sunrise, and again in the cool of the twilight, so then it was that Gian-Luca talked to them, 'Have *you* got a God?' he would ask them gravely.

The creatures would continue their artless gambols, apparently not hearing Gian-Luca; or, if they heard him, they would scamper away.

'They do not know either,' thought Gian-Luca.

There were times of innocent happiness, however, when he would feel like a schoolboy; as, for instance, when he first saw a herd of red deer in the northern part of the forest. He had wandered a long way that afternoon, and he chanced on the herd at sundown; the deer stood all together in a wide, open space, with their antlers black against the sky. Their magnificent heads were raised questioningly, their eyes looked attentive and fearful; but Gian-Luca had hidden himself behind a tree, scarcely daring to breathe in his surprise and excitement, for these beasts could seldom be taken unawares—they were hunted and had therefore grown wise. He stood so still that the deer began feeding, bending strong, chestnut necks; Gian-Luca could hear the crisp noise of their cropping and the muffled sound of their lazy movements as they pushed their way through the grass. Then he must have shifted his hand a little, for a twig snapped under his fingers, and up went every head, while the herd wheeled abruptly—in a moment it had bounded away.

Gian-Luca gradually grew familiar with nearly all the beasts of the forests—stoats and weasels, both thoroughly hard-hearted hunters with colossal appetites for birds' eggs; moles and hedgehogs, and the queer little plush-coated shrew-mice with their long, prehistoric-looking noses; foxes and badgers, who were seen for the most part soon after the evening star; squirrels, who were seen at any old time; and the shy, wild ponies who were timid at first, but who afterwards came to know Gian-Luca, so that sometimes the mares would bring him their foals, born in the forest over-night. And birds! Were there ever so many under heaven, or such a variety of songs? All day there was singing, and all night as well, for nightingales sang in the beech trees in June, and Gian-Luca must lie awake under the stars because of their splendid music. He learnt to know the songs and the habits of the birds before he discovered the names of the singers.

'That must be the fellow who shivers while he sings,' he would think, as he listened to the tremulous trill of a wood-wren swinging just above him. Or: 'That must be the bird with the little white chin—he always sounds cross like that when he feels frightened.' And sure enough out would bustle a whitethroat, furiously angry with Gian-Luca.

And then there were all the creeping things; the long, graceful grass snakes, very self-conscious and fearfully embarrassed by a stranger; the hot-tempered adders, who were better avoided because of their unregenerate nature; and the harmless but unprepossessing slow-worms, very stupid, near-sighted and inept. There was also a goodly company of beetles, and these varied in disposition; some were peaceable, others quite quarrelsome at times, and one of their number was a veritable fiend—a species of Nero, but with ten times his courage and more than ten times his cunning.

Gentle and fierce by turns was the forest, like a great, throbbing human heart. Its gentler thoughts came to life in its bracken, in its delicate mosses and silvery lichens, in its little wild berries—the food of the birds—in its pools and its glades and its flowers. Gian-Luca had come at the time of the bluebells, but out in the forest they had not depressed him; and because he had once pushed them roughly with his foot, he had knelt down beside them and buried his face in their dewy, ineffable coolness. Anemones and cuckoo-flower had been blooming, and quite soon the hawthorn had followed. Now it was June, the month of dog-roses, the month of the kingcup in damp, boggy places, the month of forget-me-nots growing along streams or clustering beside quiet water. The days held the nights imprisoned in their brightness, for the dawns broke early and the twilights were long; the darkness, when it came, must perforce reflect light in an endless faint after-

363

glow. Long before the big moon was ready to vanish, the sun would be eyeing her out of the east; then the night and the morning must love one another in a tangle of leaves and birds' wings and stars.

Below in the forest Gian-Luca would be lying with his face turned up to the sky; and the soul of the forest, always wrapt round with peace, in spite of that heart fierce and gentle by turns, would come timidly touching the soul of Gian-Luca—trying to tell him something. Then Gian-Luca would lie very still and would listen, but after a little he would sigh.

'I cannot find God—not yet,' he must answer; and perhaps he would get up to look for his God, meeting Him face to face in the sunrise, but passing Him by unseeing.

3

That July Gian-Luca fell in with some gipsies who were camping in a clearing near a pine grove; and, because by now he looked rather like themselves, the gipsies took kindly to him. The family consisted of three generations, a very old man with his very old wife, their buxom, brown daughter, their tall son-in-law, and an odd assortment of children. In addition to these latter there were three dogs, two horses, a large caravan, and some dilapidated tents; and—low be it spoken—when Gian-Luca surprised them, there was also a fire in the clearing.

'Hullo!' said the young man, whose name was Sylvester.

'Hullo!' said Gian-Luca smiling. Then he sat down beside him where he squatted near the fire, and all of a sudden he was friends with this man—friends as one tree may be friends with another through sharing a common soil.

The gipsies, it seemed, were remaining for some weeks; they talked quite frankly to Gian-Luca. They were busy, they said, making brackets and flower-stands from wood collected in the forest. These objects they would sell later on at the fairs; but they had many other occupations. At swarming time they made bee-hives, for instance; in the autumn they collected beech-mast and acorns, for which there was quite a good market. Sometimes they would go hop-picking for a change; this, they said, was great fun for the children.

'Gives 'em a chance to see a bit of life,' smiled Sylvester, glancing at his litter.

During the time that they stayed in the forest Gian-Luca was often with these people. They had strangely good manners, a kind of natural breeding which forbade them to express their curiosity about him.

'Grand place, the forest——' was all Sylvester said, as though that in itself explained Gian-Luca.

They were not over-clean, and their animals were thin, but never unkindly treated. The gipsies' worst crime was the snaring of rabbits; but this crime Gian-Luca only suspected, for even Sylvester, so frank in most matters, ignored the existence of rabbits. He was something of an ornithologist, however, and from him Gian-Luca learnt the names of the birds, their migratory habits, their matrimonial codes, the months in which they mated, the construction of their nests—this latter often touching and amazing. Sylvester, on the whole, possessed a very kindly heart, and if he killed he did so to eat; he had the woodland instinct of hunting for his young, which instinct he shared with the wild creatures.

Their names were very musical, these brown-faced, nomad people—Sylvester, Claretto, Morella, Clementina; but their children were just plain Jim, and Bill, and Maggie; there were also a Syd, a Jennie and a Bobbie—the latter a baby at the breast. For, according to Morella, their very ancient grand-dame, the traditions of the race were fast dying; it was all the fault of towns and motors, said Morella, and those devilish flying machines. Their language was now dead, she told Gian-Luca sadly, and the Romanies were passing away—then Morella spoke some soft-sounding words to Gian-Luca, in the beautiful lost language of her people.

Gian-Luca learnt a great deal from this wise old woman who was only too glad to find anyone to listen. The unwritten laws of the wanderers he learnt, and the unwritten laws of the roads and of the forests; the virtues of herbs, and what berries might be eaten and the seasons in which to find them. Then one day he must ask her what she thought about God; did she think that He really existed? But at this Morella could only shake her head; she had never thought much about such things, it seemed. She had had nine children, she explained rather grimly; four of them were alive, but five of them had died—one way and another she had not had much time, what with their father and all. Then Gian-Luca must ask her what she felt about death, for had she not lost five children? Did she think that the soul lived on after death? Did she think that her children still existed?

'Who knows?—it don't seem likely,' she told him; 'leastways, it don't to me.'

But Gian-Luca was curious; now he wanted to know the Romany word for death. He who had always been a lover of words was trying to pick up their language.

Morella surveyed him out of rheumy old eyes; 'Merripen,' she said gravely.

'And for life?' he inquired. 'What is life in your language?'

And she answered him: 'Merripen.'

One day the gipsies were no longer to be found when Gian-Luca went to the clearing; they had slipped away like shades in the night—only their wheel-tracks remained on the turf, and the guilty ashes of their fire. So now once more he had the forest to himself, except for the charcoal-burner, and he felt half glad and half sorry in his heart; he had liked that companionable, guilty fire, and Sylvester, and the old Morella. He had felt at peace with these vagabond people whose problems were all so simple; for the agèd, the quiet waiting for death, without hope, without fear, without questioning; for the young, the mating of the man with his woman, the passing on of life to their children. He envied this placid acceptance of the world as they conceived it to be, and their courage—what was it that gave them such courage? The courage to ignore, the courage not to fret—was it, perhaps, belief after all, a kind of unrecognized belief?

4

The heat of the summer lay heavy on the forest in spite of its splendid trees. The air was often a-shimmer with heat, and small, winged insects would dance in the shimmer or scud across the surface of the pools. The nights were disturbed by the hooting of owls, flying on their wide, soundless wings; but the streams grew less noisy, and by noontide the ponies must draw in to shelter from the sun. Gian-Luca continued to feed his song-birds while forgetting to feed himself—for now there was no Maddalena to remind him, and his distaste for food had been growing again lately; he never felt really hungry these days, which was strange considering his life. It began to irk him to walk into Lyndhurst —and of course the less one ate, the less one needed; there were always berries to be found in the forest, so sometimes he lived on berries. But food he must buy because of his birds, and because of a wild roan pony—a fierce little fellow, very handy with his hoofs, very anxious not to sell his free soul. And yet, as is often the case with his betters, curiosity would overcome his shyness; he could not keep away from the strange fascination of this man-thing who followed him with carrots. Once a week, when Gian-Luca went in to the post, he would purchase his frugal supplies; carrots for the pony, bread and seed for the birds, and occasionally something for Gian-Luca. His clothes were worn out and his shoes needed soling, very badly indeed they needed soling; but out in the forest he had ceased to wear shoes; he went about barefoot for the joy of the earth, and his love of the forest was increased by this contact of his naked feet with its soil.

His possessions were gradually dwindling away, and somehow they never got replaced. He had given his raincoat to a woman one evening, drenched through she had been, that poor Sister of the Road, and it always hurt him to see such women battered by the wind and the rain. Their faces were sunken or heavily bloated, their tired feet dragged slowly or shuffled to keep up with the shuffling stride of their men. They were miserable, heart-sick, home-sick creatures, the outcasts of cities, the outcasts of life.

'Men can exist without roots,' thought Gian-Luca, 'but not women; they need roots, like the trees.'

He would sometimes give away his food to such people, and then he would have nothing to eat; and his money he gave them because they were ill-clad, more so than he was himself, he fancied. They took all that he offered, and sometimes they thanked him, but sometimes they would look at him askance.

'I have not stolen the money,' he would tell them, and would know that they did not believe him.

His head had begun to ache badly at times, and at times he felt giddy and stupid; too stupid almost to think about God or to ask his eternal questions. But standing against his calm friend the beech tree, feeding its trustful birds, he could still recapture that sense of oneness with something that belonged to the birds and the beech tree, to the smallest particle of soil in the forest, to the humblest flower that sprang from that soil—to the pity in the heart of Gian-Luca. Then the moment would pass, and back he would come to earth with a kind of mental thud, with a sense of desolation more poignant than pain, so that he must sometimes cry out very loudly in his bitterness: 'God, where are You?'

The birds, grown startled, would all fly away, deserting Gian-Luca for that morning; then he would sit down and begin to cry weakly, begging the birds not to leave him.

'Can it be that you are frightened of me?' he would reproach them. 'Are you frightened of Gian-Luca, who feeds you?'

Then one day who should come but the little roan pony, and it took a carrot from his hand, and it lipped his hand, which meant: 'Thank you, Gian-Luca,' which meant: 'I am your servant—this had to be so, for my people are born servants of men.'

After that it took to following Gian-Luca about, letting him twist his fingers in its mane; and Gian-Luca loved it and would walk beside it, fondling its silky nostrils.

'Oh, well,' he would say, 'I have not found God, but I have found you, little friend of the lonely——' Then the pony would sometimes nuzzle his hand, as though it had understood him.

He began to sleep badly, for his body had grown feverish, so sometimes he would get up and wander to a stream; undressing, he would plunge straight into the water, which would strike cold against his thin body. He was always doing foolish things like this lately, grown careless of his physical welfare; he scarcely troubled to think about illness, so busy was his mind with its problems. And then there was something that was always coming nearer—nearer and nearer he would feel the thing coming, and for some strange reason this began to console him.

'Is that You, God?' he would whisper.

He would often be haunted by the memory of a poem, the memory of the 'Gioia della Luce.' The great, beautiful stanzas would go rolling through his brain until the words seemed to be a part of the forest, a part of its hope, and of other blessèd things; and one night as he murmured the poem, half asleep, he thought that the words were part of God. Thus it was that Gian-Luca, all unknowing, ratified his peace with Ugo Doria.

5

The hunting of the red deer began in July, and Gian-Luca would hear hounds giving tongue; a curious, half-plaintive, half-merciless sound, as they broke away on the scent. The faint blast of a horn would echo through the forest, the faint cry of the huntsman, the faint cracking of whips, and then, strangely enough, something quite unregenerate would stir to life in Gian-Luca. He would throw back his head and stand stock-still and listen, thrilling to that pagan music, the music of men and beasts taking their pleasure in the hot, steaming blood-lust of death. Then Gian-Luca would know that the passion of the chase lay somewhere deep down in every male creature, from the stoat who hunted his scurrying rabbits to the man who hunted his deer. He would know that death stalked abroad in the forest, even as he had done on the battlefields of France, when Gian-Luca, held in leash at the Officers' Mess, had fretted for his outraged manhood. These thoughts would give him fresh cause for speculation, fresh cause for bewilderment and sadness, and then he would remember a Romany word: 'Merripen,' meaning death, 'Merripen,' meaning life, and, turning away, he would wonder . . .

One morning a splendid red stag dashed through the thicket directly in front of his face; its flanks were heaving, its eyes staring wildly, there was blood on its lips, and it swayed as it bounded, for the creature was nearly spent.

The stag paused an instant as though grown stupid, then off it went to the left; but the hounds did not follow, the forest was silent.

'They have lost the scent,' thought Gian-Luca.

But presently he saw a couple of horsemen pressing forward through the trees.

'Seen him?' they asked quickly, observing Gian-Luca; and they urged on their beasts, leaning sideways as they did so, the better to hear his reply.

Then Gian-Luca lied, pointing in the wrong direction. 'He went off there to the right,' he told them; 'he was travelling pretty fast, too, when I saw him.'

'Oh, he's game all right!' remarked one of the riders as they swung round and galloped away.

CHAPTER TWELVE

I

IT WAS early in September when they caught the roan pony, and they caught him as he stood beside Gian-Luca. A farmer and his boy came quietly forward, and the man slipped a halter on to the pony. The beast looked surprised, but not really resentful, because he now trusted men.

The farmer nodded, grinning at Gian-Luca. 'Strong little devil,' he remarked, 'got plenty of work in him, look at his loin; no trouble with him either, it seems.'

Gian-Luca's heart gave a bound of fear. 'You are taking him away?' he faltered.

'Yes,' said the farmer, 'his turn's about come; we've all got to work for our living.'

The pony began to pull back on the halter, edging towards Gian-Luca.

'Come up!' ordered the boy.

'Steady now!' coaxed the farmer, patting the pony's neck.

Gian-Luca said: 'Where are you going to take him?'

'I've sold him,' the man replied; and he eyed this scarecrow of a tramp with interest. 'Are you keen on horses?' he inquired.

'Yes, but where will he go to?' Gian-Luca persisted, laying his hand on the pony.

'To the mines,' said the farmer; 'they most of 'em go there, that is, when they're small enough.'

For a moment Gian-Luca stood as though turned to stone, then he threw up his arms with a cry. 'No, no!' he babbled; 'not the mines. Oh! for God's sake—he will never see the light in the mines—he will go blind! I cannot let him be taken to the mines, the creature has been my friend.' He spread out his hands and pointed to the trees. 'Look, look!' he went on wildly; 'all this beauty and freedom, all this greenness and joy—the mines, they are dark, all his life in the darkness—his body full of sores from straining at the trucks, his eyes filming over for want of the sunshine, his heart breaking because he has known the forest, because he remembers and remembers——' And now he was clutching at the farmer's arm. 'Listen! per amore di Dio, but listen! I will buy him, I tell you I will buy the beast's freedom, only tell me how much and I will buy him!'

'*You!*' growled the farmer, pushing him off, and staring sceptically at him; then his eyes grew more kind: 'Poor devil, you look starving—what's the matter, you're light-headed, can't you find work, or what?' His hand went quickly down to his pocket: 'Here, take this,' he muttered, producing some silver; 'take this and buy yourself a square meal.' And he handed Gian-Luca three shillings.

Quite firmly but gently he thrust out his arm between Gian-Luca and the pony. He gave the rope of the halter to the boy. 'Get on with it!' he ordered. 'Come along, now, look sharp!'

And the pony went with them, giving no trouble, because he had learnt to trust men.

Gian-Luca threw himself down on the ground, burying his face in his hands, and he spoke to the earth, asking it to show pity.

'Let him die, let him die, let him die!' he entreated, as though the earth had ears wherewith to hear, as though it were a mother who must surely feel compassion for the creatures her bounty had nourished.

Then he told the earth, in low, broken words, of the life of the ponies in the mines; all that he knew of that life he told it, and all that his half-distraught mind must picture.

'He trusted them because of me,' moaned Gian-Luca; 'I gave him his faith, and yet I cannot save him—he is little but he has a heart full of courage—he will work until that heart breaks!'

He stopped speaking as though he were waiting for an answer, then a most peculiar thing happened; Gian-Luca heard a voice inside his own head, quite loudly it spoke, with a kind of precision.

'Merripen,' said the voice, 'death is life, Gian-Luca—it is only for such a little while.'

372

Gian-Luca sat up and pressed his fingers to his temples. 'I must be going mad,' he muttered.

2

The forest was turning scarlet and golden, touched by the first sudden frosts of autumn, and Gian-Luca felt terribly cold these nights, so that sometimes he must get up and walk. The fever had left him, its place being taken by an ever-increasing weakness, yet the thought of four walls that would shut him in, the thought of a roof that would shut away the sky, and above all the thought of leaving the trees, filled him with misery.

'If I eat more I may feel less cold,' he reasoned; so whenever he felt able he went into Lyndhurst, and while there he would try to pull himself together, smiling as he purchased his food. 'If they think I am ill they will catch me!' he would mutter; 'and of course I am not really ill——'

But when he had tramped slowly back to the forest, he would find that he could eat very little after all; his stomach had grown unaccustomed to food, and some days he suffered great pain.

'It must be that I do not need it,' he would argue; 'everyone eats too much!'

The fine weather broke and it rained a good deal; strong winds swept over the forest that October, the beech trees sighed and groaned under the storms, while Gian-Luca got wet to the skin. He must always be lighting fires, and this distressed him, for now he lived in the dread of getting caught; keepers and foresters were after him, he fancied, waiting to shut him up between walls. In the end he grew desperate, preferring to go wet than to risk getting caught by those keepers.

'The foxes have holes, and the birds of the air have nests,' he would sometimes think, smiling ruefully; and then he would wonder where these words had come from—surprised when his memory failed him.

His money was running very short by now, he had only about three pounds left; but he firmly resolved not to write home for more, he was not going to rob Maddalena.

'When it is gone I must find work in the forest, perhaps

with the charcoal-burner,' he thought vaguely. 'If I cannot find work, well then, I must beg.' And he tried to remember what the tramp had once told him regarding those signs chalked on gate-posts.

He began to have a queer feeling in his heart, his heart was constantly moving. 'Keep quiet!' he would tell it, pressing his side. 'Ma che! you behave exactly like a wild thing.' But his heart would continue to change its position, for that was what it felt like to Gian-Luca: 'Are you in bed that you have to turn over?' he would ask. 'Do not beat like the caged richiami! You turn over and then you beat with your wings—yet I am not cruel like Sisto——.'

Whenever he saw the wild ponies now, he pitied, thinking of the horror of the mines; and whenever he pitied his sick heart grew restless, beating like Sisto's richiami. Then one evening he came face to face with himself, as he walked slowly back to his beech tree. Towards him came walking another Gian-Luca, a gaunt, ragged fellow with a little cleft beard.

'Ah!' said Gian-Luca, 'I have found you at last; I have looked for a very long time!' Yet even as his arm shot out to detain him, this other Gian-Luca vanished. 'Never mind,' thought his twin, 'I shall see him again; he lives, as I suspected, in the forest.'

But this strange apparition had reminded him of God, who still remained to be found; so now he went scouring the thickets for God, and the glades and the long, green rides.

'God!' he would call softly, as he called to the ponies, 'come here, I have something to give You! I will give You Gian-Luca—he is not very grand, he is not the smart fellow who served at the Doric; but that, as You know, is because he came to find You.' And then he would hold out his hand.

'Magari!' Gian-Luca would presently mutter, having failed to coax God from His hiding: 'Magari! I am dirty, and my clothes are in rags—perhaps that is why He avoids me.'

They were saying in Lyndhurst that Gian-Luca must be starving, judging from his haggard appearance.

'Well,' said the baker, 'he certainly looks queer, but he seems to have money enough to buy bread; I changed a pound note for him three days ago.'

'He's some "new-religion" crank, I expect,' suggested the girl from the Post Office.

<h1 style="text-align:center">3</h1>

A week later, when Gian-Luca called for his letter, the girl eyed him curiously. 'An unpleasant change in the weather——' she began; but Gian-Luca had thanked her and had hurried away before she could get any further.

He shuffled along in his battered old shoes, which now felt too small for his feet; as he went he kept staring down at the letter—it seemed heavy, he thought, it was thicker than usual—and his fretful heart thudded against his side because the letter looked thicker.

He opened the letter under the beech tree, sitting with his back against its trunk. 'No wonder it was thicker than usual,' he murmured as he drew out the closely written pages.

'I am well, Gian-Luca,' the letter began—Maddalena never stooped to deception—'I am well, Gian-Luca——' but the rest of those pages were covered with the ache that was in her.

'All that I have promised I have done,' wrote Maddalena; 'no one knows this address that I write to. They worry, they question, Rosa and the others, and I answer: "Gian-Luca writes that he is well, he has gone away to think over our future, I expect him home any day now." I pray to the Madonna every night and every morning—she must surely be weary of my poor prayers, amore. I say: "Do whatever is best for Gian-Luca, whatever will bring him happiness," I say. And I pray the Madonna to give you her peace, and the peace of her blessèd Son. But oh, Gian-Luca, I am only a woman, I am not brave and holy like Our Lady of Sorrows—I am only Maddalena, who was born on the Campagna, just a poor, loving, ignorant peasant——'

Then Maddalena wrote as a woman will write to the man she has taken for her mate—all the love and the longing of her soul and her body; all the emptiness of days and the loneliness of nights; all the difficult, hopeless, yearning frustrations of a mother-of-men without child. The letter was terribly truthful and simple, as simple as the law of the forest: 'Come back to me, Gian-Luca, amore, come quickly. You are all I have in the world.'

Gian-Luca folded Maddalena's letter and slipped it into his pocket. Getting to his feet, he stood against the beech tree, then, scarcely conscious of what he was doing, he stretched out his hands, palms upwards. He stood so still that the birds fluttered down, thinking he had come there to feed them; but his palms were empty, so they lit on his fingers, waiting for a miracle to happen. But Gian-Luca was seeing the streets of a city, all the noise and confusion of crowds; he was seeing the Doric with its ignoble service—the little Milady, Jane Coram and the others . . .

'Gian-Luca!'

'Signorina?'

'Do send me Roberto!'

'Pubito, I will find him, signorina.'

He was seeing the hideous struggle for existence, with its cruelty, its meanness and its lusts; the breath of it hot and sickeningly fœtid, the heart of it cold and unspeakably callous, its body a mass of festering sores from the sins of its blinded mind. His own body shrank and quivered a little, as a bird will quiver who is thrust into a cage, for the ruthless walls seemed to be closing around him; and the dull slate roof that would shut away the sky hung over him like a pall. Nerone had shut away the sky from his skylarks, in case they should beat themselves to pieces in despair; Robert's bright eyes were the eyes of a skylark, a skylark looking through the bars of the Doric—but the child of the beggar had lost his eyes, and that surely was the fault of the world.

'I cannot go back to that world!' cried Gian-Luca; 'I cannot go back to that world!'

Yet even as he said it, he knew that he would go back, for something far stronger than the world stood beside him, the steadfast, enduring courage of mankind that draws all men up to the divine.

Then, as though a mist had been swept from his vision, he seemed to see clearly for the first time in his life, and seeing the darkness, yet perceived a great glory, shining steadily through that darkness. He was conscious of a vast and indomitable purpose to which all things would ultimately bow; he himself, Gian-Luca, was a part of that purpose as was everything else on this struggling earth—and at that supreme moment he must cry out to God:

'I have found You; You are here in my heart!'

There were spent, hunted stags; there were blind pit-ponies; there were children without eyes; and to such things he belonged by reason of his infinite pity. He was theirs, the servant of all that was helpless, even as God was their servant and their master. But one helpless thing needed him above all others, the sad, patient woman who waited—it was better to make one poor creature happy, than to mourn for the ninety and nine. He must turn and go back, he must try to find work—it would have to be humble at first, a beginning; and whatever he did must be done with great patience, patience with himself and with Maddalena, but above all, patience with the world.

He had been young and strong and had caught at the world, determined to make it serve him; he had grown very angry and had spat at the world, seeing only its sins; he had grown very sorrowful, pitying the world, seeing only its sorrows; and then he had grown frightened because he was lost, because he could not find God. And all the time God was here in himself, that was where He was, in Gian-Luca, and in every poor struggling human heart that was capable of one kind impulse. Why, God must be somewhere in the heart of Jane Coram, consoling her solitary spirit. Nothing was too base or too humble for God, He was patient and undefeated. The path of the world was the path of His sorrow, and the sorrow of God was the hope of the world, for to suffer with God was to share in the joy of His ultimate triumph over sorrow.

Gian-Luca sank quietly on to his knees, and his body fell sideways and lay waiting; for now his mind was wandering again, and he fancied that someone was stooping towards him—someone very tender who would gather him up and carry him a long way away. A peace that was passing all understanding lay in his heart and on his eyelids, so that he closed his peace-laden eyelids, like a child who is heavy with sleep. And now his body was lighter than air, he was floating above the tree-tops; and now he was down on the

377

kind earth again, lying there under the beech tree. Maddalena was coming, she was saying her prayers, her voice was all over the forest—Maddalena was saying her favourite prayer—it began—it began—how did it begin?

'Blesséd be God,' breathed Gian-Luca.

A leaf drifted quietly down and touched him, but Gian-Luca lay very still. Then a rabbit that was scampering over the grass, sat up on its haunches, staring. In the beech tree the birds began talking to each other, for now it was the hour of the sunset——

And that was how Gian-Luca returned to his country after thirty-four years of exile.

EPILOGUE

I

TERESA BOSELLI stood and faced Maddalena with the parlour table between them; on the table was lying that short official letter—the cold, white messenger of death.

'I have come,' said Maddalena, 'because it was my duty, and because Gian-Luca would have wished it.'

'You have come,' said Teresa, 'because he was my grandson, the child of my only child.'

Maddalena's face was as white as the paper, and her mothering eyes were tearless. 'To-morrow I go to Lynd-hurst,' she answered; 'Father Antonio has promised to go with me, and Rosa, who loved her foster-son, and Mario and old Nerone.' Her voice was quite steady but curiously toneless, as though a dead creature were speaking.

'I also will accompany you,' said Teresa.

'Why?' inquired Maddalena.

Teresa Boselli drew herself up, and her hard, black eyes were defiant. 'Why?' she said harshly; 'because my blood calls. Was he not the child of my child?'

Then Maddalena's eyes grew as hard as Teresa's, and her gentle face stiffened to anger. 'Too late you remember,' she answered coldly, 'you who would never love Gian-Luca.'

After that they were silent, staring at each other, while their bitterness leapt out between them; the little back parlour was trembling with it, with the dull, heavy thuds of their hearts. Maddalena quietly picked up the letter, which she thrust into the bosom of her dress, then she turned and went out of the Casa Boselli—leaving Teresa alone.

Six black-clad figures got down from the train when it stopped at Lyndhurst station.

'This must be the lot that have come for the inquest,' whispered a porter to his friend.

Very calm and noble looked Maddalena, clothed in the weeds of her affliction; she walked straight forward into her grief, like the brave Roman matron that she was. Her eyes held no hope and no resentment, they were filled with the finality of fate; and after her followed Teresa Boselli, scarcely less steadfast and upright.

Rosa was clinging to Mario's arm, and Rosa must openly weep: 'Mio bambino—mio cuore——' she wept.

And Mario muttered: 'He did all, all for me—even in his trouble he remembered poor Mario and got him a post at the Doric.'

Nerone stumped beside them with his chin sunk on his breast; he was swinging his wooden leg slowly, for his loins were no longer so strong as they had been and the wooden leg felt very heavy. And ever at the heels of this sad little flock there hovered a faithful old sheep-dog—Father Antonio, whose hair had turned silver, and whose eyes were the cloudy blue of an infant's, as is sometimes the way with the eyes of a man whose life's circle is nearing completion. He it was who drove with Maddalena in the fly, and who quietly held her hand.

'So God has taken Gian-Luca——' he said thoughtfully, and he added: 'God surely knows best.'

But Maddalena answered: 'There is doubt in my heart— I am doubting the mercy of God.' Then she put her doubts and her fears into words, while Father Antonio listened.

What would happen to the poor lonely soul of Gian-Luca? He had died all unshriven by Holy Church—all alone he had died, without priest or candle, and no one had been near to pray for his soul that it might have a merciful passing. And as she went on speaking her voice shook a little with the superstitious dread of the peasant.

'To die like that, on the cold earth——' she whispered; 'and he never received the precious body of Our Lord— there was no one to put the blessed oil on his eyelids, or on his tired, travel-stained feet——'

Then Father Antonio looked at her gravely: 'The earth has been blest for always, my daughter—God walked upon the earth in the Garden of Eden, and again on His way to Calvary. The Church is a Mother whose arms are wide open to succour and comfort her children, but God is a Father whose heart is eternal, and many a sheep that has never been penned will be gathered to the fold of that heart.' He gazed at the splendour of the woods that they were passing, all flaming they were with gold and crimson. 'England is a beautiful church,' he murmured. He often said queer things like that these days, they thought it was because he was so old.

3

Gian-Luca's body was lying in a stable attached to an unimportant inn. Some new red bricks were piled in a corner, together with a number of workmen's tools—they were going to turn the place into a garage, and the work had been hastily suspended. A silent police sergeant unlocked the door and allowed the mourners to enter; then he quietly turned back the sheet from the body, and standing aside, he waited.

'Santa Madonna!' muttered Nerone, 'this is an outrage, a scandal! No chapel, no reverence, not even for the dead; what a pagan country is England!'

But Gian-Luca lay very much at rest in his stable, with his thin hands folded on his breast; and seeing him thus, Nerone fell silent. Finding his rosary, he began to tell his beads, marking the prayers with his thumb. Then they all gathered round, those members of the clan, to say good-bye to their child.

'He was born in our midst, the Gian-Luca——' sobbed Rosa.

'Davvero,' murmured Mario, 'he was born in our midst.' And remembering the past as folk will at such times, he also could not check his tears.

Teresa went close and stared down at her grandson, and none could know what she was thinking, for her face was the face of an ivory idol in which glowed two points of flame.

'What do they say that he died of? she demanded, walking over to the sergeant.

The sergeant looked embarrassed and glanced at Maddalena. 'Well, of course, there'll have to be an inquest,' he murmured, 'but I've heard that they think he died of starvation and exposure—it's been chilly these nights.' Then, because Teresa still fixed him with those eyes, the sergeant must go blundering on: 'It's peculiar, though, we found money on the body—over two pounds—but it's not for me to talk,' he concluded hastily.

Teresa Boselli went back to the coffin and looked down at the wasted face. 'So much food in the world,' she muttered, 'and they think that he died of starvation!'

Maddalena bent forward and kissed Gian-Luca, very gently she kissed his forehead. 'He looks so strange,' she whispered to her priest, 'as though he were not here at all——'

'Why should Gian-Luca be here?' he answered. 'Did Our Lord remain in His tomb?'

And now Father Antonio took something from his neck, a little crucifix in gold, and he placed it gently on Gian-Luca's hands. 'May this Man who died and this God who lives, keep your soul unto life everlasting,' he said slowly, then he dropped on his knees by the side of the coffin and began to read the prayers for the dead.

Mario knelt down, and Rosa and Nerone, joining in those charitable prayers; but grief suddenly caught Maddalena by the throat, so that she could not pray, and it scourged her and shook her like a reed in the storm——

'He starved, he was homeless and cold and forsaken!' she cried out, wringing her hands.

Then Maddalena wept for her unborn children and for the father of her unborn children, himself so much her child. The merciful tears streamed down her cheeks unheeded, while the sharp plough of sorrow furrowed her soul; and her tears fell one by one into those furrows, nourishing the sacred seed of the spirit, the seed of faith in the mercy of God, that must come to fruition through tears.

Rosa touched Mario quietly on the shoulder, and together they left the stable. Then Nerone got awkwardly up from his knees, and he too left the stable, trying to walk softly, trying not to tap with his old wooden leg that made such a noise on the stones. But Teresa Boselli still lingered by the coffin, for she could not take her eyes from her grandson.

'So much food in the world,' she kept repeating, 'and they think that he died of starvation!'

When old Teresa had at last looked her fill, she walked away firmly with her back very upright; she scarcely appeared to require that stick, so strong, it seemed, were her knees.

Outside in the street she said to a passer: 'Where is our Catholic Church?'

'The Roman Catholic church is down there on the right-hand side,' she was told.

Teresa went into the quiet, empty church—she had not entered a church until now for thirty-four angry years. Right up to the statue of the Virgin walked Teresa—the statue that stood at the foot of the altar—and the Virgin's halo was set with seven stars, perhaps for her seven sorrows.

'So,' said Teresa, confronting the Madonna, 'so this is what you have done! I gave you Gian-Luca, the little Gian-Luca—all helpless and cold and motherless he was—and I said to you: "Take him, I give him to you, you can have him body and soul!" And you took him, and you broke him, and you starved him to death out there in the cold, English forest—and he was the child of my only child, of Olga whom you left to die in shame. And he was a fine and a lovely man, as lovely as the morning with his strange, light eyes, and you left him at a time when his heart was broken because of this intolerable world! Oh, I know very well why you did these things, you did them to break Teresa Boselli. "She will not serve me any more," you said; "very well, I will show her that it pays best to serve me; I will take all things from her and leave her alone, now that she must suffer old age." But she will not serve you; she has come here to tell you yet again that she will not serve you! He was lovely as the morning, the little Gian-Luca——'

She stopped abruptly, staring up at the Madonna, who looked down with a deprecating smile—she could not help that deprecating smile, it was moulded into the plaster.

'Answer me!' commanded Teresa sternly. 'What have you done with Gian-Luca?'

But the Virgin was silent, and her lips were composed and gentle, like the lips of the body in the stable; for not in poor, faltering human speech could the Mother of God reply to Teresa.

The first Virago Modern Classic was published in London in 1978, launching a list dedicated to the celebration of women writers and to the rediscovery and reprinting of their works. While the series is called "Modern Classics" it is not true that these works of fiction are universally and equally considered "great," although that is often the case. Published with new critical and biographical introductions, books appear in the series for different reasons: sometimes for their importance in literary history; sometimes because they illuminate particular aspects of women's lives, both personal and public. They may be classics of comedy or storytelling; their interest can be historical, feminist, political, or literary. In any case, in their variety and richness they promise to confuse forever the question of what women's fiction is about, while at the same time affirming a true female tradition in literature.

Initially, the Virago Modern Classics concentrated on English novels and short stories published in the early decades of the century. As the series has grown, it has broadened to include works of fiction from different centuries and from different countries, cultures, and literary traditions; there are books written by black women, by Catholic and Jewish women, by women of almost every English-speaking country, and there are several relevant novels by men.

Nearly 200 Virago Modern Classics will have been published in England by the end of 1985. During that same year, Penguin Books began to publish Virago Modern Classics in the United States, with the expectation of having some 40 titles from the series available by the end of 1986. Some of the earlier books in the series were published in the United States by The Dial Press.